**WITHDRAWN**

# Manhattan Alien

# Manhattan Alien

B.K. Mhatre

Copyright © 2017 by B.K. Mhatre.

Library of Congress Control Number: 2017902967
ISBN: Hardcover 978-1-5245-8685-0
Softcover 978-1-5245-8684-3
eBook 978-1-5245-8683-6

All rights reserved. No part of this book may be reproduced or transmitted in any form or by any means, electronic or mechanical, including photocopying, recording, or by any information storage and retrieval system, without permission in writing from the copyright owner.

This is a work of fiction. Names, characters, places and incidents either are the product of the author's imagination or are used fictitiously, and any resemblance to any actual persons, living or dead, events, or locales is entirely coincidental.

Any people depicted in stock imagery provided by Thinkstock are models, and such images are being used for illustrative purposes only.
Certain stock imagery © Thinkstock.

Print information available on the last page.

Rev. date: 03/09/2017

To order additional copies of this book, contact:
Xlibris
1-888-795-4274
www.Xlibris.com
Orders@Xlibris.com
757778

This book is dedicated to all past, present and future 'Aliens' in the United States of America.

I would like to express my gratitude to my family and friends who provided strong support and encouragement to me while writing this book!

-BKM.

# Contents

Prologue ..................................................................................... xi

Immigrating to the land of opportunity! .................................. 1
June 2001 Life in New York City Begins ................................. 17
I become Dr. Bond .................................................................. 35
Learning English ..................................................................... 52
Not all fat women are pregnant (and other important facts) ... 67
Fifth Commandment ............................................................... 75
The Sixth Commandment ....................................................... 88
Being off the market! ............................................................. 110
Seventh Commandment ........................................................ 118
Eighth Commandment .......................................................... 136
Once an Indian… ................................................................... 153
That's what friends are for .................................................... 168
The big interview .................................................................. 191
New Years in America ........................................................... 222
Back to work ......................................................................... 241
The long good-bye and Mumbai ........................................... 253
The tenth commandment ..................................................... 286

Epilogue ................................................................................ 309

# Prologue

As I boarded my flight from Mumbai to JFK, New York, I mentally prepared myself for the long flight ahead of me. The smell of Indian food in the aircraft was already making me feel hungry even though I had just finished eating spicy and delicious hot samosas at the Mumbai airport. Since I was one of the first few passengers to board the aircraft, I was already seated in my place without much hassle. The flight attendants were moving along the cabin and harassing the passengers who were carrying oversized hand baggage as I settled down in my seat and put on my seat belt and tried to adjust the big blow of cold air coming down on my head. As I sat down, I closed my eyes and started thinking.

For more than a decade, I had been living in the United States. First I could not believe it—had it really been over a decade? Me, Raju More, or better known as Roger Moore, or even better Bond, had finally become a citizen of the United States! As I was thinking about the whole process of transformation from Raju More to Bond or Dr. Bond, my mind went back to the memories of the whole decade . . .

# Immigrating to the Land of Opportunity!

## November 2000

Going to U.S. was a big step in my career, particularly for a physician. I had to pass two grueling exams and an English test to make sure I was qualified enough to speak English to my future patients in the United States. Following the tests, I had an equally grueling interview at the U.S. Embassy in Abu Dhabi. There was heavy security in and around the embassy. I was greeted by a man from my own country, India, who had been working at the counter. To my disbelief, he spoke to me in an American accent. No wonder since he had been working with so many Americans he must have developed the accent fairly quickly. Anyway, I filled out the forms and was waiting in the embassy waiting area for my turn for the interview with the consular official. As there were many others ahead of me, I looked around the pictures and notices on the wall, just to kill time.

I was amused to see one particular notice; it read something like this:

'If you belong to any of the following Terrorist organizations, please fill up Form L" and there was an exhaustive list of Terrorist Organizations around the world... some of which I had not even heard of. And the funniest part was the note below the notice... N.B. answering 'YES' to this question does not necessarily mean that your visa will be rejected!

I was glad that I did not belong to any of those terrorist organizations. Less paperwork, I guess.

"Please fill up Form 'L' if you belong to the following terrorist organizations"

N.B. answering 'YES' to this question does not necessarily mean that your visa will be rejected!

Soon my name was called and I appeared for my interview.

My consular official was a young pretty lady wearing a black suit and cream-colored blouse. She had just enough make-up on her face, not too little or too much, and golden nail polish on her manicured hands. She had blonde hair tied into a nice pony tail. In short, she was very attractive and I thought I missed a heartbeat when she looked at me with her deep blue eyes. For some reason, she wore a low-cut blouse exposing her cleavage. Although tempted, I decided not to look down "there" but directly to her face. What if she rejected my visa and the reason would not be something like "Potential immigrant" but "the candidate was looking at my exposed breasts or cleavage to be precise." One thing I could not understand was why these girls exposed something if they didn't want anyone to look. I thought I would learn about the American psyche after I start living there! First step was to get a proper visa so let me get my visa first. I was dressed impeccably in a black suit and bright red tie. I thought I had impressed her with my suit but this was not the right time to think about flirting with her.

"So, why do you want to go to United States?" she asked me, looking directly into my eyes. I missed another heartbeat! Not because of her question but because she was too attractive.

"I want to attend the radiology conference in Chicago," I told her. "I am planning to present a scientific paper. It has already been accepted."

"Do you have the acceptance letter with you?"

"Yes, I do." I promptly gave her the letter and she looked at it carefully. Then she asked me a few more questions about how long I planned to stay and where I was going to stay. I showed her a letter from my friend in New Jersey, answered all her questions honestly and showed her all the necessary documents. At the end of interview, she wrote her recommendation and said, "I have granted you a six months visitor's visa. Make sure you don't overstay the duration of visa." And she smiled and I missed many heart beats! A few because I got visa and other few (probably more) because of her smile. I thought of asking her what her plans for the night were but resisted and instead said, "Thank you very much, ma'am". She replied by just smiling and handing over the documents to me. At that point I thought I was having a heart attack but was glad I did not.

I was supposed to come back to pick up my passport and when I returned the security outside was much less. I opened my passport and saw that I was granted a six months multiple entry visitor's visa to the United States. Wait, if I was given six months visitor's visa, why multiple entries? I guess she knew that I was not going to reenter United States again in six months' time, but I realized that the multiple entry visa cost more than single entry. Hmm . . . I guess that was my first introduction to capitalism. I had won the first battle and I was really excited!

After coming out of the embassy I realized that I did not have sufficient time to prepare for my trip. I had to go to the malls in Abu Dhabi and Dubai to do the necessary shopping. Since at that time I was staying in one of the hottest terrains in the world and my first visit to the states was in the midst of winter, I had to get a help from a friend of mine to buy the thermal undergarments, winter coat, gloves, scarf, etc. I was also working on my scientific paper I was planning to present in the conference. The days passed by quickly and I was ready to take my first ever transatlantic flight to the United States!

My first flight was from Dubai to London, which was pretty uneventful. I had to change my flight at the Heathrow airport in London. While I was waiting for my next flight to New York's JFK airport, I decided to walk around and did some shopping. I also called my friend who happened to be in London at that time. I have to admit that it was first time I felt how I stood out in a predominantly white crowd. I was probably only one of the few in the waiting lounge with brown skin and black hair.

London's Heathrow airport appeared to be one of the busiest airports in the world. As my flight time came closer I went to the gate. Before boarding I was interviewed again by the airline security personnel. I have to admit that it was one of the harshest interviews I have had in my entire life. Even worse than the Viva exams I had done in medical school. The guy who interviewed me was fat and he looked Indian to me but had a strong British accent. I thought maybe he was originally from India but raised in the UK. I was grilled more than twenty minutes and that fatso asked me all sorts of questions.

At one point he asked me, "Sir, where do you work?"

"Ministry of Health, in Dubai."

To my surprise he asked me if I had the Ministry of Health ID with me. I remembered while packing that I was wondering whether I should take my ID with me because it was in Arabic. But finally I did carry it with me, just in case.

I said, "Yes, I do."

"Can I see it?" He asked.

"Yes, of course, but it's in Arabic"

"Does not matter, I want to see it."

I had no choice but to take out my ID and show him. He looked at it and God knows what he understood, because I was sure he could not read a single word of it. He looked at it and gave it back to me. After that he asked me many irrelevant questions, most of which had nothing to do with my trip to U.S. I have to admit that he did ask me some relevant questions, such as why was I going and where I was going to stay, etc. After grilling me for more than twenty minutes, he finally seemed to be satisfied and he stamped something on my boarding pass. He also applied some sticker on my passport. After this ordeal I was finally sure that I was really going to United States of America. I have to admit that I was excited and one of the reasons was that I believed that I was going to meet some of the most beautiful flight attendants. But soon I was disappointed to see overweight, older and not-so-good-looking ladies and to my disbelief, a few men as attendants. I was wondering where all those beautiful blondes I had seen in American movies were. Maybe they just worked in movies and the rest as flight attendants? Maybe when I get time I should plan a trip to Hollywood or LA and look for those missing sexy blondes! After a few months of my stay in the US, I realized it must be because of the "equal opportunity" and "non-discrimination Policy" or whatever. Anyway, as I settled down in my seat I looked around to see how American people looked. Most of them were white. One lady sitting in a row ahead of me was so fat that I wondered how her back side could ever fit into the airline seat. Her arms were as bulky as my thighs! My first impression about Americans was that they were really heavy weight characters throwing their weight around, literally. As the plane landed, however, all these people who I thought were American were standing with me in the line of non-us citizens. I soon realized that I had mistaken the European visitors as Americans.

As my plane began descend to land at JFK I looked through my window and saw the familiar sight of New York City's tall buildings, often shown in American movies. Wow! I thought, this must be the best skyline in the world! I also felt somewhat home sick as it reminded me of Mumbai or Bombay, my home city, although Bombay does not have as many skyscrapers as New York. Since we did not have immediate permission to land, the captain circled around and gave us a short tour of the city! He pointed out landmarks as we flew: "Look to your right to take a look at Twin Towers," he said and we all looked to the right side. I was really impressed with the Twin Towers. At that time I did not know that one could visit the towers also called the "top of the world."

The plane soon landed and I said to myself, "Congratulations, you have finally landed in the land of opportunity!"

My friend from high school, who lived in New Jersey with his wife, was supposed to come to pick me up at the airport. I was supposed to clear immigration first.

The immigration officer asked me only one question, "Sir, what is the purpose of your visit?"

"I am here to attend a conference in Chicago." He asked to show my registration for the conference and seemed to be satisfied.

He stamped my passport and said, "Welcome to United States of America."

"Thank you very much," I said.

I soon collected my bags and went outside. I could not believe that I was going to soon step out in New York City! I was very anxious. What if my friend forgot to come to airport, what if I cannot find him? While I was walking down the long corridors, I was looking at the advertisements on the glittering, back-lighted screens. I saw a picture of young blonde woman with a beautiful smile. I was stunned by her beauty and more than that her smile. I stopped to take a good look at her. I did not know who she was but I was mesmerized by her sheer beauty. I was trying to see if her name was mentioned somewhere on the screen but I could not find it. On the top of the screen was written "FRIENDS" in big bold letters. There were pictures of some others but it was her face that caught my eye. She also had a different but attractive hairstyle. I soon realized people were getting blocked as I was standing in the middle of the walkway. I decided to move on still thinking about that beautiful face I had seen. Who was she? What had she to do with "Friends?" I decided that I would ask my friend after I reached his apartment in New Jersey. I was relieved to see my friend, Girish, standing in the crowd, smiling and waving at me.

"How was your flight, buddy?" he asked. I immediately noticed his accent had changed a little bit.

"It was good except for the fact that I was really disappointed by the quality of air hostesses," I said jokingly. "Where are those hot, sexy blonde girls we used to see in the Hollywood movies?"

"Most of them are in Hollywood. Why would they work as air hostesses if they are so sexy and beautiful?" he asked. Then he smiled and added, "This is a land of equal opportunity for everyone. Let's go and get my car".

I was wearing a sports coat. He looked at me and said, "I think you should be okay in the cold outside. But make sure you wear these gloves I got for you".

We went outside and he asked me to wait at one spot with my bags. As he got his car and opened the trunk, a big burly man standing next to me lifted my bags and helped me to put them in the trunk. I thanked him without knowing he was expecting money. Girish got out of the car and tipped him. Once I was in the car I said, "I didn't know that the negro guy who helped us put the bags in the dicky was expecting money or tip. I thought he was just helping us." I did not realize I said something wrong.

# Manhattan Alien

I did not know that the 'N' guy who helped us put the bags in the 'dicky' was expecting a tip.

Girish turned around and said, "Raju, this is your first lesson in U.S. Don't *ever* say the N word. Okay?"

"Yes. I am sorry I was not aware, but what do we call them?"

"The better term is black or even better African American."

"Okay. Got it."

"Another thing, don't ever say dicky, it is called the trunk here. Dicky means something else," he said, smiling.

To be frank, I was little embarrassed. To change the topic I said, "Oh, by the way, I saw a picture of a beautiful woman with a great smile. I don't know who she is but "FRIENDS" was written on the advertisement."

Before answering my question he said, "You better use the term commercial here in U.S. And the girl you are referring to I think is Jennifer Aniston. Yes, she has a great smile."

"Jennifer Aniston... hmm," I murmured to myself.

Soon we reached his apartment. He was staying in New Jersey near or pretty close to the Hoboken tunnel. From the apartment complex compound, I could see the Twin Towers. I was really excited. The view from his apartment was even great because I could see the great New York skyline. His apartment was quite small. I was relieved because I thought only people in Mumbai lived in small apartments. When he told me the rent he was paying for the studio apartment and the parking charges, I was shocked.

He said, "This important man because Priya and I both work in NYC."

"What is NYC?" I asked.

"NYC stands for New York City, my dear. America is the country of short forms or acronyms. So get used to it, buddy. Soon you will realize that everything is simplified and shortened here. You may end up staying here. You never know."

I was hungry. Girish said, "Get fresh and we will have dinner. Priya has cooked great food."

Soon three of us were eating freshly cooked Indian food made laboriously by Girish's wife, Priya.

"Try to get good sleep. Anyway you may have a jet lag and may get up in the middle of night but don't worry. Remember it is daytime in Mumbai and night here. Tomorrow is Saturday, so try to relax. We will talk about your conference and other things tomorrow."

He continued talking without waiting a response from me. "We have just one bedroom so we have bought this inflatable bed for you. We will show you how to inflate and deflate and you will have to sleep here in the living room."

"I am used to it being from Mumbai. We have small houses in Mumbai unlike New Delhi." Priya was from Delhi and she was used to stay in much bigger houses than us in Mumbai.

As I laid down on the bed, I realized it was much different than a regular bed. But I was tired and I never knew when I fell asleep. I had a dream in which I was on flight and Jennifer Aniston was the air hostess. She was wearing a sort of mini skirt and tight skin-colored stockings or leggings or something of that sort. In short, she was looking very sexy. I was calling her frequently and would ask for water, coffee, and other stuff just so that I could see her and talk to her. In the beginning, she did not mind but at one point she got annoyed. I had asked for water and she came with a big bottle of water. She opened the bottle and poured water on my head and screamed, "Stop calling me again and again you... fucking rascal." I was shocked by her response and soon woke up and realized it was just a dream. It was already late morning and Girish was preparing breakfast for us.

"I am sorry. I think I slept for a long time, Girish," I said.

"Never mind. It happens. I am glad you did not wake up in the middle of night."

The next day, the two of us went out to New York City. Going to the city was pretty easy from Girish's house. We just had to take a ferry, which cost only a couple of dollars. We went to shopping malls, a relatively new concept to me, although I had seen a few in Dubai. I was surprised the way people were shopping. Some of them were carrying two to three bags in each hand.

I asked Girish, "How come people are shopping so much? Some of them do not appear to be very rich."

"Hey, buddy, this is America, okay? Here people buy what they want, even if they can or cannot afford it. All you need is a credit card."

"But why do you want to buy something which you are unlikely to afford? Ultimately you will end up paying for it, won't you?"

"Yes, very true, but this mentality is more like Indian mentality. Here in the U.S. if someone wants something he or she will buy it no matter what. You can pay your credit cards later."

At one point, we had to stop to refuel his car.

"I need to fill some gas," he said.

"Oh, I did not realize your car tires needed some air." I got down and started checking car tires.

"No, need some fuel for my car," he said.

"Oh, I did not realize this is petrol pump."

"Raju, in America it is called a gas station not petrol pump," Girish corrected me.

"Oh you mean your car runs on LPG, the liquid petroleum gas?" I was a bit confused.

"No, no, no. What you call petrol in India is called gas here."

"But it is liquid state isn't it? Then why is it called a gas?" I asked again as I was thoroughly confused.

"My dear, gas is a short form for gasoline. No one calls it a gasoline station, it is called a gas station. Now remember that. If you ask anyone around for a petrol pump, they will look at you as if you are coming from a different planet. Like an alien. You better get used to these things now," he warned me with stern voice.

I got down to see the price of petrol... er... not petrol but gas. I realized the gasoline was sold in gallons not liters. Hmm, everything looks and feels different here, I thought.

"Now let me take you to one of America's popular coffee shops," he said. I was excited. We stopped at one shop called Starbucks. There was a big picture of a princess of some sort on the shop.

"If you would not have told me that this a coffee shop, I would have thought that this is a pawn shop" I said.

"Really? What makes you think that this is a pawn shop?"

"Oh, because it says 'bucks' at the end of the name. Buck means money doesn't it?"

"You are too funny man. Starbucks is a great coffee shop not a pawn shop," he said. "You are about to enjoy one of the best coffees in the world."

Even just outside the shop, I could smell the coffee that was brewing inside. We went inside and I noticed the shop was full of people. Most of them had laptops or books and were chatting, studying, and having coffee at the same time. I realized that this was not an ordinary coffee shop but one that was fancy and expensive.

"Hey, Raju, this is America's favorite coffee, okay? Order whatever you want, I will be just back." Girish disappeared somewhere, I guess to empty his bladder.

I looked around and stood in the line to order. There were some people ahead of me so I had time to look at the big board behind the counter. I could not see coffee anywhere. Soon my turn came and the black boy asked me in a thick African American accent

"What kind of coffee you want? Latte, cappuccino or mocha?"

I did not know all these types. I was confused and I looked around for Girish but could not see him. I never realized ordering coffee could be so difficult a task.

Looking at the expression on my face, he said, "Sir, there are people behind you. Can you please step aside and decide and let me know when you are ready? Thank you."

I promptly stepped by the side. I looked at the menu board and could not find anything familiar. Why there are so many choices? I wished there were less choices.

Then I thought I should probably listen to other people ordering so I could get a clue as to what to order. One tall lady came and said, "One tall skinny latte, please." No clue. Okay, let me try the next one. Next was a tall white guy who ordered, "Double shot venti mocha." Absolutely no clue as to what he was ordering. I looked at the menu board again. The only thing I thought was familiar was an espresso, which in India is like a frothy coffee drink. I decided to order that.

"One espresso, please."

# B.K. Mhatre

"How many 'shots' you want?"

By that time the attendant had changed. A thin younger black girl asked me in a thick accent, "How many shots you want?"

I was really in deep trouble. I could not understand her question. *What "shots" is she talking about? Is this coffeehouse or whorehouse?*

"Sir, how many shots you want?" she asked again.

I again looked around for Girish but could not see him anywhere.

"Two shots," I said in a trembling voice.

"Here you go, sir." She handed me a big cup that was almost empty with some coffee at the bottom. I was shocked. Now what do I do with this? I also noticed that on the coffee cup it was written in bold letters: "BEWARE: CONTENTS MAY BE HOT." I promptly paid and stepped aside, added some milk and sugar and drank it.

By the time Girish came back. He stood in the line ordered a huge coffee drink and came to the table where I was sitting.

"Is this coffee only for you or are we supposed to share this?" I asked him, looking at the huge cup of coffee.

"No. This only for me. Here people are kind of big, so is there appetite. You won't get the size of small cup of coffees like you would get in India. The Americans would probably drink ten cups of those coffees at one time."

"Really?" I was surprised.

"Anyway, how was your coffee? Looks like you finished it already," Girish said while sipping his large coffee.

"To tell you frankly… horrible. I asked for espresso thinking that I will get a frothy coffee like you get in India, but instead I got something else."

"Idiot, the espresso you get in India is not the same espresso here. It is called cappuccino. Do you want another one?"

I was already pretty shaken from my coffee ordering and drinking experience so I kindly declined his offer.

But I asked him, "Why are there so many choices here? I wish I had fewer choices."

"Again, this is America, man. You can choose what you want, not only what is being offered to you. Everything here is consumer driven. Do you get it?" I nodded. I was getting too many lessons on my first ever day in US of A.

The next day, I was supposed to leave for the conference in Chicago. There was a direct flight from New York to Chicago. Before leaving I asked Girish, "They ask two questions before boarding the flight and I could not understand well because I am still getting used to the American accent."

"Raju, the answer to both questions is 'no'. She must have asked you have you received anything from anyone which you are carrying and does not belong to you. And the other question must be has anyone else packed the bags for you."

"Okay, sounds good."

I was mentally ready for the flight as well as the conference. This time I was not expecting beautiful and blonde flight attendants.

The flight was pretty uneventful. I was impressed by the large and beautiful O'Hare Airport. The conference venue was at McCormick Place in Chicago. Luckily there was guy from Mumbai, Milind, with whom I was in touch before coming to the U.S. Milind was studying at the Illinois Institute of Technology. He had told me that his dorm was pretty close to McCormick place and he had arranged for me to stay with him. His only condition was that I would need to arrange for my transport from the airport to the IIT hostel since he did not own a car. When I got to his apartment, I knocked on the door. Luckily he was in his apartment.

"Hey, come on in. Do you need any help with luggage?" he asked me.

"No, I think I am okay. It is very cold outside." I said.

"Remember Chicago is also called the Windy City. So it is not only cold here but windy too which makes it worse. But you should be fine. You will be inside McCormick place for the most of the time."

I settled in his room, which was pretty shabby and unkempt. I was frankly shocked by the way it was kept. However I did not show any expression on my face and I thanked him for the arrangement.

"By the way, what is McCormick place?" I asked him.

"Come, let me show you." He got up and took me near the window of his dorm room. It was already dark.

"Do you see those lights in the distance?"

"Yes, sort of," I said while stretching my vision as well as my imagination.

"That is McCormick place. It is one of the biggest conference venues in the U.S."

"How do I go there? Is it walkable distance?" I asked him.

"No. I mean, it is walkable in summer but not now in winter. But I did some research for you and guess what, there is a bus which goes from here across the street to your conference. All you need to do is take a bus from here and it is I think only a couple of stops. So you are all set!"

"Wow, that is great. Thanks for the research." I was happy that my transport problem was resolved.

There were at least three to four other students staying in the room with him and every one had one corner and table for themselves. Some of them shared the PC in the room. What made that room look shabby was the fact that some of them were sleeping on the floor on a mattress. Many of them had their clothes, including underwear, scattered on the bed or made into one big pile of clothes. All of them were from India. Some of them had come on a scholarship and a few secured one after coming to the U.S. Most of them were also doing some sort of campus jobs, typically in their own department.

My friend, Milind, introduced me to everyone in the room.

"This is what I have arranged for you." Milind got up and showed me an old sofa near one of the windows. "You can sleep here for the duration of your stay. I don't want you to sleep on the floor. Only problem is one of our guys wakes up in the middle of the night and uses this computer next to this sofa and he is typing for the most of the rest of night."

I thought about it and said, "That is okay with me. Once I fall into bed, I go to sleep immediately and don't wake up easily. So don't worry about it."

"Do you want to eat pizza?" Milind asked me.

"Yes, sure." I was so hungry and a hot pizza sounded great to me.

The next day I woke up early before everyone else woke up. I got ready and wore my suit. I looked at myself in the mirror. Not bad, I thought. I was a bit nervous. While I was walking to the bus stop, I thought it was raining a bit. Then I realized, it was not water; it was actually very small crystals of ice. Wow! The first time in my life I had experienced snow fall. I was amazed and excited too. I got onto the bus and noticed that there was no conductor. I had been forewarned by Milind about it. I was carrying the exact change I needed. While standing in the bus, I realized almost everyone was looking at me.

"When you board the bus, don't look into the eyes of anyone, man or a woman. Just get down at your stop and start walking. Many of the passengers will be looking at you so don't be self-conscious," Milind had warned me.

The conference venue was a huge place. I had already registered and once I got my ID badge, I was officially part of the conference. One thing I noticed during the conference was that most of the time people were walking from one end to other and trying to attend different lectures in different halls or lecture room. I went to the lecture room where I was supposed to present my paper the next day. I checked the projection system and also took a look at the dais. I was a bit nervous.

The next day I went straight to my lecture room about half an hour before my presentation. I realized that most of the other people in the room were presenters before or after me. No real audience! Before the time of actual presentation, however, there was a sufficient audience in the room. I presented my paper with confidence and everything went well as I had planned.

Most people in the audience were impressed by my paper. I happened to meet a friend of mine who introduced me to Dr. Stein from one of the reputed hospitals in New York.

"Dr. Stein is the chair, by the way," he whispered in my ears. "Chair?" I looked at him with a question mark on my face. "Well, Raju, chair means chairman which you guys call head of department or HOD in India."

He stressed the words 'you guys,' which was sort of embarrassing for me but I ignored it. I thought he must be a U.S. citizen by now and he must be referring to 'you guys' as 'you bloody Indians.' Anyway, ignoring his comments, I thanked him for introducing me to Dr. Stein.

I chatted with Dr. Stein over coffee for few minutes. He liked my paper and asked me if I was interested in doing research with him. Since I showed immense interest in research, he conducted a short semi-official interview in cafeteria and accepted me as a research fellow in radiology at the New York hospital where he was working. I was set to start my first job in the USA as research fellow on a stipend of a mere five hundred dollars! It was both exciting as well as depressing event. Exciting because I was going to do some research in United States and depressing because in spite of being a full-fledged radiologist, I would be paid a meager salary. Dr. Stein also promised me to get a furnished apartment in the hospital complex, which meant I would not have to pay the rent from my salary.

I came back to New York and gave the good news to Girish. He was happy that I had found an opportunity in the United States.

He said, "Do not worry about your salary. Once you are here you should be able to find a better opportunity and maybe find a residency in the field of your choice."

During next few days, the three of us toured the major attractions in the city including the Twin Towers, top of the world. I was already feeling at the top of the world! I fell in love with New York. I liked the tall skyscrapers, the subway, and the multi-cultural society. New York was always on the go like Mumbai. I decided to buy small gifts for friends and family for when I returned home. I thought the best gift would be replicas of the Statue of Liberty. Enthusiastically I picked up small statues, at least half a dozen. Just out of curiosity I turned the statue upside down, just to make sure they were made in United States. I was shocked to see that all of them were made in China. I went to the shopkeeper and asked, "I was looking for some Statues of Liberty made in USA. Do you have any?"

"No sir, all we have are those ones you have picked up and all of them are made in China, I believe."

I had no choice but to accept those Chinese made statues and give them as gifts from United States to my family and friends in India. After staying in United States for few months I realized that except houses, some people and some other stuff, everything else was made in China!

"Remember you are a Non-resident Alien"

# June 2001
# Life in New York City Begins

I went back to Dubai. Now the next step was to get the visa. I was supposed to get a visa called J1 visa, which is usually given to the foreign medical graduates coming to U.S. for training. However there was one glitch. Apparently there was a clause in the visa rules that I have to go back to the country of my origin before I could get an immigrant visa like H1B. At that point, however, I cared less about those issues, and my first priority was to get the visa and start research. Getting J1 visa was pretty easy, I guess because of the home country clause in the visa. I resigned from my job in Dubai and started packing my bags for USA. Some of the guys at the hospital where I was working were astonished that I accepted a research position on much less salary than what I was being paid at that time. I was happy about it as to me it was more like a stepping stone and probably best way to get into the land of opportunity and the field of Radiology. This time I decided to take a direct flight from Dubai to New York so I could avoid harassment from the officials at Heathrow Airport. I finally landed at the JFK airport again. My entry into United States was pretty uneventful. The immigration officer asked me only one question. "Why are you here in US?"

"For doing research."

"Sir, welcome to the United States of America. Remember you are a non-resident alien in this country. Make sure you do not overstay a single day in the U.S. after your visa expires."

17

Alien? I thought to myself that this is the term used for those creatures from other planets. Many times in books and comics they are shown to have one eye in the middle, no ears and big heads, like the character in E.T., or like some of the characters shown in the movie *Star Wars: A New Hope* particularly in the scene where Luke Skywalker meets Han Solo for the first time in the bar. Do I look like an alien to him? However I remembered the golden rule that someone had taught me. Never argue or confront an immigration officer.

"Yes sir," I said.

He gave me a weird look and stamped my passport and asked me to proceed.

Since I was promised an apartment in my contract, I did not have to do any apartment hunting in the city. I stayed for a few days with Girish and Priya. New York City looked even more beautiful in summer than in winter when I had visited. One of the days during my stay with Girish, he said that they were going to a car dealership to buy a car for Priya and asked me if I wanted to come. Since I thought car buying in America would a good experience, I agreed to go.

"Why do you need a car?" I asked him.

"Raju, I agree that we don't need two cars but we need at least one good car. I have to drive to the train station and park my car then catch a train into the city for my job. A lot of people stay here and do jobs in New York like I do."

"Got it," I said and we all went to one of the car dealerships close to their apartment.

The car salesman was luckily not a high pressure sales guy. But when he came to know that my friends were looking for an American car, he started protesting. "Guy, don't buy an American car, you will get into trouble. Those cars will give you more headaches than comfort, believe me."

I was surprised. Rarely would you see an American sales guy advising the clients not buy an American product! He insisted that we should buy a Japanese car or a German car. Since buying a German car was out of budget for them, they decided to go for a Japanese car. Priya liked one particular Toyota model and we decided to take a test drive.

"All right, guys, here is a short route we take for the test drives." The salesman showed the route to both of them and handed over the keys to Priya.

Priya drove and Girish sat next to her. I sat next to the car salesman in the back. He greeted me while sitting and handed me his business card. "Hello, sir, looks like you are new in this country?"

I was surprised but I said, "Yes."

"Here is my card in case you decide to buy a car, please avail yourself of my services."

I looked at the card and kept it.

"My last name is Beaver, like the animal," he said and started laughing alone. Till that time I did know an animal like the beaver existed, so I also smiled and thanked him.

He kept on talking. "Guys, how long do you plan to keep the car . . . just curious."

"At least eight years, maybe ten years or more" said Girish.

"Really." He turned to me and said, "Americans keep cars only for three to four years. We change cars every three years..." and then whispered into my ear " . . . and wives every ten years." I was shocked.

"Really?" I asked him.

He nodded and added, "Only the lucky ones . . . you know, those who are rich. They get a younger wife every ten years like new model of car!" And he started laughing hysterically again.

## EDUCATIONAL CAR BUYING EXPERIENCE'

"Americans change car every three years...
...and wife every ten years!"

My friends decided to buy that car and for more than an hour we spent time arguing over the car price. Eventually, they all agreed on one price and decided to take the car home in a week or so after the necessary paperwork was done. Finally we came back home and naturally we were all tired!

"So how was this experience?" Girish asked me.

"Well, very educative," I said.

"Really? In what way?" Priya asked me.

"Well, I learned that Americans change cars every three or maybe four years and wives every ten years, but only the lucky ones, according to Mr. Beaver." I said in single breath only to get Priya furious.

"Yes, that is why I married your friend... not an American," she said.

"Cool down, babe," Girish told Priya.

"Raju, you know something weird in this country?" Girish asked me.

"Tell me about it, there are so many weird things I have seen so far! One more to my list of those things!"

"I don't know if you heard the conversation with Mr. Beaver. He said to us that we cannot buy a car unless we buy the car insurance. What is funny and ironic is as of now it is mandatory to have car insurance but it is not mandatory to have health insurance! So if you have an accident and you don't have health insurance, your car will be replaced or repaired but you will be left to the mercy of God! Of course having said that, emergencies such as accidents are covered by the hospitals irrespective of your insurance status."

"Wow, I did not know that!" I was amazed.

Finally we sat down for dinner and chatted about our high school and college days.

After a couple of days staying with them, I moved to my apartment. Girish and Priya came to drop me off in their brand new Toyota Corolla car since I had significant luggage.

Also they didn't want me to spend money on the taxi cab in New York.

Both of them helped me with my luggage, which was pretty heavy. After settling down in my dorm, both of them took a look around. Girish was looking at my bed and he asked for my help to raise the mattress and was inspecting something under the mattress.

"What are you looking for? Bed bugs?" I asked him curiously.

"Well, the actual mattress part looks good but I was checking your box spring under the mattress."

I had no idea what he was talking about. Seeing the expression on my face he said, "You need to ask them to replace the box spring. Here the beds are quite different than the ones made in India." He started explaining to me.

"Look here, here is the mattress and under which is a box spring. Your box spring looks old and needs replacement, I guess."

"Oh so there is a box spring under the mattress. No wonder Americans are so springy in nature. They are 'made' that way," I joked as Priya entered the bedroom.

"Look there is box spring under the mattress."
"No wonder, Americans are so 'springy' in nature, they are 'made' that way."

"Raju, you are here for research, remember, don't try to make any springy babies on this bed," she warned me.

I quickly said, "I was just joking and looking at the anatomy of the bed."

"Well, Raju, it looks like you have all the basic things in the apartment you need, I guess," said Priya. After a brief survey of the apartment, it was time for them to go.

"Hey, you take care buddy" said both of them giving me a warm hug. I was bit emotional.

"Raju, come visit us if you feel home sick," said Priya, and I was really emotional.

"Thanks, guys, I am glad you are here for me," I said with wet eyes.

By the time I moved to my tiny apartment, my jet lag was almost over. My apartment was a tiny one-bedroom apartment in the hospital campus. There was just one small road in between my apartment building and the main hospital building. After which there was a parking lot. So to get to the hospital building where I was going to work, I had to cross the road and then go through the parking lot. A small grocery store was inside the campus within walking distance from the hospital or my apartment. My apartment building was mainly occupied by foreigners, "aliens" like me. There were a lot of Indians, Chinese, and Korean students, as well as doctors like me who had come for research.

I had a few days off before my job started. Staying on my own was somewhat difficult and challenging, if I may say so. I was thoroughly confused with miles, gallons and Fahrenheit. During my physical exam, the doctor asked me my weight and I said it was fifty-five kilograms. She frowned then used her calculator to convert it into pounds. I took a long time to get used to the temperature. In the beginning, I used to have a pocket calculator to convert Fahrenheit into Celsius. Gallons were equally confusing for me. Also apparently European and US gallons were not the same. I did understand the distance in kilometers but I had to think twice when someone talked about miles. The light switches were exactly opposite of those in India or Middle East which confused me further. 'ON' position in US was 'OFF' in the rest of the world.

The biggest problem was writing dates. Since in India and probably rest of the word, the day is written first followed by the month and then the year. The secretary at the hospital office got thoroughly confused when she saw the dates on my certificates. "Sir, these dates don't make any sense. They are in a weird format." I did not quite understand her confusion so we asked another lady in the office. Her confusion was resolved when the other lady who came to our help explained, "Hey girl, these dates are in European format day, month, year." After which she said, "Oki doki, now I get it."

I did not quite understand why she said "Oki Doki." Doki in my language means heads. I was pretty sure she did not know Marathi. Maybe that was New York lingo, I thought, but did not dare to ask her.

After looking at all the paperwork she said, "You are all set now. Any questions?"

"No."

"All righty." Oh, New York lingo again, I thought.

I did not quite understand in the beginning why everyone was in bad mood on Monday morning. Although everyone seemed to be in good mood on Thursday and particularly on Friday.

Anyway, soon my day of orientation arrived. I got up early in the morning, maybe because I was excited or maybe because I had not gotten over the second jet lag completely. I got ready and made some tea for myself and looked outside the window. Since I did not have an electric tea kettle, I had to make tea in the old Indian way of boiling tea leaves. It was early morning and the sun was just rising up. It was a bit cold though. I had a feeling it might rain. In fact, it was kind of monsoon season in India. I decided to carry an umbrella with me just in case it rained. I finished my tea and went outside. As I had guessed, light rain just started even before I had stepped out. Luckily it was not heavy and there was hardly any wind. I crossed the little road in front of my dorm building. I had to enter the parking lot. Lots of cars were driving in the parking lot so I was walking slowly and looking for cars around me and avoiding getting knocked down by them. As I was in the middle of the parking lot, I heard someone saying, "Hey you." I stopped and looked around. There was a car parked to the left of me with a young lady sitting in the car. I turned around to make sure she was not calling someone else.

"Hey, you with umbrella, I'm talking to you." Now I was sure that she is talking to me. "Hey, can you please share your umbrella with me and drop me to the hospital building?" I was a bit surprised.

"Sure, come along," I said. She jumped out of her car and grabbed her bag and came under my umbrella. She was wearing a cream-colored top and a short but well-fitting dark brown skirt. She was a bit short and even with her fashionable brown high heels boots she was still shorter than me.

It was dark and cloudy so I could not see her face very well. She seemed to be in a bit of a hurry. Without turning her head she said, "I have an important appointment today and didn't want to get drenched in rain."

"That is fine. Hope you are not getting wet," I said politely. She was pretty close to me while walking. I could smell the sweet feminine perfume she was wearing. Her partially wet hair rolling over her shoulders was touching my arms. Frankly, I was kind of aroused by her closeness and her smell. I wished that small walk from the parking lot to the hospital would never end. Unfortunately, the hospital building came closer and as soon as we reached the main porch of the hospital, she lurched forward and turned around. She gave me a bright nice smile and said, "Thanks, buddy. Have a great day. See you around." She walked quickly and disappeared into the crowd in front of the hospital. I had glimpse of her face; she was stunningly beautiful. For some reason, I thought I had seen her somewhere. Or maybe she resembled somebody I had known or seen before, but I could not figure out where. I was kind of speechless after I saw her face. I did not even reply to her and thought of saying something. Before I could gather my senses, she had disappeared. Wow, I thought. *My day is going to be great. I wish it would rain every day and I would get a chance to meet her again under the umbrella.* I recovered from my fantasy and was looking for signs to the radiology department. After I reached the department, I asked the lady at the front desk about Dr. Stein's office. She gave me a look and asked, "Do you have an appointment with him today, sir?"

"No, I mean yes, he is expecting me today but I am not sure if I have an appointment with him."

"Okay, let me call his secretary and please have seat and I will call you when I get in touch with her. What is your name, sir?"

"Dr. More, Mor-ay." I spelled it for her.

"Oh, Dr. Moore, please have a seat."

Gosh, can anyone pronounce my name correctly? I thought. Oh well, I am an alien anyway and how can I expect humans to know the names of aliens and pronounce them correctly? I sat down in chair and waited for her to call me. After making some phone calls she looked at me and said, "Sir, could you please come with me?" I went with her and she showed me Dr. Stein's office.

"How are you today" she asked me.

"I am doing fine, how about you?" I asked her politely.

"Well, you know, it is Monday morning. I need a few more cups of coffee to wake me up then I should be fine," she said, laughing. WTF, I thought!

After walking for a minute or so she knocked on one of the doors and opened it for me.

"Dr. Moore, this is Mary, Dr. Stein's secretary."

Mary greeted me and asked me to wait for her boss. Soon Dr. Stein came and greeted me. He asked me about my flight and my stay so far, after which he showed me my office where I would be working. It was basically a huge room with many tables and computers. Most of the room was occupied by Japanese and Chinese research fellows. Dr. Stein introduced me to almost everyone in the room. "Hi guys, this is Dr. Moore from India. He will be doing some exciting research with you guys." I was assigned one table and a computer. The guys and gals in the room were talking in Japanese and Chinese. One of the Japanese guys came to me and said in fairly good English with a strong Japanese accent "Hi, I am Akio. Welcome and get settled."

"Thank you. I am Raju. I am from Mumbai, India. Where are you from?"

"I am from Osaka, Japan."

Dr. Stein's secretary then took me around in the department and introduced me to multiple people. Mary gave me a bunch of paperwork to fill out. On one of the forms it was written "Do you have or have had sex with a stranger?" I replied to that question 'I don't even talk to strangers, forget having sex with him or her.' The secretary laughed when she read my answer but also had an objection to my answer. "Sir, this does not answer the question because you can still have sex with a stranger without speaking a word."

"Really, are you kidding me?" I thought. Finally, I had to answer to that question as 'No.' There was one more question about drugs. 'Do you take drugs?' to which I answered 'Yes.' Soon there was a small group of people with a university police officer who came to me and escorted to me a small room. The officer asked me to sit in a chair and asked me "Since you have confessed to taking drugs could you please tell me what kind of drugs do you take and how often?" I replied, "I take vitamins almost every day, Tylenol as needed, sometimes Ibuprofen when I have a bad headache."

He was stunned. He said, "Sir, those are not called drugs."

I replied "Yes, of course they are drugs. A drug is a substance that is used in the diagnosis, treatment, or prevention of a disease or as a component of a medication. Also a drug is medicine or other substance which has a physiological effect when ingested or otherwise introduced into the body."

There was a moment of silence. Then the officer said, "Do you take marijuana, cocaine or methamphetamine? Also called the street drugs?"

"I have never seen or heard about such things except maybe in Hollywood movies," I said.

"Sir, that does not answer my question. Please reply 'yes' or 'no'," said the officer angrily.

"Sir, if I have never seen them how can I consume them?" was my argument.

"Well, you can close your eyes and take them," said one of the ladies.

"Or someone can give them to you without your knowledge," said the officer.

Finally I gave up and said, "I am sorry if I have wasted your time. But I have never taken any illegal drugs, I will never take them in future. I am here to do research and not to do these kind of crazy things."

Finally, they walked me out of that small room and the officer put his arm around me and said in a friendly tone, "Listen man, let me tell you. When I saw you I knew you would not do drugs. You don't look that type of guy at all.

Remember when we say drugs, it almost always refers to street drugs or illegal drugs. Enjoy your stay here and good luck with your research."

I thanked him and also apologized for the confusion.

"No problem, bro. Take care," he said and he left.

As soon as he left, there was a lady who walked towards me and smiled.

"Hi, I am Lindsay" she said, and we shook hands. I was wondering who this new person was and what she was going to grill me about.

"I work in the university police department and I will take only two minutes of your time. I am here to ask you a few questions about your experience today with our police department and I will be very happy if you can complete this survey."

Frankly, I was in no mood to complete any surveys or anything but reluctantly I said, "Fine, please make it fast."

"On the scale of one to ten, one being worst and ten being the best, how would you rate your encounter with our police officer today?"

"Five," I said and she seemed a bit surprised.

"Sir, at any point did you feel that the officer was racially biased towards you due to your skin color, religion, or your sexual orientation?"

"No and for the record I am a straight man."

"Thank you, sir, but the last part was not necessary."

"Sir, on the scale of one to ten how would you rate the friendliness of the officer you dealt with, again one being worst and ten being the best."

"Ten," I said. She continued and at one point my patience ran out.

"Sir, on the scale from one to ten, ten being—"

I had to cut her short. "Lindsay, on the scale of one to ten in terms of boredom, I am at ten, ten being the worst and if you don't stop now, I will run away from you at the level of ten, ten being fastest," I said and got up and just walked out of the room as fast as I could.

"Sir, on the scale of one to ten how would you rate me, one being worst and . . ."

"On the scale of annoyance you get the worst, one assuming that is the worst but in terms of good looks you get the highest probably ten out of ten. Thank you and have a nice day," I said while running away. I could see her blushing from the corner of my eye.

After this dramatic episode, I was asked to fill up some forms and documents.

There was so much paper work involved that I kept on signing one document after other. Frankly by the middle of the day I was more disoriented than oriented.

I realized that it was almost lunch time and I was really hungry. Luckily I had some lunch coupons passed on to me by Dr. Stein through his secretary.

I took those coupons and went to cafeteria and selected a chicken sandwich and grabbed a water bottle. The cafeteria was really crowded and a lot of people were waiting for free tables and chairs. I decided to walk to back to the department as it was futile to wait there to eat my lunch. But on the way back I got lost. In one of the hallways I saw a room that seemed empty from outside. I opened the door slowly and the room was completely empty. It was bit cold due to strong air-conditioning. There were nice windows with colored paintings and some colored glass. I sat on one of the benches and opened my sandwich and started eating. Since I was hypoglycemic and probably in a hurry, I did not read the name of the room written outside. I was halfway through my lunch when a tall man wearing white clothes stood beside me. He was wearing huge cross around his neck. When I looked at him I realized he was angry. Out of sheer respect and maybe fear I got up.

He continued to stare at me and asked me, "My son, what are doing here?"

"Sir, I am having my lunch," I politely answered.

"I can see that. But did you see what was written outside the room?"

"No sir."

"This is a chapel. Do you know what a chapel is?"

Is he here to test my knowledge of English or religion, I thought for a second. Maybe both!

Suddenly I remembered a scene when the stabbed man in the Alfred Hitchcock movie *The Man Who Knew Too Much* mutters in James Stewart's ear "Ambrose Chapel."

"Yes, a chapel is a worship place for Christians," I said.

His temper rose and he asked me, "Do you know who I am?"

I looked at him from bottom to top and said "No, sir, but you are dressed like the Pope."

"No. The Pope is in the Vatican, I am just a priest or Father. You must a Hindu, am I right?"

I noticed he said Hindu with a hard D, not the soft D as we would say in Marathi or Hindi. Anyway I ignored it and answered his question.

"Yes"

"So do you go and eat in your Temple?"

"Yes, we do." My answer seemed to have angered him further.

"You must be a Hindu, do you eat in your temple?"
"Yes, we do"

"You might be doing that but we don't eat inside a chapel or church, do you understand?"

"Yes sir, but I must have missed the sign outside. This room was empty, quiet, and well decorated so—"

He cut me short. "So you just entered and started eating? Now finish your lunch and clean up everything and I don't want you to do this mistake again. Do you understand?"

"Yes, sir. I am very sorry . . ."

Once I said sorry he seemed to have calmed down and said, "That's okay, my son. Finish but don't do this again," and he left. I quickly finished my lunch and went back to the department. Luckily I found my way back to Mary's office.

Mary then took me to the IT department and introduced me to a lady. "Hey, Shannon, this is Dr. Moore. He will be doing research with us. Can you help him create his account and have access to HIS and RIS?"

"Hi, Shannon," I said and sat down in the chair next to her. She could not find my name because she had created the account under the name of 'Moore' but not 'More'. Finally, she realized her mistake when she read the name batch. Eventually she created an account for me and explained to me, in a strong nasal tone, the steps to sign into the HIS and RIS systems.

"Remember, your password must be at least eight characters long and must contain an upper case, lower case letter, a number and a special character."

I did not understand how a password can contain a special character. So I asked her "Special Character meaning like Darth Vader from *Star Wars*?"

She got mad at me thinking I was making fun of her but she soon realized that was my real doubt. "No, sir" and she explained me what it meant.

I selected my password and wrote it down in my small notebook.

"Good. Now the next step is to select three questions and then answer them. Remember, these are the questions you will need to answer if you lose your password." She then opened that page for me and told me to select any three questions and answer them.

"I will go and get a coffee while you do that," she said and left me. These were some of the strangest questions I had ever seen.

'What was the middle name of the girl you had first sex with?' The other question was 'What was the day of the week when you lost your virginity?' I did not answer any of those questions and looked anything which makes sense!

Security Question No. 1:
'What was the middle name of the girl you had first sex with?'

'Who was the boyfriend of your favorite school teacher?' I skipped that too.

Finally there were some sensible questions like 'Who is your favorite celebrity?' to which I promptly answered 'Jennifer Aniston.'

'What was the first model and make of your family car' I answered 'Premier Padmini' since when I was a kid, that was the only car available in Mumbai. When I was done with those stupid security questions Shannon walked in.

"Are you done with the questions?"

"Yes, I am," I replied.

"Great. Some of those questions may look somewhat strange but we want to make sure that our system is absolutely safe and secure," she said while smiling.

I was going to ask her which idiot had devised those questions, but I was glad that I did not ask her because she said, "I was the one who wrote those questions and so far no one has broken into our hospital information system." She said beaming a great smile. I said to myself 'Well good luck because I am sure there are hackers around who are much smarter than you and can easily hack into the system if they want by answering the stupidest questions you have selected.' I did not say anything of that sort. I thanked her and left her office dazed and exhausted!

# I become Dr. Bond

At the end of the day I met Dr. Stein again. He told me to report to the reading room next day where he usually reads.

The next day, I woke up early and got ready. I made some tea on the stove and looked outside through the window. It was a sunny day, no way it could rain again, so there was little or no chance I could see that beautiful girl again. Even then I decided to leave at the same time I had left the previous day. I had my tea and breakfast in the room and headed straight to the hospital. I walked through the parking lot and panned around to see her but there were too many unknown faces. After reaching the hospital building, I went straight to Dr. Stein's reading room, as he had advised me to. There was no one in the reading room. Once I was seated, there was a soft knock on the door and a young lady with glasses and a ponytail entered the room. She was wearing a white lab coat with a sky blue top beneath and was carrying a binder with a small paper in her hand. As soon as she entered the room, I could smell the perfume she was wearing, which reminded me of something I couldn't immediately identify. When I looked at her face more closely, I realized she was the girl I had met in parking lot! She looked even more beautiful today than previous day. Then I realized why I had thought that I knew her—she had stunning similarity to Jennifer Aniston, only her hair was black not blonde. I was stunned. For a moment I thought the girl from the sitcom *Friends* had walked into the room. Then I thought… it must my dream again like Jennifer Aniston as an air-hostess dream. I was about to pinch myself when she smiled and held out her right hand for me to shake. "Hi, I am Jennifer."

I was about to have a heart attack! Is this a dream?

"I am looking for Dr. Moore. Is that you?" I did not know what to do so I stood up mechanically and shook her hand and said, "Hi, I am Dr. Mor-ay… not Dr. Moore. How are you?"

"I'm good."

I realized she was standing so I offered her a chair.

"Thank you. That's nice of you to offer me a chair."

"I come from a country where women are or at least used to be well respected," I said and I sat down as she settled down in her chair.

She was surprised. "Oh, I presume you are from India. Aren't you?"

"Yes, you are right, I am."

"Let me introduce myself. I'm Jennifer, a fourth year med student here. I wanted to do some research and Dr. Stein said he had some project I can work on. So I'm here to meet him and you too. I presume you are or will be assigned some research project and I suppose I will be helping you."

"Well, that sounds good. I am here to do research too."

As I was about to say something, there was a knock on the door and both of us turned around to see who was coming in. Dr. Stein's secretary walked in.

"I am sorry guys, Dr. Stein had to go for an emergency meeting so he won't be here until nine thirty. Jen, Dr. Stein has requested you show Dr. Moore around the hospital and library, and here are some cafeteria coupons for breakfast he wanted me to pass on to you guys."

"Sweet. Thank you." Jennifer said. Jennifer looked at me and said "Well, what shall we do for the extra time we have? Shall we play 'Rock, paper, scissors?" I did not get it and I had a big question mark on my face. "Oh, man you are totally un-American! Never mind, you'll learn it." After a pause she said, "Come on, let's go have some free breakfast."

"I already had my breakfast today morning but I will accompany you to the canteen if you don't mind."

I had a feeling that she smiled about something I said.

"Did I say something wrong?" I asked her.

"Well, you should say 'this morning' not 'today morning' and second thing is it is called cafeteria not canteen. Canteen is the term used in Army and government facilities not in civilian life. Looks like you are new in this country."

"Yes, I am. I am an alien," I said jokingly.

"Alien?" Jennifer screamed in mock horror. "Like in *Star Wars*?"

"Yes, but I look like a normal human being, don't I?" I asked her.

"Yes, of course. Alien is a derogatory term for you," she said with some anger.

"Well, I am not only an alien but also a non-resident alien. At least that is what the immigration officer told me."

Both of us burst out laughing.

We went to canteen... er... cafeteria and sat down on the table. She got something to eat and I frankly did not know what she ordered.

"So how are you Dr. Moore? Oh, I am sorry, Dr. More?" Jen asked.

"I am fine, thank you for asking." And after a pause I asked her, "How about you, Jennifer?"

"Well, it's beginning of the week, you know. But I'm good," she said and I smiled.

She noticed my smile and asked me, "What's so funny?"

I realized my mistake and said with an expressionless face, "No. Nothing is funny."

"No. There is something I said that made you laugh. Tell me."

"Well, in British English, if you say I am good, it is wrong. You are supposed to say I am fine... not I am good."

"To hell with British English," she said loudly and I almost startled. In fact, the medical students who were walking next to us who heard the comment also turned around and looked at her.

She realized her mistake and said softly to me "Hey, what's your first mane?"

I also said softly "Raju, it's R-A..."

She cut me short. "Whatever, man. Listen, you are in America so you need to live, eat, drink, talk, sleep, and have sex like an American. Forget whatever you have learned in your life so far. Just wipe it out from your hard disc. Otherwise your life will be miserable." After a pause she said "Do you understand?"

"Yes, I do," I promptly replied.

"Anyway, let me get my breakfast real quick." She suddenly changed her tone from authoritative to friendly.

Jennifer got her breakfast and asked me if I wanted Starbucks coffee. Since my very first experience in the coffee shop was quite embarrassing, I kindly declined her offer. But I offered to carry her coffee to the table as her hands were full.

"Thank you. Let's go to that table where all radiology residents and fellows are sitting." I saw a bunch of white people in white coats sitting around the table she indicated. As we joined them, Jennifer said, "Hi guys, meet Dr. More."

"Hi," I said.

Literally everyone on the table gave me a weird look.

"Where are you from, Dr. More?" someone asked me.

"I am from Bombay, India"

"Where is India? Or you mean you are from Indiana? Or are you native American Indian?"

Jennifer was surprised, I was not.

When I used to call various hospitals to look for a research position, our conversation would go somewhat like this:

"Hi, I am Dr. More calling from Dubai. I was wondering if you have position vacant for research."

"Hi, Dr. More. Yes we might have an opening in near future. But where is Dubai?"

"Dubai is in Middle East."

Typically there would be a silence for a few seconds.

"Middle East? Is it East Coast or West Coast?"

"It's neither. It is in the Gulf."

"Oh you mean near Alabama or Mississippi?

At that point I would get frustrated and explain "Ma'am this an international call. I am in one of the Gulf countries and the name of the city is Dubai."

So basically I was not surprised at all.

I quietly said, "India is east of Europe."

"What do you plan to do here?"

"Research."

There was a moment of silence and may be some faint laughter.

Someone whispered, "He's fresh off the boat."

I could not quite understand that phrase but Jennifer seemed to be quite annoyed at what was being said.

Suddenly someone said. "Hey guys, it's time for the grand rounds, I think we are getting late."

"Good luck, Dr. More, and good luck for your research," someone said sarcastically.

Suddenly the table was empty and it was just me and Jennifer.

After such a traumatic experience I did not know what to say. So to start some conversation I asked, "Jennifer, what is your surname?"

"Surname? What's that? Do you mean my last name?"

"Yes. I mean your last name."

"It is Graziano. It's Italian. By the way, just call me Jen. Did you hear what one of the guys said at the table?"

"Yes, I did. Someone said I am fresh off the boat. But I don't know what it means."

"Dude, that the term they use for immigrants, particularly from Asia, like you."

"What's a dude?"

"Oh my god, you need some hard core lessons, man. Do you watch a lot of Hollywood movies?"

I did not understand the connection but replied, "Oh yes, I love Hollywood movies."

"Me too. Have you seen the movie *Terminator2: Judgement day*?"

"Oh I love that movie. It is one of my favorite movies."

"So imagine you are like Arnold Schwarzenegger in the movie and assume I am John Connor. Remember the scene where John Connor teaches him how to talk in America?"

"Yes, of course, they are in the car going somewhere," I said.

"Perfect. You have a good memory. So I am going to teach you how to live and talk here in America. You will be my 'Guru' for research but I will be your 'Guru' for your extracurricular activities. Deal?"

She smiled and held out her right hand, and we shook hands.

"Yes, deal. So teach me how to walk, talk, and sleep like an American."

"Listen. You are probably one of the smartest doctors who's come from India. But you need to be street smart too. You may excel in studies and research but otherwise you're a dumbass in day-to-day life if you don't change. But don't worry. I'll turn you into a smart ass doctor."

I was bit surprised and nervous the way she was using the term 'ass' so frequently. But I thought that is how everyone spoke here. I was in a joking mood so I asked her "So Jennifer, are you going to do an 'ass transplant' on me?"

She laughed and said, "Yes, kind of like that." See, man. You are totally un-American. I am going to give you Ten Commandments and transform you totally into an American dude. Do you know what the Ten Commandments are?"

"Yes, of course I have seen the movie. That bald guy Yul Brynner and Charlton Heston."

"Yes, very good. Looks like you are a movie buff. So you're right, Yul Brynner. Wasn't he so sexy? Anyway, leave alone the religious part because we're not talking about changing your religion."

"Yes, of course not," I replied.

"Good." Said Jennifer... I mean Jen.

Suddenly she remembered something and changed the topic of discussion. I soon realized that it was kind of her habit to change the topic all of sudden. She would jump from one topic to another one, which had absolutely no relation with each other!

"I get so mad when these guys call someone off the boat. Do you know what they call us?"

"No."

"WOP."

"WOP. What is that?"

Jen whispered, "Without papers."

I did not have the courage to ask what the Hispanics were called.

**First Commandment.**

I was ready to receive my first commandment.

I bent down and sort of folded my hands in Namaskar position.

"Here you go, dude. This is your first commandment: Thou shalt not speak English."

## FIRST COMMANDMENT

"Thou shalt not speak English"

I was a bit confused "What do you mean, Jen? Here everyone speaks English, don't they?? I even gave a Test of English when I—"

Jen cut me short. "Dude, we don't speak that damn English, we speak American. You need to learn the American slang to understand what people are talking about, otherwise you will really feel like an alien. You will be like Arnold in *Terminator II*.

"Dude means a guy or man or whatever, by the way."

"What is the female version of dude?"

"Very interesting question. I think the official version is dudette or dudess. But even 'gal' or 'babe' or 'baby' would work."

"Really? So I can call you a 'baby'? Isn't that like a small kid?"

"No, that is a very common term used here. You can call me whatever you want but I prefer that you call me Jen."

"Sure. Will do."

Later on she gave me a short lecture on the American slang. She asked me for my personal email address and assured me that she would send an email with various American slangs and their meanings. She also wrote down a website on a small piece of paper. Apparently I could go on that website and could type whatever slang I heard and the website would give me the meaning in simple terms.

"Today, Dr. Stein is going to be late so we can talk and I can tell you as much slang as you need to know, but you really need to do your homework, okay?"

As we were talking, I was distracted by an attractive girl in the cafeteria wearing a short skirt. I was looking at her and Jen realized I was not paying attention to what she was saying.

She got mad. "Hey, man, are you feeling woody?"

"Woody, no I feel pretty fine." Jen busted out laughing. I was confused.

"When you go to your apartment and check on the website what woody means and tell me tomorrow, okay? Don't do it from your office computer, do you get it?"

"Okay, I got it, this is my homework."

"Don't use terms like surname, canteen, whatever you learned so far in British English or in India," she instructed me. After a brief pause she asked me "By the way, are you Maha . . . rash . . . train?"

She spoke in broken words and I could not understand so she repeated. I still could not understand. She got somewhat annoyed and asked me "Do you speak Marati at home?"

"Yes, I do. How do you know?" Now it was my turn to be surprised.

"I saw your CV and that you are from Mumbai. I had several friends in my high school whose parents were from Bombay and they told me they speak Marati."

She changed the topic of conversation and said, "Before I give you any more commandments I have some suggestions for you. Remember, these are just suggestions and you don't have to follow them if you don't want to."

"Sure. What do you have in your mind?" I asked her.

"Get rid of your glasses and wear contact lenses. My other suggestion is to shave off your mustache and if you don't mind we can go to my hairstylist and have some better suggestions for you for your hair. Your hair is so curly."

"Will this transformation make me look like an American?" I asked her.

"Not necessarily, but it will definitely give you a cool look instead of a nerdy look. Again, as I said these are only suggestions. No force. Hope you understand."

"Yes, I don't mind trying. But contact lenses would be expensive, I am not sure if I will be able to afford it."

"You have university or hospital sponsored insurance I guess. You might want to check with our Ophthalmology department. They do give semi soft contact lenses for throw away prices for residents and hospital employees. As far as a hair stylist is concerned, she is my friend so she won't charge a lot. In fact she may do for a very reasonable rate."

"Sure, I don't mind doing it," I said.

"Great, what are you doing today after work?"

"Nothing planned."

"I'll come to your office and we can go to Susan, my hairstylist, and start working on it."

"Sounds great, Jen"

"Fine and by the way, if for any reason if you don't like the hairstyle, you can always revert back to what you have now, so no loss."

Soon we got news that Dr. Stein had to go for some emergency hospital committee meeting so the reading session got cancelled.

"Oh boy, what should we do now?" Jennifer asked me and I gave her blank look.

That evening I went out with Jen to her hairstylist. She turned out to be a very nice Vietnamese lady. She made some minor changes and cuts and changed my hairstyle a bit.

The next day I enquired about contacts and it seemed there was some hospital promotion by a company and they were giving out contacts for throwaway prices. So I got the eye exam done and got new contacts and got rid of my old glasses.

I started wearing contacts over the weekend and on Monday I came to the hospital with my new hairstyle and no glasses and of course I had shaved off my mustache over the weekend, some people did not immediately recognize me. I think I heard some soft whistles from some gals.

"Oh, Dr. Moore. You look great. I did not recognize you at first," said Dr. Stein's secretary.

I went to the research office and got a similar response from my co-research fellows.

After which I went to my own table and started my computer and checked hospital email and my personal email. As I started looking up some scientific papers, there was a knock on my door and I looked up and saw Jen.

"Hey man, I would not have recognized you, you look great."

I stood up and she gave me a friendly hug.

"Thanks, do I look cool?"

"Cool? Are you kidding me? You look sexy!" she said while winking.

I was flattered.

"Dr. More, my serum caffeine level is dangerously low. Let's go and have some coffee"

"By the way, I always try to have Starbucks. You know the saying, 'Bad coffee is like bad sex . . . it is still better than nothing!' But I say 'Bad coffee is like bad sex . . . it better be good or nothing."

"It's early morning and you are talking about sex?"

"Don't get me started. But early morning sex has its advantages! Let's go." She forced me out of my office and went straight to the coffee shop.

"Let us go and sit down there," she said, after we'd gotten our coffee. Someone was already sitting at the table she indicated and we joined him. "Want to see some fun, just do as I say or nod." I did not know what she was up to!

"John, this is my friend Dr. More and this is John from Texas."

"Hi," I said.

He looked at me and said, "Como estas?

I thought he was speaking Italian because I was with Jennifer.

"He is fine," Jen replied.

"Where are you from?" he asked me.

"I am from Bombay, what about you John?" I asked him.

"I'm from West Texas. Where is Bombay?"

Even before I could answer Jen said, "Bombay is in East Texas." I was shocked to hear her answer but as instructed, I just nodded.

"Really, I have heard about small towns like Paris and Italy somewhere in Texas but never heard of that town. Must be really small. Huh," he said.

I just nodded as per instructions from my Guru.

We then chatted for some time. He had a different accent than New Yorkers. At least that is what I thought. When he said Sunday, Monday . . . it sounded more like Sundi, Mondi. At one point he said, "What are ya'll doing this weekend," which sounded more like Youll. John was telling us how he missed his Texas. At one point he looked at me and said, "In New York you must be feeling like a foreigner, right?"

Which was true for me so I said, "Yes, I do."

"I haven't met anyone from Texas until now, I am glad I met you," he said while looking at me.

"We're buddies from today." He made a fist in front of me and I did not know what to do but Jen signaled me to do the same and he hit his fist on mine and said, "Amigo, glad to meet you, we should get together some time and have a Texas size wild party with bunch of hot girls."

I was sweating but I said, "Yes, sure, count me in."

"Hey, you must be a Cowboys Fan!"

He was about to leave but he turned around and said, "Hey, you must be a Cowboys fan?"

I was going to say that I have watched all Clint Eastwood western movies and I loved them but I got a feeling that he might be referring to something else so I looked at Jen. She winked at me so I said, "Yes, of course. Without doubt."

"Listen, guys, I have to go now but I will see y'all around." he said and left. I again noticed his "Youall" with a drag at the end of the word.

I gave an angry look to Jen and said, "Jennifer, you are going to land me in trouble. Since when is Bombay in Texas?"

"Don't worry. You probably know by now how great our knowledge is about world geography. We'll play this game for some time and at one point I'll tell him the truth. I'll take all the blame if he gets mad at you so don't worry."

"No. I am really worried. What if he finds out that I am from India and not from Texas and shoots me. I will be dead."

"Hey, listen, calm down. He won't shoot you if you're with me. And if you meet him again, tell him your father is a farmer and grows corn. He may ask you what kind of pickup truck you have so tell him you have Ford F-150."

"What? Are you crazy? I have never driven any kind of truck and I have not been on any kind of farm in my whole life, let alone corn field."

"Why don't you play this game with me? Just for a little while."

"Okay, wait, let me write it down." So I wrote down all her suggestions in my small notebook.

"Oh and if he asks you what news channel you watch, tell him that you watch Fox News."

"Okay, Fox News, got it. By the way, what is this thing about Cowboys? Was he referring to the cowboys movies?" I asked her.

"No, no, no. Cowboys is a football team. I'll tell you one day about the game. We are arch rivals because I'm a New York Giants fan."

"Lord, I only know David Beckham and no one else," I said.

"No," she said firmly. "That is soccer. This is American football, which is somewhat like rugby. I'll explain it to you sometime but just pretend to be a Cowboys fan okay?"

"Sure, I think I should start wearing a bullet proof vest tomorrow. I am sure the day when John comes to know that I am not from Texas, not even from United States but a foreigner, that day will be the last day of my life!" I said in a depressing tone.

"Don't you worry. I'm here to protect you."

"Are you going to jump in to save me from his bullets when he shoots me, like they show in Bollywood Movies?" I asked her with a bit of anger.

"I don't watch Bollywood movies but I might just do that to save you. But don't worry, that's not going to happen. One day we will tell him the truth, and as I said I'll take the blame. I'm sure he won't shoot a woman."

"Thank god," I said. There was a long pause and I decided to change the subject. "So where are you from Jen?"

"I am of course an American. But my grandparents came from Italy. That's where my last name Graziano comes from."

"So you are Italian-American."

"Yeah, you can say that if you want, but I'm American." Suddenly she remembered something. "Oh, I wanted to ask you something. Do you have a cell phone?"

"Cell phone? You mean mobile?"

"No, not mobile. Cell phone. That is not what it is called here and remember that, okay?"

"Yes, I will. No I don't have mobile... er... cell phone."

"Well, here is mine." She wrote down her cell number on a piece of paper. I looked at the number and realized it was pretty easy to remember. Some of the digits resembled my apartment number and the rest were like my birthdate but in the reverse order.

"You can call me and if I don't answer, just leave a message. I am usually busy in the evenings but I do listen to all messages and I will try to call ASAP."

"What is ASAP?" I asked.

"As soon as possible."

Looked like we had hit it off immediately. I was closely listening to her and was already feeling that she was my 'Guru' of American culture and everything else.

"Listen Dude, this is a country where people don't have much time for things other than watching TV, sleeping, eating, and having sex. So everything else, including work, is secondary. We use short forms for everything. It saves time and energy. So remember to use and understands acronyms, AKA short forms. Oh by the way, AKA is 'also known as'."

"Thanks. I was going to ask you anyway what is AKA," I said.

"Here is your Second Commandment: Thou shalt always use short forms and acronyms. Dude, here in America everything is simplified and shortened. Like that girl's short dress you were looking at. So Jennifer is Jen, Amanda is Mandy, James is Jim, David is Dave..."

## SECOND COMMANDMENT

"Thou shalt always use short forms and acronyms!"

"But David is such a short name itself. Why is there a need to shorten it further?" I interrupted her and asked my stupid question.

"Oh man, David is too long to say. Dave is good."

"Also for example Bay Area Rapid Transport is too long to say so we call it BART. Dallas Area Rapid Transport is called DART. Guess what Farmington Area Rapid Transport is called?"

I immediately said, "FART." I said it so loudly that some of the guys and gals sitting next to us got up and left the table.

"No, I was just joking. There is no such transport service," Jen said, laughing. "But you just made some people leave from cafeteria so I'm glad there are more empty tables now."

Then she changed the topic to something totally unrelated.

"By the way, I've been calling you either Dude or Dr. Moore ever since we met. What's your first name?" Jen asked.

"It is R-A-J-U., pronounced as Raa-joo and my last name is not Moore it is Mo-ray"

"Listen, whatever . . . your name is totally un-American and so hard to remember."

"What can I do? If my parents knew that one day I would immigrate to America, maybe they would have probably named me something simple which can be Americanized."

"No harm done. We can still change it, let me think. So your name is Raju Moray... hmmm... sounds like Roger Moore, the guy who played James Bond back in the sixties. How about if I call you Dr. Bond?"

'I BECOME BOND'

"Your name sounds like Roger Moore...
the guy who played 'James Bond'... That's it!
You are Dr. Bond or Bond for me and everyone else!"

"Well, it's up to you," I said.

"Well, that's it. You are Bond or Dr. Bond for me and everybody else."

The world soon spread around and all the research fellows and everyone I was working with started calling me Dr. Bond or just Bond. I was baptized by an Italian American, Jennifer Graziano, from Raju More to Roger Moore alias James Bond, or more precisely Dr. Bond.

# Learning English

After our cafeteria rendezvous we were heading to the reading room. I asked Jen on the way, "Do you know where is the toilet?"

"Whaaat? Jen screamed and then softly in my ears "Dr. Bond, it is called a restroom here, not toilet. Don't ever use that word. Why don't you go in there and I'll wait for you in the lobby, otherwise you'll get lost in this maze," Jen said and I nodded.

After coming out from the restroom I said, "Now I understand why it is called a rest room. My bladder was really full and I felt really rested after relieving me."

"Dude, I think we're getting late. Let's go fast, otherwise we will get screwed."

"What do you mean? Maybe you will and I won't."

"Dude, that's just a saying. Nobody is going to screw anybody."

By that time we had reached Dr. Stein's reading room. The room was full of radiology residents and fellows, some of whom I had seen in the cafeteria. Dr. Stein introduced me. "Guys, this is Dr. More from Bombay, India. He will be helping us with our research." Most of the residents looked at me as if I was a piece of furniture!

I could see that some of them were kind of pitying me. He asked me to sit with him during the reading session. Jen was also in the same room but in the corner where most of the junior residents and medical students were sitting.

After the reading session me, Jen, and Dr. Stein went to his office. On the way, Dr. Stein asked me, "So what do you think of the reading session?"

Without thinking I said, "Dude, you were awesome!"

Jen was about to faint but Dr. Stein took it lightly. He smiled at me and Jen, who seemed to be petrified. "All right, let me get coffee and I'll join you guys in my office," Dr. Stein said.

As soon as we entered his office, Jen closed the door and hit my back side with her binder.

"Ouch."

"Idiot, that's a wrong way to use the word dude. You have failed in your first test of becoming a Yankee."

"Why? You just said today morning that dude means a guy or whatever so isn't Dr. Stein a guy?"

"First of all don't say 'today morning,' use the term 'this morning' instead, okay? I told you that earlier. And dude is more like what you call your good friend or buddy or maybe someone younger than you, not a respected and senior person like Dr. Stein."

"Alright, I am sorry. I will apologize to him."

As I was speaking Dr. Stein entered with a big cup of coffee.

"I am sorry, Dr. Stein. I just learned this word 'dude' today. But I used it in the wrong way. I apologize."

"That's alright, dude." Dr. Stein said. "Foreigners like you often make mistakes without realizing the real term or the meaning.

"I liked the paper you presented at Chicago and I want you do to further research on diffusion tensor imaging. We have the time, money, and manpower as well as the latest machines at your disposal. Ms. Graziano will help you in your research."

After a brief introduction to his research ideas and a brief talk about his vision for future research, he left and we went back to the research office. "I'm sorry, I should have told you when and how to use the word dude."

"I think it is my mistake also. I shouldn't have used that word the way I did. Anyhow, can you tell me who Ms. Boobs is?

Jen burst out laughing. "Yes, of course. I know her because I have been in and around the Radiology Department for the past few months to work on research related work. Good thing you asked me. Oh my god, her name is not Ms. Boobs, her name is Ms. Sherry. She is in the office on the second floor right above your office. Come on, I'll take you there."

When I saw Ms. Sherry I understood why she had that nickname.

"Who told you her name is Ms. Boobs?" Jen asked.

"Akio said."

"Son of a bitch," Jen said. "You'll get used to the lifestyle here eventually, Dr. Bond. Let's go get more coffee. I still have two coupons Mary gave us."

At that point I thought I would take her into confidence and open my mind. I just felt that she wouldn't laugh at me. I told her about my experience in the coffee shop when I ordered espresso.

Jen could not control her laughter.

"Bond, I think you were too confused when you looked at the coffee menu. Your friend should have helped you but you can just ask for coffee and you will get black coffee to which you can add sugar and cream."

After that she requested the coffee menu from the store. We sat down in the corner and she went over the coffee menu with me and explained all the types of coffee available.

"You can order a latte which is basically a coffee mixed with hot milk. You can get nonfat milk if you want. From what I understand from your description you wanted a cappuccino, which is basically a frothy coffee drink, which is probably called espresso in India. I usually don't drink cappuccino because I think it's a waste of money to pay for the froth. Do you want to try cafe latte? Remember, order confidently as if you've been drinking coffee since you were drinking breast milk. They'll ask for what size you want. I would go with small size which for some reason is called tall. So let us practice. Repeat after me, 'I want a tall nonfat latte.'"

Like an obedient student I repeated what she said. "I want a tall nonfat latte."

"Bond, don't ever forget the magic words in America."

"Magic words? You mean honey or something?"

She cut me short saying, "No Bond, try again."

I thought for a moment and said, "Bitch?"

"No," she screamed. "How can you think of that as a magic word? 'Please' and 'Thank you' are the two magic words you need to remember."

"Got it. 'I want a tall non fat latte, please,'" I said.

"Good, you are learning. Now remember that some drinks are called 'skinny,' which means the same as nonfat milk. As you try different drinks, you should get confident in ordering. Let's go order. And always remember to say thank you when you get the drink from the barista."

So I ordered a cafe latte and she ordered a mocha. As we were having coffee, I noticed a warning in big bold letters on the cup:

CAUTION: THE CONTENTS MAY BE EXTREMELY HOT AND MAY CAUSE BURNS.

"Jen, can I ask you something?"

"Sure, go ahead Bond."

"Why is there a warning on all the coffee cups that the contents may be hot?"

"My dear, once a woman ordered a coffee and spilled it on herself and got burned. She sued the company and guess what happened ?"

"Of course she must have lost because when you order a hot coffee it is supposed to be hot and you need to be careful."

"Wrong. She won the lawsuit because there was no written warning on the coffee cup that the contents may be hot."

"What?" I just could not believe it.

"America is a lawsuit friendly country. Here is your third commandment Dr. Bond: Thou shalt be careful of lawsuits and lawyers."

# Manhattan Alien

## 'THIRD COMMANDMENT'

"Thou shalt be careful from lawsuits and lawyers."

"Sure, I will remember that. By the way, is there a warning on cold coffee or ice cream that says 'This product might be too cold. You may get frostbite of the tongue?'"

"Well, Bond, I like that idea, but to tell you frankly, there is no such warning on ice cream or cold coffee. Maybe they'll have one if and when someone sues them," Jennifer said, laughing.

While we were walking back to the research office, we saw several signs that said "wet floor".

"Do you see those signs?" Jen asked.

"Yes, I do."

"No one really cares if anyone falls but these signs are here so that no one can sue the hospital if someone falls due to wet floor."

"Really. In that case I think the hospitals should keep that sign up all the time. Because no one can sue the hospital if the floor is not wet despite the "wet floor" signs. What do you think?" I asked her.

"I do like that idea but I don't know why they don't do it,"

As soon as we reached the office, Jen confronted Akio.

"Hey Akio, if you play another trick on my friend Dr. Bond, I'll do a bilateral orchiectomy without anesthesia, you get it?"

Akio was shocked by her language and so was I.

"Why did you tell him to see Ms. Boobs?" she asked him.

He said apologetically "I am sorry, I did not know he is your friend. Don't worry, I shall not play another trick on him."

Then he said, "I thought his name was More."

"Not anymore. He's my friend and his name is Dr. Bond. So don't mess with me or you will face my wrath."

Later I told Jen, "I think you should have been somewhat polite to him."

"Polite, my foot. For what? He could have landed you in trouble. I am here to protect you."

"Alright, Jen, thank you very much. I need to get back to work."

"By the way, how much are you getting paid for this job, if I may ask?"

"Five hundred dollars per month and the apartment is free. Dr. Stein also said that most of the days he will arrange for some coupons for me to have lunch in the cafeteria. So I should be okay."

Jen was visibly shocked. "You're getting paid just five hundred bucks! If I was in your situation, I would have said 'Kiss my ass.'"

"Really, why would you want anyone to kiss your backside?"

"Bond, it's slang. What I meant was I would have flatly refused. You can't do anything with that money. How are you going to buy a car?"

"I don't need one right now. Plus, moving around in New York is not a big deal as you have subways."

"That's right. And if you need some help I can help you sometime."

"Oh, that reminds me. I have to go to social security office to get a social security number. Can you help me?"

"Of course I can. Let's go right away. Do you have the necessary documents you need?"

"Yes, I do. I came prepared today. Let's go. But I don't know the nearest office location. Let me ask Mary."

"No. You can find almost everything on the Internet, buddy." She sat on my office chair and opened the Internet "See? Here is the nearest office. It is East and Twentieth Street." She showed me while pulling the location on the website.

"How do we find it?" I asked since I was still new to the city.

"James Bond, look here." She took me near a huge subway map on the wall.

"The whole city is divided into streets and avenues, which are at right angles to each other. So if you want to go to a particular address, all you need to find out is the cross intersecting street and avenue and boom there you are! Then once you find the location, next step is to find the nearest subway station. See this one here. So now we need to figure out how to go to that subway station from here. See, it's so simple!"

I was impressed. "Wow, that's great."

"Dude, about five percent of the genius men and women in this country have made things simple for the rest of the ninety-five percent of not so intelligent people like you and me."

"Is that supposed to be the fourth commandment Jen?"

"No, not exactly. This is just how things run here. I'm just giving you a tip. Come on, move your ass. We need to go there early, otherwise the office will be crowded."

"Move my...? What do you mean?"

"That's just a saying. I'm just teaching you the lingo. Wait, I need my morning caffeine. Let's grab a coffee on our way, do you want an espresso?"

I knew she was teasing. "No, thanks I am done with that."

We ventured out to the social security office. While getting out of the hospital campus, I saw a sign on one of the streets "Ped Xing" and saw a bunch of Chinese students crossing the street.

"Oh, does that sign here say 'xing' because so many Chinese students cross here?"

"No, my dear, 'xing' is a short way to write 'crossing.' Remember I told you that America is country of short forms and acronyms. And by the way, nobody says social security number here. They'll ask you what's your social or last four digits of your social. Sometimes they may refer to it as SSN."

"Alright, got it."

We took the subway, although the office was not very far from the hospital.

"Why don't you go upstairs to the office and I'll do some window shopping here in these stores," Jen said.

"No problem," I said.

As soon as I entered the Social Security Office, I saw a big reception desk and a large burly man standing near the desk. His pants were down and so was his underwear. I was shocked to see him proudly displaying his butt crack. I guess he was totally unaware of it. For an alien like me that exposure was quite shocking. But I just went ahead and picked up my number and waited for my turn.

Soon my turn came and I met an old sweet lady in her mid-60s.

"Hello, dear, how are you today?"

"I am doing great. How are you, ma'am?"

"Let me see your documents, honey."

I showed her all the documents I was carrying.

"Were you born here or do you happen to have permanent residency in United States?"

"No, ma'am" I said.

"Then you are a non-resident alien." She reminded me of my official immigration status in the United States, confirming what the immigration officer had told me.

"You should receive an official SSN within two business weeks from today."

"Alright. Thank you, ma'am. Now I need social security number every day at work. I cannot get anything done without it. Is there a way to get this number earlier?" I asked.

"No. I cannot give this number on the phone due to security reasons, honey." she said.

"Alright, now what happens when my status changes to a green card or a permanent resident status?"

"Honey, you will be then called a Resident Alien," she said.

"Even then I will be an alien?" I was surprised.

"Yes, dear. I am so sorry. I think you were simply born in wrong country."

Although I did not like her comment, I did not see a point in arguing with her at that point. I again thanked her and left her office to look for Jen.

"How was it?" she asked.

"Horrible," I said.

"Why, what happened? Did they refuse to give you SSN?"

"No," I said. "First as a welcome sign I had to see a man's butt crack. And the lady in the office said I won't get social for at least two weeks and you know I cannot get a single damn thing done in the hospital without SSN."

"I know. But you can still do your exciting research. And as far as butt cracks are concerned you will eventually see a lot of underwear and butt cracks and cleavage even if you don't want to see them," Jen said while laughing.

"I don't think this is very funny, Jen." I was slightly mad at her.

"Yeah, I know, but you need to get used to things like that in the USA . . . like looking at something you don't want to see."

"Alright enough about butt cracks now. Let's go back to the hospital. How was your shopping? And thanks for waiting for me," I said while changing topics.

"Not a problem, Dr. Bond," she replied and we headed back to the hospital.

On our way back she pointed out at a bunch of high school kids whose pants were sagging and we could see their underwear.

"Look at that. This is what I was talking about."

"That is disgusting," I said.

"Yeah, it is. But now I'm used to it."

We soon came back to our research office.

"What next? What is your plan today, Bond?"

"I need to go to some place called 'Human Resources.' Sounds like a scary place. Do you know what that is?"

"Again it's more of an American thing. Basically, it's personnel management. I call it 'Inhuman Resources' because most of the people who work there, except a few, have little talent and skills. Most of them care more about the piles of paper in front of them rather than the human beings. All they care about is if the paperwork is complete or not and they can put check marks on their piece of paper. You can almost be a moron or stupid and get hired and on the other side you may be the most intelligent dude but you may not get hired!"

"Really, I am shocked!" I said.

"I heard they're planning to rename their department Talent Management, which I think would be a joke!"

Anyway I came back from the 'Inhuman Resources' office and luckily the experience was better than I had expected.

When I returned to the main research office, I bumped into Akio and he gave me a good news.

"You will be occupying the next office soon, maybe starting now. By the way, what visa are you on?"

"I am on J1 visa," I said, as I quickly moved into my new office, which was more spacious.

### Fourth Commandment

Jennifer must have heard my conversation with Akio. As I was settling down in my office, I asked Jen, "I suppose you know what a visa is?"

"Of course I know. In fact, I know exactly what a J1 visa is and I was about to give you my fourth commandment."

"What it is?"

'FOURTH COMMANDMENT'

"Thou shalt work hard to get rid of J1 visa as soon as possible"

"Here you go. This is about your visa, and frankly I have heard this from someone who came here like you, Bond. J1 visa is like having an HIV infection, easy to get but very difficult to get rid of. So here is your fourth commandment: Thou shalt work hard to get rid of J1 visa as soon as possible."

I could not control my laughter. "Well, that's a good way to put it, and I will ardently follow it."

"I think among all my commandments I've given you so far, this is the most important commandment, so make sure you don't forget it, my dear."

"Alright, I think I've wasted enough of my time and yours so I should probably go back and read something about diffusion tensor imaging."

"Yes, that does sound like a good idea to me. Thanks for your help today."

"You are always welcome. And make sure you have my cell phone and if you need anything give me buzz. See you tomorrow morning. Bye."

She started to leave but stopped. "Oh, by the way, 'give be a buzz' means call me, just in case you didn't know."

"Thank you! Hasta La vista, baby," I said, remembering Arnold from *Terminator II: Judgement Day*.

"Great, I am glad you're learning. I think that is enough education for today. You already have received Four commandments from me in last the past few days. I don't want to overburden you and your memory," she said while leaving my office.

I looked around my new office. It was much more spacious than the old one and the best part was that office was meant for me alone!

I made a list of things to do. I planned out what I needed to do the next day and headed back to my apartment. I finished dinner in the cafeteria on the way so I wouldn't have to worry about it after reaching my apartment. My apartment was fully furnished by the hospital so I did not have to worry about buying any furniture. I thought of only two things that I would need, a laptop and an electric kettle. Dr. Stein had promised me that as research fellow I would be entitled to a laptop from the research fund that would be mine to keep at the end of my tenure. He also promised me that I could carry it back to my room at the end of the day and use it as needed. So now the only thing I needed to buy was an electric kettle to make tea in the morning. I thought I would ask Jen the next day if she had any idea where to buy one so that I could have my morning tea in my room. So far I had been boiling water on the electric stove and did not want to do that any further. An electric kettle was a better option. I was tired, but then a thought came to my mind. How am I going to remember all the commandments which my 'guru' gave me? I decided to write down all the commandments and I opened my diary, wrote the date, and wrote down all the commandments she'd given me so far. I got about four in about a week and I thought that was more than enough!

The next day, I went straight to the main or common research office and logged on to my computer. One by one my new colleagues showed up. James was from Australia, Ibrahim was from Egypt, Robert was from Philippines, and Francisco was from Argentina. So there was a great mixture of cultures from around the world. Most of them were new immigrants or aliens to be precise, like me. Everybody spoke in a different accent. For the first few days it was difficult for everybody to understand one another, but soon we got used to everyone's accents.

I was preparing to go to Dr. Stein's reading room at eight that morning. He usually arrived sharply at eight. I got ready and headed for the reading room. I was just reading my plan for the day when I bumped into Jen.

"Hey there, how are you, Dr. Bond?"

"I am great, how are you doing this pleasant morning?"

"I'm good. I'm glad you're learning the American lingo. By the way, did you look up what feeling woody means?"

"No. I did not get time."

"No problem, tell me when you look up." She winked.

Both of us then entered the reading room. No one was in the room except for both of us. Jen, being a med student, preferred to sit in the corner.

Soon the room filled with radiology residents, fellows and medical students. Dr. Stein entered in the room at eight with his big cup of coffee. The first case he looked at was a tough one. He asked the differential diagnosis and no one, including the fellows, could come out with what he wanted. He looked at me and said, "Dr. Bond do you have an idea?"

I said "From the given history and the imaging findings of bilateral T2 and FLAIR weighted hyperintensities in the putamina which also appear bright on diffusion weighted images, I would strongly think of Creutzfeldt-Jacob disease. Although I would also consider extra-pontine myelinolysis, if there is a history of rapid correction of hyponatremia."

There was a stunned silence in the room. How could a research fellow from a third world country diagnose a case?

Bond: "I would strongly think of CJD"
Dr. Stein: "I am wetting my pants!"

"I am wetting my pants," Dr. Stein said. Everyone in the room except me burst out into laughter. I noticed the girls enjoyed that moment or joke even more than the guys. I was little embarrassed as I did not quite get what he said. Was I right or totally wrong?

"Excellent, Dr. Bond," Dr. Stein said and I was relieved.

From that day onwards the residents and the fellows stopped looking at me like I was a piece of furniture. Although some of the fellows were jealous of me, I started getting more respect in the department. Residents would stop by my office or reading room and ask my opinion on a tough neuro case they were looking at. Medical students would stop and say "Good morning" to me and would ask me how I was doing. Jen was also impressed. Some of the female residents stopped and introduced themselves and some of them gave me a tight hug. Frankly, it was embarrassing for me but I did not say anything. Female anatomy in the chest region being significantly different than male anatomy, every time each one of them hugged me I could feel their soft breasts against my chest! Soon the word spread around that I diagnosed a tough neuro case which even fellows could not. The secretaries and clerks came to know about my heroism and they would stop and give me a hug. Even Ms. Sherry started doing that. She was pretty tall and when she would hug me my face would come invariably in between her two large breasts and I would get suffocated! I told my experience to Jen "You know what I call her?"

"No, tell me . . . must be something funny"

"Well, I call her Boobie Trap," I said upon which Jen just could not control her laughter.

"Oh man, you are so funny. But do you know the real meaning of that?" she asked me.

"Yes, I do."

After that, any time Jen would see Ms. Sherry, she would say "Bond, better run away, your boobie trap is coming over here!"

I spoke to Jen about my embarrassment about females hugging me tightly. She laughed and said "If you're so embarrassed I'll give you a sideways hug."

"That sounds good to me"

Anyway, after the marathon reading session Jen and I went to the cafeteria for a coffee. A bunch of fellows also accompanied us.

"Hey, how did you nail that case man?" someone asked and I knew it was coming.

I did not know what to say and Jen said, "Dr. Bond has vast experience. He is a radiologist who was trained in Mumbai, India and he also worked in the Middle East."

"After your research, what do you plan to do?" one of the residents asked.

"I am not sure, but maybe I'll do a fellowship or residency here if I get one," I said softly.

"Hey man, are you crazy? Not a single brownie like you has got radiology residency here in this hospital for last ten years. You better start packing your bags after your research or whatever you are doing is over," one of the fellows said.

"And you, madam?" That fellow turned his attention to Jennifer. "Since when are white people interested in research? Research is meant to be done by those nerdy people from China and India."

Jen was furious and she gave him an angry look.

I did not quite get the term 'brownie,' but I decided to reply to him.

At that point, someone said, "Forget about residency. See, America has never had a black president."

"Really, I thought . . ."

At that point Jen stamped my foot so badly, I shouted, "Oh shit . . . that hurts".

"Yes, that hurts man . . . I'm sure one day we will see a black president," said one of the African American med students. Anyway, since my policy was to not talk about politics, I decided to change the topic. "You never know, I might be the first brownie to get residency here," I said, upon which no one really reacted or commented although I heard some muted laughter.

Soon everyone left and it was just me and Jen at the table.

"I liked the way you answered that SOB. He was really rude to you," Jen said.

"That's alright, Jen. Don't get mad. I am sort of used to this now. By the way, what's the meaning of what Dr. Stein said?"

"What do you mean? He said so many things in the reading room. Which one are you referring to?"

"He said 'I am wetting my pants.' I did not quite get it and everyone in the room laughed."

"Why don't you look up online, buddy?" Jen said and she wrote down name of another online American slang dictionary web site. "And don't forget to look up woody too!" she said while winking at me.

"Alright, ma'am" I said.

"By the way, you were awesome this morning."

"Thank you for the compliments. Now let's go back to the research office and let's get started on the research."

# Not all fat women are pregnant (and other important facts)

As we were walking through the hospital corridor, I saw a beautiful lady walking in the opposite direction. She looked at me and smiled. I thought she was looking and smiling at someone else, so I looked around. Jen was busy talking to someone on her cell phone, so I presumed the lady was indeed looking at me. I smiled back at her and she asked "How are you?"

"I am fine, how about you?"

"Good," she said and she went ahead without any further conversation. By that time Jen had finished talking on the cell phone.

"Jen, can I ask you something?"

"Sure, go ahead"

"Why do people smile at strangers in this country?"

"I don't know. I don't find it strange. Maybe you do since you are still new in this country."

"Yes, I do find it weird. Also when someone totally unknown to you calls you honey."

"Let me explain to you something, Dr. Bond. Here people do smile at complete strangers and they love 'small talk.'"

"What is a small talk?"

"Let's say you're in an elevator with a group of people and then maybe you talk to someone about the weather, a game, or your or their weekend etcetera. People here just love small talk. We're about to enter an elevator now so maybe you can talk to someone about something. It's just one of the ways getting used to the culture here. Do you want to try?"

I was a bit tense. Smile at strangers and even talk to them? Was the next step having sex with strangers? But I had not much choice since I had decided to follow the advice of my 'Guru' Ms. Graziano.

"Sure, I will," I said reluctantly as we entered the elevator.

There was no one except me and Jen. Then on one of the floors one of the radiology secretaries walked in and recognized me. "Hi Dr. Bond, how are you doing?"

I was glad that at least this lady was kind of known to me. I said, "I am good. How are you?"

At that point Jen pushed her elbow at my waist signaling me to say something. So I said something which came to my mind. "Hey, looks like you put on some weight."

At that moment her face turned red and she frowned at me "Excuse me, what did you say?"

I was terrified and did not know what to say so I looked at Jen. Jen was mad at me but she tried to do some damage control

"Maybe it is your hairstyle, honey."

That seemed to work.

"Oh dear, I don't think I should get this style again." She walked out as her floor came.

As soon as she left, Jen pinched me. "Bond, as a golden rule never tell a lady that she put on weight. Ever. Do you understand? And that includes me too"

"But she did look fat to me today," I said.

"Yes, but don't ever say it and remember that, okay?"

"Sure, baby, don't worry. I will not do that again," I said apologetically.

"Let's see, you can try once more." Jen said as the elevator stopped and another fat lady entered the elevator. She was totally unknown to me but I guess she was some hospital staff. She smiled at me and said, "How are you all are doing?"

"Good," I said. At that point Jen again pushed her elbow against my waist and signaled me to say something.

I turned around and said, "So when is the baby due? You must be really excited about it." I thought I had scored big points, but the lady was furious at me.

"Who the hell are you? I am not pregnant." She stood there in stony silence until the elevator door opened on the next floor and then walked away.

After she left, Jen coldly said, "Bond, she was not pregnant . . . she was just fat! You should not have said whatever you said!"

Since my first experiment with 'small talk' was such a big failure, I decided not to do it again.

The rest of the day I was busy in planning my research activity. Dr. Stein wanted to present a scientific poster on diffusion tensor imaging in an upcoming big radiology conference. So I was supposed to submit my abstract, get approval from local IRB, and enroll volunteers in the study for the research project.

Jennifer helped me with great enthusiasm to get this done in an orderly and timely manner. Finally, we got the IRB approval and we were ready to enroll new patients for the study. I was excited since it was going to be sort of a dream project for me. Jen was excited too as doing research was going to boost her chances of getting into a radiology residency at this hospital.

Within a few days I had noticed interesting features about American people. The most amazing thing for me was they were multitaskers, unlike me! Another thing I realized was that this country was a country of 'gadgets.' Americans were so heavily dependent on the gadgets that they would be almost functionless without them. Imagine a day in the hospital if the computer system went down! The hospital wouldn't be able to do anything. One more thing that sort of surprised me was there were multiple 'drive in' stores, coffee shops, and restaurants. I am sure someday there will be drive-in MRI clinics where you can just drive in and get a head MRI while you get a free foot massage or vice versa!

'FUTURE MRI CLINICS'

Soon after I began my position, I realized that I need to buy some things from the grocery store so I could have my breakfast in my own room. I asked Mary about buying groceries. She said, "Dr. Bond, since you need pretty much basic stuff and you don't have a car, I recommend that you go to the small store on the first floor of this building. It's run by the hospital trust and the prices are very reasonable." I went to the first floor or at least what I thought was the first floor and I could not find the grocery store. I asked one of the hospital staff and she said, "You're one floor above dear. Go down these green elevators and you'll find the grocery store right in front of the elevators. You won't miss it."

"I thought this is the first floor and the one you are referring is the ground floor," I said.

"Are you new in this country?" she asked with a frown.

"Yes, I am an alien," I told her jokingly.

"Really, you don't look like one. Anyway, in this country whatever you are referring to as ground floor is called the first floor and then the one above is called second and so and so forth," she explained to me.

"Thanks." I went to the green elevators. I realized that in spite of the U.S. being a literate country everything here was color coded. The elevators in the hospital were green, purple, and orange. No one referred them like south side or north side elevators. Most of the trains in the country were also color coded. Even the entry into our radiology department was color coded. So if someone asked me the directions to radiology all I had to tell them was to follow the blue line on the floor and they would end up in X-ray department. Even within our department there were color coded lines on the floor. Green line would go to MRI, purple line would go to ultrasound. Cool, I thought!

I took the south . . . oops, the "green" elevators and found the grocery store right in front of the elevators as the lady said.

I went in and picked up a small shopping basket from the corner and went straight to the section of bread. When I grew up in Bombay, when you ask for bread you get only one type of bread but maybe by different manufacturers. Here the bread section was full of a variety of breads. Not only do they come in different sizes and shapes but there were so many different types. I looked at the whole section with some kind of astonishment. A store associate who was passing by and saw the confused look on my face stopped and asked me if I needed help.

"Yes," I said.

"How can I help you?"

"I need bread."

"Sir, what kind of bread do you need? Here is brown bread, here is white bread, here is a section of bagels, here are hot dog rolls and on the other side you'll find New York style Bagels, which are pretty famous here."

I think I heard something like dog bread so I said, "No, no. I need bread for human consumption not for dog consumption. It is for me not for my dog. I don't have one."

She was trying to hide her laughter. "All the breads here are for human consumption, sir." Then she gave me a five minute lecture with live demonstration on the types of bread. At the end of her lecture, I was thoroughly confused. Finally at the end of the lecture she said, "Now it must be clear to you which bread you want!"

"Yes, of course, thanks for the discourse on the types of breads." I said, and then selected a wheat bread with no sugar or preservatives.

Next I went to the fruit section and wanted buy some apples. Again there were so many types of apples. Gala, Fuji, Red Delicious, and Pink Lady to name a few. I had never seen such types of apples. Finally I decided to try Red Delicious hoping they would be delicious. The cheese section was even more confusing. There were more types of cheese than I could have ever imagined. There was cheddar cheese, Monterey Jack cheese, and mozzarella cheese to name a few. They also came in different forms; cheese sticks, cheese slices, shredded cheese. I bought some cheese slices after spending about fifteen minutes in that section. The vegetable section was also interesting because most of the vegetables were in hypertrophied form. The green peppers were at least one and half times the size I had seen in India. The average size of the people shopping around was at least twice the size I had seen in India. I was amazed to see how much fat can be put on the body. There was one guy whose belly was so enormous that it reached almost his knees. I saw one lady with wearing a low cut dress revealing a significant portion of her cleavage. What was funny that when she turned around, her back was kind of exposed in a strapless dress. To my disbelief she had so much fat on her back that she proudly displayed cleavage on her back too! I called her "a lady with two cleavages!" Maybe she was proud of the fact that god had given her two instead of one cleavage. I thought maybe there is something in these vegetables and food that makes people assume those ginormous sizes. I asked one of the store associates about the vegetable sizes. She asked me, "Do you eat organic food?"

I did not quite understand what she was asking so I replied, "I am not sure. I think I eat inorganic food" upon which she smiled and took me to the food section labeled organic food. "Sir, the vegetables you saw in that other big section of the supermarket is kind of modified food so the sizes are big. Here you will find naturally grown vegetable products, but let me warn you that they are much more expensive than the other type."

"Really, why?" I asked her.

"Sir, I don't know the answer. Are you new in this country?"

"Yes, I am." I confessed to her.

"Let me tell you something you should probably always remember. In general, junk food is much cheaper in this country than the healthier food. So I guess that answers your question about organic food," she said while smiling. I realized that what she was saying about junk food was true. When I looked around in the city and airports I realized that this was probably the only country in the world where poor people were fat and the rich were less fat! In the rest of the world it was exactly opposite.

"Is there anything else I can help you with?" she asked me, distracting me from my thoughts.

"No, but thank you so much for your time." I went back to the inorganic food section, as the prices of organic food were too expensive for me. Maybe once I started earning enough money I could afford the organic and healthier food, I thought.

One thing I realized after coming to America was everything in the grocery store had an expiration date, which included fruits, eggs, even the salt and sugar. I guess even human beings had expiration date, only it is not stamped on us!

After my exhaustive shopping experience, I went back to my room. I set some of the inorganic food I had brought from the store into my fridge. I made some chai for myself and sat down. Since there was nothing else to do, I switched on television and was surfing channels. On one of the channels there was heated discussion going on about some apparently important issue in the schools. There were a lot of speakers on the show. Each of them was arguing about something and trying to prove their point. I watched for a while, but at the end of the show the issue they were discussing was still unresolved. No one offered any solution to the problem. Each one of them was trying to prove his or her opponent wrong. I changed to another channel. There were a lots of women of different ages (and sizes) arguing about the morning after pill. Apparently this pill is designed for those women who want to prevent pregnancy after they had unprotected sex. There was fruitless discussion for about half an hour without any amicable solution. I switched to another channel and there was almost a war between two political opponents who were arguing over voter ID laws. At the end of the show, the host had to physically separate the two opponents as they almost tried to wrestle with each other coming literally to blows! In between these programs were advertisements of some kind of drugs for various types of diseases. One of the advertisers warning was something like this:

"Please consult your doctor before starting this medication to determine if you are healthy enough to take this medicine. As a result of this medicine you may experience side effects such as dizziness, stuffiness of the nose, headaches and palpitations. Some rare adverse reactions can be skin rash, nausea, vomiting, diarrhea, or an erection lasting for more than four to six hours. In case of these adverse reactions please go to the nearest emergency room immediately and consult the doctor." Then the person on the advertisement continued with further warnings. "If you do any of these activities such as driving, walking in park, using a computer, taking a bath, or taking a shower this drug may not be suitable for you!" I was literally shocked! If I was the patient suffering from that disease who might need that drug, I would be better off with the disease itself rather than side effects of the medicine! There was also a commercial for a drug treatment for erectile dysfunction which showed a number of horses entering the stable. Was that supposed to be a subtle indication of coitus? I wondered. I also saw some commercials for some so-called medicines or drugs which said:

"These statements have not been evaluated by the FDA. This drug or medicine has not been approved by FDA for diagnosis or treatment. Please consult your physician before starting this medication . . ." I was tired and I did not know when I fell asleep on the couch. I woke up suddenly due to some loud commercial on the TV. It was a bunch of overweight people justifying spending thousands of dollars for weight loss surgery or pills. After which there was another commercial which had many thin or relatively thin people dancing and telling their success stories about weight loss. A lady came on the commercial and said, "I lost thirty pounds" and started dancing. Then there was another guy who came on and described how miserable his life was when he was over 250 pounds and after losing one hundred-something pounds how his life has changed. Oh my god, I realized that the weight he had lost was almost as much I weighed at that point. So he lost one adult human being's weight! How did he gain so much weight in the first place? I then realized that problems are quite different in different parts of the world. Some countries have problems with people being undernourished while some have problems of being over-nourished and overfed. I switched the channel to the next one and it was some kind of shopping channel in which a bunch of fat ladies were convincing the viewers to buy some things to save money. On some other channel, there was a commercial about some drug lawsuit. A lady would come on the commercial and tell how her husband suffered by taking some medications and he developed some kind of cancer. Following which a lawyer and his pretty secretary would come on and give their number for the proposed lawsuit against the company. First of all the husband of that lady took some medicine which was not really indicated so the pharmaceutical company made money. I guess the doctor who prescribed made money and so did the pharmacy. Now that he developed cancer, the hospital made money! Now that he is dead from taking the medication, which was not really needed, the lawyer and his wife will be making some money. Any way I switched of the idiot box and had a sandwich and went to the bedroom.

The next day we were going to start enrolling people for our study so I was excited. I went to bed and never knew when I fell asleep.

# *Fifth Commandment*

Jen had listed some patients who were likely volunteers for our study. She would meet them and get basic information, explain to them the research project and brain MRIs they would undergo. It was my duty, however, to get their signature on the consent form and answer any questions the patient might have about MRI scans or anything else.

There was a sweet eighty-something-year-old-lady who was one of the first few volunteers. Jennifer had interviewed her and explained basic things about our project.

I was sitting in my clinical research office where typically I would see patients, talk to them, and get the consent form signed. There was a soft knock on the door.

Jen walked in with this old lady and introduced me. "This is Dr. More who is conducting this research."

I got up from the chair and shook her hand and welcomed her. "Nice meeting you. I hope you are doing well," I said to start the conversation.

"I'm doing fine, thank you, doctor," she said in a somewhat feeble voice.

"I guess Ms. Graziano has already gone over and explained to you the consent form. Do you have any questions?"

"Yes, I do." she said. "Here it is written that I need to 'avoid sex for two weeks before and after chemotherapy.' Why is that?"

I was shocked because that was the last question I was expecting from her. But I kept my expression neutral and explained to her, "Ma'am, we are going to do MRI scans before and after chemotherapy. This situation arises because they don't want you to be pregnant while you receive chemo for your tumor. In your case, this situation does not arise because you are post-menopausal."

"Are you currently sexually active?" Jen asked. I was shocked and I thought Jennifer was insane to ask this question. But I was even more shocked by the old lady's answer.

"Yes, I am dear. I have an eighty-four-year-old boyfriend," she said, and I was about to faint.

She finally signed the consent form and thanked me. When she got up from the chair, I noticed that she was pretty frail, had curvature in the spine and walked with a cane.

"Thank you, ma'am, have a great day!" said Jen.

"Oh, by the way, I have one more question," The lady turned around and looked at me.

I stood up and was ready to listen to her. "Sure, go ahead."

"Is the sixty-nine position okay for sex during your clinical trial?"

I was stunned and did not know what to say. I looked at Jen who was covering her smile with the consent form.

Finally Jen replied, "Ma'am, should be okay, I think."

"Thank you dear," she said and left.

As soon as she left, Jen busted out laughing and said, "I wish I had a camera to take your picture when she asked you about the sixty-nine position. You had such a weird look on your face, man. This is so hilarious. Looks like I am going to enjoy this research project with you."

I was speechless though. Then I thought and said to Jen, "Maybe the sixty-nine position was kind of ideal for her."

"Why do you say that?"

"Because of her kyphotic curvature of the spine the six is already formed, only thing remaining is how to fit the nine from her eighty-four-year-old old boyfriend in that curve!"

Jen could not control her laughter and said, "Oh, my god. That is so hilarious. You have a great sense of humor, Bond."

The very next day I met a thirteen-year-old boy. There was a question on the consent form about being sexually active. I was going to check not active but on second thought, I asked him, "Mike, are you currently sexually active?"

"Yes."

"How many sexual partners?" Jen asked.

"I'm not sure. Four, maybe five." His mom was sitting next to him and her face was red and I was surprised.

"Mike, we need to talk about this when we go home, okay?" his mom said.

I soon realized why some movies are PG-13, which means for immigrant parents like me, a boy or a girl greater than thirteen years has to accompany the parent, just in case the adult parent had some questions. So PG-13 to me meant the thirteen-year-old kid was giving guidance to his or her parents.

I was also quite depressed after realizing that both the 13-year-old and the 80-something-year-old were more sexually active than I was at that time. Jen picked up my thoughts and said, "Bond, I need you to hook you up with someone." I stopped her from making any further comments.

"Jen, let us concentrate on research."

The other day, Jen introduced me to a seventy-four-year old male patient who would be our prospective volunteer for the study.

I went over the consent form with him and asked, "Sir, do you have any questions?"

"Yes, just one question. I have a penile implant, will it be okay if I get an MRI?"

I had heard about breast implants but not about penile implants so I did not know what to answer. As usual, Jen came to my rescue. "Sir, thanks for informing us. If it is a metallic implant then it is probably a problem. But we need to look it up. If you know the type of implant you have then we can probably tell you more. We'll check that before you actually go in the scanner." After which both of us looked up online about penile implants and MRI compatibility.

"Oh man, looks like I am going to learn more about sex lives of other people and sexuality during this research project than anything else," I said.

"Dude, this is America. People want to have sex as much as and as long as they want. There is nothing to get ashamed of or embarrassed about."

"That's okay, but I thought after the age of seventy or eighty years people will have different priorities on their minds other than sex."

'FIFTH COMMANDMENT'

"Thou shalt have sex as much as and as long as thou can!"

"Here is the fifth commandment for you, Bond: Thou shalt have sex as much as and as long as thou can."

"Alright, Jen, you are almost half-way through your ten commandments."

"That's right. Bond, your life seems to be pretty boring. Do you want me to hook you up with someone?" Jen was persistent despite my reluctance.

"No. I am fine the way I am."

"Why not just give it a try. I'll give you tips as to how to talk to girls here in America."

"Jen, I have a lot of things to do before this conference and I am barely ready. It gives me shivers as we have to submit the abstract in about two month's time. If I don't get this research project going well, I will be out of this hospital and out of this country also. Do you understand that?" I said in a stern and authoritative voice.

"Yes, I do. Don't get mad at me. I was trying to help you."

"Jen, I don't get mad at anyone and definitely not at a beautiful girl like you."

Jen seemed to be surprised by my comment but she did not say anything.

The very next day I was going through some papers and Jen walked in my office and she started saying something, but I interrupted her and said, "Wait, let me finish writing this email and then you can talk."

"You can write as I talk. You are using your ears to listen to me and your hands to write the email. You see? Americans are multitaskers!"

"I am not. I can only do only one thing at one time so I can either finish this email or listen to you. What do you want me to do?"

She gave up and said, "Okay, Bond, you win. I'll keep my mouth shut till you are done."

After I finished my email, I looked at her and said, "Okay, now tell me."

"First of all, as I was telling you, Americans can do multiple tasks at one time. For example, I can drive while I talk on my cell phone and at the same time I am putting on some make up! If you want to live here you need to be a multitasker. I know some men can drive while talking on phone, smoking, and take some pleasure from their girlfriends, which I prefer not to mention here in your office."

I paused for a moment and I said, "Jen, my brain cannot do that. Maybe it is just me. I cannot listen to music and read at the same time. I don't think I can change that now. Too late! Anyway, tell me what you were really going to tell me, please."

She seemed to understand and maybe gave up on me and said, "We have a volunteer, probably a normal person for the control part of our study. She had a CT scan of the chest, abdomen, and pelvis today. Do you want to check her scan to make sure she doesn't have any metal or any other problems such as cancer or weird infections before we enroll her?"

"Sure, let's go to the reading room and I will look at her scans," I said while getting up. Finding 'normal' volunteers was the difficult part of our study so I was excited.

We went to the reading room and I logged in on one of the PACS machines and opened her study. Jen was sitting right next to me.

Before looking at the patient's CT scan, I opened her chest X-ray. She had big breasts, which were pretty obvious on the lateral view of the chest. Before I could say anything, Jennifer said, "She is big."

I smiled, turned around, and said, "I have heard this before. When one woman looks at other woman's chest or chest x-ray and says she is big. Does it always refer to her breast size?"

Jennifer smiled and said, "The short answer is, yes. I mean, look at her boobies. They must be almost reaching her belly button! Come on, don't tell me you didn't notice them, Bond! I know that all male radiologists look at breast size on chest x-ray!"

I simply smiled and did not comment and decided to close her chest x-ray and open her CT scan.

When I opened her chest CT scan, I noticed that there was some kind of linear metal on her chest.

"Are you sure that this is an out patient, Jen?"

"Yeah, I am pretty sure. Why do you ask?"

"Look at the ECG leads on her chest." I showed her the metallic curvilinear things on her chest.

"Let me see." Jen took the mouse from me and scrolled and said, "Oh by the way, FYI it is called EKG not ECG in this country. Oh you know what? This is not what you are thinking. I think this is her underwire bra. See how those lines follow her boobs all the way?"

"What is that?" I asked her.

Jen looked around and said softly, "Bond, let us go to your office and I will explain to you. But can we enroll her as a volunteer?"

"Sure we will. Let us go to research office."

"No, first we'll go to your office and then to the big research office," she insisted.

"Fine, let's do that." When we got to my office, I sat down in my chair and Jen locked the office from inside.

"What are you doing? Why are you locking the office from inside?" I screamed at her.

"Shh, keep your calm, I am not planning to rape you or seduce you. Now listen to me about what I am going to say. As women get older, the breasts start sagging so there is a need to wear an underwire bra to lift the breasts up. Do you understand?"

I nodded. Then she cupped her hands and held her both breasts and then lifted them up.

"See, when I was twenty-five these were up here and now..." she put her hands down, "...that I am almost thirty-five they are here, understand?"

Frankly I was quite embarrassed but I kept my cool and said, "Yes, thanks for the demonstration. It made my learning experience somewhat embarrassing but much more easy and more interesting. By the way, I'm not sure if it's appropriate to ask, but are you really thirty-five?" I asked her.

"Bond, you should not probably ask any other women her age but it is okay with me because I know you pretty well. I was a nursing student before I was a medical student so I am not a young med student; I am much older than most of my classmates or batch mates. I just couldn't imagine me working as a nurse and besides I always wanted to be a doctor."

"Oh thank god. I am also not very young, probably much older than the residents and fellows out here. I always thought that I am too old to start residency here."

She unlocked the door and said, "Bond, this is America. You are never too old for anything here. Especially for sex! Always remember that."

"Thanks, baby," I said. After that day I felt that we were going to be great buddies.

The very next day Jen entered my office as I was working and said, "Bond, I got something for you, you might want to look at it," and she closed the door and locked it again. I was a bit annoyed but she ignored me and gave me a large envelope.

"Why do you keep locking the door and what is this supposed to be? Did you bring me a *Playboy* or something like that?" I asked while opening the big envelope. There was a clothing advertisement, particularly women's underwear and bras.

"These are pictures of lingerie! Why are you giving this to me?" I almost screamed at her. I said 'lingerie' the way it is spelled 'linge-rie'.

She corrected me. "Bond, it is correctly pronounced 'lahn-zhuh-rey'."

"Whatever, I really don't care how it is said. Bottom line is, it is what women wear inside. By the way, no pun intended when I said 'bottom line '."

"Got it. Bond. Don't get mad at me. These are things you should know if you live here. These might be useful to you in day to day life, you never know," she said while smiling. "Why don't you go to your dorm room and study different types of these women's undergarments so you won't get confused between an underwire bra and EKG leads in future."

"Thanks. I am going to get a PhD in what women's underwear looks like. By the way, since we are talking about bras, one of the states in U.S. sounds like the name of bra in the old Indian ancient language Sanskrit," I said.

"Really, which one? Tell me."

"Kentucky. It sounds like *Kanchuki*, which means a brassiere in Sanskrit."

"Yeah, it does. This is hilarious," Jen said.

While we were enrolling a new volunteer for the study, I happened to walk into the room where Jennifer was interviewing the lady and taking her consent. As I passed by, I noticed the lady showing Jen pictures of some kids. Jennifer introduced me to the young, good looking lady. "This is Dr. Bond. Dr. Bond, this is Rachel. She's enrolling in the study."

We shook hands and I happened to notice the photos in her hand.

"Oh, nice kids," I said.

"Yes, these are my grandkids," she said, and I was astonished. I looked at Jen and she signaled me to walk away. "It was nice meeting you," I said and I left the room and went to my office. Soon there was a soft knock on the door and my American Guru entered the office.

"Bond, I should have again photographed your face when she said those were her grandkids," she said while entering.

"Yes, she looked so young and sexy. I cannot imagine her being a grandmother!"

"Dude, this is America! She was probably sexually active in her late teens, got pregnant when she was around eighteen may be twenty and guess what, her daughter does the same. So at the young age of forty, she is a grandmother! And if she eats and exercised right, she would look young and sexy!"

"Oh, I get it now. I am sorry about the expression, but it was really hard to believe that she has grandkids. She did not look like a grandmotherly type," I said.

"No, she is not. I was chatting with her. She is divorced but has a boyfriend . . ."

"You mean a man-friend, because he would be of her age or older so no more a boy," I cut her short.

She smiled and said, "Yes, you can say that. But she is still young and very much sexually active and active otherwise too. The point I'm getting at is you will meet women who are around forty who can be grandmothers."

"Yes, I got your point, Guru. Which means she is only five or six years older than you . . ."

She cut me short and said, "Bond, don't remind me of my age and don't say it in public."

"Alright baby, I am sorry."

The very next patient who was enrolling in our study turned out to be man in his early fifties but who looked much older than he was. I happened to walk into the consent room while Jennifer was explaining to him about the research project and the scans we were doing.

There were young kids with him. To start some conversation I said, "Looks like the kids are happy with their granddaddy taking care of them," and then I introduced myself. At that point Jen gave me an angry look.

He said coldly and bluntly to me, "Sir, they are my kids not grandkids."

I was so ashamed and I said, "I am sorry."

"No problem. I got married a little late and had kids later so that is why I look older." Thank god he enrolled in our study in spite of this incident.

Jen was furious at me. "Bond, we would have lost a normal volunteer. You know I am working my ass off to get normal people to enroll and it looks like you are out to screw that."

"I am sorry but how the hell I am supposed to know at what age these people start having sex, get married, and produce kids. That previous lady looked so young so I thought the pictures she is showing were of her kids but they turned out to be her grand kids. This guy started late so he looks so old so I thought they are his grandkids!"

"Bond, in such cases you should politely ask them before commenting spontaneously. This is America so—"

I cut her short and said, "Oh, I know your usual lecture . . . I got it."

She seemed to have cooled down and said, "Okay, I am going to enlist the next volunteer who is already here. You stay here and I'll report to you."

"As you wish," I said while resting my feet on the table.

She came back in few minutes, this time quite furious.

"What happened? He refused? Don't worry, we will get someone else." I said, trying to calm her.

"No. We enrolled him but what makes me angry is something else," she said.

"What? Did he ask you if you were single or married?" I used my best judgment.

"No. That would have been okay. He thought I was a nurse! And this is not the first time this has happened. I've been on clinical service and I walk into a patient's room and he would say 'I want to see a doctor not a nurse.' That makes me mad."

"Calm down, baby. It's okay, don't get mad."

The next volunteer for the study was a drug addict. Since I did not have great knowledge of street drugs, I tried to page and then call Jennifer on her phone but she did not respond back to me. I think her cell phone was switched off or out of range. Since we also needed some drug addicts as volunteers, I decided to go talk to him to enroll him for the study. I was looking at the form he filled for enrollment and he wrote that he was a cocaine addict. I had no idea about cocaine addiction. I wanted to look up on the internet but the internet in the hospital was extremely slow so I gave up the idea.

I walked into the room and introduced myself. He was shabbily dressed, his beard was grown and unkempt and he had a trashy girlfriend with him who was wearing a mini skirt and t-shirt so short that her cleavage was exposed as well as her pierced navel. I was frankly embarrassed. I ignored her and her multiple piercings, including the exposed belly button, and spoke to him. I looked at his arms and hands and could not see any injection marks or any skin injuries.

He was curious and asked me, "Doc, what are you looking for?"

"Where do you inject cocaine? I am trying to see injections marks."

Upon which both of them started laughing hysterically.

His girlfriend got up from chair and came close to me. I could smell tobacco smoke and alcohol. She whispered in my ear and said, "Hey, handsome, you don't inject cocaine, you snort it. Do you want to try some?" That's when Jennifer entered the room and looked and me and that trashy girlfriend.

Hey handsome, you don't inject cocaine, you snort it...
Do you want to try some?

I said, "Of course not." I explained to him about what was going to happen and what he was supposed to do. Jennifer then took him to show him the scanner as he was bit claustrophobic while I checked the form for its completion. While I was alone with his girlfriend, she said, "Hey, Doc, that nurse with you is so hot. Are you flirting with her?"

I was a bit annoyed and said, "Look, first of all, she is not a nurse and I don't know what you are talking about."

She did not give up and asked me a question that I thought came straight from the movie *Basic Instinct*. "Hey, handsome, have you ever fucked on cocaine?"

I was furious and looked at her angrily as she winked at me. I was going to say something but that moment Jennifer and our future volunteer entered the room so I just ignored her and asked her boyfriend, "So what do you think? Can you undergo the MRI scan? Or is it too scary for you?"

"No. It's not bad at all. I have no problem. Where's the form? Let me sign it. Oh I have one more question. I don't have health insurance. Is this going to be paid out of pocket? In which case I won't be able to afford it."

I was clueless. Jen came to my rescue. "No, sir. This is our hospital research project so all the expenses are covered for the MRI scan. You just have to show up."

"Thanks," he said and signed the form. While leaving, his trashy girlfriend gave me a big smile and said, "Thank you, handsome! You might want to try what I asked you." And winked at me.

Jen was furious. "Hey, Bond, looks like you have been flirting with her while I was gone with her boyfriend to show him the scanner. Did you hit on her?"

"No. Absolutely not. I have a better taste, come on!"

"I thought so. So what was she talking about?"

I hesitated a bit and then said "She called me handsome, winked at me, and after you had gone she asked me if I ever fucked on cocaine."

"Wow, she was hitting on you! So what was your answer, Bond?"

"Nothing. I was stunned. Before I could answer anything you and her boyfriend entered the room."

"Thank god I entered the room at the perfect time. Anyway, you should have told her your libido is so strong that you don't need cocaine and maybe asked her what she was doing tonight," she said while smiling.

"Oh, really?" I was amazed by her response.

"No, Bond, I'm just messing with you," she said while giggling.

The next patient we were supposed to scan was in neurosurgery ICU. I did not know the exact location so I decided that Jen and I would go together to see him. Before going up to the ICU, I decided to review the CT scans he'd had so far. He'd had an extensive brain surgery to remove a tumor. He was not waking up after his surgery so the neurosurgery service wanted to scan him and do diffusion tensor imaging to see if we could figure out why he was not waking up. I had discussed this case with Dr. Stein and he had given his green light for scanning for the research. His scans I reviewed looked pretty bad, but I did not see any major hemorrhage in his brain.

We went to see the patient in neurosurgery ICU. He seemed to be in pretty bad shape. Frankly, I was shocked to see him and so was Jen. While we were looking at his chart the neurosurgery resident came to talk to us. "Hey, guys, can I have his chart, please?"

He wrote a note in the chart that did not say much. All it said was "post op day #3. VSS stable, moving all extremities." And then he scribbled few lines which were illegible. I am sure neither I nor he could have understood! I asked him, "Hey, how is the patient doing?" just to start some conversation.

"He's doing fine. He's still recovering from his surgery. He's moving all four extremities. Are you planning to scan him today?"

Wow, I thought, this patient is intubated, on a zillion drips with multiple catheters and tubes coming out of his body, his skull is partially open and this resident says he is doing fine! I was shocked out of my wits! Before I could recover from my thoughts, Jen replied to him, "Yes, either today or tomorrow. We'll inform you guys. Thanks."

Afterwards in the elevator I said to Jen, "Oh my god, I was stunned by the neurosurgery resident's interpretation of the patient status."

Jen smiled and said, "I figured that out, Bond. Look, they see so many bad patients every day that their threshold for being normal is pretty high. Just pray that you and I will never have a horrible brain tumor."

"Well, I hope so," I said while coming out of the elevator.

It took me a while to recover from that incident!

We ended the day by enrolling many volunteers for the study, including so called normal people. I was happy and so was Jen. We decided to call it a day and meet the next day.

# *The Sixth Commandment*

It was Friday morning. Everyone seemed to be in a good mood on that day. We actually started scanning a few patients that day so I was in a good mood too as the research seemed to be going well. Jen and I were getting friendlier and closer too.

During lunch time we sat down with bunch of radiology residents and fellows. They were discussing politics, which I never enjoyed and never commented on. But I decided to open my mouth on that particular occasion.

"Hey guys, I am so surprised that there are only two options available for choosing a candidate, either Democrat or Republican. Isn't it weird that there so many choices in everyday life such as . . ." and I got a thought block and I could not think of an example. But I continued with some effort, "...such as common things like... women's underwear. There are so many choices but when it comes to politics there are just two!" Some of the female residents laughed while some others were bit annoyed.

One of the female fellows asked me, "Bond, are you comparing politics to women's underwear? That is so disgusting!" Another resident said. "Why are you thinking about women's underwear at this time of the day? Are you dreaming about it?"

Jen tried to support me and said, "Hey, guys, maybe it's a bad example but Bond does have a point. There are so many choices available in everything in day-to-day life but when it comes to politics there are only two or very few."

Someone else commented, "Oh, by the way, we spend billions of dollars on these elections and that money can be spent on something else more worthwhile."

One of the cute female residents spoke. "Apparently, the money America spent on Halloween was kind of equivalent to the money spent on the elections. Isn't that bizarre?"

It was my turn to speak. "Yeah, absolutely. I have watched a particular trend in elections. The White House goes to Democrats and Republicans every eight years. So why not let Republicans rule for eight years and then followed by Democrats for another eight years? That way you can get rid of elections and use that money for something else."

Everyone was sort of stunned by my comments! Then someone broke the silence. "Hey, Bond, a lot of businesses depend on elections. There is a lot of money involved. And imagine what the folks at the major news channels would do for a living if they didn't have politics and elections to talk about."

So finally it boils down to only one thing I thought— money! That is root cause of all problems and still everyone is working their asses off to get it.

After lunch, I compiled the list of normal volunteers and another list of patients with cancers and other diseases. At the end of the day I updated both lists. Just when I was about to wrap up my work there was a soft knock on the door and I knew it was Jen.

"Come in," I said.

"Bond what you doing this evening?" she asked as she walked in.

"Nothing. Probably go back to room and maybe watch a movie on my TV or something."

"Okay. Get ready at around seven and come down. I'll pick you up and we'll go to a bar. I suppose you drink?"

"I can have a beer. Not a problem."

"See you at seven, then. Wear something cool. Bye."

"Scrubs are okay?" I asked her.

"No, Bond, of course not. Wear like jeans and T-shirt. No scrubs . . . do you get it?"

I was ready at seven and went downstairs. Jen soon showed up in her car and waved for me to get in. I was stunned to look at her short party dress and hairstyle. "You look great," I said.

"Thanks."

When we were at the restaurant and seated, Jen looked around and said, "See that beautiful girl in black dress at the bar? Go talk to her." Then she had a second thought. "Wait, let me go and make sure of something. I'll walk over there but, Bond, you stay here, okay?"

"Sure," I said obediently.

She walked to the bar, talked to the bartender, and from that distance it looked like that she said "Hi" or something like that to the girl and maybe talked to her before returning to our table.

"Now you can go, Bond," Jen said.

"Why did you walk over there?" I asked her.

"I just made sure that she's not a hooker," Jen said. "I didn't want you to be in trouble. Now you should go and talk to her."

"How did you figure out that she's not a hooker?"

"She's wearing a T-shirt that says 'I am not a hooker'," she replied.

"Really?" I asked her like a fool.

"Bond, I am being sarcastic. I can figure out some things that you cannot even though you are much smarter than I am," she said and then almost pushed me off my chair.

"What?" I protested. "I thought you and me were going to have beer together. Are you trying to hook me up to someone?"

"No, I'm just teaching you how to talk to girls here, the American way. Come on, don't feel shy. I'll go to the ladies room and spend some time there so you are not conscious of me being around."

"But I even don't know her."

"I'm not telling you to have sex with her, man. I mean, eventually and hopefully you should, but right now just go and talk to her. Come on, she is so beautiful and she is alone now and this is your best chance."

"What should I say to her to start conversation?"

"Just introduce yourself and say anything, tell her how pretty she looks and offer her a drink."

She almost pushed me again and I had to go. Reluctantly, I went to the bar and sat next to her. She was smoking and first of all I could not bear the smell of the smoke. However, I controlled myself and said, "Hi, how are you?"

"Good and you?"

"Great. You look so pretty."

"Thanks. I'm Mandy," she said and held out her hand.

"Hi, I am..." I was going to say Raju but probably it would have been too un-American for her so I said, "I am Bond. Nice to meet you, Mandy."

"Bond . . . like James Bond? Interesting," she quipped.

I was going to offer her a drink but she said she needed to go to the ladies room. I was terrified as she would meet Jen there so I said, "I also need to go to restroom." I was sweating.

I went to restroom and was thinking what conversation if at all must be going on between Mandy and Jen.

I purposely waited for long time even though I had finished hoping Mandy would be back at the bar. I went back and was glad to see that she was back at the bar.

I noticed that her top was up and there was a tattoo on her exposed lower back. Her jeans were way down, just short of revealing her butt crack and she was wearing a string-like panty. I sat next to her and thought she may not be aware that her panty is being exposed, so I said softly in her ear, "Hey, Mandy can I tell you something if you don't mind?"

"Sure," she said.

"I think you need to pull up your jeans a little bit because your panties are getting exposed and everyone can see those."

Her face turned red and she said, "Fuck you. You don't even know how to talk to girls."

At that moment I was so embarrassed, I decided to walk out of the bar and went straight to Jen's car.

Jen came out after few minutes, infuriated. "Hey dude, what happened? I met that girl in ladies room but I didn't say anything because I didn't want to spoil your chances."

I did not say a word. She realized something must have gone wrong.

I said, "Can you drop me back to my apartment, please?"

She got into the car and so did I. On the way back, neither of us spoke a single word. That ten-minute journey seemed like forever.

She dropped me back and I thanked her.

"Hey, what's your apartment number?"

"It is six fourteen."

At around nine the next morning there was a soft knock on my apartment door. I knew it was her. I opened the door and it was Jen.

"Hi."

"Hi, come in please."

She came in and looked around. My apartment was very clean and tidy. There was a laptop, which was my connection to the rest of the world, sitting on the table in the living room. I also had a kettle in the kitchen and some other minor stuff. I went to grab something from the fridge. "Do you want a diet coke or OJ?"

"OJ is fine. I see that you are picking up the American slang."

"Yes, but not the American life I guess."

Before she could ask, I said "First of all, I am sorry about yesterday night. I guess I screwed up your evening and night. Now let me tell you what happened."

I told her everything. I was wondering what her reaction would be. She giggled at first and then started laughing uncontrollably.

"Oh man, you're too much. First of all, those panties she was wearing are called thongs. You can check online or the thing I gave you the other day, if you want. Secondly, she purposely wanted to flash them to attract guys."

"Why would she do that? Isn't underwear supposed to be an *under*wear so that no one sees it?"

"Dude, how would ever anyone know that the girl is wearing a thong unless she shows off? I think time has come to give you the sixth commandment. Here you go man: If thou have got it, thou shalt flaunt it."

I did not quite get that one.

## 'SIXTH COMMANDMENT'

"If thou have got it…
Thou shalt flaunt it"

"Can you explain in layman's language?" I asked her.

"It means that if you have got something, you have to flaunt it so that others would know. This is America, man. Learn the American psyche."

"Alright, understood, but I have one small request."

"What is it?" Jen asked.

"You don't have to try to hook me up with anyone. I am fine the way I am."

"Alright. No problemo. I was just trying to help you."

"Let's have cup of spicy tea also known as Masala chai," I said, changing the topic of our conversation.

I made two cups of chai and we sat down and chatted.

"Do you want a biscuit?" I asked her.

She seemed surprised. "I didn't know you ate a biscuit for breakfast!"

"Yes, I do." I went inside the kitchenette and got her Britannia Marie Biscuit.

"Here you go Jen. This biscuit tastes great with chai!" I commented.

"Bond, this not a biscuit. This is some sort of cookie," she said.

"Well, this is what we call biscuit in India," I said while smiling.

"Bond, remember this is a cookie not called a biscuit here, okay?" she said in a stern voice.

"Alright, my guru, I will remember that," I said in an apologetic tone.

At one point she started looking around for something while eating her "biscuit," or cookie, to be precise. I asked her "Do you want a tissue paper?" She almost sprayed the tea in her mouth on me.

"Bond, tissue paper is for wiping butt. I definitely don't need that. Oh my god, you almost killed me!" Then her hysterical laughter came to halt and she said "Wait, this is a teaching point for you." She got up from her chair and went straight to bathroom and brought a roll of tissue paper in her hand.

"Okay, Bond, let's get our basics clear. This is called tissue paper in the USA to wipe your butt after—"

I interrupted her. "Yes, I know after what, you don't have to tell me"

"Okay, good." Then she held another object in her hand and said, "This is called a paper towel to wipe the opposite end, i.e. the mouth. And the larger and sturdy ones also called Bounty are used to wipe table or to absorb spilled water."

"Got it, sorry I was unaware of the subtle differences! Thank you for the illustrative lesson Guru!"

We slowly moved into the living room.

She was getting more comfortable and cozy in my apartment. She removed her shoes and kept her feet on the tea table. I noticed the tiny socks she was wearing.

"Jen, what is that?" I asked, pointing at her feet.

"My feet, anything wrong with them?"

"I know those are your feet. I am asking you what are you wearing?"

"These are tiny socks. They hide under my shoes so people don't see them," she explained to me.

"Wow, great! Which means it is okay if people see the underwear which is supposed to be an *under*wear but it is not okay if the socks are exposed?"

"I don't show off my underwear. Have you seen it?" Jen asked me, infuriated.

"No, not yet," I said calmly.

"What do you mean not yet?" she screamed at me.

"I meant . . . No."

"Then your question or whatever does not apply to me. Go ask that girl, Mandy, if you want," she said.

"Don't get mad. It was just a curious question. And I hope I don't run into Mandy again anytime because she will recognize me. I hope she is not a med student or some hospital employee," I said to calm her.

"I don't know. Hope she isn't," she said while relaxing.

There was a long awkward silence. Both of us did not know what to talk about after that heated debate. After that, Jen asked me something to break the silence and changed the topic. "Do you have any relatives here in the U.S.?" Jen asked.

"No. I have many classmates and friends who are scattered in different states. I have a friend in New Jersey who is physically closest to me. How about you, Jen? Where are you from and who is in your family?"

She opened up and started talking. "My parents are divorced. I grew up with my mom who is a nurse. I am from upstate New York, a place called Rochester. I have one sister who is currently doing residency in internal medicine in Michael Reese Hospital in Chicago."

We just kept chatting and did not realize how the time passed.

"It's almost lunch time, Jen. Want to go to the hospital cafeteria and eat something?"

"We can go to a nearby fast food restaurant and grab something to eat and come back here or go to my apartment if you want."

"I don't mind; let me have a quick shower and change. Do you mind waiting over here?"

"No. Not at all. Can I watch something on the TV to kill time?"

"Sure. Go ahead. Here is the remote."

Once I was ready, we headed out. Jennifer said, "Let's go to a place that's a very good example of my sixth commandment."

I was bit scared. "Are you taking me to some place where there are naked or topless waitresses?" I asked her with shivering voice.

"No, man, trust me. Nothing of that sort. No topless or nude girls, I promise. So don't worry, everyone including ourselves are fully clothed in this place."

We went to a place called Hooters. While we were entering the place, she asked me, "Bond, do you know what hooters means?"

Frankly I did not know but going by the tradition of our med school, we always answered confidently even if we did not know the answer. So I said, "Yes, I do."

Jen was surprised and said, "Really? Tell me what it means?"

"It is an owl wearing sunglasses," I said and Jennifer burst out laughing.

"Bond, this is hilarious. You just saw the logo outside, right? Wait till you see when we go inside."

The door was opened by a young girl wearing tight, low-neck T-shirt and mini shorts and some sort of stockings or leggings. "Welcome to Hooters," she said while opening the door for us.

After we sat down, a girl came to our table to take our order. She was beautiful and wearing a low-neck T-shirt exposing nearly one third to half of her breasts.

At one point I thought that she was purposely bending down and showing her assets.

"What do you want, Bond?" Jen asked me.

The other day I watching TV and dozing off and I heard something like a filibuster in one of the shows. I thought that is the name of some new burger.

So I said "Can I have one chicken filibuster, please".

"Whaaat?" Jen shouted. "There is no such burger as a filibuster. Are you in your senses? You eat chicken right? Let me order something for you."

She ordered some kind of a chicken crispy burger for me and a beef burger for herself.

I was feeling somewhat nervous and shy.

"Bond, don't feel shy. You can look at them but don't try to touch them," she explained to me.

"Why do you think I will touch to try them? Why did you bring me here in first place?"

"Well, Bond, this is the perfect example of my latest commandment: if you got it you have to flaunt it. Plus the food is not bad."

Our waitress brought our order and started chatting with us. Jen was chatting with her but I was nervous as every time I looked at her my attention would go to her breasts rather than her face.

"Sir, do you like these?" she asked me at one point.

I was going to say something like, "Yes, they are big and beautiful" but I thought she was asking about something else. I looked at Jen who said, "She is asking how are the french fries?"

"Oh, fine, I mean very fine. Delicious." After sometime I got somewhat comfortable with her breast show and everything else. So I also started chatting with her.

"How long have you been working here?" I asked her.

"This is my kind of an extra job. Where do you work, sir?" she asked me, smiling.

I decided to answer all her questions by looking at her face but not looking down there. At one point even she said, "It is okay to look. Just don't—"

I cut her short "I won't touch them, don't worry."

At one point during our conversation, Jen got annoyed. After the girl went to attend to some other customers, Jen said in soft voice, "Bond, stop hitting on her. She is being nice to you for a good tip."

I, too, was annoyed. "Look, you got me here in first place and now you are telling to not to chat with her?"

We soon finished our lunch and Jen said, "Oh by the way, Hooters means big breasts. I suppose you know by now."

"Yes, I have guessed it," I said.

"Let's go to my apartment."

At the entry level of her apartment there was a big burly guy who happened to be the manager on duty.

She stopped by his desk and asked him if she had any mail or parcels to pick up. She also introduced me to him. "Scott, this is Dr. Bond, my friend."

"Hi, Scott, nice to meet you," I said, shaking his hand.

After I went ahead towards the elevator, he called Jen again and whispered something in her ear. She smiled and said something to him.

"What was he saying?" I asked.

"Nothing. Something about mail," she replied and I knew she was lying.

While in the elevator I noticed there was no thirteenth floor.

"How come there is no thirteenth floor?"

"People are superstitious. Since thirteen is an unlucky number no one wants to stay on the thirteenth floor. So there is none. As simple as that, doc."

"But the fourteenth floor is actually the thirteenth, isn't it?"

"Yes. But it is not numbered as thirteen, which is the point."

While up on the fourteenth floor I noticed that the apartment numbers were in weird order. The door with 215 did not follow 214. All even numbers were on one side of the corridor and all the odd numbers were on the other side.

"Jen, all odd number apartments are on one side and all even numbers are on the other side. I guess this is also an American psyche?"

"Well, it is. By the way, did you notice that the all the odd numbered highways run north-south and even numbered highways run east-west?" Jen asked.

"No. I never noticed that!" I was surprised that I never noticed it.

As we went into her apartment, I nearly stumbled on a pile of dirty clothes. Every surface was cluttered with objects—books, dishes, newspapers, old magazines. There were empty cans and glasses scattered around the sofa and on the table. She saw the look on my face.

"Hey, I'm sorry but this how I live."

"Do you need any help? I am kind of a neatness freak."

"I don't mind, but let's have some dessert because I'm still hungry."

Both of us continued talking, rather I was listening and she was talking. She wanted to become radiologist so that she could earn a lot of money and have a good lifestyle. While talking to her, I also realized that she really missed her dad as a child. When she came to know that he left two young girls with her mom and married a younger lady, she was mad. She asked about my family in India.

"Do you feel lonely here?" Jen asked.

"Yes, I do. But I guess I am getting used to it."

"Do you have a girlfriend?" Jen asked.

I knew it was coming. I said, "Well, do you see one?"

"No, of course I don't. But what if you had one in India?"

I guess now it was my turn to ask the same question to her.

"Jen, who is your boyfriend?" I asked.

She seemed to be surprised by my question.

"Why do you assume that I have one?"

"Most of the girls of your age or even younger than you will have a boyfriend."

"Yes, they do. I had kind of a boyfriend earlier but we broke off. I found out that he was cheating on me." Jen said. "But I am seeing someone now." I did not ask the details.

After a pause she said, "Guys don't get attracted to me because I don't have a big rack" and she looked at me.

I did not quite get what she said and I looked around her apartment and I did not see any big rack.

"Why don't you buy one then?" I asked her.

"It is very expensive," she said.

"Really, how much?" I was surprised.

"At least five grand for each one and it's not covered by insurance."

"Each one? Why do want two, just buy one and insurance? What has a rack to do with insurance?" I was even more surprised.

Jennifer probably understood my confusion. She sat up and said, "My dear Bond, rack refers to breasts. What I was saying was guys don't get attracted to me because I don't have big breasts."

"Oh, I get it now. I am sorry, I thought you are talking about like a piece of furniture."

"Oh, no, I thought you were asking me to get a boob job to enlarge my breasts so I said it costs about five grand for each one and it is not covered by insurance."

We had a good laugh after I realized my mistake.

"Bond, what do you guys call girls with big breasts in India?"

I thought for a while and could not come up with an answer. "I don't know but I know what guys in India call a girl with tiny breasts."

"What is it, Bond. Tell me."

"Carom board or Manchester," I said.

"What is Carom Board? Never heard of it." She frowned.

"It is like a small square board which is square and flat," I tried to explain to her but she was confused. "Basically it is like a small pool table you can say."

"Oh, I get it now," she said.

After a long pause, I said, "Guys should also look at the inner beauty too."

"You know what, Bond, most guys don't care about inner beauty, I wish someone did," she said with a big sigh.

I soon realized that it was close to four in the afternoon and that there was nothing in my apartment for dinner and I also realized that one of the Indian girls in the apartment building had asked me to buy something for her from the grocery store.

"Jen, when you drop me back can we stop at a grocery store on the way?"

"Sure, I will. Have you made a list?"

"Yes, I have. I have to buy some vegetables and some other stuff."

"Veggies? For what? You don't have utensils to cook in your apartment. Are you going to eat them raw?" Jen almost shouted.

"No. There is this Indian girl I met in the lift—"

Jen cut me short "What is a lift?"

"I mean elevator. Anyway, she requested me to get some stuff and she is going to cook dinner for both of us tonight."

"Hmmm... looks like something is else is cooking between you and her. Is she single, is she good looking, what does she—"

Now it was my time to cut her short.

"No. There is absolutely nothing between us. She is just a friend. Since the cafeteria is closed she invited me over for dinner. That's it. Nothing else. But why are you getting so curious?"

"I'm just curious, you know. Okay, let's go. After I drop you and I am going to see my current BF so I don't want to be late," said Jen.

Soon we landed in a grocery store. She explored the store while I was shopping. When I was done, I signaled Jen and I went to the cashier for a check out. Since I had less than fifteen items, I stood in the line for express check out. Jen joined me and we were waiting for our turn. There were two ladies behind me. One of them looked at the cart and whispered something to the other.

Soon Jen turned around and said, "Hey ladies, let me tell you something. This gentleman here is more educated than both of you put together so he very well knows how to count items and we are in the right lane. So keep your mouths shut."

Both of them were somewhat embarrassed.

"Oh I am so sorry. He is from India isn't he? What is his education, if I may ask you," one of the two ladies asked politely. I decided to avoid her question by looking straight and by not turning around.

Jen answered for me. "He has a PhD in sexology from Harvard and he is an associate professor of sexology at NYU and he is the world renowned authority on sex and especially on Kama Sutra!"

I was about to faint but I gave an angry look to Jen, which she conveniently ignored.

"He is an Associate Professor of Sexology at NYU…
And world authority on *Kamasutra*"

After that the two ladies whispered something to each other and one of them said, "Is he seeing new patients now and can we have an appointment?"

I was stunned.

"No. He is very busy right now and his appointments are booked until Thanksgiving so you may try sometime next year." Soon my turn came and I moved my cart to the cashier.

"Good luck, ladies. See you some other time," Jen said and we moved forward. I simply did know understand what ticked her off. I looked at her and she signaled me to keep quiet. I went to the cashier who happened to be a young black girl. She had long nails painted with a bright red nail polish. While I was looking at her nails, she asked me, "Sir, what is this?"

"Ladies fingers," I said.

"Whaat?

"Ladies fingers," I repeated.

She was mad at me. Jen looked at me and said, "Bond, this is not called ladies fingers here. It is called okra my dear."

Then she turned to the black girl and said, "I'm sorry. He is new in this country and I think this is called ladies fingers in his country."

I soon realized my mistake and said, "I am sorry."

"That's okay," said the cashier girl and gave me a big smile. "I thought you were just mesmerized by my finger nails."

Soon we went out of the grocery store. Just outside the store there was a tall African American man selling something. As were approaching the parking lot, he looked at me and winked and said "Hey, I got something for you." I stopped and looked at him. He was carrying some small booklet with lot of pictures.

"What is that?" I asked him.

"One hundred fifteen sex positions assured to give you and your sexy girlfriend pleasure. Its only ten dollars, do you want one? You can try a few positions tonight," he said while pulling out one copy.

I was going to say something but Jen intervened.

"Screw you buddy, we know a hundred twenty positions already so your booklet is a piece of junk." Then she grabbed my hand and pulled me to the parking lot. I was frankly shocked by her reaction but kept quiet.

As I was getting into Jen's car I decided not talk about this small incident and asked her, "Hey, what happened with those ladies behind me? Why were you so rude to them?"

Jen smiled and said, "Dr. Bond, you probably didn't hear what they were saying. One of the ladies was looking at your shopping cart and was saying to the other lady that you had more than fifteen items in your cart and still you're standing in the express lane. So I got mad at them and… you know what happened, right?"

"Oh, I see. Now I know why you got so mad at them."

"And how did you invent this thing of me being the associate professor of sexology at NYU and an authority on Kama Sutra? You could have landed me in trouble."

"I'm sorry, Bond, but I thought I would just mess with them. See, they believed me and they were interested in getting an appointment with you," Jen said while laughing uncontrollably.

"Thank God they did not ask me any questions on sexual positions or something."

"I'm sorry, Bond." Jen said.

"That is alright. No harm done. I hope I don't see them again in that grocery shop," I said with a sigh of relief.

She dropped me at my apartment building. "Bye, good night. Tell me how the dinner was, or rather, the after dinner adventure," she said, winking at me.

"Jen, as I said, there is nothing between us. She just happens to be from Mumbai and speaks Marathi. Go and see the new man in your life. Good luck with that."

"Thank you. I'll see you Monday morning. Bye." She zoomed away in her car.

I carried the grocery bags to Madhuri's room and knocked on her door. She opened the door with a great smile.

"Come on in. Thanks for doing the shopping for me."

"You are very welcome. But I hope I am getting dinner in return," I said jokingly.

"Of course you are. We can chat while I make dinner," Madhuri said.

"I need to work on my project little bit and I will be back. I haven't worked on anything since morning," I said apologetically.

"What were you doing since morning?" Madhuri asked.

"I was chatting with my friend Jennifer," I said in a flat tone.

"Oh, I see. You were flirting with her then and now it's my turn to talk to you and you don't have time but you need me to cook dinner for you?" Madhuri seemed little bit annoyed.

"There is nothing between me and her. She just happens to help me in my research project and frankly it is going to help her to get a radiology residency."

"This is how the things start and slowly the boy falls in love—"

I cut her short and said "Okay, fine. Let me just go to my room and I will be back to chat with you. Just give me half an hour."

I was soon in my room. I looked through some research papers and I heard a knock on my door. I was somewhat surprised to see Madhuri.

"Bond, I have to go to the hospital as something has gone wrong with the reaction I had set up in the morning. My assistant just called me. But I promise to you that we will have dinner at my place. Only thing, it will be bit late," she said and left in a hurry without giving me a chance to ask a question her.

I just sat on the sofa and opened my laptop to read a journal article about diffusion tensor imaging and started reading. I was bit tired and was feeling sleepy. I did not realize when I fell asleep and suddenly woke up as the phone was ringing. It was pitch dark outside. It was Madhuri calling to say she was still stuck in the research lab and basically asked me to make arrangement for my dinner. I looked at my watch and it was almost eleven. I was wondering if there was something in my refrigerator to eat. There was practically nothing. I was thinking, now what to do? It would be stupid to call Jen at this weird hour. I then realized that there was a fast food place a stone's throw away from the campus. I quickly got dressed, grabbed my wallet and ran out the door as I was worried it might be closed. By the time I reached McDonald's, it was closed and there was a big board at the front door.

"Sorry we are closed now. Only drive through option available."

I was wondering what to do since I did not have a car. I looked at my watch, it was eleven fifteen. Again I thought Jen would be busy on a date or something so she may get furious at me if I call her, but I was really hungry. I looked around, but there was no car in sight. Finally out of sheer helplessness I decided to walk through the drive through lane. I ordered a chicken sandwich and went walking through the lane to collect my order, of course on foot. I reached the service window and I was preparing to get my wallet out, but the girl at the counter screamed loudly and said "Hey, someone call nine-one-one. There is a guy walking through the drive thru lane." I was shocked. I had not committed a crime of any sort… I was just hungry. Is being hungry a crime? Probably not.

"Hey, someone please call 911…
There is a guy walking through the drive through lane!"

I thought of running away but the girl just grabbed my hand and soon two big burly guys came and escorted me inside. Soon a big black police officer arrived and looked at me and took me away in his car.

"Hey man, are you new in this country?" he asked.

"Yes, sir. I am an alien".

"Really? But you look normal," he quipped.

"Where do you work?" came another question.

"I am a physician and currently I am working in the hospital. I am doing some research."

"Do you know I can arrest you and put you in jail?" he asked.

"Yes, sir. But I am sorry but I was very hungry and since I do not have car, I had no choice."

Then at that point I briefly told him what had happened. He just could not control his laughter.

"Oh man, you are just too much. I'll let you go with only verbal warning, but I need someone here who can vouch for you and that you work in the hospital and you won't commit this stupid mistake in future."

"I promise you that I won't do it again and I can show you my ID tomorrow or on Monday to prove that I work in the hospital."

"Nope," he said. "Get someone here now, otherwise I am grabbing your ass and you are going to jail."

The thought of going to jail sent shivers down my spine. I think in my last ten generations no one ever had gone even near a jail. The only exception was my great great grandfather who went to jail because he protested against the British rule in India, which was basically for a good cause. I had no choice but to call Jen.

"Can I go in the restaurant and call my friend?" I asked.

"Sure. Go ahead but don't try to run away," he said.

"No sir. I won't." He seemed to believe me. I quickly ran into the restaurant and tried to recall Jen's cell phone. I was really worried at how she would react. Luckily I could remember her phone number and I dialed it with trembling hands. Luckily she answered immediately.

"Hello, Jen?"

"Bond, what on earth are you calling me in this wee hour for?" she asked in a sleepy voice.

"Jen, I am really sorry but I want you to come here right now."

"Whaaat? Do you know what time is it? And what happened? Did you screw up something with that Indian girl during dinner?"

"No," I said and then I briefly explained to her about what happened.

She was shocked. "Alright, I am coming right away. Don't worry."

I went back to the police officer's car.

"A friend of mine is coming in less than ten minutes," I said to the officer.

"Alright. Sit in the car till she shows up."

Those ten minutes were like a hundred years for me. Luckily the officer was very nice. He chatted with me and told me how he loved Indian food. Soon Jen came. He was astonished by her beauty.

"Hey man, she is smoking hot. Are you banging her?" he asked.

"No. I guess my bad luck is banging me," I said.

The officer seemed to like my joke.

"You Indians seem to have a good sense of humor!" he commented and stepped outside his patrol car. I was surprised that my sense of humor was alive even in that horrible situation.

He spoke to Jennifer for a couple of minutes and before letting me go he warned me, "Hey, don't do this again, okay? Have a good night both of you."

"I am sorry, Jen. But the officer gave me no choice. He said he would put me in jail," I said apologetically.

"No problem but why didn't you call your Indian girlfriend?" she asked. I knew she was furious.

"Madhuri was stuck in the research lab due to some reaction gone wrong. Plus I do not know her phone extension in the lab. Luckily I could remember your phone number."

"Oh... so her name is Maduri! So are you mad about Maduri?"

"Jen, come on, I am hungry. This is not a time to crack jokes. My blood glucose is probably in the low fifties. Can we please go in your car and order something and would you please drop me off?" I begged.

"Sure. Looks like it's just not my day today."

We went through the drive thru and met the same girl who was holding my hand during the ordeal. While giving the sandwich she said, "Tell your boyfriend not to do this again."

"He is not my boyfriend," Jen shouted.

"Doesn't matter. He's hot," she said and winked at Jen.

"Shut up and just mind your business," Jen yelled and we went to my apartment building.

She started parking and I said, "Why are you parking? Just drop me off."

She did not say anything and I understood she wanted to come up with me. I did not protest but my heart was pounding as to what was going to happen next. It was almost midnight and I was feeling hypoglycemic.

We went in my apartment and I just started eating the sandwich. I offered her the French fries and she gladly accepted.

After I nearly finished my sandwich I asked her, "How was your date?"

She looked at me and I knew something was wrong.

"He stood me up," she said.

I was confused as I did not quite understand the phrase.

"Oh, so he kept sitting and eating in the restaurant and you were standing all the time?" I asked her innocently.

"No, Bond. Remember my first commandment? This is American, not British English, which means I kept waiting and he never showed up at the place we were supposed to meet."

I did not dare to ask her any further details. To change the topic. "Jen, thank you so much, you prevented me from going to jail."

"Yeah, tell me about it, Bond. If I wouldn't have come, your mug shot would be all over the internet with the big caption 'Indian doctor jailed for breaking the law.'"

"Mug shot? Why would anyone take a picture of my mug?" I was confused.

"My dear, sweet Bond, that is not what a mug shot is called. It is your picture from front and side on the police record," she explained to me.

"Oh my god, I did not realize that!" I shriveled with the thought of that happening.

"But why is it called mug shot instead of like face shot?"

"Bond, I have no idea. Maybe you can search on the internet," she replied.

"Thank god you came in time! Otherwise I would have been kicked out of this country."

"No problem, but don't do this again. I am more upset because you did not call me earlier. I could have easily come and got food for you rather than coming later after all that mess."

"I am sorry but I thought you were on a date," I said apologetically.

"To hell with this dating," she said to my disbelief. "You hardly know a guy and even before you start liking him, he ditches you."

I simply kept quiet as I did not know how to respond.

"Jen, it's getting pretty late," I said to change the topic.

"Yes, I know. But I want to talk to you about what happened today with me."

"Go ahead," I said.

She then told me in great detail about what happened. Frankly, it seemed quite boring to me at one point but she was speaking with so much intensity and emotion that I simply did not dare to stop her. Basically, she apparently had liked this guy and he did not show up and was not answering her phone calls either.

"I was so pissed off," she almost shouted. "How come you are not saying a word?"

Frankly I did not know what to say. Then I thought of something. "He simply does not deserve you, Jen. You are so nice at heart. You deserve a better guy than this jerk," I said after a long pause.

"I am so glad you said that," Jen said.

There was a long and uncomfortable pause. "Jennifer, can I ask you something?"

"Sure, go ahead."

"How do you have sex with someone you even don't know well?"

She seemed stunned and surprised by my question. "What do you mean? I do know the person I am or will be having sex with. I don't randomly pick up strangers from street and have sex with them."

"Wait, when you say that you know someone, how well do you know a new man before you sleep with him? Chatting in a bar or meeting in a restaurant is not really knowing someone because potentially you and the other person are seeking sex and nothing else."

"Looks like you have taken your title of professor of sexology a bit seriously, Bond. Are you preaching me on dating, sex and sex education?" Jen asked me as she stood.

"No, I am not. I am just trying to understand the logic," I explained to her.

After some time she asked me, "Do you mind if I spend the night here?"

I was shaken out of wits but I could not refuse.

I said, "Alright, Jen. Let me get my Cashmere shawl and I will sleep here on the sofa. Why don't you go inside and sleep on the bed."

She seemed to agree. I asked if she wanted to change her clothes.

"No. I sleep naked so don't worry," Jen said and I was about to faint. "I'm just joking, idiot. I'll sleep in my jeans. I'm used to that. Get what you want from your bedroom."

"Do you want to chat more?" I asked, hoping she would say no.

To my disbelief she said, "Yes, sure. Can I ask you to make some special masala chai?"

I had no choice but to make some tea for us as both of us were pretty sleepy. Our chatting was pretty much one way; she was talking continuously and I was listening trying to ward off sleep. All she wanted to say was how guys are so ruthless and worthless. Finally at one point I gave up and I never knew when I fell asleep. Next morning I woke up and realized it was almost eight thirty. I knocked softly on the bedroom door.

"Yes, I'm awake and I'm not naked so you can come in."

I went inside and she was almost ready and looked great as usual.

"Thank you so much," she said.

"I think I should thank you for helping me; otherwise I would have been in the jail."

"That's okay. By the way, I used your bathroom without asking your permission."

"That's okay. You don't have to be so formal with me Do you want to take a shower also? I have some extra towels."

"No. I think I'm fine," she said and was about to leave. From her expression I thought she wanted to say something and I guessed it.

"Do you want to meet over lunch?" I asked her.

She was bit surprised. "Yes, sure. Where do you want to meet?"

"I will be in the hospital to get things started for tomorrow, so I guess in the basement cafeteria."

"Fine. I'll meet you in your office then. What time do you plan to start working?"

"Around ten."

"Good. I will see you at ten then," said Jen and left.

# BEING OFF THE MARKET!

I got ready still recovering from last night's nightmare. I reached my office and found out that my computer was not working, my pager battery was down, and I found a note on my desk that read something like this:

"Bond,

The new MRI scanner is not working.

Hopefully sometime next week.

xoxo

Jen"

I did not understand xoxo part.

I was upset as I had spared some time on Sunday morning and nothing was working well at that hour.

As I was contemplating what to do next, the phone bell rang. It must be Jen, I thought as I picked up the phone.

"Hey doc, what's up?" It was Jen.

"Nothing is up everything is down," I said in a depressed voice.

Jen busted into laughter.

"Bond, that is just a way of asking what is going on. You should have learned it by now," she said.

"Nothing seems to work here today so you can drop your plan of coming here."

"No. I'm coming there and I just called you to tell you that I'll be bit late. We can always find something to do to get ready for tomorrow."

"Don't worry. Take your time."

Soon she arrived and I told her we had a potential candidate in ICU for our research study. Since I had no idea where the ICU was, both of us decided to go there and check on our potential patient.

"By the way, I found a note by you which basically said that the scanner is not working, but the part I did not understand was why would you curse me at the end of the note." I told her in a somewhat bitter tone.

"Curse you? I did not . . . why on earth would I curse you? Show me the note," she demanded.

I opened the note and showed her. "See here, you said xoxo, which I thought I read in some online conversations where people instead of cursing or using the F-word make up some characters instead."

She started laughing and hugged me. "Honey, that is meant to be hugs and kisses. I thought you would feel bad after reading my note so I said xoxo, which literally means hugs and kisses."

"Oh, I am so sorry. I totally misunderstood you. Thanks for the clarification," I said apologetically.

"Just for FYI, you can practically look up everything on Google. You should have just Googled it," she said while releasing me from her hug.

"What is FYI, Jen," I asked her.

"Again you can Google it, but it means 'for your information' or sometimes 'for your interest.' Got it?"

"Got it, my guru. Thanks for your help, now let us go to the ICU."

When we reached the door of the ICU, Jen said, "Bond, why don't you go in and I'll join you in couple of minutes. I need to take a dump."

"What?" I screamed at her.

"Why don't you look that up too," she said while rushing towards the restroom.

So I went inside the nurse's station and approached a nurse on duty. "Hi, I am Dr. Bond from radiology. Do you know where this patient is?"

I showed her the details of the patient and she said with a big smile, "Sure, doc, come with me and I'll show you the patient." I went with her and to check patient's chart, I went to the main desk. Soon I was surrounded by pretty, blonde nurses.

"He is so hot," someone whispered in the back. One of the good-looking nurses handed over the patient's chart and said, "Hi doc, I'm April, this patient's nurse."

"Hi, I am Dr. Bond from radiology." I shook her hand and took patient's chart and sat down to check the details.

"Let me know if you need anything," she said.

Soon another blonde nurse came to me and said, "I need his chart after you're done."

"Alright, no problem."

Soon I found myself surrounded by beautiful nurses. Jennifer entered and saw the possible danger. She went and whispered something to one of the nurses. I did not hear it quite well. When she joined me I said. "Let's quickly go and check the patient." I went to April, his nurse, and said, "I need a torch, please."

She said in disbelief, "A torch? Whom do you want to torch, doc?" and started laughing.

Jen realized I was probably using a wrong term. "Bond, why do you need a torch?"

"I need to check his pupils. What's so funny about it?" I asked.

"It's called a flashlight here not a torch. A torch is the one they carry from one country to another. Like the Olympic torch. Do you get it?" Jen asked.

I guess now it was my turn to laugh. "Oh, I see. I am sorry, I am still getting used to American lingo. I need a flashlight please."

I went near the patient's bed and checked his reflexes and pupils. While I was checking him, a monitoring alarm went off and April went to his bedside as Jen stood outside the patient's room. April checked patient's IV and switched off the alarm. She said to me, "So, doc, I understand you are off the market."

I did not understand her question; I thought she was talking about the stock market.

"Hey Doc, so I understand you are off market?"

"Stock markets are really risky, I don't invest and I would strongly advise you to not put money in any stocks. I suppose that answers your question."

Before she could answer, Jen showed up and April quickly left. I was left somewhat confused. The next day, when I went to ICU to see the patient again, I realized that not many nurses were hovering around me. I saw April and asked her about your conversation yesterday.

"April, you were talking about some market yesterday. Frankly I don't know much about stock markets and also I hardly have any money to invest."

"Looks like you are just off the boat, doc. I wasn't talking to you about the stock market," she said and was about to leave, but then she turned back. "By the way, your girlfriend is pretty hot!"

I was shocked. "April, what are you talking about? Which girlfriend? I don't have—"

She cut me short and grabbed my scrubs. "Oh come on, I am talking about that sexy med student Jennifer."

I was about to have a heart attack. I said, "No, we are—"

She cut me short again and pulled me aside and whispered in my ear, "Hey do you get hanky-panky almost every night?" I did not understand the term so did not know what to say.

I wanted to talk to patient's physician so I went near the ICU nurse's station. Luckily, the resident doctor was writing some notes on another other patient's chart. I went to her and introduced myself. "Hi, I am Dr. Bond from radiology. Are you the resident taking care of this patient?" I showed her the chart.

She acknowledged she was, then stood up and shook my hand. "Hi I'm Lauren, nice to meet you. What do you need?"

"We are scanning some patients with neurological disorders for research purposes and your patient fits in our criteria so we will be scanning him tomorrow in our research magnet sometime in the morning."

"No problem. He's quite stable so I wouldn't worry about him going in the scanner although I will ask April to accompany him as per our protocol".

"Thank you so much," I said and went to put patient's chart in the place.

I saw April again and she winked at me and smiled and said, "Can I tell you something funny about my patient?" Soon she was joined by other blonde nurses.

"Tell me," I said in a rather flat tone not expecting what was going to come.

She came near me and said, "My patient has a tattoo on his penis."

I was really shocked and I said, "Really?"

Immediately the other nurse said "Why? Do you want one, doc?" and everyone including April started laughing. I was embarrassed and stunned.

"April, why don't you show doc his tattoo so he will have an idea how and where to get one!" said another blonde and sexy nurse. There was another round of laughter.

I was frankly embarrassed. I said, "No thanks" and quickly left ICU without interacting with anyone else.

Later, I met Jen on my way to my office. "Jen, I want to talk to you."

"Okay, talk. I'm in front of you and listening."

"No. Not here, in my office," I said. From my tone she guessed something was wrong.

We went in my office and luckily there was no one else around. I closed the door and asked Jen

"So, I am your boyfriend? Since when? Can you tell me please so I can also go around and tell everyone that you are my *hot* girlfriend and also we get hanky hanky or something like that every night?"

Jen kept her cool. She smiled and said, "Bond, don't get mad. I did it to protect you from those women. Remember the very next day when you went to ICU and no one was hovering around you?"

"Yes. I do," I said after thinking for a bit. My anger was slowly melting.

"Remember what April said to you that you are off the market?"

"Yes. Did you hear that? I thought you were not around."

"I was right outside and trying to listen to what April was saying. Those women thought you were single, which of course is true, and they were trying to hit on you. So to discourage them, I told them you are my boyfriend and you're super-hot in bed. And also we get hanky-panky almost every night."

I soon realized my mistake. I said apologetically, "I am so sorry. I completely misunderstood you." I felt somewhat ashamed.

Jen came close to me and grabbed my coat and whispered in my ear, "Doc, I suppose you don't know what hanky-panky is. Do you want me to show you or you will look up online?"

She came so close that I was feeling very uncomfortable. I could smell the sweet feminine perfume she was wearing. My heart was racing and I started sweating. "Jen, I think I will look up online. Can you please let me go now?"

"Sure, but only if you tell me tomorrow what hanky-panky is. That's your homework today, doc." Jen released my coat and I was relieved.

She started laughing and said, "This is America, Dr. Bond. Be an American."

"I am nine-to-five American," I said.

"No. You need to be a full-time American man. More so at night. Otherwise you won't survive here. Oh, by the way, I found out one more reason you should stay away from that sexy nurse April."

"What is that? Don't tell me that she is too sexy for me."

"No Bond, she is certified crazy."

"Certified crazy? What do you mean?" I was puzzled.

"Bond, there are many women in this country who suffer from mood swings and depression, and I truly feel sorry for them. But with April it's kind of a different story. She's on regular meds and there is something more."

"What is it?" I was really curious.

"There was a male nurse on the same floor who once was her boyfriend." She continued. "He told me that she stabbed him with scissors on his arm once when they had a fight."

"Wow, she looks so nice and cute," I said.

"She also has a child, and guess where the father of that child now?"

"Where? In the ICU?" My curiosity was at its peak!

"No, Bond. The ICU would have been okay. He is in jail and for some serious crime, can you believe it?"

"Wow." I was stunned. "You really saved me from her! Thank you so much, Jen." At that point Jennifer looked like a goddess to me.

"No problem, Bond. See? Looks are so deceptive!" she said, smiling.

"By the way," Jen said, "There is a possible new volunteer. Her only issue is back pain and she may have had some back surgery. Do you want to see her scans?"

"Yes, of course." We went to the reading room, but all the PACS stations were busy so we went to one of resident's PACS station and requested her to pull up the scan.

It was a lumbar spine MRI. I looked at plain films and then pulled up the MRI. The resident was doing a neuro rotation and was quite inquisitive. "Bond, can I ask you a question?" Julie the resident politely asked me.

"Yeah, sure go ahead."

"Do you see this kind of edema in the posterior soft tissues, fat to be precise, on the T2-weighted images?" she said while pointing out the changes on the scan.

"Yes, I do see what you are trying to ask. So what is your question?" I asked.

"Is that normal or pathological?" Julie asked me.

"It definitely physiological but I have seen this commonly in obese individuals with a lot of fat around their belly and back. For some reason it is called 'tramp stamp edema,'" I said without knowing what that term meant. Upon that Julie and Jen both burst out laughing. I looked quizzically at Jen upon which Julie said, "Jen why don't you teach Dr. Bond about tramp stamp edema!"

"Sure, my pleasure! But can we enroll her as volunteer so I can start the paperwork?"

"Yes, of course, go ahead," I said as I stood. "Julie, thanks for sharing your workstation."

"Always a pleasure, Bond. Good luck with your research!" Julie said.

"Thank you," I said.

"Bond, let's go to your office for a second," Jen said, winking at me.

I knew something was coming but kept calm. "Sure, let's go. I guess it is about tramp stamp edema?"

"You are so smart, my dear," she said. As soon as we entered, she asked to sit on my chair and locked the door. She turned her back towards me and lifted her top to expose her back and told me to hold onto the top with my hands. I was confused. "Just do it, Bond, as I tell you."

Then she slightly unzipped her jeans and slowly lowered them "What are you doing?" I screamed at her.

"Don't worry, Bond. I have to be careful as I don't want to expose my underwear or my butt crack but do you see that tattoo on my lower back?"

"Yes, it looks like a butterfly. But why do you have tattoo there?"

"Because I wanted one! Okay now let my top go." She pulled her jeans up, zipped again, and lowered her top.

"That tattoo you just saw is called 'tramp stamp' that's where the name comes 'tramp stamp edema.' Get it?"

"Oh wow, I always knew the term but never knew what it meant. Thanks for the demonstration but you could just have shown it to me on the 'net.'"

"Well, Bond, just wanted to make this more interesting and sort of personal," she said while winking at me.

"Oh well, now I know one secret place on your body which has a tattoo!" I said.

"That's fine, I trust you, Bond."

# SEVENTH COMMANDMENT

We went to cafeteria and got some coffee and were looking for a free table. There were only few so we went to a table where John, the fellow from West Texas. I always thought that he was very unhappy to be in New York though I didn't know why.

"Hi Bond, hi Jen, how are y'all doing?" he asked with his Texas drawl.

"We're just fine. How are you?" Jen said.

"Well, I am counting my days of fellowship and waiting to return to Texas."

"Don't you enjoy being in such a great city?" I asked.

"No. I miss Texas." John said.

There was a newspaper in front of him and I glanced at it. There was some news about the presidential race. While I was looking at the newspaper Jen started talking about politics. Jen and John did not agree over something and they almost started fighting.

I tried to calm both of them. Finally I convinced Jen to keep quiet.

"By the way, are you Republican or Democrat?" I asked John.

John's face turned red. He looked at me as if I had asked him something very personal and private. I did not think it was a wrong or an insulting question. Jen realized the seriousness and said to John, "Hey, John, don't pay attention to what he said. He's just kidding, okay? By the way, how was your weekend?" Jen said quickly to change the topic.

That seemed to have worked. John described how he spent the whole weekend with his girlfriend, including the details of how they had great sex. At one point, he started describing various positions they assumed while doing it. Jen was kind of enjoying the conversation, but I was embarrassed. I kept wondering 'Which one of the questions was more embarrassing? Mine or Jen's?' Anyway, then he started describing how they went on a drive in her SUV and she gave him oral pleasure in the SUV. Jen was listening intently and I was even more embarrassed.

Suddenly, he realized he was getting late for the tumor board so he said, "Have good day, y'all. I have to go for this stupid tumor board."

After he left, I asked Jen, "By the way, what is an SUV?"

"SUV stands for Sports Utility Vehicle, what did you think?"

"From the kind of activities he was doing, I thought it stood for 'Sex Utility Vehicle.'" I said.

Jennifer could not control her laughter. "That was a good one, Bond. I like it. You have a great sense of humor."

'SEVENTH COMMANDMENT'

"Thou shalt not ask one's political affiliation"

Soon we headed back to my office. On the way Jen said, "Doc, it has been a long time since I have given you a commandment. Here is the seventh commandment for you: "Thou shalt not ask one's political affiliation."

"I still don't understand why John got mad at me. I did not ask anything wrong."

"You did. Never ask anyone about his or her political affiliation unless he or she is close to you. People here don't like it for whatever reason. Secondly, it is pointless to ask that question to someone from Texas. But I will spare you on that one since you're new in this country so you don't know this country's geo-political map."

"And he does not mind discussing the dirty and exquisite details of his sexual adventures in public. For me that was more embarrassing than the political affiliation question," I said angrily.

"Calm down, Bond, and start working on your project."

It was a fine Tuesday morning in September. I went to my office, and Jen said "I'm trying to get hooked up to a guy. I'm going to go to meet him and I'll be back."

"So I believe this a new guy in your life?" I asked.

"Yes, any problems?" Jen turned around and asked me.

"No. Absolutely not. Good luck. Bye."

It was around nine in the morning. I barely started working when I got paged. *Who the hell is paging me?* I thought. I called the number and said. "Hi, this Dr. Bond. Did someone page me?"

"Hey, it's me." It was none other than Jen.

"What happened? You barely left from here. Did your new guy already dump you?" I quipped.

"No. A plane just hit one of the Twin towers. Turn on the TV in your department."

"Oh my God. What kind of plane? What happened? It may be an accident." I said.

"No. It must be a terrorist attack on us." Jen almost shouted on phone. I ignored her and started working. Frankly I did not think it was an act of terror. It just seemed impossible to me.

After ten to fifteen minutes, Jen stormed into my office.

"Hey, Bond, another plane just hit the other tower. Now do you believe it's a terrorist attack?"

I was shocked and got up from chair. She grabbed my hand and said "Let's go to the lobby where everyone is watching the news."

There was a huge assembly of people in the lobby and everyone was watching in disbelief. The hospital emergency system was activated since we were expecting some of the injured and burn victims. I was not really affected as I worked in research only. But I saw all trauma surgeons, ER docs, and literally the whole hospital getting ready for an unprecedented emergency. I could not concentrate on the work. I went in the lobby and started watching TV as everyone else not involved with emergency services or management was doing. Apparently the first impact left a gaping, burning hole near one of the top floors of the 110-story skyscraper, instantly killing hundreds of people and even worse trapping hundreds more in higher floors. As the evacuation of the tower and its twin got underway, television cameras broadcasted live images of what initially appeared to be a freak accident (at least to me and probably many others). Then, about fifteen to twenty minutes later after the first plane hit, a second plane appeared out of the sky, turned sharply toward the World Trade Center and sliced into the south tower near the top of the tower. This was seen on live television and re broadcasted as by that time all the channels were showing the attack on twin towers. The second collision caused a massive explosion that showered burning debris over surrounding buildings and the streets below. It was unbelievable to watch and one of the most emotionally traumatic experiences I have ever had in my entire life! There was no doubt that America was under attack. The whole world was watching the Twin Towers on fire! I was thinking about the people trapped in those buildings. It was disheartening to watch some people jumping from the towers to save themselves. Jen and I were visibly shaken, so were the people around us.

"Bond, I'm going to ER and see if I can help them with something. I need to change into these scrubs real quickly, can I use your office?"

"Yes, sure."

"Don't come in while I am changing," she warned me.

"No, I won't Jen. In fact I will stand here so that no one else enters too."

She came out and said, "I kept my clothes in your office cupboard. Please remind me to take those home. I am rushing to the ER now . . . see you later Bond," she said while almost running to the elevators.

Jen went to ER and I went to my office. I started working on the project but could not pay attention as I was quite disturbed. I went to see Dr. Stein but he had gone for some hospital emergency meeting. I decided to take rest of the day off and went back to my room, switched on the TV and watched the news. I did not realize how the time passed until there was a knock on my door. It was Jen. She was wearing scrubs and looked somewhat tired.

"How was it?" I asked.

"Can you please make some masala chai for me?"

"Sure, I will." I went and made two cups of tea as she described to me some patients who came to the ER with injuries and burns.

"Those were some of the lucky ones who survived," she said, crying. I tried to calm her down.

She wiped her tears and said, "Oh by the way, I went to your office before coming here. You weren't there so I got my clothes. After a small pause she said, "Anyway, I am not letting you stay here alone. Grab your stuff for couple of days and come with me in my apartment."

"What? Are you crazy? I am fine here and nothing will happen to me. There are so many foreigners here like me." I almost shouted.

"I don't care about the rest of foreigners. But I do care about you. You don't have a choice. I have a spare bedroom with an attached bath so you shouldn't feel awkward."

"But nothing is going to happen here. I am—"

She cut me short.

"If you know someone else in the city, I have no problem if you stay with him or her. But he or she should be an American like me, not a foreigner like you. Do you have anyone in mind?"

I could not think of anyone.

"Then go and grab your stuff for a few days only. Once I feel it's safe to go back I will let you go," She ordered.

I went to my bedroom and grabbed everything from toothbrush to socks and whatever I could remember.

"I got my clothes from your office, can I put these with your stuff here?"

"Sure, go ahead."

Jen helped me to pack the things and soon we headed to her apartment.

Her apartment was small but enough for both of us. It was quite messy though. I looked around and said, "I cannot live like this. With your permission I will clean up things in my room and living room. Tell me the things you don't want me to touch or disturb. I won't enter your bedroom and clean up unless you want me to."

"You can do whatever clean up you want in your room and living room but not in my bedroom. I like the way the things are. I am going to take a quick shower and will see you after that."

I started cleaning up the living room and in about ten minutes it had a totally different look. Much more nice and tidy.

Then I took charge of my bedroom and arranged things and sorted out stuff.

After Jen came back from shower, she was surprised and happy to see the living room.

"Nice. Thank you so much. I think I'll let you stay here every couple of weeks so you can clean up."

"I can come to help you clean up whenever you want. You don't have to offer me to stay here."

"Come let me show you around." Jen grabbed my hand and took me around the small kitchen and her bedroom, which was much larger than mine.

"Do you mind helping me clean my bedroom?" Jen asked.

"Sure, I will. I thought you said no earlier."

"Yeah, I know. I was just being stubborn and maybe stupid. But I liked the way you arranged my apartment. I think I am going to be more organized and neat from now on."

We soon cleaned her bedroom and it had a much better look than before. She was happy and so was I.

Her apartment was close to Central Park and a subway station was right next to her apartment building. There was a huge glass window with beautiful view of the city. I was standing there looking at the beautiful skyline when she handed over an extra key to her apartment. "Please return to me before you leave."

"Sure. I will." I said.

"I love New York City," I said. Jen was holding my hand.

"I love it too."

"Tell me why do you love New York so much?"

"It's a very lively city. Always on the go. It also reminds me of Mumbai," I said.

"Do you drink wine?" a totally unrelated question came from her.

"Yes. I do."

"Let's have red wine and then we will have dinner," Jen said.

She opened a bottle of red wine and poured into two wine goblets.

"Let's drink to… what?" Jen asked.

"Of course to our friendship."

"Yes, of course to our friendship, how come I did not think about it?"

We sat down in the living room and started talking.

"Can I ask you something?" I asked her.

"Sure, go ahead." Jen said.

"Jen, you have barely known me for about two months. How come you trusted me and invited me to your apartment to stay? I mean… how do you know if I don't have an ulterior motive or something."

Jen started laughing. "Ulterior motive? You? You must be joking. What would you do to me? I'm sure you won't kill me. And even more sure that you won't rape me either."

I kept quiet.

"In fact, if I strip in front of you right now, what will you do?" She stood up and mimicked the action of removing her top.

"I guess I will run away," I said, laughing.

"There you go. Remember the first time we met in the reading room? I instantly knew that you are a very simple and straight forward guy. So ulterior motive is the last thing I'm worried about."

"I was just worried that there may be some violence against foreigners. So I decided it is my duty as a good friend to protect you," she said.

"Well, that makes me feel better."

"Do you want to eat something like Middle Eastern food?" Jen asked.

"Sure."

She took me near the window of the living room and asked me to look down.

"Do you see that white truck? That's where you get good Middle Eastern food. Let's go down and get something to eat." We went down and ordered some phila-phil. The owner of that cart was Egyptian. Since I knew some Arabic words, I greeted him in Arabic.

"Salam Alekum, Ke Phalek?" He was impressed and asked me if I was from the Middle East. "No, I am from India but I worked in Dubai for a while, so I know a few Arabic words." I explained to him.

"You speak very good Arabic with almost correct pronunciation."

"Shukran" I said. He gave us some free stuff and Jen was impressed.

We went upstairs and sat on a small dining table and ate together.

"I didn't know you could speak little Arabic," she commented.

"I wanted to learn the language but I was not in the Middle East for a long time so I only picked up a few words like good morning and how are you."

"Hmm, interesting." she said.

We chatted till late. Finally I said, "Jen, tomorrow is not a weekend. I am working tomorrow and guess you are too. I usually don't sleep too well in a new environment. So let me go to the bedroom and try to get some sleep."

"Alright, I'll get up in the morning to exercise. If you need something just knock on my door and I'll wake up. Don't just barge into my room, as you know I sleep naked," Jen said while laughing and I knew she was joking.

I went to bed but could not get a good sleep as I kept thinking about the Twin Tower collapse and all the innocent people who died. Also to make the tragedy even worse, there were another two planes which went down, one in Pennsylvania and another one in the Pentagon killing additional innocent lives as well as damaging property. I woke up early in the morning with the sound of door closing as Jen went out. I realized that she must have left for her morning exercise. I woke up and went to the bathroom. To my surprise, I saw a bunch of magazines there. *Seriously*, I thought. Americans are fast in every aspect of life except maybe this.

After I was dressed for work, I realized that I could not walk to the hospital as I used to do. I would have to take the subway or depend on Jen to drop me to the hospital. Soon she showed up, we had breakfast together, and she said, "Let me take a quick shower and we'll take the sub to the hospital. I'll show you today where to get down and we'll come back together but tomorrow, you can do it on your own."

"Sure."

"Did you sleep well?" she asked me.

"No." I told her frankly what happened.

"Don't worry you should be able to sleep well tonight I guess."

That day in the hospital everyone was talking about the attack on the Twin Towers. People had different theories and opinions. It was difficult to concentrate on the work. I also got a few emails from my friends and relatives in India. I replied to all of them reassuring them that I was safe. When I finished the day's work and was thinking about leaving, there was a soft knock on the door.

"Come on in," I said, although I knew it was her.

"Oh my god, Bond, I am so tired. Can I sit here?" She sat in her usual position without waiting for my permission.

"Can I ask you something?" I asked her, as that morning's experience was still lingering in my head.

"Yeah, sure what's on your mind, Bond? Spit it out."

"This morning I went to the restroom and I saw some magazines." I barely spoke and she interrupted me.

"Sorry, Bond, I don't have *Playboy* or something like that in my apartment. Were you looking for that?"

"Jen, that's not my question. All I am asking is if Americans are crazy about fast cars, fast food, fast sex, and fast everything... then why is that process in rest room so slow? So slow that they can read a whole magazine?"

"No, Bond, you're wrong. We're fast in that process too. But I guess some men and women like to scan through some articles and some light or trashy magazines during that time! I don't know the real answer, though, but it is an interesting question. Anyway, let's go home. We can discuss constipation and other bowel disorders on our way, if you would like."

"It is nice of you to come here looking for me. I thought you might have already left."

"Yeah, I was going to but I thought I'd pick you up if you'd finished work for the day. By the way, do you have clothes to work out in a gym?" Jen asked.

"Yes, I do. I remember packing them."

"Let's go to the gym. It's right across from our apartment."

I was bit surprised by the term "Our" apartment but I kept quiet.

After reaching the apartment we both changed and got ready to go to the gym. I had to register as a guest. While registering, the lady at the desk whispered something in to Jen's ears and I knew she was commenting on something about me but I just ignored her.

"I am going to exercise for at least one hour, so if you finish early go to the men's lockers and you can take a shower if you want," Jen said.

"Alright. Sounds good."

I looked around. This was one of my first visits to an American gym. I noticed that the girls in the gym wore much shorter and tighter athletic wear than men. Almost everyone was flaunting their curves as well as skin. I recollected what Jen had said in her sixth commandment, 'If you have got it, flaunt it.'

As Jen had expected, I finished quite a bit earlier than her so I decided to have a shower in the gym. I chose a locker and was about to go to shower when I heard someone behind me.

"Excuse me, my locker in right next to you." I turned around and was shocked to see a completely naked man behind me. "Hi, how are you?"

"I am fine." I thought of asking him, "Why aren't you wearing any clothes, man?" but kept quiet. I moved to the side to let him open his locker. After he finished, I kept my belongings in the locker and went to the shower area where I saw a bunch of naked men moving around.

I finished my shower but was careful to cover my waist with a towel when I stepped out. I went to my locker area again and changed into my clothes and was sitting down to put on my shoes. As I was about to pick up my socks a guy came in and stood in front of me. He smiled at me but I did not recognize him.

"Hey, you're that research guy from India who nailed that tough case while reading with Dr. Stein."

I looked up and said, '" Yes, I am that Indian guy."

"Hey, I'm sorry but what's your name?"

"Bond."

"Oh, like James Bond?"

"Yeah . . . you can say so," I replied but I was not much interested as our conversation seemed to go nowhere!

"I'm Dave, by the way," he said and unwrapped the towel around his waist. He was not wearing anything underneath. Frankly, I was embarrassed because of his nudity! But he kept on talking.

"You must have done residency in India?" he asked me still being in naked state.

"Yes. Can you please cover yourself?" I requested.

"Sure, but I'm the one who's naked not you" he said while putting on some clothes.

I decided to leave and told him, "See you around."

"Hey, Bond do you live around here?" He was persistent.

"No. I live near the hospital in the dormitory," I replied reluctantly and grabbed my bag.

"How come you came so far in this gym?" he asked me.

I wanted to leave from his barrage of questions and his curiosity into my personal life but was forced to answer him. "I am currently staying here with a friend of mine, Jennifer, who lives across from the gym. That is why I am here. Alright, see you later."

"Oh, Jennifer, I think I know her. So she is your girlfriend?"

"No. She is not my girlfriend." I was about to leave that area but he could not stop his questions.

"So are you dating her?"

At that point I turned around and said, "Listen dude, there can be a relationship between a man and women where you are neither sleeping with her nor she is your sister. Do you get it? We are just friends and now please let me go. Bye."

He murmured something but I totally ignored him and left the locker room.

I went back to gym entrance and waited for Jen. She arrived soon and noticed something must have gone wrong by looking at my face. "What's up, Bond? Did something go wrong?"

"No. But I was kind of shocked to see naked men moving around in the men's locker room."

"Why? Are you getting inferiority complex?" she asked me, smiling and winking.

I took me a second to understand her joke.

"No of course not. In fact, it may be the other way around."

"Bond, this is America. There are naked girls in women's locker room. There is nothing to be ashamed about."

"Do you remember what the main character in the movie *Blame it on Rio* said?" I asked her.

"Nope."

"He said he feels uncomfortable about nudity, including when he has to see himself nude in the mirror. I'm kind of like him. So I felt terribly uncomfortable with all those naked men moving around me."

"Oh come on, I'm sure you'll get used it," Jen said.

"But why can't they wrap a towel around or at least cover their…"

"Dicks?" Jen supplied.

"Yeah, that is what I wanted to say."

"What else did you see or not see, shall I ask?"

I thought for a while and said, "I saw a man without penis today. I call him MWP!"

"*What?*"

"Yes. This man's belly was so big and he had a huge pile of fat hanging down covering his pelvic area. So I could not see his penis. Maybe if I had lifted the fat…"

"Did you?"

"Of course not," I said.

"What else amused you in your American gym experience?" Jen asked me.

I thought for a while and said, "Let me think. Yeah, I also saw a man wearing a bra!"

"No way! What did you see?"

"I saw a man on the elliptical and on his back was a strap like a bra strap."

"Bond, I don't think so. What you must have seen was a telemetry strap, which measures your heart rate. I am pretty sure it wasn't a bra. Hope you didn't ask him that question!"

"No, I did not know him; otherwise I am sure I would have asked him!" I said.

Soon we reached her or rather our apartment and we sat down on the sofa to watch the news.

"Jen, there seems to be no news about violence against foreigners. Do you still want me to stay here?" I asked her.

"What's your problem here? You are getting everything here… except of course sex, which you wouldn't get in your dormitory anyway, and I'm taking a good care of you." Jen said with a bit of anger.

"No. I have no problem but your current boyfriend or the new man in your life may have a problem with this and I don't want to spoil your relationship."

"No, man. There is nothing serious between us right now so don't worry about that."

"What do you want for dinner? Do you like Chinese? If you like, we can go down and walk a couple of blocks and there is another van that serves Chinese food," Jen said.

"Yeah, let's do that." I replied. "Man, this is awesome. That's why I like New York City so much."

Jen looked at me and said, "Don't get so madly in love with the city. You haven't experienced the winter here yet. Maybe in winter you'll start hating Manhattan."

"Nope. I was here in winter for a short while and I guess it wasn't that bad."

"You haven't seen the worst yet, Bond! Okay, let's get into some decent clothes and go to eat."

We soon changed and went out for dinner. "This outfit looks good on you. You look great," I said, appreciating the dress and the boots she was wearing.

"Thanks, Bond. I was expecting that earlier though. By the way, I had given you some homework. Did you do it?"

"I don't recollect. What homework?" I was confused.

As we were talking, some teenage girls entered the elevator on one of the floors. They were dressed up and looked as if they were going for some party.

Ignoring them Jen said, "I asked you to look up hanky-panky and you promised me that you would."

The girls, all of them at once, burst out laughing. One of them turned around and said, "Dude, hanky panky means having sex." And then everyone, including Jen, had a great laugh. I was bit embarrassed.

When we came back to her apartment Jen asked, "Why were you so embarrassed?"

"I wasn't." I tried to pretend that I wasn't.

"Come on, you were. Tell me why?" Jen persisted.

"Well. I admit. I was. Mainly because a totally unknown girl who happened to be much younger than me turns around and talks about sex to me."

"She is younger, but that doesn't mean she's still a virgin," Jen said.

"Yeah, I guessed that reading her eyes."

"This is America, man. But I'm happy that you're getting Americanized, although bit slowly," Jen said while laughing.

After reaching her apartment, I switched on the news and sat down on the sofa.

"I'll change my clothes, slip into something comfortable, and join you," Jen said while entering her bedroom.

"Please wear something which will not make me uncomfortable being with you here," I said jokingly.

She came back in PJs and T shirt. "Is this decent enough for you?" Jen asked.

"Yes, it is. Can I ask you something?"

"Sure. Go ahead." Jen looked at me and she knew something was coming.

"Why do ladies here in the U.S. wear low-neck shirts and T-shirts revealing the cleavage? And more importantly, as men, are we supposed to look at the revelation or heed it?"

Jen started laughing.

"Well, the answer to your first question is that women do that to look attractive, you know. The answer to your second question is that you can look at it, but women won't like it if you keep staring at their cleavage."

"Staring at it? It is so distracting. The other day I was talking to one of our research assistants and she was wearing a shirt with top two buttons open and big boobs and big cleavage. She was talking to me and I could not keep my eyes off her cleavage. I did not understand a single word she was saying." Jen could not control her laughter.

"Idiot, don't ever do that. Women won't like that. Remember Bond, looking at cleavage is like looking at sun. Don't stare at it unless you are wearing sunglasses."

"Don't stare at cleavage unless you are wearing sunglasses"

"Alright, was that a commandment?"

"No, that was kind of an educative statement, I would say."

"All right, point well taken. So do you recommend I should walk around the hospital wearing sunglasses all the time so I can look at cleavages?" I asked.

"No, of course not. I didn't mean that."

Soon we sat down and watched the news.

The news coverage was all about the 9/11 attacks and aftermath of it. At one point, I switched channel to watch the weather.

Soon the weather report started. It seemed they were expecting tropical storms the next day in the Florida peninsula.

"Why do you guys call normal rain a tropical storm?" I asked Jen.

"I don't know."

"To me it sounds like a normal maybe somewhat heavy rain. We get that every year in Mumbai but we never say that there will be tropical storm tomorrow," I persisted.

"The situations here in U.S. are always somewhat hyped up, so you have to take everything with a grain of salt," Jen said, yawning.

"So my guess was right. I always thought but never said openly as I thought Americans may not like it. Looks like you are bit tired. Do you want to go to bed?"

"Yeah, I think so. I have to get up early and jog. Soon the winter will start and then most of your activities will be indoors. Aren't you sleepy?"

"I will watch some CNN and then go to sleep," I said.

"Oh, okay. Bye and good night, Bond. We'll go together so wait till I come back and get ready." Jen said, heading toward her bedroom.

"Good night, Jen."

I kept surfing channels and was watching the weather channel. The guy talked about the tropical storm and then he talked about hurricane season. He showed us some map and talked about some "Erin" coming hitting off the New York coast. I kept wondering which "Erin" he is talking about and why is she hitting New York? Like the blonde nurses hitting on me? Then I realized he was talking about Hurricane Erin. It seems in America they give name to all hurricanes and in alphabetical order. Suddenly, I remembered an email that I had received from a friend of mine in United States a few days ago. It read like this:

Hurricanes with feminine names are more dangerous than with masculine names!

Like ladies, when they come they are wild and wet and when they go, they take away your home and car!

## 'HURRICANES WITH FEMININE NAMES'

'When they come, they are 'wild and wet'
When they go, they take away your home and car!'

A few days later we had this discussion during lunch hour with some residents and fellows from the department.

I asked, "Why do you give names to hurricanes? Isn't that stupid?"

"No, it's not stupid. In fact, it's very smart," quipped one of the radiology residents. "Names help us identify storms and let us know which ones are going to be bad."

"How does that help? You can just say that the storm which is coming this week from New York or Florida is going to be a bad one," I protested.

"No, this is the American way, dude. What do you call them in your country?" someone else asked me.

I smiled and said, "Dude, we don't have time to name all hurricanes. That's lot of work! We just collectively call them monsoon!"

No one reacted but there were some muted laughter.

Anyway, I suddenly shriveled with fear. My first hurricane season in USA and what if a hurricane hits New York and takes my home away! Luckily I did not have a car, I thought. I quickly switched off the TV and went to bed.

# E*IGHTH* C*OMMANDMENT*

The next day as usual, Jen woke up early and went for a jog. By the time she came back, I had showered and was ready. After she got ready, she asked "Breakfast?"

"I will have some bagel and cream cheese. What do you want?"

"I'll have the same and if you can make some masala chai for both of us, which would be great."

"Yes. I think I had packed some tea bags when I moved over here." I went to my bedroom to get some tea bags. "Am I getting Americanized or are you getting more Indianized, Jen?"

"I like Indian and spicy food... and masala chai too. You must have noticed that American food is very boring and without real spice."

"What about Indian men?" I asked her and she seemed to be bit surprised by my query. She did not say anything but just smiled at me.

We finished breakfast and soon arrived at the hospital by subway.

I was working on the abstract of our poster. We had scanned quite a few patients by now and I had the preliminary data to write our abstract. I was updating Dr. Stein by regular meetings and emails and he seemed to be happy with the progress of the research project. Jen was helping me in all possible ways. Jen and I went to Dr. Stein's research office for weekly and sometimes biweekly research related meetings. After the meeting was over Dr. Stein asked me and Jen to come to his office.

"I wanted to make sure that you are in safe surroundings after the attack on Twin Towers. I should have asked you earlier but if you want I have guest bedroom in my house. You can stay there for a few days if you want. You will be part of our family."

"Thanks for the generous offer Dr. Stein but I think I am safe where I am right now."

"Where are you staying? In the dorm? I don't think that is a safe place . . ." Dr. Stein commented.

Jen noticed my hesitation and said, "No sir. He is staying with me right now. I'm taking good care of him."

"Oh, I didn't know that. Thanks for doing that," Dr. Stein said and soon left for a board meeting.

We went back to my own research office and started working. Jen was good at typing so typically I would dictate and she would type. At around noon, we decided to break for lunch. We went to the cafeteria and found it crowded. I grabbed a sandwich and Jen got some Mexican food. We selected a table and Jen introduced me to her friend, Angela, a pretty, tall blonde from Jen's class. Soon Jen and Angela started talking and to my surprise Angela was talking about some girl Jill, who she likes. At one point, she said, "I want to sleep with Jill soon." I was drinking water and when I heard those words I almost choked and started coughing.

"Bond, are you okay?" Jen asked me. I nodded yes and wiped the tears coming from my eyes.

"There's Jill. I'm going to go talk to her. Nice to meet you, Bond," said Angela. I just weakly smiled at her and waved. I was not sure if I heard her properly.

After she was gone, Jen turned to me and said, "I should have told you that Angela is a dyke."

"What is a dyke?" I asked her as her comment confused me further.

"She is a homosexual, lesbian to be precise."

"Means same sex lovers?" I asked.

"Yes. The men are called gay and the ladies are called lesbians."

"I heard and read about them but never encountered one," I said.

"I'm sure there are gays and lesbians in India too. But they are not as open because the Indian society or culture probably won't accept them. You have to learn to accept them and respect them as well."

"I do respect them, but the whole idea seems bit bizarre to me."

"Where is your gender located?" Jen asked me, and I was quite embarrassed.

## 'EIGHTH COMMANDMENT'

"Thy gender is not between thy legs...
But it is between thy ears"

"You don't have to tell me or show me but here is my Eighth commandment: Thy gender is not between thy legs but it is in between thy ears.'"

"In between ears?" I was even more confused.

"Look, Bond. You are a man not just because of your physical characteristics but also because how and what you think. Do you get it?"

"Yes, I think I am getting what you are trying to say."

"So, Angela is a female by physical features but she is a man by her nature or mind. That is why she likes other girls and not guys."

"Oh, alright, I get it now. Thanks for explaining Jen," I said with a sigh of relief.

There was a long pause as I became lost in my thoughts and Jen seemed to have picked up that.

"Jen, I have a question," I finally decided to ask her.

"Go ahead, Bond. I presume it is about homosexuality." She guessed it right.

"I can understand how two men can have sex. But I am just curious how two girls have sex."

She was drinking water so she just raised her index finger and middle finger as a sign. "Get it? Or sex toys," she said.

"Where do you get sex toys? Toys 'R Us?"

"No. Try something else, use your guess work."

I decided to use my imagination. "Toys 'R Sex?"

"No."

"Sex 'R Toys."

"No. Enough, Bond. You get them in adult shops," she said.

"Thank you so much for an explanation, Jen," I said.

"As always my pleasure, Bond," Jen said, smiling.

Our discussion was interrupted by call on her cell phone. She was talking to some guy, I thought.

"Alright, Bond. I need to go as I have to meet someone," she said while getting up.

"Good luck with your new relationship, Jen. Hope this one works out well for you," I said and Jen was shocked.

"How the hell did you know that I was talking to a guy and I am going to meet him?"

"I can read your mind, most of the time. In fact, I can read minds of most other women too," I answered her calmly.

"Really, tell me what am I thinking right now?"

"Right now you are thinking of seducing me and sleeping with me tonight," I said jokingly and Jen busted into laughter.

Jen left in a hurry and I went back to my office.

As I was finishing the day's work, there was a knock on the door. I thought it must be Jen but it was Madhuri.

"Where were you for so many days? I was worried. I came to your apartment so many times but you were never there." As she was speaking Jen also entered the office.

"Madhuri, meet my friend Jennifer Graziano," I said.

"Hi Jen, I am Madhuri. Nice to meet you."

"Hi Maduri, nice to meet you too. Bond is staying in my apartment," Jen said, and Madhuri was surprised and shocked too. Jen looked at her and seemed to read her mind. Jen added, "I have a separate bedroom for him. So don't worry. He is not sleeping with me or I'm not sleeping with him either." At that point Madhuri barged out of my office without saying a word.

"You shouldn't have been so blunt with her," I told Jen.

"After looking at the expression on her face, I thought it better explain to her in plain simple English. Anyway, I am going out with this guy I met today for dinner so I am leaving now to get ready. That's why I came here to make sure you have your key to our apartment and to make sure that you find way back home."

"I have my key to your apartment and I won't get lost. So don't worry. As far as dinner is concerned, I will eat some Middle Eastern food so I should be fine," I reassured her. "Thanks for stopping by and letting me know. And good luck as always."

I stood up and gave a quick friendly hug.

"Thanks, Bond," she said and disappeared.

I reached her apartment without getting lost. On the way I grabbed some food to go. When I reached it I was surprised to see Jennifer in the apartment.

"What happened? Aren't you late for your dinner?" I asked her.

"No. He had to go somewhere so we're meeting a bit later. How do I look, by the way?" Jen stood up and asked me.

She was wearing red dress with noodle straps. She wore very light make up and pink lip gloss. Her hair was tied in a ponytail. She was wearing contact lenses. She was carrying some small but fancy looking purse. For a moment I thought I skipped a heartbeat.

"Great as always. But I think you should let your hair free rather than tying a pony tail."

"Really? Let's see." She removed her hair band and asked me, "Is it better now?"

"Awesome. Your red dress is great too! I really envy the guy who is going out for dinner with you," I said spontaneously, and I thought Jen was a bit surprised by my comment.

"Won't you be lonely here?" Jen asked me.

"No. Actually I was going to watch my favorite sitcom *Friends*," I said while switching the TV on.

"I know you always watch that show. I think you have a crush on Jennifer Aniston."

"Yes, I do," I admitted without any guilt.

"Alright. You stay close to your Jennifer Aniston and I'll come back after dinner. Bye," she said while closing the door.

I ate my dinner while watching *Friends* and enjoyed every bit of it, especially Rachel or Jennifer Aniston, after which I switched on a news channel and watched the news and weather. It was almost ten and I was bit worried about Jen. As I was thinking of calling her, she barged through the front door and went straight to her bedroom without speaking a word to me. I was surprised and shocked. I guessed something must have gone wrong. I went to her bedroom but she had slammed the door shut. I knocked on her door, worried about what her response would be.

"Bond, I'll be with you in a second. I'm changing so don't come in," she shouted from inside.

I went back to the living room, sat on the sofa, and switched off the TV.

Soon she showed up in shorts and T-shirt. She had a cigarette in her hand too. I was bit surprised as I had never seen her smoking.

"I don't fucking care if you get embarrassed by my short shorts," she said as she sat on the sofa in front of me. She was really mad, as she never used that kind of language with me earlier.

"I am not embarrassed, but tell me what happened. What went wrong? And why are you smoking?"

Jen got up and started walking up and down the hallway.

"Well, I do smoke sometimes, very rarely though. This not tobacco, this is pot," she said calmly.

"Pot?" I was surprised as I had never heard that term before. The only pot I knew was the earthen pots they sell on the streets of Mumbai.

"Bond, this is marijuana, also known as pot," she explained to me.

"Smoking Pot? Isn't it illegal?"
"Everything is legal in Love and War"

"Oh my god, this is supposed to be illegal, isn't it?" I was bit shocked and surprised.

"Everything is legal in love and war, I don't fucking care," she yelled at me. She was using the F word without any reservation.

"But . . . is this love?" I asked her in a fearful way.

"No. This is an outright war," she shouted and took one more puff of whatever she was smoking.

"Do you want to try?" she asked me and I politely declined.

I decided to ignore her pot smoking and asked her, "So what happened?" to start some reasonable and logical conversation.

"This guy shows up late for dinner. That is okay. But before he shows up I get a call on my cell phone from Angela. She told me that this guy has been dating Jill for a few days now and is in a steady relationship with Jill. Jill is the girl Angela is interested in," Jen said while fuming with anger.

"When I asked him to his face, he refused to admit it. Fucking bastard." I was taken aback. Jen was in a totally different mood altogether today. I had always thought of her as a sweet girl but what I saw today was totally different Avatar.

Finally, I got up and went to her and said, "Jen, I think you should stop smoking that cigarette or pot or whatever that is right now." She did and I grabbed her hand and said, "Calm down. Sit here with me."

She burst out into tears and hugged me. I was, frankly, very embarrassed. But I thought it may make her feel better so I slowly disengaged myself from her arms and sat down with her on the sofa.

"Look, Jen, it is better that you found out now rather than later on in your relationship. To hell with him. You will still find a nice guy, I am sure."

"I was so mad, Bond, I felt like kicking his balls," Jen said. I was again shocked thinking of what would have happened if she really had done that!

"What happened finally? Did you really kick his balls?" I asked her after a pause.

"Well, no. But I wish I had. I asked him if he was in steady relationship with anyone else and he said no. Then I asked him about Jill and he was surprised. First, he tried to deny it but when I told him that I know from reliable sources, he had to admit it and said he just wanted to have dinner with me, nothing further. A fucking liar."

By this time, I was getting used to her F-words.

"I would have been okay if he had admitted that he has been dating Jill. I would have had dinner with him and left. Why would he lie?"

"I don't know," I said since I had absolutely no idea whatsoever.

"He wanted to screw me, it's obvious. Don't you get it?" she screamed at me, and I realized now naive I was.

I thought I got some strong smell of alcohol while she was talking as her mouth was pretty close to me.

"Alright. Now let me ask you if you ate anything or just have been drinking?"

Jen did not say anything and I understood. "What do you want me get for you? Chinese, Indian or…"

She cut me short and said, "I am hungry. Can you get me some Indian food from the restaurant across the street?"

"No problem. Do you want anything else?" I asked her while leaving.

"No. There's some cash on the table in my bedroom."

"I got my wallet, baby, so don't worry," I shouted from the corridor.

Soon I got hot and spicy *'chhole bhature'* for Jen.

She ate voraciously as I watched her. She was still sobbing in between wiping her tears.

After she finished, we sat down on the sofa. I held her hand and asked her, "Are you okay now?"

"Yes, I guess so. Thanks for all the help. I'm sorry that I used so many f-words. I know you don't use them or like it either. But I was so upset; I just couldn't control myself. I feel so sorry," Jen said.

"That's okay. I know that your anger was directed towards him, not me. I think you should go to bed and get some sleep now. How much alcohol have you had, Jen?"

"I don't know. Quite a bit I guess. How did you know?" Jen asked me.

"I can smell it since you came in. Aren't you cold in these shorts?" I asked her.

"No. I'm used to it. I just don't wear them because I feel shy and I thought I would make you feel uncomfortable," Jen said with a yawn.

"That's okay with me if you are comfortable. Come on, let me help you to your room." I grabbed her hand and almost pulled her up and helped her to get to her bed.

"Bond, thanks a lot. I was so glad that you were here for me today. I don't know what would have I done without you."

"Not a problem. See? You helped me and now I am helping you, right?" I said trying to convince her.

"Bond, I think you should go to your bedroom. I need to go to the bathroom too. Thanks and good night," Jen said while opening the door of her bathroom.

"Good night, Jen. Let me know if you need anything in the night," I said while leaving.

"I will."

I woke up next day and noticed that Jen did not get up early to jog. While I was in shower I realized it was Friday. I wanted to move back to my dorm room, so I packed my bags.

I got ready and went in kitchen to fix some breakfast. I made two cups of masala chai. There was no sign of Jen, so I went to her bedroom and knocked. "Hey, Jen are you awake? I made some chai for you."

"I will be there soon," she called

She came out in her shorts and said, "Thanks for waking me up. I love the masala chai you make."

"Are you okay?" I asked her while sipping hot chai.

"Yeah. I'm okay, I just have a hangover, I think. I'll take some Tylenol and I should be fine. I'm so sorry about my behavior yesterday, including my F-words." I think Jen was very much embarrassed as she apologized to me a bunch of times.

"Don't worry about it Jen," I reassured her.

I got my bag from my bedroom. Jen looked at the bag and then looked at me. I could very well read her mind. I said, "I don't have leave today if you want. But maybe on Sunday."

"Bond, how the hell could you read my mind? I was feeling so sorry that you'll be going back today and was just wondering how to convince you to stay for a couple of days more. Sunday would be fine. But I would definitely feel lonely if you had to leave today."

I did not say anything and kept my bag back in my room.

"Jen, why don't you get ready and we will go the hospital together. After I move back, I will miss our short commute."

"I'll get ready soon. Just give me a few minutes," Jen said while almost running towards her bedroom.

While in the subway Jen said, "You're welcome to come and visit me or maybe stay for couple of days. I'm going to miss your masala chai."

"Don't worry. I will get some teabags for you and today I will teach you how to make good chai, but remind me."

"Sure, I'd love to learn from you."

We worked hard the whole day and our abstract for the conference was almost ready. I was happy and so was Jen.

On our way back in the subway I said, "Jen, you like chicken biryani right? Do you want to try some awesome biryani today? My friend has given me the address but I never went there. Only thing, it is not a fancy place."

"If it's good and hygienic I don't mind trying it," Jen replied.

When we reached her apartment, I took her to the kitchen and explained to her in step-by-step fashion how to make masala chai.

"Boil the water; pour in the cup with this special masala tea bags. You can add sugar as you like and I usually add non-dairy creamer or skimmed milk but you can use half and half for a good taste. That's it. Chai is ready." She was impressed.

We sat on the breakfast table and I said, "Let's make a plan. Let's go to the Brooklyn Bridge for a walk. From there we will go to this biryani place, eat, and come back. Maybe on the way back we can stop at Times Square and get some ice cream." Jen seemed impressed by my plan. "See, you don't have to spend a lot of money to enjoy life. We go by subway so we can save money," I said enthusiastically.

"Wow, you sound like a New Yorker. I can't believe you just came to this country only few months back," Jen said.

So we had a great evening. Luckily it was an unusually warm day. Our walk on Brooklyn Bridge was great, the biryani was awesome, and the ice cream was delicious. Jen was in good spirits and was talking almost continuously and as usual I listened patiently.

At one point, I said, "Let's go back to your apartment."

"Bond, why do you always refer to it as 'your' apartment and not 'our' apartment?" Jen seemed a bit annoyed.

I knew this was going to come up at one point. I said, "Jen, in reality it *is* your apartment not ours. I am not your boyfriend or husband. We are not living together in a real sense. I am sort of guest only for a few days. So that is why I refer to it is your apartment."

"I know that but for the time being it is our apartment."

"Okay, fine, let's go back to *our* apartment. Are you happy now?" I said, and she seemed convinced.

After we reached the apartment, we sat down in the living room and chatted.

"Jen, do you know why we enjoyed the evening we spent today?" I asked her.

"No, you tell me." Jen obviously had no clue what I was about to say.

"Well, we have been friends for how long now? Little over two months, I guess. I don't have any expectation from you and neither have you from me. Our friendship is so pure and non-committal. Many times, I read your mind and I have noticed you too read what's in my mind. I am not doing anything to please you just to sleep with you. Basically, there is no expectation from each other. No fancy gifts, no expensive restaurants. Absolutely nothing. When you go with no commitment and no expectation then you start enjoying each other's company. Because the pleasure comes from the sheer presence of somebody and it comes from within too." Jen stared at me in disbelief.

I kept on talking. "There is only one expectation which comes naturally."

"What is that?" Jen asked me.

"To help each other in need. Which you have done and I have done too. But helping each other also gives you immense pleasure. Ask me why."

"Why?"

"Simply because you are helping a friend. And it is almost assumed without doubt that the person I am helping today will help me when I need him or her the most." Finally I finished talking.

"Wow, you speak so well. I think from here on I should keep quiet and let you talk more. By the way, your English is good too."

"English is a very simple language."

"What? I have never heard that from a foreigner," Jen said, surprised.

"Yes. Compared to some other languages, English is very easy to learn. I learned Sanskrit when I was in middle school, which is very tough. Compared to that, learning English is relatively simple."

Saturday morning, I decided to go to temple. I got up early and had a shower. I was wearing an Indian Kurta and jeans. Jen came back from jogging.

"Where are you going?" Jen was surprised.

"I am planning to go to Ganesh Temple in Flushing."

"I'll come with you, if you don't mind," Jen said and I was a bit taken aback.

"I thought of asking, you but you are a Christian, I believe—"

Jen cut me short. "So what? Does that mean I can't visit a temple? Am I forbidden because of my Christianity?"

"Of course not. You are most welcome. Let's go. And after that we can have lunch at a place where we can eat some south Indian food. It is called Dosa Hut. It's on Lexington Avenue. Would you like to try it?"

"Sure. I like to try new things. Since you're recommending, it must be good. What should I wear?"

"Well, don't wear a short or mini skirt or shorts either."

"I have an Indian top and I'll wear jeans, is that okay?" Jen asked.

"Should be fine."

"Alright then, give me few minutes and I'll be ready," Jen said and disappeared into her room to change.

When we reached the temple, Jen was impressed by the architecture and cleanliness of it. I explained to her about Hinduism and also Ganesh, also known as the elephant headed god.

After I prayed, the preacher at the temple applied sacred red tilak on my forehead. He asked Jen if he could apply some on her forehead and to my surprise she said yes.

We sat in the temple for a while. We went to Dosa Hut on Lexington Avenue and enjoyed hot masala dosa and hot sambar and chutney. Jen seemed to like the south Indian delicacies.

"Hey, can we make these at home?" Jen asked.

"I would rather come here and eat. Cooking Indian food is very laborious," I said. "You have to understand that vegetarian food as such does not have a flavor or taste by itself. That's why you have to add so many spices and other things to make it delicious. Meat has its own taste so cooking western or non-vegetarian food is relatively simple."

"Wow! I never thought about it. But I love dosa, let's come here again sometime."

"Sure. I love dosa too. Jen, I seriously think you are getting more and more Indianized," I commented, laughing.

"Let's go for a walk along the East River," Jen said and I agreed.

While we were walking Jen said, "Oh man, tomorrow is Sunday and you will move back and I am going to feel weird for a few days."

I tried to change the topic and said, "We have to submit our abstract next week so we will be busy and we will meet in the hospital."

"Hmm."

"By the way, Dr. Stein has asked me to apply for a radiology residency at our hospital and he said he will try to get me in the program," I said nonchalantly.

"What? When did this happen and how come you never told me?" Jen stopped walking and was almost shouting.

"I am telling you right now. This happened last week and you are the first person I am telling. No one else yet knows other than you or me," I said.

"That's a great news man. I am so happy for you." Jen said while hugging me in the middle of our walk.

"Do you know Dr. Stein is on the residency selection committee? Usually if he says he wants someone, pretty much no one can refuse." Jen was excited.

"And Jen, if you get residency in the same program, we will be together for at least four more years," I said while looking at her reaction.

"Yeah, I know. That would be great, wouldn't it? And you can do my weekend calls while I relax," Jen said jokingly.

I shook my head. "No. I won't do that for sure."

"I was just joking, man. We can help each other by at least exchanging calls."

"Yeah, so you can go on a date and I can rot in the hospital," I said.

"I hope I would have found the man of my dreams by that time," Jen said in a hopeful tone.

"I thought you already have found one," I said very seriously and she did not understand what I was hinting at.

So finally Sunday came by and as I expected Jen was depressed. She came back from her jog and I was ready to go with my bag packed.

"I'll drop you off with my car. Don't go by subway."

"Fine with me."

"I'll be ready soon," she said while entering her bedroom.

I waited for her and soon she came out wearing a stunning black dress.

"Let's go. My car also needs to be driven, otherwise it is just lying in the parking garage all week," Jen said while in the elevator.

After we reached my apartment I realized that I had not retuned the key for her apartment.

"Jen, before I forget again, here is the key to your... er... our apartment. I think you should keep it in case you get locked out."

"Bond, I think you can keep the key with you. If I get locked out, I can get help from the apartment manager," Jen said, and I was surprised.

"What will I do with the key?" I was puzzled.

"You can visit me whenever you feel like it, and remember, you promised me that you'd clean my apartment once in a while... oh come on, I'm messing with you," Jen said, laughing. "Can we have lunch together?"

"Sure. Let's go to some fast food place and have some sandwiches. I need to start working on the abstract after I come back."

While we were eating at Subway, I asked her, "Can I ask you something, Jen?"

"Sure, go ahead."

"In general, men do not understand women. I come from a different culture and background."

"I don't know what are you getting at, Bond." Jen looked puzzled.

"Well, the other day when you came back from your date, you had a totally different look and avatar. It wasn't the Jen I knew. Basically I have failed to understand American women so far. Can you explain me in simple words so that I can understand American women better? I certainly know that they are different than Indian women I have known."

"Bond, I really don't know how to explain. But let me think about it." I could tell she was thinking how to best explain to me.

"Well, here is the answer to your question. We are almost like men. Women here like to work, smoke, we do curse like men do, and we also like and crave sex. We are not like those sari-wearing women in India. They used to be passive but I guess with time they are changing too. Although we do also have strong feminine characteristics. We love shopping and eating out, spending money too. And there is one more thing we like to do that Indian women and most men don't do."

"What is that one thing, Jen?"

"We like to show off our curves and skin," Jen said while laughing.

"Alright, now I think I can understand American women better I suppose," I said then took a bite of my sandwich.

"But why do you ask me Bond? Are you in love with some American girl?"

"Yes, I think I am," I said, and she was astonished.

"Who is it Bond? Tell me. How come you never told me about her? I'd like to meet her." Jen sounded somewhat curious and maybe little bit jealous.

"No one, I was just joking. I just wanted to see how you would react," I said, laughing. "How could you believe that I am in love with someone and you don't know about it? You are almost constantly with me."

"Yeah, that's true but you never know what men are up to. They're such creepy characters." Jen reply was tinged with anger.

"You cannot blame the whole male community just because you had bad experience with a few men." I tried to convince her. "Alright Jen, time to say good bye, at least for now. I will walk back to my apartment."

"Alright. Let's walk to our car," Jen said as we left the restaurant.

I could tell she was sad, so I was not surprised when she said, "Give me a hug please."

As we hugged, I whispered in her ear, "Thanks for everything you did for me."

"No, I think I should thank you for supporting me during the difficult times."

"I will see you tomorrow, Jen. We have to submit the abstract ASAP after Dr. Stein reviews it."

"I'll be there to help you, Bond. Bye," Jen said putting her car in reverse.

I went back to my apartment and while unpacking my bag I thought about the last few days. The attack on the Twin Towers had changed the world quite a bit. The days in Jen's apartment passed so quickly that I never noticed that I stayed there for almost a week.

Later that day, I went to my office and checked my abstract again for any spelling mistakes before returning to my room and switching on the TV to watch some news. I was thinking about Jen. *What is she doing now?* I decided to call her and she answered immediately.

"Hello?" she said.

"It's Bond."

"Hey, Bond."

"I was just thinking about you," we said almost simultaneously and started laughing.

"I thought I would just give you a call to see how are you doing. Are you lonely?" I asked her.

"Yes and no. I just came back from the gym so if you would have called me like two minutes ago, I wouldn't have answered."

"See? Telepathy works. I also came back from my office and was thinking about you."

"You worked today?"

"Yes, I did. I just finished the final draft of the abstract. Checked it twice and we should be able to submit it tomorrow after Dr. Stein reviews it."

"Wow. That sounds good."

"Jen, what about your residency application? Are you applying anywhere else?"

"I'm applying mainly in all New York City hospitals and some other places in Northeast. But I think my best chance would be our hospital."

"I can speak to Dr. Stein and tell him what a great help you have been in this research project so far."

"That would be great. I think that will definitely help my chances of getting into a radiology residency. But why do you ask?"

"I guess because we can spend four more years together as co-residents."

"Yeah, and I can have your help on call because you are already a radiologist," Jen said while laughing.

"Why do you always think of calls when the subject of residency comes up?" I asked her as I was really curious.

"That is one thing I am most scared of during the residency. The night calls at our hospital are pretty busy being one of the topmost level I trauma centers in the city."

"There is nothing to be scared of. Calls are most important in the residency. That's when you learn the most. Particularly when you miss something." I gave her a few words of wisdom.

"I guess you are absolutely right. I'll see you tomorrow, Bond." Jen said, seemingly ignoring my advice and comments.

"Bye, see you tomorrow."

The next day I went in early to my office and showed my abstract to Dr. Stein who was happy and approved the abstract with some minor changes.

"I am so happy that I hired you, Dr. Bond. I will personally make sure you get residency here," he said.

"Thank you so much Dr. Stein. But I have to say that I did receive great help from Ms. Graziano also. Without her help, I would not have been able to complete this research and the abstract. She is very hard working." I tried to praise Jennifer as much as I could.

"That's true. She is good," said Dr. Stein.

"Is there a good chance that she will get residency here?" I asked him directly, and he was bit surprised.

"She does have a good chance, I must say. Bond, I am sorry but I have go for the ENT tumor board now, so will you please excuse me? By the way, submit that abstract and start packing your bags for the conference in Chicago," he said as he left the office.

As I opened the door to my office, I was surprised to see Jennifer waiting in my chair. I told her about my conversation with Dr. Stein, then submitted the abstract online. I was the first author, Jennifer was second, and Dr. Stein the third.

"Coffee?" Jen asked.

"Sure. Let's go."

# Once an Indian...

We reached the café, which was pretty crowded even at that time of the day. We grabbed our coffees and luckily found room at a large table that was already partially occupied. Most of the occupants happened to be radiology residents and fellows so I knew at least some of them. When we joined the group, they were discussing about different ethnic groups.

"Indian Americans are one of the most prominent and influential ethnic group of doctors in America," someone said.

"Yeah, most of them are already trained and they are good. They come here and get trained further! Some of the doctors I was trained under were Indian docs and I loved working with them," one of the girls said.

I jumped into the conversation and diverted the topic somewhat.

"So, Mike, where are you originally from?" I asked one of the neuro fellows.

"My grandparents came from Austria but me and my parents were born here."

"So technically you are Austrian American," I said.

"Yeah, technically yes, but I am American," he said firmly.

"What about you, Rachel?" I turned to one of the residents.

"My great grandparents migrated from Germany but the rest of us, as you know, were born here. I've never been to Germany so I don't even know which part we come from!" Rachel replied.

"So you are German American?" I asked her.

"Yes, technically I'm German American but in reality I am American."

One of the residents got a bit annoyed and said, "Hey, Bond what are you getting at?"

"No matter how long you stay here, you and your kids and even their kids will be called Indian American. That is because you are—"

Jennifer cut him short and said, "Stop it, Gregg. Enough of that. Let's talk about something else, otherwise we're leaving."

"You can leave, no one is stopping you," said someone else sitting at the table. At that, Jennifer grabbed my hand and both of us stormed out of the cafe. We went straight to my office and Jennifer was fuming with anger. "Rascals," she commented.

"Cool down, babe."

I sat down in my chair and Jen sat on the table in her usual position.

"I'm sorry, Bond," were the first few words she uttered.

"Sorry for what? It's none of your fault. In fact, it is nobody's fault. I guess the system and mindset of people and the community is at fault."

"Bond, the truth is no matter what, you and your kids and your grandkids will be called Indian American because you are—"

I cut her short and said, "Yes, I know what the guy at the table and you are getting at. It's fine with me if everyone calls me an Indian American but it's not fair to call my kids and grand kids the same who will be born here."

"Yes, Bond, I completely agree with you but that's how it is. Unless of course you end up marrying a white girl and produce white kids. Then hopefully they will not be called Indian Americans!"

"Wow! What if the kids turn out to be like me! Anyway, let's talk about something else. Frankly I am not bothered. Even if I am Indian American, I can still do research".

"Well, of course yes," she said and we started talking about something else. We chatted about some hospital gossip and soon it was time to go to cafeteria for lunch.

While in the cafeteria we chatted about possibility of going to Chicago for the conference. Jen said she might come for a day or two as the conference coincides with the Thanksgiving holiday and she wanted to visit her family in Rochester, New York.

### I had a nightmare!

That night I went to bed early. While lying on the bed, I was thinking about the conversation we had in the cafe that day. That night I had a strange dream, in fact a nightmare! I woke up in the middle of the night sweating and with palpitations. When I woke up, I realized it was just a dream. I went to bathroom and went back to sleep.

The next day I woke up a bit late but got ready on time. I went straight to my office and checked my personal and hospital email, and while I was doing that, I heard a knock on the door. I knew it was Jen. She entered with a big smile and said, "Hey, Bond, good morning."

"Good morning! You are early today!" I was surprised.

"Yeah, woke up a bit early. How are you?"

"Well, I had a nightmare. My great great grandkids were walking with their mom and dad on the New York streets and people were pointing at them saying 'Look at the Indian American family!'"

"Oh, come on, Bond. Get over it. I'll find a nice white girl for you, you marry her and hope the kids will be all white. In case they turn out to be brown, make sure they marry a white spouse so on and so forth. So by the time you have great great grandkids, hopefully all will be white! See, end of your nightmare!"

"That's not the solution, Jen. We have to change the mentality of the people."

"Who is going to do that? You? No way, you want to become another Gandhi from a Bond? Come on, get off your ass and we'll have coffee so you'll feel better." She almost pulled me from my chair.

"Okay, sure. Let me grab my lab coat," I said, getting up.

While we were chatting in the cafe over the coffee, I was distracted by a young woman. She happened to be Jennifer's friend.

"Hi, Jen," she said as she sat at our table.

"Hi, Kelly. How are you? Meet my friend, Dr. Bond," Jen said.

"Hi Dr. Bond, I'm Kelly."

We shook our hands and I replied, "Hi, Kelly, nice to meet you."

I was impressed by Kelly's beauty. She had a great figure too. She chatted with us for a little bit and then she had to leave for some class.

"She is beautiful," I said and I thought Jen was bit annoyed.

"Well, she's all fake beauty from top to bottom," Jen quipped.

"What do you mean?" I was somewhat puzzled.

"Let me start from the top. Her hair is not really blonde, it is dyed. She has fake eyelashes. She used to wear glasses but now recently she had Lasik. Her luscious lips are not real; I guess some kind of plastic surgery or injections. She usually wears very heavy make-up. Her boobs are fake, she had a tummy tuck, and I believe she also had butt enhancing surgery. She also had a laser hair removal. And that's all I know so far." I was astonished.

"Butt enhancing surgery? Never heard of that! I also wonder how her husband or boyfriend must be feeling while touching her breasts. Would they feel natural?"

"I don't know because I don't have implants and I have never touched anyone with fake breasts so I can't answer your question."

"Oh by the way, I have heard and read so many blonde jokes that I can't believe that these girls pay money to look dumb," I said and immediately realized I should not have said it.

"Don't ever say that in public. It's okay with me, but even I have dyed my hair in the past at least couple of times to look blonde, although I am not stupid," Jennifer said.

After a pause I said, "I don't believe in fake beauty."

"I completely agree with you. But you will learn soon that in the United States no one cares much about real or inner beauty. Most of the beauty in the U.S. is fake, not real. Plastic surgeons make a good amount of money here. You might not be aware that most of these surgeries are not covered by insurance. So for a typical plastic surgery job, you'll cough up anywhere between five to ten grand, depending on the surgeon."

"How can she afford that kind of money?" I was shocked.

"Her husband is a lawyer and I'm sure he earns well enough to pay for all those surgeries," Jen explained.

After finishing our lunch, we went back to our office. Since we had submitted our abstract we had some free time. I had already started working on the scientific poster itself and submitted primary data and images to Margaret, our department's artist.

"I guess we keep working on our poster assuming it will be accepted?" Jen asked.

"Yes, of course. We have to keep it ready in power point format. Can I ask you something, if you don't mind?"

"Go ahead, Bond."

"I have never asked you a personal question before." I was bit hesitant to ask her.

"Go ahead, man, I don't mind even if it is personal question." I saw that Jen was getting a bit restless. "If it's too personal I won't answer it. As simple as that."

"You are good looking, in fact very attractive. You are intelligent and soon going to be a radiologist. And most important you are very nice person," I began.

"Thank you for the compliments, but that's not a question," she said and seemed even more curious.

"I was just wondering why you keep failing in relationships? At least the ones I have witnessed."

She was not mad, which was a relief. She looked around and made sure there was no one else in the office.

"I think we talked about this briefly earlier. But you are right. In spite of having beauty and brains, I have consistently failed in getting into a steady relationship. I don't know the real reason myself. Maybe because I don't have big boobs or a seducing ass. Everyone is interested in getting me into bed more than having a great relationship or friendship for that matter. I really don't know what else to say about it," Jen said with a shrug.

I was quietly listening to her and preferred not to say anything on such a sensitive issue, particularly since I was definitely not an expert on it.

At that point she started adjusting her bra straps over her shoulder. I was bit embarrassed. "Hey, can you not do that in front of me?"

"I didn't get that. What do you want me not to do in front of you?" she asked.

"Can you not adjust your bra straps in front of me, please? It is embarrassing for me."

"What's embarrassing? If you men were not around always staring at our boobs all the time, I'm sure that the whole girl community would stop wearing bras! It is sort of imposed on us by you guys. Do you know how uncomfortable it is to wear a bra all day? If you want to try it, you are welcome to wear one when you come to our apartment. I can lend you one. Just wear it for a day and let me know, okay?"

I was stunned by her response. After a pause, I said, "First of all, I don't stare at your boobs, and secondly I would prefer to look at you adjusting your bra straps rather than listen to your lecture!"

"Thank you, Bond. And for the record, you did stare at my boobs the first few times we met. I noticed it but didn't mind at all." Anyway, that topic ended there and we never spoke about it again.

As the days passed by, I was getting a bit nervous. Dr. Stein was pretty sure that the scientific poster would get accepted. I checked my mail daily for any updates on the poster. One fine day I did get an email about the acceptance of our poster. The moment I saw it, my first reaction was to pick up phone and call Jen on her cell phone. But I guess the phone was switched off and I didn't leave a message. I paged her and she returned my page.

"Hey, Bond, what's up?"

"Jen, I have great news for you." And without waiting for her response I told her, "Our scientific poster has been accepted for the conference. Come down to my office immediately."

"Oh wow! That's great news; I'll come to your office right away," she screamed in excitement.

Soon she barged into my office and I showed her that email. "Congratulations Bond," she said, then hugged me.

"Let's go to Dr. Stein's office," I said.

"Yeah, let's go."

I took the printout of the email and went to Dr. Stein's office who was luckily not busy at that moment.

"Congratulations to both of you. Your hard work has paid off. I was quite sure that it was going to be accepted. Now you need to work hard on the poster," he said, smiling. "By the way, we plan to interview both of you for a residency position here right after Thanksgiving, so start preparing for the interview also. Of course, a paper or poster getting accepted is a big boost for your applications. I would say it's more than likely both of you will be accepted here. And Dr. Bond, I have talked to Dr. Weinberg, the chair of surgery, to get you a spot for an internship also. Only thing, a surgery internship would be bit hard, but I am sure you can do it. As far as Dr. Graziano is concerned, I don't think she'll have trouble finding an easier internship like a transitional year unless you want to a surgical internship. In that case I can talk to Dr. Weinberg about you too."

Without much thought Jen said, "Sir, I would prefer to do surgery too. So can you please—"

Dr. Stein cut her short. "Sure, I will talk to Dr. Weinberg to get two spots for us instead of one."

Soon we left office and I asked Jen, "Are you crazy? Why do you want to do surgical internship rather than something simple?"

"Because I want to," she said and I was surprised.

"See, it is difficult to get anything else for foreigners, or to be precise, for aliens like me. We always end up getting what is left that no one else wants to do, which is fine with me." I was trying my best to explain to her.

"That is fine with me too. I would probably learn something too." She was being stubborn.

"But you could have taken something—" I was trying to convince her and she cut me short.

"I wanted to be with you in the same program, so that's why I opted for the surgical internship. Any problems?"

I stopped walking. So did she, and I looked at her. I was looking directly into her eyes and trying to read her mind.

"So what do you think, Dr. Bond?"

"What do you mean?" I asked her as I was not completely sure what she meant.

"As usual, I guess you are trying to read my mind. So what is it that I am thinking? Can you figure it out, Bond?"

At that moment, I lowered my gaze and I was trying to look somewhere else. I refused to speak about what I figured out from her facial expression or body language and said, "I need to go back to my office and start working on our poster."

"Fine. I am coming with you," Jen said and we started walking again. I did not speak a single word on the way and I opened my office door. I started my computer and sat down on the chair.

"So you did not answer my question, Bond."

"Jen I did not understand what was in your mind." I gave up.

She sat on the table right in front of me and stared into my eyes. "That is very unlikely of you. I guess you don't want to tell me."

At that point, I looked at her directly into her eyes and said, "Yes, you are right Jen. I did read your mind but I don't want to talk about it. Let's talk about something else. This topic is over. You are doing a surgery internship with me."

And we never talked about the whole incident.

The football season had started and it looked like almost everyone had their favorite teams. Jen also had one called New York Giants. One fine afternoon when I was working on the poster, there was a soft knock on the door and I knew it was her.

"Come on in."

"What are you doing on this Sunday evening, Bond?" she asked me as she barged into the room.

"Why? Are you planning to hook me up with somebody?" I asked her jokingly.

"No, man, I'm done with that. The Giants are playing against the Cowboys. Why don't you come to my apartment and we can watch the game together?"

"I don't understand anything about the game. It is like if I invite you to watch a cricket match," I flatly told her.

"I know cricket. It's something like baseball. But don't worry, I can explain to you whatever I know and I understand," she persisted as usual. "You know, Bond, I read somewhere that cricket is a game for gentlemen played by gentlemen. Football is a game for gentlemen played by hooligans. Rugby Union is a game for hooligans played by gentlemen, and Rugby League is a game for hooligans played by hooligans."

"What?" I screamed without much understanding what she was saying. Finally I said, "Alright. I will be there. What time do you want me to come?"

"Why don't you get your stuff and plan to stay overnight at my place? Anyway the next day would be a Monday and you can go to work from our apartment, I suppose?"

"Yes, that should work" I said. "But I have to know who else is coming."

"No one other than you," Jen replied and I was relieved because I would have looked totally dumb as I did not know anything about the game.

On Sunday around seven, I rang the doorbell to Jen's apartment. She opened the door and was wearing a New York Giants T-shirt and shorts and looked stunning as always.

"You look great," I said.

"Thanks, Bond. Come on in. The game is about to start."

"Why don't you put your stuff in your bedroom and I'll get you a beer," she called as she went to her kitchen. "I have your favorite, Kingfisher, the Indian beer."

I was surprised. "Where did you get Kingfisher beer?"

"This is New York, baby. You can pretty much get anything. By the way, I also like Kingfisher beer."

As we sat down, the game started and she explained the game to me in great detail. It seems there were players like quarter-back, tight end, wide receiver and running back.

I must say that even though it was the first game I watched, I enjoyed it. Or maybe it was her company which made it more enjoyable.

"Bond, do you know what American people's religion is?"

I was somewhat stumped by her question. I thought and said, "Christianity, Jesus . . ." I mumbled something like that.

"Here Football is like a religion"

"No. Football is also our religion," Jen said firmly.

"Football?" I was thoroughly confused.

"Yes, here football is like a religion. People talk about it and if you don't participate in the discussion, you will feel like a fool," Jen explained to me.

The doorbell rang and I looked at Jen.

"I ordered a pizza for us," she said while getting the door.

The smell of hot pizza was really tempting. We sat down and finished the pizza in no time.

I soon realized that Americans had also Americanized all British games too. Rugby was changed to American football, cricket was modified into baseball. I guess they could not change tennis, soccer, and golf otherwise we would have had the American versions of these games too! The next day, I named some of the medical students, residents, and fellows with football player's names.

"Do you know we have a tight end, quarter back, and wide receiver in our department?"

"Whaaat?" Jen almost shouted.

"See the girl who always wears tight jeans? I have started calling her tight end. See the other girl with a tiny ass? She is quarter back."

"Why quarter back?" Jen asked.

"Because her back side is so tiny, almost size of a quarter," I replied.

"And who is wide receiver and why?"

"The girl who is wearing white top because I was told she has tons of boyfriends."

"How the hell did you think of those names? You are absolutely crazy!" She could not control her laughter and as usual, suddenly changing the topic, she asked me, "By the way what are your plans for Halloween?"

By this time, I knew what Halloween was so I did not need an explanation.

"I guess Halloween and our Hindu Festival of Diwali is clashing. So I prefer to attend the Diwali celebrations at the temple."

"Fine. I'm going for a Halloween party at Angela's house and she has invited you too, so why don't you drop in? And then you can go to the temple."

"Let me think and I will let you know. Are you going alone or with someone?"

"I am going to meet someone at the party, I guess. I'm sure there will lot of guys looking for girls."

"Alright! Let's go back to my office and start working" I said, getting up.

"Sure," she said and we soon headed to the office.

As we were walking towards the radiology office, we bumped into John.

"Howdy," he said.

I could not understand what he was saying but Jen replied, "Howdy, John!"

John looked at me and said, "Amigo, you must be sad due to the Cowboy's loss."

I put on the saddest expression I could put on and said, "Yeah, John, probably the worst day in my life. I am sad too."

"I think the Cowboys need to work on their defense strategy, don't you think so?"

I had absolutely no idea what he was talking about. "Absolutely, their defense was pretty dismal," I said to please him and that seemed to work.

"Anyway, let's hope we win the next game against the Packers," he said.

Packers? Why would Cowboys play with some packing company? I was thinking but I nodded and said, "Oh, yeah. I am sure the Cowboys will get over it and beat the Packers."

At that point Jen realized that I was getting into the really slippery territory. She tried to warn me but John continued, "I can't believe you are so friendly with someone who supports our biggest rival," he said, looking at Jen.

"I tolerate her because of the research project, otherwise—"

John cut me short and said, "Hey, why don't you come over my place to watch the next Cowboys game? We will gather bunch of hotties and some fellow Texans and have fun. What I really miss is the tailgating parties we used to do at Cowboy Stadium. Did you ever to go to any tailgating parties?"

I had no idea what he was talking about. Anyway, I could not imagine going to John's place to watch a Cowboys game. He would immediately know that I knew nothing absolutely nothing about football. And he would also figure out that I am a foreigner. I was perspiring but Jen came to my rescue as always and said, "Bond, remember we have to submit another abstract for the upcoming conference?"

"Oh yeah, thanks, Jen, for reminding me. Sorry, John, maybe some other time. That's why I keep her company, because she takes care of my schedule."

"Hey, no problem, buddy. Maybe you can join me for a Halloween party. See this picture from last year's Halloween?" John was persistent and he pulled out a picture from his scrubs and showed me and Jen.

He looked like C3-PO from *Star Wars* and there were a bunch of girls around him in different costumes. He whispered to me, "Some of the girls were not wearing their tops, this is body paint."

I realized that most of the women had very large bosoms. I started perspiring again and Jen noticed it but before she could say anything John said, "Everything is big in Texas," and he winked at me.

"Bond, it's getting late," Jen screamed at me and almost pulled me away from that picture and John.

"I will think about it, John, thanks," I said while leaving.

While walking away from John I asked Jennifer, "Hey, from what I understand isn't tailgating driving too close to a vehicle? How can you do a tailgating party in a football stadium? Does it mean everyone follows others' cars too closely or something?"

"Bond, you're so funny. Do you remember my first commandment?"

"Yes, I do: Thou Shalt not speak English," I answered like a good student.

"Exactly. What you are saying about tailgating is British English, which of course we don't speak. We speak American. So in our language tailgating sometimes means having a party, typically in the parking lot of a sports stadium, where beer and barbecued meat is served. Get it?"

"Oh, I get it now." I felt like Newton or Einstein.

After a couple of weeks, I happened to bump into John in the cafeteria during my morning coffee break. Unfortunately, Jen was not around. He said, "Howdy, Bond."

"Howdy," I replied.

"I was just curious what kind of car do you drive in Bombay, Texas?"

I recalled my notes which had answers to all possible questions a Texan can potentially ask.

"Ford F-150," I said in trembling voice.

"Wow, even I have the same truck, although little old now. What does your family do in Bombay?"

"We grow corn . . . er, we have large corn fields," I said almost immediately, although I had never seen one in my entire life. I was wondering how long this harassment was going to continue.

"Do you get Fox news in your dorm?" John asked.

I was not sure of that but decided to say, "Yeah, of course. I watch it all the time, although recently I have been pretty busy so no time to watch TV." I started sweating as this one seemed like a test to see if I was a true Texan. But my answers seemed to have satisfy him so I guess I had passed the Texas residence test at least for the time being.

He suddenly changed the topic and said, "I am planning to go to Texas for a week for hunting, do you want to join me?"

Hunting, I thought for a moment . . . oh my god, I am in deep trouble! I looked around to see if I could see Jennifer was anywhere but she was not if the cafe.

"John, I am quite busy with the poster and other research stuff. When are you leaving?"

"In a week or so." Then he reached inside the pocket of his scrubs and pulled out some pictures.

It showed him in some Army-like costume with a big gun and a truck. Then there were some pictures of wild dead animals lying on the ground. In one picture, he was standing with his foot on the dead animal. I had never seen so many dead hunted animals in one picture and I started perspiring. I quickly wiped the sweat beads on my forehead making sure he was not paying attention. Then after that he showed me pictures of some animal heads stuffed and mounted on the wall in his house.

"That one is the biggest deer I have hunted."

At that moment, I thought of telling him the truth that I am not from Texas and not even from United States, in fact I am an alien not from another planet but from another country! I had a second thought, though and decided not to open my mouth and let Jen handle that job later.

He kept on talking and describing to me those pictures. I was not really paying any attention and was painting a picture in my mind. I imagined that soon my head would be mounted on one of the walls in his house with a big caption: "Head of an alien who was not from Texas, in fact not even from this planet!"

I felt dizzy and I thought the whole room was spinning around and I started profusely sweating.

"Hey, are you alright, Bond?" John asked me.

"I am aversive to deer. They make me sick."

'Levito-Casablanca Syndrome'

"I get vertigo and feel dizzy"

"What happens?"

"I get vertigo and feel dizzy."

"Even with pictures?"

"Yes, even with pictures, it is called . . ." I paused just thinking about what to tell him. "It is called Levito-Casablanca syndrome, extremely rare." I could finally come up with some name that may seem like a rare syndrome!

"I'm sorry, I shouldn't have shown you those pictures." He put those pictures in his pocket again and pulled out a round small box.

"Hey, Bond, do you want to try this?" he asked me.

"What is that?" It looked like I was in trouble again.

"This is chewable tobacco, want to try? You just have to put some in the corner of your mouth. Only thing is you have keep spitting in a cup or trash can," he explained.

Oh my god, I thought. One lie is leading me to another one! If I start spitting in my department I am sure I will create "Spitting Image" of myself.

"No thanks, John. I am fine with caffeine, which also takes care of the Levito-Casablanca syndrome. So I am bueno. Thanks anyway. Gracias!" Thank god I had learned from Jen some Spanish words, which came to my rescue!

"Okay, amigo. I'll see you around. Keep praying for a Cowboy's win when you go to church," he said while leaving.

The chances of me going to church and praying for the Cowboys was pretty rare but to please him I said, "Yes, I will, don't worry, amigo."

Then I said to myself, "I will probably go to temple and pray for a Giants win." Anyway, that episode was over and he never brought up the topic of hunting again and never showed me pictures of dead animals.

# THAT'S WHAT FRIENDS ARE FOR

Soon Halloween arrived. I politely declined the party invitation and went to the temple instead with a bunch of Indian guys and girls. After the prayers and dinner, we returned back to the dorm. I changed and watched some TV. I realized that the festival of Halloween must have been started by some candy companies to boost the sale of the candy. Luckily being in the dorm, there were no kids trick or treating to bother me. As I fell asleep, I wondered how the party at Angela's house must be going on.

Suddenly I was awakened by the phone ringing loudly. It was almost one in the morning. Who the hell is calling me now? I wondered. I picked up the phone and said "Hello" in a sleepy voice.

"Hey Bond, sorry to call you at this weird hour but this is Angela," the female voice on the other side said.

"Yeah, Angela I am sorry I am not coming to your party, I thought Jen—" She cut me short.

"Bond, the party is over. I am calling from the ER of our own hospital. We had to admit Jen to the ER, she is in bed thirty-two. Can you please come down ASAP?"

"Sure." I thought of asking her about Jen but I thought I will meet her anyway in the ER.

I got up quickly, dressed in my scrubs, and went straight to the ER. I met Angela and Jill at the entrance. They were holding hands.

"Thanks for coming. I'm sorry to call you, but Jen had to be admitted for abdominal pain. The party was almost over and she started throwing up. I guess she had too many drinks." Angela explained to me in great detail about what happened and how they got her here.

We all went inside and Jen was in a hospital gown and was sleeping I guess because of medicine. She had a nasogastric tube placed and an IV line too.

Soon her doctor came and said to us, "We are doing a CT scan just to make sure she does not have appendicitis. We need someone to sign the consent for her treatment since she was so drunk when she came to ER." Everyone looked at me.

"Are you her boyfriend?" the doc asked me.

"No. But he's her best friend. He is Dr. Bond," Angela said before I could say anything.

"Hi, I'm Dr. Chen. Can you please sign on this line and I'll counter sign," the doc said and I signed.

Angela and Jill left the ER, and I believed they were going to sleep with each other. I suppose they had acquired enough sex toys to play with from Toys r Sex or whatever store Jennifer mentioned to me.

"Do you work here?" Dr. Chen asked.

"Yes, I am doing research in radiology."

He gave me a weird look and said, "Great. Maybe you can go and check the CT scan results after it is done. Hopefully we will get a fast read because of you!"

I waited in the on-call radiology room with the on-call resident. Luckily, the scan was done pretty quickly and was a negative study too. I came back to the ER and informed Dr. Chen of the results. He also took a quick look at the CT and agreed with the interpretation.

"I don't see any cause of pain on the CT. Her labs are okay. Her belly was non-surgical by clinical exam too. But I can't release her now because her blood alcohol level is too high. Let her get sober and I'll let her go," said Dr. Chen and I agreed.

I went back to her bed and could see she was getting back to normal.

"Hi Jen. How are you feeling now?"

She was surprised to see me. "Bond, what the hell are you doing here?" was her first question.

"Angela called me and asked me to come here. I guess you had abdominal pain and were throwing up. That's all I know," I said in a flat tone.

"Where the hell is Angela then?"

"I guess she is sleeping with Jill," I said bluntly.

"Oh well. I guess the guy I met at the party is sleeping with someone else. And they just dumped me here and they called you because they knew you wouldn't refuse. Great!" she said sarcastically.

"If you want to call someone else, I can call."

"No, no. You're fine. I'm just thinking about my other so-called friends who dumped me here and left."

I looked at my watch. It was almost four!

"Are you feeling alright? If so I can drop you off at your apartment in a cab," I suggested.

"Yeah, I am feeling fine now. Can you please ask the nurse to get my clothes so I can get out of this stupid hospital gown?" she asked me.

"Yes, sure." I went to her nurse and she promptly brought her clothes in a bag, as well as her belongings.

I gave the bag to her and said, "Here you go. While you change, I will arrange for a taxi cab."

By the time she was ready, I had gotten a cab and was waiting at the ER entrance. Soon her nurse brought her in a wheel chair and we headed to her apartment.

"Thanks, Bond."

"No problem. There is a saying in the old Indian language Sanskrit that you come to know who your real friends are at the time of crisis or emergency. Everyone with whom you were partying deserted you. Your so-called friends," I said sarcastically.

She did not say anything but seemed to agree with me. She seemed to be annoyed at herself and also her friends, or so-called friends.

Soon we reached her . . . rather, our apartment.

"I think I will stay overnight here, if you don't mind. I guess I still have some stuff in my bedroom." I sort of invited myself.

Jen said, "You guessed my mind as always"

"I am staying here for two reasons, first of all it's pretty late, and secondly, if you start feeling something weird, I would have to come here in the middle of night."

"I was also thinking along the same lines, Bond."

"If you need something at night just call me," I said while entering my bedroom.

"Thanks, Bond, for everything. Good night."

"Good night, Jen."

The next day, I woke up around nine. Although it was Thursday I had taken a day off from work, just by coincidence, so I need not have to worry about going to the hospital. I peeped through the partially open door of Jen's bedroom and saw that she was asleep. I quietly entered her bedroom and looked at her face. Even in sleep she was stunningly beautiful. I adjusted her blanket and came back to the living room. I switched on the TV and started watching the news. After some time, she arrived in her PJ's.

"Good morning, Bond," she said while sitting next to me in the love seat.

"Good morning, Jen. You look much better now. How are you feeling?" I asked her while switching off the news.

"I am alright. I'm sorry you had to come in the middle of night."

"No problem, Jen. Remember you came to rescue me when I walked through the drive-in lane a few months ago? So, that is what real friends are meant for."

"Yes, a friend in need is a friend indeed," we said almost simultaneously and laughed.

"By the way, the ER department at our hospital is FUBAR, in case you did not know," Jen said after a long pause. "Hope you don't have to visit it like I did yesterday!"

"The ER of our hospital is FUBAR!"

"What is FUBAR, Jen?" I asked her innocently.

"Fucked up beyond all recognition," she said, straight-faced.

I was shocked.

"Who fucked it?" I gathered some strength to ask her.

"No one, they themselves. They've had three chairs in last eight to nine months," she said with sarcasm.

By this time I very well knew that chair meant chairman.

"I don't blame them. It is one of the busiest ERs in the country. I was glad I came out safe and alive!"

"Come on, it can't be that bad. We are in New York City." I felt the need to support them.

"Yeah, I know, maybe I am overreacting or exaggerating," she said, yawning.

"Do you feel hungry now?" I asked her, as I thought she had very little to eat or probably vomited most of it last night.

"Yes, I do. In fact, I was going to make an omelet and you can make some masala chai for us and we will have breakfast together," Jen said, jumping up.

"Alright, sounds good to me." I also got up from the love seat.

"Your chai is awesome. I cannot make chai like you," Jen commented while sipping hot masala chai.

"Cooking is an art. You have to pour your heart into it," I quipped.

"Hmm . . . I never thought about cooking in that way. For me cooking is pretty boring."

After we finished breakfast, Jen changed and came out with her car keys.

"I'll drop you at your apartment," she said, putting on her shoes.

"Jen, I will take the sub. You don't have to worry," I protested.

"No, come on. I'm fine now and I'm going to drop you off. I can do at least this much for you," Jen insisted and I had to give up. We drove to my dorm building and she parked her car in the parking lot.

She got out of the car and said, "Bond, I need a hug." She hugged me and to my surprise planted a kiss on my cheek. "You are such a sweet person, Bond. Probably one in a million. I wish the world was like you."

"Thank you for the compliments and the kiss. I am flattered," I said and I noticed that she was blushing a bit as I stepped back. "All right, time to say goodbye to you."

"All right, Bond, see you tomorrow."

I went back to my apartment and was wondering what to do next. One interesting thing happened in the beginning of November! They suddenly changed the time due to some winter time change, which apparently happens in fall.

I was furious and annoyed. "What is this all about?" I happened to ask Jen on one of the days.

"We change time in fall and spring. The easiest way to remember is we fall back one hour in fall and spring ahead one hour in spring," she explained to me.

"It is getting dark earlier nowadays and this time change adds to the misery! I don't get it," I complained.

"Yeah, I agree with you. Well, Bond, you may want to go to Arizona or Hawaii. Those states don't change time zones!"

Of course I did not want to leave New York and go anywhere else so the discussion ended at that point. Anyway, since November had already begun, I decided I'd start working vigorously on my poster. After a brief lunch, I went back to my office and started giving final touches to my scientific poster. The day passed quickly and soon I was back to my apartment and watching TV. Soon the telephone rang and I thought it might be Jen. While I was getting up, I accidently spilled some tea on my jeans and had to quickly clean that before I could pick up the phone.

"Hello," I said.

"Hello, Bond, how are you?" It was Jen on the other side.

"Fine."

"What took you so long to pick up the phone? Were you jerking off?" She almost shouted.

I did not get that comment and I said, "I am not a jerk" and I could hear some laughter on the other side.

"That's not what I said, Bond. Look up on the Internet when you get chance. Anyway, where were you all day?"

"I was in my office working on the poster. I'm going to submit this scientific poster to Margaret tomorrow morning so that she can start working on it ASAP," I said proudly.

"What is the chronology of authors?" Jen asked curiously.

"I am going to be the first author, you are the second, and Dr. Stein is the last author. There are a few research fellows whom Dr. Stein wanted to be included so their names would be in between."

"Wow! So, I'm going to be the second author?" Jen sounded surprised.

"Yes, dear, you are going to be the second author." I was as equally excited as Jen.

"I'm really looking forward to this conference. I hope our poster gets an award or something."

"Since we've put in so much effort, we deserve an award don't we?" quipped Jen.

"I guess, we do."

The Thanksgiving holiday came and I was getting ready to leave for Chicago. Jen was going to fly to Rochester, NY to see her mom. On Thanksgiving day I got a surprise call from Madhuri.

"Hey, are you going for the Black Friday sale?" she asked.

"No."

"Is Jen going for the sale?" she asked and I was both surprised and annoyed.

"I don't know. She might be going shopping in Rochester, New York," I replied in a calm tone.

"Oh, so Jennifer is in upstate New York! I thought you might be accompanying her to Macy's or something."

"Look, Madhuri, I don't like to shop and definitely not in the crowd. My needs are pretty limited and I am content with whatever I have right now," I said bluntly.

"I was thinking of going to Macy's tomorrow for the Black Friday sale and I was wondering if you can accompany me as I wanted some guy with me."

"I am definitely not coming, but I am sure you can find someone else to accompany you."

"What would you have told Jennifer if she had asked you the same question?" Madhuri was persistent and I was really annoyed.

"My answer would have been the same," I said while putting the phone down.

The next day I woke up late as I did not have to get up to go shopping. I made some masala chai and put on my television to watch some news. As I was surfing the channels, I saw one channel where a bunch of ladies were discussing about how the holidays could be stressful for everyone including the pets! *Are you kidding me?* I thought. Then they discussed and offered some advice for stress free holidays for humans as well as pets. *WTF*! Anyway it must have been a pet-friendly channel or something. At the end of that stupid show there was a commercial about ordering holiday pajamas for everyone in the family including matching pajamas for pets. I could imagine a family picture of everyone including pets wearing same type of pajamas!

'Holiday pajamas for everyone including pets!'

Anyway, I switched to the news and similar channels. All across those TV channels there was news about the huge Black Friday sale. Some of the shoppers were waiting outside the stores from the previous evening. There was an ugly stampede in some of the shops to grab the so called "crazy deals." One of the TV channels showed people rushing in the shops at five a.m. I thought some had the looks of people from a drought-affected country who had not had food for a few days or weeks or even months. Some of the news channels showed fierce fighting between people over some TV or computers. I was shocked to see that. The phone rang and I wondered who the hell was calling me.

"Hey, Bond. Good morning, how are you?" It was Jen on the other side.

"Hey, what a surprise, where are you? I guess in some store."

"Yes, I'm shopping at Best Buy now and planning to go to Target next. What are you doing?"

"Happy shopping and thanks for calling. I am having masala chai and watching the news. I am glad that I am not in one of those shops with crazy shoppers. You be careful," I said.

"Thanks, Bond. Happy Thanksgiving to you." She had to shout on her cell phone.

"Thank you and wish you the same. Bye," I said, putting the phone down.

The time passed quickly and I went to Chicago on the Saturday after the Thanksgiving as the conference always started on the Sunday after the holiday. I went a day early to set up the poster in the scientific poster display area. Jen was supposed to fly in the next day. The conference was in a big place called the McCormick Place near downtown Chicago. Apparently, it was one of the largest medical conferences in the world! I was all suited and booted for the opening day of the conference. Either I or Jen were supposed to stand near the scientific poster to answer any questions the visitors might have. On Sunday morning, which happened to be the very first day of the conference, there were a lot of radiologists who visited our section and there were a lot of questions from them. There were also a lot of international radiologists mainly from China and South Korea who were curious about our poster. On that day when Jen saw me near the poster, her first reaction was, "Wow, you look so sexy in that gray suit, Bond."

"Thank you, you look great..." and after a pause said ". . . and sexy too."

"Wow, I like what you just said, Bond," Jen quipped.

"I thought it might be offensive to say to some girl that you look sexy."

"It depends who you say it to and how you say and under what circumstances, Bond. In fact, I have been waiting to hear that comment from you about me and my dress," Jen said in almost one breath.

I tried to change the subject a bit. "I guess we are used to seeing each other in the scrubs. So we look much better in these clothes!"

Most of the time I would stand near the poster and answer any questions from visiting radiologists. Most of them were very sharp and asked me intelligent and sometimes difficult questions. In between I would take a rest and Jen would answer any questions from the visitors. I tried to be available, though, as Jen was just a fourth year med student.

During one break, we headed to the food court.

"Jen, tomorrow the scientific committee will decide about the awards. I am very nervous. I probably won't sleep tonight" I told Jen after we got our food and were seated.

"Don't be nervous, I'm pretty sure we'll pick up some award. There has been so much buzz about our research and our poster," she said in a reassuring tone.

"I know, but I guess that is just my nature. How was your Thanksgiving, by the way? I'm sorry I almost forgot to ask you," I said to Jen, suddenly changing the topic like she did most of the time.

"It was good. Oh, my sister is going to come here to see me this afternoon."

"Is she a radiologist?"

"No. Remember I told you that she is doing her internal medicine residency here in Chicago. She couldn't come for Thanksgiving as she was on call. So she's coming here to see me and I guess to meet you too."

"Meet me?" I was a bit surprised.

"Yup."

Soon we decided to head back to the poster display area.

In the afternoon Jen's sister visited us.

"Bond, this is my sister, Emily."

Emily was standing right next to Jennifer. She was slightly taller, a little bit on the plump side although definitely not fat. She did look little bit older than Jen. She was casually but artfully dressed. I looked at her eyes which were quite similar to Jen's eyes. In fact, if I would have met her accidently, I would have probably guessed that she was her sister. She wore light make up. She had a charming smile. We shook our hands.

"Nice to meet you Bond," Emily said.

"Nice to meet you too, Emily. My real name is actually…" I was about to tell her but Emily cut me short.

"I know. Jen is always talking about you when we chat. I probably know more about you than you know about yourself," Emily said, and I was taken aback by her comment.

"How is your residency going on?" I asked her to start some conversation.

"I am kind of a senior now so less calls but more responsibility," Emily replied.

"Jen is going to be a bright radiologist soon," I said while looking at Jen.

"Thanks, Bond but I haven't even started residency. Why don't we all go for a cup of coffee?" Jen suggested.

We went to nearby coffee shop and after Jen ordered coffee for all of us, we sat down to drink our hot coffee.

"What do you plan to do after your residency, Emily?" I asked Jen's sister.

"I'm planning to do a GI fellowship, I fact I have already started applying," Emily replied.

"That's great. You are going to be a rich doctor," I said.

"It's not about only money. I like Gastroenterology."

"I think that is the most important thing you've said. It's good to like the field you are in."

"What do you plan to do after your residency, Bond?" Emily asked me.

"I will probably do a neuroradiology fellowship assuming I get residency," I replied.

"What after your fellowship? Do you plan to go back to India?" Emily was persistent.

"Most likely not. I will plan to stay here and work on my Green Card and then the citizenship. But why do you ask?" I was getting a bit suspicious.

"Oh no. I was just wondering what your plans are for the future," Emily said while looking at Jen.

We chatted for some time and I looked at my watch and said, "Jen, I think it's time to go back to the poster area."

We all walked back and there were so many people walking around that even Emily was surprised. "Wow, there are so many people here."

"Yes, it's the largest medical conference in the world," I explained.

When we reached our poster, suddenly there was big crowd around our poster. I saw Dr. Stein walking to us.

"Congratulations, Bond, we have won the prestigious 'Magna Cum Laude' award for the scientific poster. Great job by you and Jen! Both of you please join us for dinner tonight at the Crystal Ball hall. We should celebrate in style," said Dr. Stein while shaking our hands.

I could not believe that we won an award so prestigious! I received hugs from both Jen and her sister. I had tears in my eyes. The hard work of so many months had finally paid off.

"Congratulations, Bond," both of them said almost simultaneously.

I was on cloud nine.

"Thank you so much. Jen, you helped me lot. Without your help, this poster wouldn't have been possible."

"Bond, I think you are being modest. It was Dr. Stein's idea and your hard work which pulled this off. I did help you but most of it was minor in nature," said Jen.

Then Emily joined her in praising me. "Yes, Bond, you deserve the credit for the award. Jen is just a med student right now. She wouldn't understand complexities of the research you've done."

"Emily, why don't you join us tonight for the dinner? Let me ask Dr. Stein. I am sure he won't mind."

I asked Dr. Stein if Emily could join the celebration and he said jokingly, "If she is joining as your guest I can let her but probably not as Jennifer's sister."

I replied immediately, "Well, in that case she is my guest."

"Thank you so much, Bond." Jen seemed to be very happy.

"Not a problem. I am glad that she will be with us."

That night both Jen and Emily dressed up for the party and I could not take my eyes off them.

"Both of you look gorgeous," I said, welcoming them to the party. The party comprised of a small group of people from the radiology department at our hospital. I knew most of them and Dr. Stein introduced those I did not know.

"Please meet Dr. Moore. He is better known by his nickname Dr. Bond, coined by this beautiful young lady Ms. Graziano," said Dr. Stein while introducing me to one of the General Electric executives.

"You know, Bond, GE has many projects and they are thinking of starting a big neuroradiology research project with us and I thought you might be interested."

I spent a lot of my time talking to the GE and Siemens executives about future research projects. Finally, I settled down with a drink and food and joined the two beautiful ladies.

"I am on cloud nine. I have won an award and I have the company of two beautiful ladies," I said as I sat.

"Bond if you had to choose between one of us who would you choose?" That was a totally unexpected question from Jen.

"That is a very difficult question to answer. Both of you are beautiful, charming, and intelligent." I was trying to avoid answering the question, but Jen persisted so I gave a diplomatic answer.

"Promise me that both of you won't take my answer personally."

"No, we won't," Jen said.

"I just met your sister Emily today. I find her very attractive and charming. But if I have to make a choice between two of you, I would probably choose Jennifer as I know her pretty well," I said, the wanted for their reaction. Both of them seemed to be pretty happy with my answer as I had pleased both of them.

I added, "But if I start meeting Emily more and get to know her then more than likely my answer will change."

Jen was shocked and said, "In that case I'll make sure that you don't meet her again." At that point Emily and I burst out laughing.

Dr. Stein made a brief speech about the achievements in research and possible future projects in neuroradiology. To my total surprise, Dr. Stein called me to the dais to speak a few words about the research project and my experience. I was totally shocked as he had not given me the slightest hint.

To add to my nervousness, he whispered in my ear, "Bond, the program director is also in the crowd. Make sure you impress him with your speech."

I went towards the mic and my hands were trembling and I was sweating. I then thought for a while and realized this is my moment, let me make the most of it!

I started speaking confidently and clearly.

"Thank you Dr. Stein for the opportunity to speak on this great occasion. It always feels great to win prizes but this one is special for me. Frankly, I thought our poster would win some prize but never thought it would win the prestigious Magna Cum Laude award. First and foremost, I want to thank the radiology department and Dr. Stein for giving me this opportunity to do this research. I had all possible amenities while doing this research and a great team of professional MRI technologists in our department, and my special thanks to them. We worked hard and will continue to do so to put our department and research in the forefront! I want to thank Ms. Margaret from our IT department who did the great job of helping us put the collected data and images in a pleasing format on this scientific poster. Last but definitely not least I want to thank my good friend and coauthor Jennifer Graziano for all the help I received during the research. Jennifer, will you please stand up?" Even from the distance I could see tears in her eyes and knew her heart must be pounding! She stood up and I said, "Jen, without your help we wouldn't be able to achieve what we achieved today. Thank you so much for your hard work and help." The crowd gave her a round of applause.

I finally ended my speech by saying, "And to all the company executives here, GE, Siemens and others, I would like to say that we are looking forward to working with you on some exciting research projects in future. As always thank you all for your support in the past and future endeavors. Thank you all for your kind attention!"

At the end, there was a moment of silence. Dr. Robinson, our program director, stood up and said, "Wow, that was a great speech. Please give a hand to Dr. Bond."

Drs. Stein and Robinson came forward to shake hands again with me and Dr. Stein said, "Bond, that was awesome."

Dr. Robinson said, "I look forward to seeing you as a great resident in our department, congratulations once again."

I went back to my table and received hugs from Jen and Emily.

"That was too good, Bond," Emily said.

"Bond, thank you so much. I probably didn't deserve so much praise and attention," said Jen, wiping tears.

"No Jen, you did. You may think your contribution was small but it did make a big difference. Really, I mean it," I said.

The party was over soon and we all went back to the hotel.

We hired a cab and dropped Emily to her apartment and went back to the hotel.

"Tomorrow afternoon I am going to fly back to New York," I told Jen.

"I'll be with Emily for a couple of days and then I'll see you in the city. Have a safe flight back home."

"You too, Jen."

We said good night to each other and went back to our respective rooms.

Before leaving Chicago, Dr. Stein suggested to take a few days off, so when I returned to New York, I decided to go to NJ to spend some time with Girish and Priya. Both of them were more than happy to learn about my progress so far and were excited to know about my chances of getting residency.

"That is why America is called the land of opportunity, buddy. You are going to make it, Raju," said Girish even though he was aware of my new nickname.

"It has been a while since someone has called me by my real name," I said, then took a sip of beer.

"I have been watching you since you came back. You have got an accent. Looks like you are getting Americanized," Priya observed.

I told both of them about Jennifer and how she helped me in my research and how she had been coaching me about the American way of living.

"Looks like you like her," quipped Priya.

"No. We are just good friends," I protested.

That evening we had dinner together.

"Wow! This food tastes so good. I am sure Jen will love this kind of food too," I said spontaneously.

"Next time you should bring her with you. I would like to meet her," Priya said.

"Sure, I will. She will love to meet you guys too. But like I said, we are just friends." I was trying to downplay our relationship.

I ate a lot and finished all chapatis Priya made. I also had my favorite, Bedekar mango pickle for the first time in a long time. Noticing my voracious appetite, Priya said, "I think you have been missing Indian food for a long time. You should come more frequently since you are so close to us."

"Yeah, I know. I have been to a few Indian restaurants but you don't get the authentic taste of home food in a restaurant. Priya, you are a very good cook," I said, then let out a burp.

"Thank you, Bond," said Priya, and each one of us had a good laugh.

After dinner, we sat down in the living room where we had a good view of the city.

"I love this city," I said, looking outside.

"Raju, we also love this city and you know why," said Girish.

"Because it reminds us of Mumbai," we said simultaneously.

"Bond, I think you should go back and visit your family before you start your residency," Priya suggested.

"Yeah, buddy, I think Priya is right. Once your residency starts, you are going to be really busy. You won't find time to scratch your ass!" Girish said, laughing.

"I think that is an excellent suggestion. Once I go back to city, I will talk to Dr. Stein and get couple of weeks off and go to Mumbai. I have not seen my mom and dad for a long time!" I said, yawning.

"Bond, it is getting quite late now. I think you should go to sleep. Tomorrow we can go to a nice Indian restaurant and have lunch, come back for a nap and in the evening we can go to the Brooklyn Bridge," Priya said as she started the dishwasher.

"I guess you guys still have my inflatable bed?" I asked as I got up from the sofa.

"Yes, we do. It is right here." Girish pointed out to the place where the bed was kept in a bag.

"Great!" I got up and with the help of Girish I set up my bed.

"I still remember those days when I came new here and used to sleep here," I said while lying down on the bed. "Good night guys. I think I am going to fall asleep pretty soon."

"Good night, Bond," Girish and Priya said almost simultaneously while entering their bedroom.

The next day, everyone got up so late that it was too late to have breakfast and too early to have lunch so we decided that we would have brunch at a nearby restaurant. I was not too hungry, though, since I probably had overeaten the previous day. We chatted and ate and soon came back for a nap as all were still sleepy.

I was really freshened up after that afternoon nap and was ready to go to Brooklyn Bridge. Priya made masala chai for all of us.

"Jen likes the way I make masala chai," I said while sipping the chai.

"Looks like you are missing her. Why don't you call her?" Priya said.

"I am not missing her but I will call her now." I picked up the phone and called her cell phone which I had memorized.

"Hi Jen."

"Hey Bond, what's up?" Jen almost shouted.

"Nothing. We are having masala chai so I remembered you."

"I love the way you make chai. When are you coming back?"

"Well, I just came over here. Let me spend some time with my buddies. How are you doing?"

"I'm doing great. I spent some time with Emily and now I'm back to the usual stuff. Nothing new. Preparing for the interviews I guess. How are you and your buddies?"

"We are doing great. We are planning to go to Brooklyn Bridge. Luckily, today it is going to be unusually warm for this time of the year so we thought of taking a walk. Do you want to join us?"

"No. May be some other time."

"Oh, I guess you are busy with your dating stuff?" I asked.

"No. Nothing of that sort."

"Alright then. I will see you soon, bye."

"Bye, Bond, have a good time." Jen said and disconnected.

That evening we went to Brooklyn Bridge for a walk. It was unusually warm and hence not surprisingly extremely crowded. We did enjoy our walk along the bridge. We chatted and I told them about the research project and possibility of doing residency in the hospital. Both Girish and Priya were excited.

"Man, once you get through your residency, you will mint money," said Girish.

"Bond, you are living an American dream," said Priya.

After our walk, Girish took us to some place where we had an excellent chicken biryani. It seems that place was being run by some guy originally from Afghanistan.

After our sumptuous dinner, we wanted to walk so we decided not get a cab. We all walked to the subway station and went all the way to Ground Zero. From there we got a ferry to New Jersey. Soon we were back at their apartment complex.

"Oh my god, the New York skyline looks so unattractive without the Twin Towers!" I said while were at the bottom of the apartment building.

"I know, Bond."

"I remember I had taken a nice picture of the Twin Towers right from here." I was emotional.

The next day, we were supposed to go to Bronx Zoo but we cancelled our plan as it was going to be a cold and rainy day. So we decided to go to the

Museum of Natural History instead. After spending almost a whole day there, all of us were pretty tired.

I decided to go back to my apartment the next day. Girish was bit surprised.

"I need to work on something before I start my day on Monday morning," I told him.

"I think you are missing Jennifer," Priya said and I knew she was teasing me.

"Nothing of that sort. In fact, I am quite comfortable here. Once I go there I will start feeling lonely," I explained to both of them.

"All right, buddy, we won't stop you. Next time you come to meet us you should bring Jennifer too," Girish said firmly.

"I will. I am sure she would like to meet you all too," I said in a reassuring tone.

The next day I was back in my dormitory. I made chai and sat down on the sofa and started thinking. It was the beginning of December. I was thinking about my future in the U.S. Due to the award I received at the conference, my residency was almost assured. This meant I would have to start my grueling internship in July. I liked surgery in the past so I had decided to do surgery. Jen's chances of getting into residency were quite high in general and more so in the same program due to her research. Suddenly my thoughts were interrupted by the telephone ringing. I was so deep in my thoughts that I was startled.

"Hello," I said in a soft tone.

"Hey Bond, so you are back from your mini vacation. How was it?" It was Jen on the other side.

"It was good. I ate some homemade food. We went to Brooklyn Bridge for a walk." I was kind of excited while talking to her. "Oh, Girish and Priya would like to meet you so we can go to New Jersey to meet them and then we can go to this biryani place too."

"Yeah, I would love to meet them. Are they from Mumbai too?"

"Yup, Girish is my high school buddy. Priya is from New Delhi, which is also a big city."

"Yes, I know Delhi is the capital of India, isn't it?"

"Yes, it is. But it is quite different than Mumbai. New Delhi is like Washington, DC and Mumbai is like New York," I explained to her.

"Oh, by the way, what are you doing for lunch?" Jen asked me.

"Well, it is too early. I have not thought about it yet." I said.

"I'll pick you up around noon and then we can go for lunch. How's that?" Jen asked.

"Sounds good to me. I will prefer to go a place which is less crowded and we can sit and chat while we eat. I would prefer not to go a fast food restaurant."

"Sure. I know one place that serves Indian food and is close to where you live."

"That would be great. I will have shower and get ready and I will wait for your phone call."

I got ready and was waiting for Jen's phone call. Soon the phone rang and it was her.

"Bond, I am in the parking lot of your apartment."

"I will be there soon." I said.

When we met in the parking lot, we hugged each other and said almost simultaneously, "It's been only few days but it feels like a lot."

We had lunch in this quiet and less crowded Indian restaurant. The food was not very good but the place was not crowded, so we could talk at leisure.

I told her briefly about my visit to New Jersey as she was listening with a lot of interest and interrupted me with her questions.

"Both of them want to meet you so whenever you are free we can go to their place and have that famous chicken biryani too," I told her enthusiastically.

"Sure, I want to meet them too, but Christmas is coming up and I'm going to be busy shopping. Maybe sometime after Christmas we can plan to visit."

"Alright, after this sumptuous lunch, I need to take a nap," I said in a sleepy tone.

"Alright, I'll drop you at your apartment or do you want to come to ours? I've been missing the chai you used to make. After your nap, we can have chai and then I'll drop you to your apartment."

Frankly I wanted to go home. But that might have made her unhappy so I agreed and we headed to her apartment.

I was surprised to see her apartment well organized and well kept.

"Looks like you are getting more organized," I commented as soon as we entered her apartment.

"Yeah, thanks to you, my apartment now really looks pretty. You can take a nap in your bedroom," she said, opening the door to the guest bedroom.

I immediately fell asleep. When I woke up, I went to the living room where Jen was talking on her phone.

"Hi Bond, Emily is saying hi to you."

"Tell her I said hi too. I will make some tea for both of us."

"Sure, go ahead. You know where the things are."

"Yes, I do," I said while entering the kitchen.

I made two cups of masala chai and both of us sat down in the living room.

"Wow, that is a wonderful chai, Bond," Jen said, after sipping the hot chai.

"Thanks. How is your preparation for the interviews is going, Jen?" I asked her while settling down on the love seat.

"So far so good. I guess my main chance will be here in our hospital. I have some more interviews in the Northeast. If I don't get residency in Manhattan then my second choice will be in Chicago so that I'll be close to Emily."

"What about internships?" I asked her.

"Dr. Stein has promised me that he will try to get me in surgery but I am trying at other hospitals too, here as well as Chicago. What about you, Bond?"

"My only chance for both internship and residency is here. I am applying to some places around where Dr. Stein has asked me to."

There was moment of silence. I broke the silence and said "I will miss you Jen if you don't get residency here."

She was a bit surprised by my comment. But she said almost immediately, "I'll miss you too, Bond."

"Let's hope that won't happen," I said in a reassuring tone.

After our brief chat while having chai, I decided to take off. Jen dropped me in my apartment's parking lot and we departed with a warm hug.

The next day I woke up at seven and reached the department by eight. Almost all my research fellows congratulated me for my poster and the award. Some of the radiology residents also made a special visit to my office and congratulated me. As I was talking to one of the residents, my pager started beeping. When I called the number, it was Mary on the other side.

"Hey, Dr. Bond. Can you please come to Dr. Stein's office ASAP?"

"Sure, I will be there in less than a minute." I said and almost rushed out of my office.

I was a bit surprised to see the program director in Dr. Stein's office.

"Good morning, Bond. How are you doing?" asked Dr. Stein, while sipping a cup of coffee.

"I am doing well. How about both of you?" I was wondering what was coming.

"We thought we should tell you that we are going to rank you higher in the match process. Of course we are not supposed to tell you so treat this as a confidential matter. We will make sure that you get into the residency here. I have also talked to the surgery program director to get you a spot for your internship. We'll interview you in the latter part of this week and you can meet with various faculties in the department. You should plan to start your residency next year with your surgery internship in July."

I was astounded and did not know how to respond.

"Thank you so much Dr. Stein and Dr. Robinson. I do not have words to describe how happy I am today and how happy my parents will be to hear this," I said, holding back tears.

"Not a problem, Bond. You have worked hard to get this and we think you deserve this." This time it was Dr. Robinson who spoke.

"Do you have any questions?" Dr. Stein asked.

"Not really. I just wanted to go back to Mumbai and see my family before I start my residency here."

"That should not be a problem at all. You can take about two weeks off. Will that be enough?" Dr. Stein asked.

"Yeah, it should be," I replied.

"One more thing, please do not talk about this to anyone outside. Maybe the only exception I'll make is Ms. Graziano since both of you are good friends. But make sure she does not let it out," said Dr. Stein while opening the door. "And congratulations to you."

"Thank you so much, sir," I said as I left the office.

My first instinct was to call Mumbai and talk to Mom and Dad and give them the news. So I rushed to my office and talked to them for about twenty minutes. Both were very happy to know that I would be getting residency in the United States. My Mom in particular was ecstatic.

"Now you should seriously think about getting married," she said, not unexpectedly.

"Mom, let us talk about it when I reach there," I said, cutting her short and ending our conversation.

My next reaction was to call Jennifer and tell her about it. I was about to call her when she barged into my office.

Before I could say anything she said, "Bond, your phone was busy for such a long time. I have been trying your phone for almost fifteen minutes."

"I was talking to my parents in Mumbai," I calmly replied.

"You and I are going to be interviewed this week. Do you know that?" she almost screamed.

I got up from my chair, grabbed Jennifer's arm, and said, "Jen, let us go to cafeteria and we will talk. I have something to tell you." She seemed a bit surprised by my behavior.

"Tell me now," she demanded.

I looked around and said softly, "Not here. There are other research fellows here. Let's have a coffee." I grabbed her arm and almost dragged her outside.

We went to cafeteria and got our coffee. I wanted to sit in a remote place so I led her to the corner-most table in the cafeteria near the window where only two people could sit.

Her curiosity was at its peak. After we settled down in the chairs, she asked me, "What is it, Bond? Tell me now, fast. I am so freaking out to hear. No one else is here to hear us."

"Promise me that this stays strictly between you and me. No one including your best friends or Emily should know about it," I said calmly while smiling.

"Bond, I promise I won't utter a word about it to anyone. Now don't stretch my curiosity or I will die."

"This morning, Dr. Stein called me in his office. When I reached his office, Dr. Robinson was sitting there as well. Dr. Robinson as you know—"

She cut me short and said, "I know, Bond, he is the program director and one of the most influential doctors in the hospital."

"Dr. Stein said that the program is going to rank me pretty high to make sure that I get spot in the radiology residency here. He has already spoken with the surgery program director to assure me a spot in their program for the mandatory internship." I finished talking in almost one breath.

Jennifer was ecstatic. She held my both hands and said, "Bond, that is awesome news. You have done something that's almost impossible to achieve. Congratulations, I am so happy for you. In the last ten years or so, no foreigner like you has got into the residency here."

"Thanks, Jen. I must say that the poster at the recent conference was a key factor for me getting this residency and that would not have been possible without your help. Thanks for your help."

"Yes. But it was your hard work that did the magic. My part was maybe five percent . . . at the most ten percent. Your parents must be really happy."

"Yeah, my mom was particularly ecstatic. She also bought up the topic of marriage," I said plainly.

"So what did you say?"

"I cut her short and told her I would see when I land there. Oh, by the way I am planning to go to Mumbai for a couple of weeks."

"Really, you never told me about it! When are you leaving?" I could tell she was surprised and bit annoyed.

"Hell, not now. The ticket prices are pretty high now. I will probably leave in February or early March when tickets are cheaper. I thought it is a good idea to go visit my family before I start my residency here as it is going to be very busy. Anyway, enough about me now. What about your plans, Jen?"

"I would prefer to get residency here. My second choice will be Chicago or maybe Rochester for obvious reasons. I'm sure that I want to do my internship over here. The radiology residency is not entirely in my hands."

"Have you talked to Dr. Stein about it?" I asked.

"No, but—"

I cut her short and said, "Why don't you talk to him?"

"OK, I will... if you insist," she said reluctantly.

"Yeah, talk to Dr. Stein. I personally think that your chances are pretty high since you are one step above the rest of your classmates due to your research. So go ahead and meet Dr. Stein and let him know that you are interested in doing residency here and most importantly that you wish to do research even during your residency," I told her.

"I won't get as much free time as I am getting now." She seemed worried.

"Don't worry. You don't have to do big research. You can do small projects, letters to editors, small case reports."

"Yeah, you're right. Thanks for the free advice, Bond," Jen said, smiling.

"It's not completely free. I need you to come with me to buy a suit for my interview. I have one old gray suit but I need a black one."

"I'm free right now for couple of hours. Do you want to go now?" she asked and I was surprised.

"Yeah, I don't mind. I will just let Mary know that I will be out for couples of hours."

"Bond, I drove here today so let's drive to the nearest JCP store and I will drop you at your apartment so that you don't have carry your suit in the sub," Jen said.

"That is so nice of you, Jen," I said.

We drove to the nearest JC Penney store. Soon I was in the suit section of the store. The man in the store was very nice, and with tips from Jen, he realized exactly what I was looking for. He got a black suit for me and gave me a white shirt to wear underneath since I was in scrubs. When I came out wearing the suit, Jen looked at me and whistled and said, "Here comes a lady killer. That one looks really good on you! Now wear a red tie with it."

Soon we got a nice and sober red tie and my shopping was done!

"Do you want to buy anything else?" Jen asked me.

"Nope. Not me. What about you?" I asked her.

"I need to save some money for the last minute Christmas gifts," she said with a giggle.

When we were driving back, Jen said, "Bond, why don't you go to your apartment and keep your suit in a nice place and come back down. I'll wait for you and then we can drive back to the hospital."

"Will do, baby," I said.

Jen said, "You are getting more and more Americanized, Bond."

"Thanks to you, baby." I said and both of us burst out laughing.

After we dropped off my suit, we drove back to the hospital. The whole process took about one and a half hour.

"I don't feel like you did any shopping. You should see how I shop," Jen commented while driving back to the hospital.

"I know. I do not wish to experience it."

She was astonished by my reply. "I drove you all the way from the hospital and helped you shop. I think it's pretty lame that you won't come shopping with me."

I realized that I'd hurt her pretty badly so I said, "I was just joking."

That seemed to calm her down a little bit but she threatened, "I am going to drag you with me when I need to finish my Christmas shopping." We reached the hospital parking lot so the discussion kind of ended there and I was happy that it did.

# THE BIG INTERVIEW

After I reached my office, I sat down in my chair and Jen sat on the table in front of me and asked me, "Dude, have you done any interviews in the past?"

"Yes and no. I was informally interviewed for the current post by Dr. Stein," I calmly replied.

"I think it will be useful if you do a mock interview before the actual interview this week."

"That's a great idea. I never thought about it. But who will do it for me?" I asked, instantly realizing it was a stupid question.

"Idiot, I will do it for you. Not that I have great experience but I am definitely better than you and I have also read some books about the tactics," Jen replied.

"Alright, but when and how?"

"I can use your office for the interview. But the only problem is that there will be people around so we have to do it early morning or late evening. I would personally prefer late evening," Jen said.

"Then let's do it today. Do you have any plans for the evening?" I asked her.

"No, not really. I have a great idea," she said, "Why don't both of us dress up like we are being interviewed and we will interview each other."

"Why do we have to do it here? We can do that in my apartment or yours."

"Yeah, that's right. Let's do it in our apartment, in the study room. I'll pick you up from your apartment around five. Make sure you're ready and bring your coat. Then we'll drive to our apartment and conduct a mock interview and I'll give you some helpful tips." As she talked to me she looked at her watch and screamed, "Oh Shit! I'm late. I better rush now." And without giving any clue as to what she is talking about she stormed out of my office.

I said to myself, *So typical of Jen!*

I laid out my suit, my white shirt, and the red tie. I showered and put on a nice deodorant and I shaved. I was just sitting down to watch TV when my phone rang. It was Jen.

"Bond, it's me. I am waiting for you in your parking lot. Do you have everything you need?"

"Yeah, baby. I got everything I need."

"Hey, listen, why don't you plan to stay overnight at my place, which will be convenient for me too. I'll drop you back in the hospital in the morning."

I had no choice but to say yes to her. "Okay, I will pack few things real quick."

When we were settled into her apartment, Jen said, "Here is the plan: We'll both go change and I'll meet you in the living room and let you know what is going to happen next. Oh, and don't forget to wear your black shoes."

I changed into the black suit and was ready to be interviewed. I was feeling a bit nervous. When I went back to the living room, Jen was already there. She wore a black jacket and skirt and I guess some skin-colored stockings. She wore a white shirt underneath and her cleavage was somewhat exposed. She looked stunningly beautiful.

"Bond, first lesson, do not stare at someone's cleavage during the interview," she almost shouted at me.

"Yes. Understood dear."

"Good. I'm going to go in the study room and close the door and in about a minute or so you will knock the door and enter the room. I am the Associate professor of Radiology Dr. Graziano and I will conduct your interview. Then we'll switch places and you will interview me."

"Sounds good to me," I said.

She entered the study room and I knocked the door after some time.

"Come on in," she called.

I entered and said, "Good evening. I am Dr. More."

She held her hand out and said, "Hi, I am Dr. Graziano, please sit down. How are you doing?"

"I am doing very well, Dr. Graziano, how are you," I said as I sat.

During my mock interview, which went on for almost half an hour, she grilled on various things, including my current and future plans. She took notes while nodding as I gave her my answers.

"So, Dr. More, I understand that you are an immigrant."

"Yes, ma'am," I said politely.

"After you finish your residency in radiology on your J1 visa, what do you plan to do?"

"Well, it is too early to say for certain, but I am planning to do a fellowship in neuroradiology"

"That sounds great. What after that, Dr. More?"

I did not understand what she was getting at so I was confused. Since the interview was not officially over, I could not ask her as a friend. At that point she pushed her chair back and the back of the chair touched the wall behind her. As she was sitting, her skirt looked even shorter and nearly one third of her thighs were exposed. After asking me that question, she smiled and uncrossed and then crossed her legs.

"That sounds great. What after that Dr. More?"

It reminded me of the famous scene straight from *Basic Instinct* when Sharon Stone uncrosses and then crosses her legs during her interrogation. For a moment, I thought Jen was trying the same trick on me so I got nervous. I started sweating and prayed to god and hoped she was wearing something underneath. She uncrossed and crossed her legs again and said, "Dr. More you look nervous. You did not answer my question." By that time I had totally forgotten the question. I took out my handkerchief and wiped the sweat over my forehead and asked, "Dr. Graziano, can you please repeat your question . . . if you don't mind?" She repeated the question after which I said, "I plan to stay in academics and teach residents and fellows in radiology."

"I like that, Dr. More. I think we are done now. It was very nice meeting you today."

"Nice meeting you too, Dr. Graziano," I said.

Soon the interview was over and she led me out of her study room door. I was perspiring at the end of the interview.

Jen came out and said, "You did pretty well, although I have to go over a few things with you." She gave me a smile. "Tell me the truth, Bond. Why were you sweating when I uncrossed and crossed my legs?"

I decided to be frank with her. "I thought you were playing a Sharon Stone trick on me so I got nervous and started sweating."

Jennifer started laughing uncontrollably "Oh man, you are just too much. Did you think I would interview you without wearing anything underneath? I was just watching how you react and you reacted inappropriately. Never look down there if someone uncrosses or crosses her legs in front of you. Especially when you are being interviewed. Get it?"

"Yes, I got it," I said, smiling.

She then thoroughly went over the whole interview process and pointed out my mistakes and gave me some broad guidelines. She also gave me a book on residency application and the interview process. "Bond, why don't you start reading this book tonight and at least start going over the important things I have highlighted."

"Thanks, Jen. I think this going to help me a lot."

"Oh by the way, you look pretty hot in that suit," Jen said, winking. "Now it is your turn to interview me. Make sure you ask me some tough questions."

I went and sat in her office and Jen knocked the door and I welcomed her. I asked her all sorts of questions I could think of and I realized she was sweating at the end of the interview. I asked her some detailed questions about the research project, which actually was done by me.

After I finished she let out a sigh of relief.

"How was it Jen?" I asked her.

"You know the saying that when rape is inevitable, you should lie back and try to enjoy it! So I did the same thing."

"Oh I am sorry. You thought I was sort of raping you?"

"Oh, Bond, you were brutal. But it was good. I think I sort of needed that and frankly I really enjoyed it."

"Jen, you need to look up stuff about the research project because almost everyone is going to grill you over it," I said, handing over the notes I made during the interview.

"Go over these things in particular where I thought you were pretty weak. Oh, by the way, you look stunningly beautiful in that suit."

"Thanks." She said. After a brief pause she said "Bond, do you know what happens after the interview? Do you know what NRMP is?"

"No. I have absolutely no idea, please tell me," I said.

"Well, let's sit here for a while and let me explain to you briefly," Jennifer said.

Soon we sat down in her study room. She was sitting across the table from me and pulled out a blank paper and started writing on it.

"Bond, see here. After your interviews are over then you rank different programs in your order of preference, no matter what they think about you or how they would rank you."

"Ok, got it" I said.

"Then the programs rank the candidates depending on whom they like. From the best to worst. This is their order of preference. Do you understand?" She asked and I nodded.

"You submit your match list on a website. Then what happens is called a 'match process' in which the lists are submitted to a computer or maybe a supercomputer and the computer matches the programs and the candidates and spills out a list of selected candidates. That's when you come to know if you got accepted in a residency program or not!" She continued talking as I was listening intently.

"This whole process is called National Resident Matching Program or simply NRMP and you need to register for the match process in addition to everything else, so don't forget to do that, Okay?" She stressed.

"Yes, I won't" I reassured her.

"This so called 'match day' is usually mid to late March but there is a different deadline to submit your match list, which usually near the end of February. Get it? So read online more on these websites," and she scribbled down the names of a few websites on a piece of paper.

"If you have any questions after reading the info on websites just ask me and I will explain to you. But don't forget to submit your match list before the deadline and most important register for the NRMP if you haven't done already." She finished.

"I completely got it," I said while grabbing the paper from her.

After a brief pause she said "Oh boy, I am so hungry! Let's eat now."

"What are we eating?" I asked as I loosened my tie.

"Anything. We can go down and eat a Subway sandwich if you want."

"I don't mind but let me change into something comfortable," I said as I removed my coat.

"Sure Bond, I'm going to change too."

After, we went down to Subway and I ordered chicken sandwich and Jen ordered some big sandwich. She kept on talking, as usual, and I finished my sandwich.

"Jen, I think you need to stop talking and eat the sandwich. I finished mine," I said calmly.

"Not a problem. I'll keep talking and we can carry this to our apartment." Jen stood up and grabbed her untouched sandwich. I noticed that more than once she would refer to her apartment as our apartment.

After reaching the apartment, she finally took a break from her talking and started eating.

"Why don't you talk about something," she said with her mouth full.

"I think I'm better off listening to you," I said quietly.

"You are such a…" She left her sentence unfinished.

"Bore." I finished her sentence.

"Thanks. I did not want to…" Another unfinished sentence.

"…insult you." I again finished her sentence.

"Thanks again," said Jen as she finished her late bite.

"You are most welcome Jen. I think it is pretty late and I think we should go to sleep."

"Yeah, Bond, you're right. I'm tired too. In two days we'll be interviewing. I can't believe it, Bond. I just met you six months ago and we might be doing residency together in six months or so," she said while yawning.

"I can't believe it either. It would be so much fun to do residency together."

"Alright, Bond, I am sleepy and tired. I'm going to my bedroom to crash. Please wake me up if I don't. I'll drop you to your apartment or we can always take a subway," Jen said as she headed to her bedroom.

"I would prefer to go by subway so you will save some money and gas as well as the hassle of driving."

"Alright, Bond, whatever you say. Good night."

"Good night, Jen. See you in the morning."

I was tired so I fell asleep pretty quickly. I woke up at around six and checked if Jen was awake. I knocked on her bedroom door softly and she said, "Thanks Bond. I'll get ready and try to fix some breakfast."

When I got ready and went to kitchen, I was surprised to see Jen ready and already making some breakfast.

"Bond, I made an omelet for us. Can you please fix some chai for us? You know where the stuff is right?"

"I do, unless you have moved it."

"No, I haven't."

"Jen, do you have masala chai when I am not around?" I asked her, while pouring boiling water in the cups.

"I will be very frank with you. I don't because I can't make it like you do," she said as she sat at the table.

We finished our breakfast and Jen said, "Bond, I realized that you need to carry your suit, so I'll drive you to your apartment and then go to the hospital after dropping you off. Going by subway is not a good idea today."

"Yes, I agree. I did not think about it. Wow, I am so fortunate to have a beautiful lady to help me select my suit, take my mock interview, give me breakfast, and drive me around. I cannot ask for anything more, I love it. Thank you so much for taking such good care of me."

"You are most welcome, Bond. You deserve it."

Since there was not much work to be done in the hospital, I changed into my scrubs and went to my office and started reading the book on residency interviews given to me by Jen. It was quite useful to me. The day passed by slowly and around lunch time there was soft knock on my door and soon Jen barged in my office.

"Get off your ass and let's get something to eat. I am starving." I was now quite used to her language and manners.

We went to the cafeteria and ate food and as usual she kept talking about something and I listened to her quietly.

The cafeteria was full but there was one table where a few Indian residents and fellows were sitting. I knew some of them and I noticed a few empty chairs.

"Do you want sit with my fellow brownies?" I asked jokingly and she gave me a look.

"Come on Bond, don't insult your own race."

"Sure. But Asian is not exactly a race, actually we are Aryans."

She frowned and said, "Let's sit with your fellow Indians." It sounded more like an order, which I followed without question.

"Hey guys, can we please sit here?" Jen asked while sitting without even waiting to hear an answer.

"Hi, please join us," Aditya, one of the ENT fellows, said.

Everyone introduced themselves. Most of the residents were already trained in some sort of residency in India. Some of them were repeating their residency while a few were doing totally different residencies in the U.S. Jen was amazed!

"Wow, most of you guys are already trained docs. Aditya is doing a fellowship in ENT, which is pretty difficult to get!" she commented. "By the way, I have a question for you guys and Bond you can answer too." Suddenly everyone was more attentive. "What is the difference between South Indians and North Indians?"

There was pin drop silence as no one wanted insult anyone as the crowd was sort of mixed.

"Hey guys, I am sorry, but is that such a difficult question to answer? How would you explain to a white girl or guy about these differences? Come on!" Jen persisted.

Finally, Aditya, who was from Mumbai like me, answered. "Jen, it is very simple. As you go from south India to north, the color of the skin improves but the I.Q. goes down!"

While some of us enjoyed the joke, Amandeep, who was from Delhi, was furious. "Aditya, that is an insult to us. How can you say that, that too in front of a foreigner!"

We had to calm him down. "Come on, Aman, that was just a joke. Cool down," I said.

"Wait, let me make something clear," Jen said in an authoritative tone. "I am the local person here, white and truly American. All of you are foreigners. Is that clear? Maybe you meant white girl and not foreigner!"

"Cool down, babe," I said and that seemed to work on her and everyone gave me admiring looks.

"So Bond, which category do you fit in?" came an obvious question from Jennifer.

"Well, neither. Because we are in the middle and sort of from the west coast," I said while looking at Aditya who nodded in agreement.

Someone asked a random question, "Hey, do you guys know when the ENT department graduation party is next year?"

Aditya said, "Yaar, it's too early. Why do you ask?"

"I am planning to go to India and probably getting married. I did not want to miss the graduation party as I will be leaving this program to do fellowship in John Hopkins in Oncology Surgery."

I jumped in the conversation and said, "These resident graduation parties always remind of one festival in my state of Maharashtra."

Suddenly everyone was attentive. "Which festival? Diwali?" Jen was curious.

"No. Diwali is celebrated all over India. This festival is unique in Maharashtra and it is called 'Pola,'" I said. Some of the guys who knew this festival busted out laughing!

Amandeep was unaware of this festival. "Bond, what is Pola? Can you explain and why is it so funny?"

I started talking and there was silence on the table. "In Maharashtra there is lot of agriculture and for that we used bulls for ploughing. Aman, you know that right?" I asked him.

"Yes, even in my great state of Punjab," Amandeep replied almost instantaneously.

"So these bulls work all year and the work is pretty strenuous, they never get a single day off in a year. But there comes a day called 'Pola' when they are not ploughing or working, they are worshipped, covered with colorful clothes and given supposedly delicious and sweet food to eat. That festival is called 'Pola'!" As soon I finished talking there was applause and another round of laughter.

"Wow, Bond, you are so accurate. The graduation party does resemble Pola," Amandeep said. Some of the residents even got up and shook hands with me and said, "Bond, your observations are so meticulous."

Even Jen was impressed. "Wow, Bond I was going to say the same thing. You have very diligent observations!"

The discussion changed to hospital politics and then to accents among different immigrants!

This was an interesting topic especially for me.

"Guys, have you noticed how Hispanics confuse between B and V? When they say bowel it sounds like vowel!" I said.

"Really? I never noticed," Jen said.

"I worked in the Middle East for some time and those guys pronounce P as B so a Middle Eastern guy will say betrol when he is trying to say petrol!"

"Wow, that is amazing," someone quipped.

"Well, Bond, it's your turn now. I've noticed something about Indians too, want to hear?" Jen asked and everyone encouraged her to explain her observation.

"You guys are confused between V and W. And you use it interchangeably!"

Some guys nodded while others tried to think and some refuted the charges!

Soon the discussion topics varied from politics to sex to anything.

"Why are you Indians guys so paranoid about having premarital sex? I've heard most of the boyfriends and girlfriends in India don't have sex before marriage! Why is that?" Jen asked a sensitive question and there was some silence on the table.

Venky, one of the internal medicine residents said in typical South Indian accent, "Jennifer, it is kind of complex."

"What is complex? Having sex? I don't think so!" Jen interrupted. Almost everyone laughed.

"No no . . . I don't mean that. I mean the answer is kind of complex. Well, let me think . . . to be frank with you . . . a very brief answer is that we have superior but different culture."

"Why are you guys so much paranoid about pre-marital sex?"
"We have superior but different culture!"

There was some muted laughter.

I did not quite understand what he said but that seemed to have ended discussion on that topic!

"Hey, since we are talking about sex, can I tell a non-veg joke?" asked one of the Indian guys.

"What? I don't get it. What is a non-veg joke?" Jen asked.

"Jen, I will explain to you later but in India it means a dirty joke," I explained to her.

"Oh I get it. Since most of you guys eat vegetarian diet, non-veg joke is sort of forbidden joke," Jen said. "Go ahead, I'm all ears. I don't mind at all. I eat non-veg food every day!"

Suddenly someone said, "Hey guys, I have to go for a tumor board. I am presenting cases today." Suddenly everyone else realized they were getting late for their own tasks or duties and almost everyone left. Soon the table was empty except for the two of us.

We moved closer together and after a long silence Jen asked me, "Bond, you know why I like meeting you?"

"Yes, because I am so sexy," I said seriously.

She almost choked. "Bond, do you want to kill me?" she screamed so loudly that everyone around out table started looking at me. After taking a sip of water she said, "Nope. Because you listen to whatever crap I talk about. Anything from about my sister to the hospital gossip."

"Yes, I get the local news and all the hospital gossip sitting here with you. And it's all free too!" I said in one breath.

"That is the other way of looking at it, I guess," Jen said, getting up.

We went back to our office and from there Jen went to the library and I went back to reading the book on residency.

The day of our interview came pretty fast. I spent the night before the interview without much sleep. I woke up early and as we had decided, I gave a wakeup call to Jennifer.

"Hi Bond, thanks for waking me up," Jen said in a sleepy voice.

"Did you sleep well?" I asked her.

"Nope. I didn't sleep too well. I think I need your masala chai or Starbucks coffee to wake up. What about you, Bond?"

"I spent a restless night. But I am fine. I will see you in the hospital. Good luck for your interview in case I don't see you."

"Thanks and good luck to you too," she said, then disconnected.

I got ready and went straight to the conference room in the radiology department where the candidates were supposed to assemble before the interview process. The conference room was filled with well-dressed and well-groomed men and women. There was a mixture of male and feminine perfume that lingered in the room. It was not difficult to find Jennifer, as she was undoubtedly the most beautiful girl in that room.

"Hi Bond, someone is looking so smart and sexy today," she said, giving me a hug.

"Yes, and someone is looking so beautiful that I cannot take my eyes off her."

"Thanks, oh here is your packet for today." She handed over me a small folder containing a bunch of paperwork.

"Bond, let's go in that corner and sit," she ordered and I followed her like a robot. We sat down and she quickly went over the important papers in my packet.

"Look at this," she said, handing over a paper to me. "This is the list of people who are going to interview you today. Go through the list carefully and make a mental note of what questions you might be asked and what you need to ask. I think Mary will come now and will go over some of the details of the interview. Dr. Robinson will..." At some point I lost track of what she was saying and kept staring at her face.

"Bond, where is your mind? Pay attention to what I am saying. Stay cool, okay?" she almost screamed at me while shaking me and grabbing my shoulder.

"Sorry, I just got lost. I do get what you are saying. I will be fine. Jen, thank you so much and remember what I told you too. You will be asked about our research. Are you prepared to answer any questions about it?" I asked her.

"Yes, don't worry about me. I should be fine."

As we were chatting Mary entered the room and briefed all of us about the interview process.

Soon Dr. Robinson entered and he briefed us about the radiology department and various current research projects.

"I wish I could give every one of you a spot in residency today. Our department, as you might be aware, is academically and research oriented. We are looking for hard working residents who can handle the day-to-day work as well handle calls. Let me tell you, radiology calls are pretty tough and nasty. If you are expecting light calls this not the place you want to be. Our hospital is a level one trauma center; our ER is one of the busiest in the country. Also it is expected that the future residents take part in scholarly activities, including writing papers and scientific posters." He went on for a few more minutes.

Soon the interviews started. We were divided into small groups and each of the groups was given a tour of the department by selected senior residents including the chief residents. Jen was in a different group of med students, but we occasionally bumped into each other during the tour. She handed over a small note to me and I opened it.

*Let's meet in your office after the interview -Jen.*

I looked at her and nodded in approval.

I was interviewed by several faculty members, most them I had known or seen in the department.

One of the staff radiologists began by saying, "Dr. More, you are already a radiologist. You have been in our department for a while and I have heard a lot of good things about you. I do not have any questions for you but if you have any questions, please let me know." Most of the faculty members were nice to me and just talked about my future plans. The last person I was supposed to meet was Dr. Stein.

"Come on in, Dr. Bond," he said, then offered me some coffee, which I gladly accepted. "How was it so far?" he asked while handing over the coffee cup to me.

"Thanks for the coffee. It has been very good so far," I said while sipping the fresh hot coffee.

"As you know I am the last person to interview you today. Do you have any concerns or questions?"

"I just have one question about the internship."

"I will personally guarantee you that you will earn a spot in the surgery internship here. There is absolutely no doubt about it," he reassured me. "Anything else?"

"I guess not."

"Then I think you can proceed back to the conference room where the lunch is ready for you guys. Dr. Wang is giving a lecture on head and neck CT anatomy."

I went to the conference room, which already buzzing with a lot of interviewees. I grabbed my sandwich and drink and was looking for a seat. I saw Jen waving and went straight to her.

"Hey, Bond, I sort of reserved a seat for you," she said, lifting her folder from the seat next to her.

"How was it?" we asked almost simultaneously.

"I think it was good overall. I had no problems," I said and then looked at her.

"Mine was good too but I need to talk to you in your office after we're done."

I guessed that she needed more words than I did to tell me what happened.

Dr. Wang entered the room and greeted us.

"Hi guys, I am Dr. Wang. Hope your day has been going pretty well so far. I am going to give you a brief lecture on the CT anatomy of the neck." He started his PowerPoint slides and gave an excellent review of the anatomy of the neck and larynx.

After the lecture Mary entered and said, "As you know, the interview process is over. There is an optional tour of the rest of the hospital in brief. If you are interested, please stay in the conference room. We understand that you may have to go to airport to catch a flight or go back to your hotel. In which case, you can see me in my office right across from the corridor and I'll help you. Thank you for coming and best of luck to you all."

Neither I nor Jen was interested in the hospital tour so we glanced at each other and Jen whispered in my ear, "Bond, let's go to your office."

We slipped out of the conference room quietly and went straight to my office.

I removed my coat and hung over the back of my chair, loosened my tie, and offered my chair to her which she declined. Jen removed her coat and hung it on to the hanger and sat on the table right next to the computer. She crossed her legs and signaled me to sit on the chair.

"Oh my god, I am so tired. Let me tell you what happened." And she started from the time she started the tour of the department and told me briefly about her interview.

"Some of the faculty members asked me a lot of questions about our research and I could answer most of them, thanks to you. One of them, a lady, was not very nice to me but other than that it was fine."

"I think tomorrow you should meet Dr. Stein and ask him frankly about your chances here," I told her.

"Yes, I will. I have to leave in a couple of days to go to Chicago and then Rochester for the rest of the interviews."

"Oh by the way, you looked so beautiful today; I almost had a heart attack when I saw you."

"Oh I'm glad you're still alive then," Jen said while getting up from the table and fetching her coat. "I'm going to back to the apartment and taking a nap, then start packing for my short trip."

"I am going to back to my apartment too and taking a good nap." I stood up and put on my coat and helped Jen into hers.

"Thanks, Bond."

"Good luck to you for your other two interviews and send me an email or call me after each interview and say 'hi' to Emily."

"I'll call you to talk," she said. We hugged and she left my office.

I went back to my apartment and was pretty tired. I took a nice nap and then called Mom and spoke to her. It was bit early in Mumbai and my mom did not complain about my waking her up.

I told her that most likely I would get a residency spot in radiology in the hospital I was working. She was very happy and so was my dad. Luckily she did not bring up the topic of marriage this time.

I also called Jennifer in the late evening to wish her best for the upcoming interviews.

"Did you finish your packing?" I asked her without preamble.

"I knew it was you when the phone rang. I finished my packing except a few last minute things so don't worry."

"I forgot to ask you earlier. What time is your flight?"

"It's mid-morning. I'll be flying to O'Hare and Emily is going to pick me up. The interview is the next day, and then I'm coming back here. My interview in Rochester is just before Christmas and I'll be back after Christmas."

"Oh boy, you will be gone for a long time! I am going to get bored," I said and there was a silence on the other side.

"You can join us for Christmas if you want. You can meet my mom, and Emily will be there too."

"Meeting Emily excites me but no, I am fine here. I may go to New Jersey for a week around Christmas if Girish is not planning to go anywhere," I said, politely declining her offer.

"Oh by the way, did you call them about your interview here?" Jen asked me.

"No, I haven't, but I will call Girish as soon as we finish talking."

We chatted for few minutes and I said at the end of conversation, "Have a safe flight and good luck with your interview again. Make sure you talk about doing research in future and that will be a plus point for you."

After I finished the conversation with her, I called Girish. He was not at home but I spoke to Priya. She was excited to know about the interview "That's great news! When do you come to know for sure?"

"We should come to know on the match day, which is mid-March, I presume."

"I will tell Girish you have called. He will be late today so he may call you tomorrow if he cannot call you today. By the way, how is Jennifer?"

"She is fine. She interviewed with me today and she is interviewing at other places too."

"We hope to meet her soon," said Priya.

"Sure, maybe after the interviews are over we can drop in over the weekend or so. Oh, are you guys going to India around Christmas time?"

"No. We are here and you are more than welcome to join us. Bye and see you soon."

"Bye, Priya." I thought having Girish and Priya so close to me was a great advantage for me.

They supported me when I came to this country for an interview and continued to do so.

The next few days passed by pretty slowly. As my residency spot was almost assured, I decided to look up some ads for radiology jobs. I had to finish residency before I could start any job but I was just curious.

The job market apparently was pretty hot at that time. Lot of residents could join private radiology groups without any fellowship, I was told. Radiology ads were very interesting, at least that is what I thought. Most of the ads would mention very little about the actual job and there was lot of description about "extra-curricular activities" and other totally unrelated things. Some sample ads were something like this:

*Very large private practice group in New Hampshire. Partnership track is currently being offered to new recruits. 8 to 5 job Monday to Friday. No after five work. Calls only once in 8 weeks.*

*Very picturesque location of practice, 10 weeks of vacation. Close to world famous ski resorts. Lot of golf courses in the surrounding area. Great place to bring up family, great public schools, no traffic problems of a big city. Nice weather all around except few months of winter. Lot of lakes around for Watersport activities in summer. Big shopping malls in nearby city just 30 minutes of driving distance.*

Wow! I thought the selling points of such job would be mainly the activities you would do after work! Some of the radiology jobs would specifically mention: No mammography, No Angio.

Some of the outpatient practices would stress on the fact that the job was only eight to five, Monday thru Friday. No calls on weekdays, no weekend calls. Some of the jobs would mention the potential salaries up front and would also offer huge signing bonuses. Well, I thought, if this is all true and hopefully remains the same for at least few years then this would be the perfect time to join a radiology residency!

The other thing on my mind was my India trip! Since my interview was over and there was no need to start working on a new research project, I spent time looking for good airline deals to go India. Since New York and Mumbai had a lot of connections, it was not difficult to find a good deal in the not-so busy-month of February. While I was looking up the deals, the telephone rang.

"Hello?"

It was Jen on the other side. "Hey, Bond. My interview is over here in Michael Reese."

"How was it?" I asked her.

"It was good. Some of the faculty members I interviewed with showed a lot of interest in our research project and the poster so most of the time was spent on that, which is good. I did answer most of the questions related to the project and research. I also told the chairman that I would like to continue doing research during residency." As usual she was continuously talking and I was listening.

At one point I had to cut her short and ask her, "Where are you calling from, Jen?"

"I'm in Emily's apartment. By the way, Emily says 'hi' to you. Do you want to talk to her?" As usual she gave me no choice and handed over the phone to Emily.

"Hi Emily, how are you?" I asked her to start the conversation.

"I'm doing well, Bond. How are you?"

"Great."

"How was your interview?" Emily asked me with curiosity.

"It was good. Now I have to wait till mid-March to see what happens next. Is your little sis bothering you?"

"No. Not at all. It was nice talking to you, Bond. Here, talk to Jen now." She handed over the phone back to Jen.

"How is the weather in Chicago?" I asked Jen.

"Well, what do you expect? Cold and windy. Thank god it's not snowing too bad here. Anyway, I'll be back tomorrow."

"I will see you, Jen," I said then put the phone down.

It was kind of a festive atmosphere in the hospital and in the country as Christmas was approaching fast. There were a lot of sales in the stores around the city and the shopping frenzy was at its height.

I was busy planning for my upcoming trip to Mumbai. While I was looking up something on the 'net in my office, there was a soft knock on the door and Jen stormed into my office. There was some paperwork right next to the PC where she used to sit. She held the paperwork in her hand and handed over to me.

"Is this place reserved for you?" I asked.

"Yes, just a little place for my tiny ass. Do you have a problem?"

"No absolutely not, as long it stays tiny. Now tell me in person what happened in Chicago," I asked as I knew she wanted to talk about her trip and interview.

"It was great as I met my lovely sis and the interview also went pretty well. The faculty who interviewed me were very nice and I faced a lot of questions about our research. I did answer most of them to their satisfaction. In general, I made a great impression about the program and I believe they also liked me."

"That's good. So now how many more interviews?"

"There are quite a few, but the important one is coming up in Rochester at the Rochester General and Strong Memorial Hospital. I was born in Strong Memorial Hospital, so I have warm feelings about that hospital. Bond, let's go to the cafeteria. I'm starving," she said while getting down from her special seat.

We went to the cafeteria after grabbing a sandwich and drink and sat down at the table with bunch of radiology residents.

"Welcome guys, I guess should I say the future Radiology residents?" someone quipped.

I declined to say anything but Jen said, "You can say that if you want. It won't hurt us."

Soon the discussion started about Christmas and Christmas shopping.

One of the radiology residents, I believe his name was Jim, looked at me and asked, "So Bond, what are you doing for Christmas?"

I had to answer something so I said, "Nothing special. Probably visiting a friend of mine in New Jersey."

I hoped that the conversation would end there but there came another question. "Which church do you belong to?" I did not know what to say now so I kept quiet but he would not give up and asked me the same question again. This time Jen came to my rescue.

"Jim, Dr. Bond is from India and he is a Hindu, which is a different religion."

Jim was shocked and he looked at me and said "Really?" He gave me such weird look as if I was from a different planet, making me feel like an alien.

"Jim, you should be aware that there are other religions in this world just like there are different languages."

Someone else commented, "I know little bit about Hindus. They worship idols and don't eat cows."

Now it was Jim's turn. "Really? Why don't you guys eat cows?"

At that point I thought the discussion was fruitless and was going nowhere. So I decided to get up as I had finished my sandwich. But Jen decided to answer his question and said, "Because of their religious beliefs. Bye guys."

Jim persisted and said, "Do you guys put red color on your forehead after you visit temple, isn't that funny?"

"Jim, come on, don't you put some ash on your forehead on Ash Wednesday? Now should we say that's funny?"

Jim did not say anything.

I did not utter a single word and left the place and Jen followed me.

"I am sorry about his questions. Are your feelings hurt?" she asked on the way out.

"No. Not at all. I am fine," I reassured her.

After reaching my office and assuming our usual positions, me in the chair and Jennifer in her 'little' space next to PC, she asked me, "Can I ask you something?"

"Jen, since when do you need a permission to ask me a question? Go ahead."

"Do you feel racial discrimination because of your Indian origin or your religious beliefs?"

"No, not so much as how I sometimes feel in India or when I go to an Indian community function here in the USA."

She seemed surprised by my comment.

"What do you mean? I don't get you."

"For you we all are alike and Indian. But that is a broad term. While in India or here in the Indian community, people start classifying you based on your language and state of origin. That is why I feel more discriminated in India than over here. After meeting fellow Indians, they start classifying you as first as North Indian or South Indian but I am in the middle. From a last name they would classify you as Marathi speaking, Gujju who speak Gujrathi, Tamilian, Telgu and so on. No one thinks of you as an Indian first. In addition, there are so many religions and castes in India, it is just mind boggling and frustrating."

"So if I may ask, what caste do you belong to?"

"I am a mixed caste; my mom is a Brahmin and my dad is from a warrior caste also called Kshatriya in Sanskrit. But to tell you frankly, I don't believe in castes."

"Wow, that is so amazing. I did not know these subtle differences in Indians."

"Yes, there are indeed. And there are basically two types of Indians in United States," I replied.

"Really? What two types?" Jen asked.

"These types are what I have observed so far. These are not based on their castes or place origin but their behavior and their attitude towards the fellow Indians," I continued.

She leaned forward and said, "So interesting. I like when you talk because you rarely talk. But when you talk it totally makes sense. Anyway, please continue. Sorry to interrupt you."

"The first type of Indians are those care about fellow Indians in the USA. If you bump into them in elevators, cafeteria, and other places, they will at least will give you a smile, make an attempt to talk to you, maybe get to know you and sometimes even help you. And it does not matter if they are first generation immigrants like me or someone who is a second generation Indian who are US citizens by birth.

"The other type is, as you must have already guessed, is exactly opposite. They will not make eye contact with you if you bump into them, they don't want to acknowledge that they are Indian or of Indian origin. They will many times put on an accent to mingle into the white crowd they are with and if you ask them if they are Indian, guess what? They will plainly refuse to accept that fact! In fact, they may get annoyed or irritated and try to run away from you! And believe me or not they will always marry a white spouse so they can feel superior and different to the rest of brown people."

"Really? You have very good observations, I must say." After a small pause she asked, "So which type do you belong to Bond?"

I jumped out of my chair and grabbed her arm and said, "Are you kidding me? Of course the first type who cares about fellow Indians."

She laughed and said, "I know that Bond! I just wanted to see how you react, so cool down."

"I knew you were kidding," I said, settling down in my chair.

"So, Bond, does that mean that you won't marry a white girl?" That question came out of blue and I was surprised.

"No, of course not. I don't believe in manmade barriers like caste, race, and religion!" I protested.

Suddenly I remembered something when I was in the Middle East and I smiled.

"Why are you smiling?" Jen asked me.

"I was in the Middle East for some time as a member of Officers Mess of Air Force of UAE. I used to meet a British officer in the bar. Till that time I used to think all Brits are Brits. But when he used to talk about some of his friends he would call them not British. Oh, he is not British he is Irish. So and so guy sitting next to the bar man, he is Scottish, so on and so forth. The funniest part was when he talked about his own country."

"Why is that?" Jen was curious now.

"Once I asked him how often he goes back home and you know what he replied?" I raised her curiosity even further.

"No, tell me Bond."

"He said he almost never or rarely goes to the U.K. It is too expensive to live, it rains all the time, the weather is horrible. Instead, he goes to Mumbai and he had a girlfriend in Ghatkopar!"

She was amused. "No wonder Brits go all over the world! What is Ghatkopar?"

"It is a suburb of Mumbai," I clarified.

To change the topic altogether, which she usually did, I asked her, "Oh by the way, I haven't heard anything about your new or old boyfriends? How is the dating scene? Have you found anyone so far?"

"Oh, no time right now as I'm so busy with interviews and other stuff going on. But thanks for asking. I'm single and unattached and like the way I am," she said while getting down from her position. "Alright buddy, time to go. I'll see you tomorrow."

The next few days were pretty boring for me as Jen had gone out of town for her Rochester interviews and was going to come back after Christmas. I made sure to get her home phone number in Rochester so I could wish her Merry Christmas. I started wondering if there was an Amtrak train from New

York to Rochester. Unfortunately, the website was partially shut down for some reason and there was a large display asking the customers to call the following number: 1-800-AMTRAK.

I was puzzled! How do I dial an alphabet from a phone! I had never done that before. I took the handset and then I found some letters on the key pad. I tried to dial the number 1-800-AMTRAK.

"Hey, are you feeling 'horny' tonight?"

There were some beeps and then I heard a sexy voice on the phone. "Hey, are you feeling horny tonight?"

I was puzzled. "No. Not really. But I am feeling like traveling actually," I replied.

The voice on the other side laughed and said "Oh, so you feel like traveling into the wet pussy land, honey?"

I was even more puzzled. I had heard of Disneyland but not this kind of land. "No, your website is down so I was wondering—"

The sexy voice on the other side cut me short and said, "No Babe, my website is on with all the sexy shots you want to see."

I was a bit suspicious and then realized that this must be some paid phone sex line or some sex talk line. Anyway, after realizing my mistake I said "Oh, I am sorry. I think I dialed a wrong number."

"No problem, sweetie pie, I'm always available to you, particularly when you start feeling horny. Good night, hot stuff," and she hung up. I was relieved then I thought I would ask Jennifer about how to dial the alphabet from the phone.

The next thing on my mind was to buy something for Girish and Priya. I did not have a big shopping list as others did, so did not have to go to malls to spend my time and money. I was looking forward to going to New Jersey and eat some home cooked food.

I reached Girish's house on Christmas Eve, carrying a small gift for them.

Girish opened the door for me and said, "Welcome home, come on in. Seems like we are meeting after ages! Congratulations on your interview."

"Thanks, buddy. I guess the job is half way done. I have to wait till mid-March to see what happens next," I said, giving him a hug. "Thanks a lot for your help."

"Well, we did not do much. It was your effort all the way which brought you here."

"Yes. But I could not have done it without your help. Oh, I bought this small gift for you guys. I am sure Priya will love it," I said, handing over the gift to Priya.

Priya entered the living room from the kitchenette.

"Hi Raju, congratulations!" I was startled as it had been a long time since someone had called me by my real name.

"Thanks Priya and thanks for reminding me of my real name. Almost everyone calls me Bond."

"Hey man, we need to celebrate," said Girish.

"Yes, but not so soon. Let me get residency. It is too early to say anything."

"What about your friend, Jennifer?" queried Priya.

"She did interview with me but I am not sure how will they rank her."

"Let's hope for the best. Do you want a drink? Should I get you a martini, shaken not stirred?" asked Girish, teasing me.

"No. I am not James Bond in real life. I prefer scotch with soda and easy on the ice, please."

Three of us sat down in their living room. I was enjoying my scotch, Girish and Priya were enjoying a glass of red wine.

"So what is the next plan of action?" Priya asked me.

"As of now I am going to wait till the match day which is mid-March and if I get residency, or even if I don't get, I am planning a short trip to Mumbai. If things go as I have planned, then for the next four to five years I will be doing residency in Manhattan."

"Now what happens, just in case, you don't get residency?" came the expected question from Girish.

"In that case I still go to Mumbai but come back and continue with research on the visa I currently have. I hope that if not this year then next year I should get spot in residency. Another better option is to do a fellowship in neuroradiology."

"But how can you do a fellowship without doing residency here?" Girish asked me and I was expecting that question.

"Apparently there is currently a shortage of the fellows in the U.S. so the governing body in radiology has decided to open the fellowship spots to foreign medical graduates, also called the FMGs, provided you have done radiology residency in the country of your origin," I answered almost in one breath.

"Bond, I think that is probably a better option than continuing the research." Priya was super smart and I knew that.

"Yes, I know. I hope I get residency, otherwise I will go ahead with my fellowship plan."

"What about Jennifer? What are her chances of getting a residency in the same hospital?" Priya asked.

"Most likely she should get residency spot in the same hospital but there is tough competition. She may get it somewhere else like Chicago or Rochester, NY."

"Why don't you bring her here next time you come here and we all can go around and have some fun," Priya said. "We want to meet her and I am sure she would like to meet us too."

"Sure, I will. I have already told her about how great a cook you are and she loves eating Indian food. She will be going to Rochester, New York for an interview around Christmas and should be back before the New Year."

"Why don't you guys spend the New Year's weekend with us? We can go to Times Square for the New Year's bash. Unless both of you have a different plan in which case we do not want to be 'kabab me haddi,'" Girish suggested.

"First of all there is absolutely no 'kabab' between us so there is no question of 'haddi.' I am okay with the plan as long as Jen is okay," I replied but was a bit annoyed.

"We have always thought that there is something cooking between the two of you," said Priya.

"There is absolutely nothing between us. We are just very good friends. She had and will in the future have boyfriends."

"Does she currently have a BF?" Girish asked.

"No, right now she is too busy with interviews and other stuff so does not have time for dating. At least this is what she told me." I was trying to explain.

"Anyway, let's eat. I will heat the food. I have made some chicken masala for you Bond," Priya said as she got up from couch.

"I am very hungry and have been looking forward to eating home cooked food after so many days. I am sort of sick of eating American unhealthy and tasteless food in the hospital cafeteria," I commented while filling up my glass with another drink.

We had a sumptuous dinner, and afterward sat down in the living room where Priya served dessert.

"Oh man, I think my stomach is going to burst now," I said as I finished the delicious ice cream.

"So Bond, what is your further plan?" Girish asked.

I was about to say something when Priya interrupted me. "I guess he wants to know about your plans, including marriage."

"I don't know about marriage right now so it is kind of difficult to say. Frankly, I have been so busy with research studies and planning for residency so far that I did not get enough time to think about the whole thing. But I guess I will get married sometime during residency." I immediately changed the topic and made sure that I didn't get bugged about it.

We spent the next few days roaming around city. Priya did a lot of shopping and we did lot of eating. On Christmas we woke up pretty late as we were watching a movie till late night. By the time I woke up and made some tea for me, it was almost ten o'clock. I called Jennifer and she was exited.

"Merry Christmas, Jen," I wished her.

"Merry Christmas to you too, Bond."

"How was it?" I asked in spite of knowing that she would talk to me for about thirty minutes without my prompting. She described everything including Christmas Eve, her last-minute shopping, and what they had baked for Christmas. I also spoke to her mom briefly.

"I know you don't celebrate Christmas but maybe sometime in future you can join us," her mother said.

"Sure, I will," I assured her and she gave the phone back to Jen.

"So what are you doing for Christmas, Bond?" Jen asked me as soon as she got hold of the phone.

"Well, nothing in particular. Eating and sleeping a lot. So you may notice some extra pounds on me when you come back."

"Same here. I haven't jogged for quite some time. I guess I am truly enjoying the holidays."

"Anyway, I won't bother you more. Enjoy the time with your family and good luck for the upcoming interviews," I said to finish the conversation.

"Thank you so much for calling and Happy Holidays to you. I'll see you before the New Year," she said. As we finished our conversation, Priya and Girish walked in.

"So who were you talking to in your early morning phone call?" asked Girish.

"Early morning? It is almost eleven o'clock! I called Jen to wish her Merry Christmas."

"It is kind of early morning for us being the holiday weekend. So how is Jennifer doing?" Priya asked.

"She in Rochester with her mom and sister, enjoying the family time. She also has a couple of interviews lined up in Rochester."

"You should really come here for the New Year weekend," Girish reminded me again.

"Yes, I will talk to her as soon as she is back in the town after her interviews," I assured both of them.

We decided to skip breakfast and had lunch at home since almost everything was closed on the Christmas day. After spending a few lazy days, I went back to my apartment, which was pretty boring. Although the hospital was working it was kind of a holiday atmosphere throughout the week between Christmas and New Year. Dr. Stein was also on vacation and was apparently out of the country. There was a skeletal staff in the department and not much work.

On the day I was expecting Jen back, my phone in the office rang.

"Hey, Bond. I am back in the city." It was Jen on the other line.

"Welcome back, where are you?"

"I'm at the airport right now but should be in the apartment soon."

"It is almost the end of day here. I am about to go back to my apartment. Do you want to meet me in my apartment?"

"No let's meet in our apartment. You still have the key, right? Why don't you grab your stuff and go there and go in even if I haven't reached it yet and I'll see you there."

It was almost like an order and I did not mind at all as I was getting extremely bored in my apartment.

I packed some clothes and headed to Jen's apartment. When I arrived, she had not yet reached the apartment, so I entered with my key, sat down on the love seat, and switched on the TV. As I was watching CNN, Jen entered the apartment. On CNN there was a news story about an eighty-something-year-old businessman getting married to an attractive and young girl. I was watching the news and was quite amused. As Jen came, I switched off the TV and said, "Welcome back, Jen."

She walked past me with her wheeled bag and said "Thanks, Bond. I am so glad to be back." She went straight to her bedroom and said, "Let me freshen up and I'll see you in a bit. I also need to pee. My bladder is about to burst."

I switched the TV on and continued watching the news about the old man getting married to the young girl. Soon Jen came back to living room.

She sat down next to me and said, "Bond, can I ask you to make some masala chai for us?"

"Sure, you can order me. Why don't we talk in the kitchen?"

"Yes. I have to tell you about lot of things. How was your Christmas holiday?"

"It was good. Oh, by the way, Girish and Priya have suggested that we can visit them around New Year."

"That is a fabulous idea!"

I poured the old water from the kettle and filled it up with some fresh water before switching on. "Tell me what happened in Rochester."

She started and as usual was talking non-stop for at least thirty minutes. She told me everything from her interviews to her Christmas celebration.

"Did your mom like the gift you bought for her?" I interrupted her.

"Yeah, she did. She wants to meet you some time, maybe next Christmas or maybe even earlier in summer."

"Why does she want to meet me, Jen?" I asked her.

"I don't know. You can ask her if you want." She seemed bit annoyed.

"Well, I don't have to. I can meet her; I have no problem with that."

We went back to the living room and Jen switched the TV on again. This time it was some Hollywood news/gossip channel. There was again this news of an old man getting married to a young girl.

"I wonder if he can still do it at his age," I commented.

"Even if he can't, he can do with the blue pill."

"I wonder how these young women get married to these old men who would be as old as their grandfather or father?"

"Bond, this man has been married at least three times now. This is his fourth or fifth wife."

"But she is so young . . ."

"I haven't given you a commandment for a long time. It's been a while so I've lost track of how many commandments I've given you so far to Americanize you."

"I believe this will be the ninth commandment."

'NINTH COMMANDMENT'

"Thou needs only money and lots of money to get married and remarried…
For everything else there is the 'Blue Pill'!"

She stood up and said.

"Thou needs only money and lots of money to get married and remarried. For everything else there is the Blue Pill," she said in authoritatively.

"All right, Jen, thank you for the ninth commandment."

"I think I am running out of the commandments now. I may have to stop at nine commandments. I wonder if I can ever give you the tenth one."

"Jen, nine may be enough."

"Well, Bond, I may find something for you just to complete Ten Commandments."

"Or maybe I will give you the tenth commandment!" I said jokingly, and Jen gave me a look.

"So what are we doing for New Year?" Jen asked me, changing the topic.

"As I told you, Girish and Priya have invited me and you to their apartment in New Jersey. That is of course if you don't have any other plans or can suggest something better."

"I would love to meet both of them. I have heard great things about her culinary skills from you."

"Then let's make a plan. We will go there and stay for a couple of days, attend the New Year bash and come back here on the New Year's Day. How does that sound?"

"It sounds good except for the fact that we're much closer to Times Square than they are. So it may be wiser to come back here after the New Year celebration than to go back to New Jersery."

"I think you are probably right," I said after a long pause. "Can I make a phone call to Girish from your home phone?"

"Of course you can. You don't have to ask for my permission," she said, handing over the cordless phone to me. "Do you remember the number?"

"No, I don't but I have my pocket diary in my bag. That is my way of storing numbers and it works!" I went inside my bedroom to get my pocket diary. I called Girish's house and Priya picked up the phone.

"Hi Priya, this is Bond."

"Hey Bond. What a surprise! What's up?"

I spoke to her about ten minutes and chalked out the plan. Basically, we decided that Jen and I would go over to them on the thirtieth and stay overnight and next day we would come back to Jen's apartment and go to the Times Square for the New Year celebration. On that night, Girish and Priya would stay overnight and the next day basically do whatever we wanted to. At the end of our conversation I said, "Let me discuss with Jen. If she agrees I will not call you back. If she disagrees or has something else to suggest I will call you back."

After listening to the plan, Jen said, "That'll work for me. I have nothing else to do anyway."

We chatted for some time and ate the pizza we ordered. After eating, I could see sleep in Jen's eyes so I said, "Jen, I think you are tired. So why don't you go to bed. I will watch some news for some time and then I will do the same."

"Alright Bond. Good night," she said letting out a yawn before entering her bedroom. "Please wake me up. I would love to have masala chai in the morning."

"Good night. I will make some chai and wake you up."

# New Years in America

The next day I woke up and made some chai for us. I knocked on her bedroom door and Jen said, "Thanks Bond. I'll be there in a few minutes."

She came in the living room and we had hot chai.

"Bond, your chai is so good that without it I don't feel like doing anything."

At that point I told her a story of a Marathi stage actor who happened to be a doctor from the same medical school I went to.

"He would come home drunk at odd hours in the morning and wake up this particular guy who used to stay in boy's common room. He would get up at four a.m. or something, get milk, and make chai for this doctor-turned-actor. Only after drinking his chai only, would he leave."

"Wow! I can see in the future that I'll be doing that to you. I'll wake you up at four when I'm on call and order you to make chai for us."

"Yes, I can see that too. But I will have no problem making a chai for you."

Since Jen was a bit tired, we decided to go to the gym for some light exercise. After I finished my exercise, I went to see what Jen was doing. She was working out on a leg exercising machine. After she finished she said, "Do you know why this machine is so favored by all the women in the gym?"

"Yes, I can guess," I said, smiling.

"Then tell me, Bond." She seemed somewhat surprised at my quick reply.

"Because it involves spreading legs," I said and waited for her response.

"Shut up, Bond. Of course not. It's because it tones up legs and helps make us look more sexy," she almost screamed at me.

After our workout, we came back to the apartment, had shower, and decided to have lunch together before Jen dropped me back to my apartment.

The next few days went past pretty quickly. On the thirtieth, I was supposed to go to Jen's apartment and from there we were going to Girish's house.

We basically took a cab to ground zero and took a ferry to New Jersey. As we entered his apartment complex, I stopped and turned around to see the New York skyline.

"What happened, Bond? Why did you stop?" Jen asked me as she almost bumped into me.

"Jen, when I came here for the first time I always used to stop here for a moment to take a look at the Twin Towers. I can't see them anymore and I miss that part so much!"

"Tell me about it, Bond."

I sighed and we went to their apartment building. His apartment was on twenty-fourth floor. Priya greeted us, "Welcome home Bond."

We went inside and I formally introduced Jen to Girish and Priya.

"We already know a lot about you from Bond. You were the one to give him his American name I guess?" Priya asked.

"Yes, that was me, mainly because his name is difficult to remember and kind of difficult to pronounce."

"I can smell some good food, Priya," I said while entering kitchen.

"Yes, there are lots of good recipes I made."

Jen handed over a big wrapped box to Priya and said, "Priya, this a small gift for you guys."

"Come on, you don't have to be so formal but thank you."

Jen and Priya hit it off instantly. At one point they both went in the kitchen and Priya showed her the recipes she had made. Jen was amazed.

When she came back to the living room Girish told her, "Jennifer, there are no formalities in our house. Eat as much as you want and if you go hungry that is not our fault."

"You can call me Jen and I'm sure I won't go hungry."

We chatted for some time and then had sumptuous lunch. Jennifer praised almost everything she tasted including Priya's homemade mango pickle. After the lunch, since I was feeling so heavy, I wanted to take a nap.

"Why don't both of you go and sleep for some time. Jen and I will chat here for some time." Priya practically ordered me and Girish out of the room.

We were more than happy to take nap and woke up around four to find Priya and Jen asleep in the living room on the sofas.

When they woke up, they demanded masala chai from us and we had no choice but to make them what they wanted.

Looked like Jen and Priya had been talking for a long time. Since both were avid talkers, I was wondering who spoke and who was a listener. I guess both had an equal chance. Jen asked her bunch of questions and was trying to get know more about her past in India.

After our masala chai, we decided to go out early. We went to eat biryani at some local restaurant Girish liked in particular. All of us relished it, particularly Jen. Later on, we decided to go to a mall as outside it was bitter cold. Jen and Priya were talking almost continuously. I guess they had a lot to ask one another. At least that is what we figured out. Girish and I talked mostly about his work and my future plans.

We came back home, our stomachs full from the sumptuous lunch and dinner we had.

We decided to watch a movie and there was disagreement over which movie to watch. Girish and I wanted to watch an action movie and Jen and Priya wanted to see a romantic movie. Finally, we decided to watch a Jennifer Aniston romantic comedy, which was of course suggested by me!

After the movie was over, Priya and Jen wanted to talk so we sat down in the living room and chatted till all of us were sleepy. As I had expected, Priya ordered the men to sleep in the living room. Looked like Jen and Priya were going to sleep in the bedroom. They still had the inflatable bed and I happily agreed to sleep on that while Girish decided to grab the sofa. We were too sleepy to talk.

"Morning Guys, wake up," Priya called to us the next morning.

I was first one to get up. Since there was only one bathroom, I went in first to brush my teeth.

"Bond, why don't you make chai for all of us? Jen was praising your tea a lot. Even I want to taste it now," Priya said.

"It is not that great. I think Jen likes it because she is gori mulgi," I replied, using the term for 'white girl.'

I made four cups of hot chai and brought it to the living room. By that time everyone was awake and waiting for my tea.

"Wow, this tea is awesome!" Priya said, taking a sip. "I think now on whenever we meet, Bond will make chai for all of us. What do you think, Jen?"

"I fully support this motion," Jen said with a giggle.

"Now you are our official tea maker, Bond," Girish added.

"Alright guys, I will make tea for all of us. If I don't get residency, I will at least start my chai shop in Manhattan," I said jokingly.

"Both of us will be your first customers for sure," said Priya while laughing.

"Alright, I think we talked enough about chai. Now let's plan what we are going to do tonight," I said as I wanted to change the topic.

"We have the food from yesterday night so we will eat right here guys," Priya said.

"Yeah, let's have lunch here and then head out to our apartment in the city," Jen said.

Both Priya and Girish looked at me when Jen referred to her apartment as "our" apartment.

Priya winked at me. I did not show any sort of reaction and ignored both of them.

By the time all of us were ready to go, it was close to eleven, so we decided to have lunch.

"Wow, this food tastes awesome today," Jen commented.

"Jen, it is like eating chicken biryani. It always tastes better the next day," I said.

"We haven't been to that place where you get awesome Indian food. Last time you promised me we'd go," Jen said, while Girish and Priya exchanged glances.

"Let the weather get little better and I will take you there. In fact, Girish was the one who introduced me to that place!"

"Look at your friend, he just makes empty promises." Now it was Girish turn to face Jen.

"Yeah, I think Bond is right. Just wait for a couple of months and you will enjoy it more. In fact, we can come to the city and we can go there. That guy knows me very well. He speaks good Hindi too," said Girish.

"Oh, is that your mother tongue?" Jen asked.

"No. All of us speak Marathi but Priya being from New Delhi is more comfortable with Hindi," I said.

"But she is from a Marati-speaking family, isn't it?" came one more question.

"Yes, I am but since I lived in Delhi almost all my life, we spoke Marathi at home and I am more comfortable with Hindi and English," replied Priya.

After the lunch, we decided to get ready and ventured out to the Jen's apartment in the city. We took a ferry to Ground Zero and then we took a cab from there to Jen's apartment.

The guy downstairs knew me pretty well so to Girish and Priya's surprise he welcomed me and said, "Good to see you again, doc!" At that moment Girish and Priya again exchanged glances which I conveniently ignored. Jen's apartment was pretty tidy and clean.

"Guys, let me show you around and then you can make yourself comfortable," Jen said, as she slid open the curtains.

"Thanks to Bond, our apartment is clean and tidy. Otherwise it would be pretty messy."

She took both Girish and Priya around and I sat down to watch some TV.

The plan was to go to Times Square for the New Year's celebration but we had not planned anything for dinner.

When Priya asked, "What is the plan for dinner guys?"

I said, "Jen is going to cook for us tonight!"

"I wish I had the skills like Priya has. We can order a pizza if you guys are okay with that. I have some beer in the fridge, also some wine and whiskey if you want."

We all agreed on pizza and since we wanted to eat all veggie pizza, and Jen also decided to try it.

"Let me warn you, Jen, there is no meat in that pizza so may not like it," I told Jen.

"Yeah, I know Bond, but let me try it something without meat."

"You never know, she may like it," Girish said coming to her rescue.

"Are yeh Gore log subah se sham tak meat khate hai," I said in Hindi, which irked Jen.

"Bond, excuse me, no Marati here. You have to speak in English."

"That was not Marathi, I spoke in Hindi," I replied.

"Whatever, Bond. No Hindi or Marati please. By the way, what did you say?" Jen demanded an answer.

"Jen, cool down. All I said was you guys are used to eating meat from breakfast till dinner."

She looked at Priya and asked, "Is that truly what he said?" and Priya nodded. Since I had given a truthful answer it seemed to calm her down.

"I'm glad you're so frank, as always," Jen said.

"Okay guys, cool down. We don't want to start a fight here" Priya said, intervening.

"We are not fighting, Priya, so don't worry," I said and smiled.

"By the way, Jen, you are a minority here. We all are Indians you are the only one who is gori mulgi," I said to Jen and that seemed to fuel more anger.

"Bond, thanks for reminding me, but I know very well that I am in the minority. And what was the meaning of those Hindi or Marati words at the end of your sentence?"

"I told you, remember? Gori means white and mulgi means a girl. So gori mulgi means a white girl."

At that point Priya said, "Jen, have you ordered pizza or we have to order one?"

Due to the sudden change of topic, Jen walked away from me and said, "No Priya, we have to order one. Let's do it."

We sat down and chatted for a while. Jen and Girish had beer while Priya and I had wine. We decided to head out at around nine to avoid the big rush and get a fairly good spot in Times Square. Since it was the first New Year's party after the 9/11 attacks, security was pretty tight. We spent time walking around and were lucky to get a place in an ice cream shop that was packed to its capacity. We decided to sit there and enjoy ice cream till around eleven thirty. We could get a good spot in Times Square for the last countdown. At midnight everyone cheered and wished each other a Happy New Year. We all hugged and then started heading back. The subway was pretty crowded but the frequency of the trains was pretty good. We reached the apartment at around one thirty and all of us were pretty tired.

After returning to the apartment Jen said, "Do you want to chat or sleep?" Girish and I looked at each other and said almost simultaneously, "Sleep!" I guess she wanted to chat so Jen seemed pretty disappointed.

"How are we going to sleep?" Priya asked.

"You guys can use the other bedroom that Bond usually uses. And Bond, you'll have to sleep tonight on the sofa, or I have an inflatable bed you can use if you find it comfortable."

"Yes, I am used to it," I said, which stimulated laughter from Priya and Girish.

Jen got confused. "Why are you guys laughing?"

"Oh, that is because Bond always sleeps on the inflatable bed we bought specially for him when he visits our apartment."

"Bond, can you help me get that bed from my bedroom?"

I went in her bedroom and got the bed out. We had to move the tea table to make space for the bed.

"Alright guys, good night. Tomorrow morning we will once again have the opportunity to drink masala chai made by Dr. Bond."

I was too sleepy to comment on that so I just nodded and soon crashed onto the bed and started snoring. Next day I was the one to wake up first and switched on the news with low volume so as not to disturb others. Soon Jen joined me in the living room.

As she sat down next to me I said, "I am sorry about the meat eating comment yesterday, I did not mean to offend you."

"Oh Bond, I don't get offended so easily," she said in a sleepy tone.

"Okay, then I should try something harsh next time I guess," I said jokingly.

"Hope this year will bring happiness in our lives," Jen said.

"I am sure it will, Jen. More than likely both of us will get residency in radiology. Once we get in, our lives will be set. Don't you think so?"

"Yes, I want to make a lot money and have lots of kids," she said.

"A lot of kids? How many kids do you want to produce?" I asked her.

"At least three, maybe four. What do you think about that?"

"I prefer to have a small family, two kids should be enough!" I commented.

"But why are we talking about kids?"

"I don't know, you started the topic." I said, at that moment Girish and Priya entered the living room.

"I just overheard you guys talking about kids," said Priya as she entered the room.

"Yeah, Jen was saying that she wants to have a lot of kids and make a lot of money," I explained to both of them.

"What about you guys? How many kids do you plan to have?" Now it was Girish and Priya's turn to face Jen.

"I want at least two kids," Priya said. "Definitely not four but maybe three."

"Does it matter to you guys if they are boys or girls?" Jen asked.

"No. It does not matter, Jen. It can be two girls or two boys. All we want is healthy kids. But why do you ask?" Girish asked.

"Well, don't get mad at me, but I've heard that many Indian families prefer boys over girls," Jen explained.

"You are right, Jen, but we not one of those families," Priya clarified.

"Bond, what about you? Do you prefer boys over girls?" Jen turned towards me.

"No. Of course not. I would though prefer to have one boy and one girl. Unless I have a wife who is as beautiful as you, then I will prefer girls over boys hoping they would not look like me but like their mother." Jen seemed to be surprised by my answer. "Well, I am going to make masala chai for you all and you can continue the conversation about kids." I was glad to find an excuse to run away from the future conversation which seemed to go nowhere.

After I made four cups for all of us, Jen said, "Wow, that's a great tea, Bond! Probably the best I have ever had since I started drinking tea."

"Thank you so much but it is probably due to the half and half instead of the non-dairy creamer I usually use," I clarified.

After our tea and breakfast, we decided to watch some TV. While we were watching TV, Priya reminded us about the time.

"Guys, it is already almost eleven. We need to think where we are going to have lunch."

"I'm not too hungry so we can eat dosa or something," Jen said. "Another option is to go to have Mediterranean food at the mobile cart."

"I am not too hungry either," me and Girish said almost simultaneously.

"I think there is tiny south Indian place not too far from here. We can have dosa or idli there," I suggested.

"Alright then we can all get ready and head for the dosa place," Jen said, getting up.

"I think we will have shower when we will reach our home in New Jersey," Priya said.

"I'll have a quick shower and get ready. What about you, Bond?" Jen said as she entered her bedroom.

"I would like to have a shower too before we head out," I said and headed for my bedroom.

"Bond, get ready and we will pack our stuff later," Priya ordered. "We will watch some TV till both of you get ready."

Jen got ready quicker than I and almost everyone was waiting for me when I came out.

"You take more time than a girl to get ready, Bond," Priya commented upon my arrival to the living room.

"Yeah, on the holidays I prefer to be in water for a longer time than usual. Sorry to keep you guys waiting."

"And thus increasing Jen's water bill," added Girish.

"That's okay, guys. Stop teasing him. He is so nice. Bond, I don't mind paying few extra bucks for you," Jen said.

"By the way, why don't you guys stay here after lunch and can go home after having tea or coffee in the evening."

"No, I think we will head out home after lunch. Thanks for the offer though," Girish replied.

"What about you, Bond?" Jen turned towards me.

"I have nothing else to do when I go back to my apartment. I would rather stay here unless you have any other plans to do, in which case I will go back."

"No. I don't have any plans."

"I had made plans to stay here for at least two nights," I said.

"That is absolutely fabulous. We'll go to the hospital together tomorrow morning," Jen said.

Soon we all headed to the dosa place. Since almost everyone was not hungry, we all ordered plain dosas.

"Wow, this is fabulous! I just love the variety of veg food you guys have in the Indian cuisine." Jen said, while relishing the dosa.

"Thanks, I will take the credit for introducing you to the great Indian cuisine."

"Thanks for doing that. I think without the Indian food, my life would have been spiceless! Literally."

After lunch, Girish and Priya decided to take a cab home, and we all parted.

"Bye, Jen, it was so nice to meet you. You can come and visit us any time you are craving for Indian food, either with or without Bond. Only thing is just give some notice so I can cook some extra food for you," said Priya while hugging Jen.

"Thanks for the offer, I would love to come," Jen said. "You guys should also come over to our apartment more frequently, definitely before we start our residency."

"Bond, you take care and see you soon. I think I am going to forget your real name soon," said Girish.

"Thanks to Jen who has baptized me. In fact, most of the staff in my department do not know my real name. Almost everyone calls me Bond," I explained.

"Let us know what happens about your application for residency. I hope both of you get residency here," Priya said. "By the way, when will you guys will come to know?"

"We have to submit our choices by the end of February. The match day, which is the day the results are released, will be somewhere in mid to late March. I forgot to tell you that I will be making a quick trip to India, Mumbai to be specific. If you guys need anything, let me know."

"Really, when are you leaving?" Priya seemed surprised.

"Of course when the tickets are cheaper. Probably the last two weeks of January or early February. I want to be back in the USA well before the match submission."

"If I remember something I need I will let you know. But unlike the past, you get almost everything here, particularly in New Jersey," said Priya.

"Let me know. You can email me if you remember something when I am in Mumbai," I said.

"Bye, Jen see you later."

"Bye, guys. We had a great time," Jen said.

Both of us went back to Jen's apartment.

"So Bond, what's the plan?" Jen asked me while settling down on the sofa.

"I think I am going to take a short nap since we were up late last night, if you don't mind," I replied.

"Nope, I don't mind at all. In fact, I'll probably do the same. If you wake up early just knock on my door and I'll do the same if I wake up before you," Jen said as she entered her bedroom.

Soon I was sound asleep and I was awakened by the knock on my door.

"Bond, it's time to get up."

I came in the living room rubbing my eyes.

"What time is it, Jen?"

"It's almost five, can you believe it?"

"No, I can't believe we slept for such a long time! Let me make some chai for us," I said.

"No, just sit down and we can have chai later on."

"So what's on your mind?" I asked.

"Nothing, just wondering what's going to happen in March?"

"You and I are going to be co-residents." I said in a steady tone.

"Bond, how can you be so sure? Let me reframe my question: how can you be so sure about me?"

"I am pretty sure that you will get radiology residency and more than likely you will get it here," I told her confidently.

She kept mum, and it was clear she did not know what to say.

"Jen, you have done research in this institute, which puts you ahead of everyone else. Not a lot of med students do research."

"I agree, Bond. But there are a lot of good applicants who want to be in our hospital. Many of them have very higher USMLE scores and they come from prestigious med schools like Duke and Stanford to name a few. What if I don't get in here?"

Frankly, I had never thought of that possibility. I was speechless.

"Jen, I am pretty sure that you will get residency somewhere in the country," I said, not knowing what else to say.

Jen did not say a word and stared at me. I could not face her stare so I got up on the pretext of making some more tea.

"Wait, Bond. Would you like if I get residency somewhere else and not here?"

I sat down again. I did not know what she was getting at.

"No, probably not," I murmured.

"Probably? Or definitively?" she persisted.

Oh boy! I was in an awkward situation. Finally I decided to turn this conversation into a funny one.

"Definitely not, because you won't find anyone else to do your calls." I said that while laughing and hurried into the kitchen and switched on the kettle to boil water. Obviously my answer did not satisfy her at all but gave me an opportunity to run away from her and her questions and probably from reality also. Luckily she did not follow me in the kitchen. When I came back to the living room with tea she was watching the news.

"What's in the news, Jen?" I asked her a stupid question hoping not to go back to the topic we were discussing earlier.

"On nothing great, the usual stuff. Main news is about the New Year's celebration from around the world. Right from Australia to United States. When do you leave for India?"

I was sort of stunned by her question. "I am planning to leave in late January or early February. Why do you ask?"

"Bond, be here well before the final date of submission of the NRMP match. I don't want you to get stuck somewhere in India and not been able to submit the list before the final deadline."

"Don't worry, Jen. Even if I get stuck, I can do it from India. Internet is available in India, although it might be somewhat slower than here," I reassured her.

"I know, dear, but it is better that you are here. What I'm saying is make your plans in such a way that even if you get delayed by a few days, make sure you will land here well before the application deadline."

"Thanks for your advice and concern, Jen, but I will be here much before the last date for submission."

After watching the news for some time, we got bored. It was getting dark and cold outside.

"Do you want some wine?" Jen asked me.

"Sure, if you have red wine I would love that."

"I think I do. Come with me."

I followed her into kitchen.

"Wow, this looks like an expensive French wine!" I said while admiring the wine bottle.

"Yes, it is. I got it during the Christmas sale from one of the nearby stores. Now it is your job to open it, Bond. Hope you know how to open a wine bottle."

"Yes, as a matter of fact, I do. Where is the bottle opener?" I asked her while I looked around for one.

"Here you go Bond. Now show me your skills." Jen handed over the bottle opener to me.

I carefully removed the wrapper on the top of the wine bottle and with great precision screwed the cork right in the center, while being careful not to let it drift to the side. After the cork had been penetrated enough, I held the wine bottle with my left hand and with gentle force I pulled the cork. Soon there was a pop and the bottle was open. Not a drop of wine fell on the table!

"Wow, that was awesome!" Jen said clapping.

"Thank you, now if I don't get residency, I hope I will find a part time job in a restaurant to support myself," I said jokingly and suddenly Jen was serious. I could not guess what she was thinking about.

"Bond, can I ask you something, if you don't mind?" Jen asked with a very serious expression.

"Come on, Jen, since when you have to take my permission to ask me a question? Go ahead and ask me whatever is in your mind." I was trying to defuse the seriousness of the situation.

"Have you given a thought to what happens if you don't get residency? Are you going to continue as a research fellow? What about your visa? Oh my god, I am so worried about you now!" She was dead serious.

"Yes, let me explain to you. Now the first thing I want you to do is relax. Let me pour some wine into the wine glasses," I said and poured wine into two goblets.

We went in the living room and settled down in the sofa.

"First of all, chances of that happening are pretty low. Just for the sake of possibility, let's say I don't get a spot in residency here. I have thought about it. There are many options. I can continue as a research fellow and I will get a visa extension also. There is also an option of me getting into the neuroradiology fellowship as I have done radiology residency in India. And the last option is to go back to Mumbai, and I am fine with that too! I have nothing to lose."

"But what is the point of you coming all the way across half of the world and then going back empty handed?" She seemed really worried.

"Well, Jen, if you think about it, I have nothing to lose. I am pretty sure that I will get fellowship in neuro if I don't get radiology residency. I would assume I have sort of wasted a year or so in my career, which is nothing. Most importantly I have found a great person and a very good friend like you. Isn't that worth something?" I tried to convince her and that seemed to calm her down.

"Really Bond, I find it amazing that I have a great friend from a faraway country who I can trust with almost everything. It is hard to believe that we've lived our lives separately for so long and now we are so close to each other!" Jen had tears in her eyes.

"I would say the last few months and the next few months to come by have been the most fruitful months of my life! Of all the places in the U.S., I landed here. I met you just because you were interested in the research project which I was working on, Dr. Stein assigned you and me together for the same! Jen, I strongly believe that we met each other because we were destined to meet. Don't you think so?" I asked her.

"Yes, I do believe in destiny, Bond. But what scares me is what is going to happen to me in the future. I'll feel just horrible if I don't get residency here with you."

"Jen, stop worrying about it. Why don't you speak to the program director or Dr. Stein as the interviews are over now?"

"Bond, don't you know it's against the rules? I cannot talk to them and vice-a-versa. That would spoil my chances of residency for sure," she said.

"In that case, let me speak to Dr. Stein. He knows that we are good friends and—"

She cut me short and said, "Don't you ever do that. You have a much better chance of getting residency here than me and no way would I want you to spoil your opportunity."

"As you wish, Jen, I was just trying to help you."

"Yes, I know, but if I don't get residency here that's not the end of the world for me. I'll get a radiology residency somewhere else. No big deal," she said casually.

"No big deal! Of course it is big deal for me, Jen. What would I do without you?"

She seemed a bit surprised by my reaction.

"Have you booked your ticket to India?" Her question was obviously meant to change the topic suddenly. I knew her tricks pretty well by this time, but I decided not to show my real emotions.

"Yes and no."

"What do you mean by 'yes and no,' Bond?"

"Jen it's an open ticket. I have a date range during which I am supposed to fly," I explained to her.

"So when are you planning to leave?" came one more query.

"As soon as schools start here. That's because the planes are pretty empty and flight tickets are also cheaper," I answered, anticipating her next question.

"Thanks for answering my unasked question too," Jen said with admiration.

"Can I ask you something, if you will give me a frank answer?" Jen asked, looking into my eyes.

I kind of knew what was coming.

"Go ahead."

She took a big breath while looking at the floor, then she turned her gaze towards me and asked, "Will you be getting married or engaged when you're in India? I mean, would your parents force you to get married?"

I was expecting that question from her and decided to give very frank answer. "Jen, that issue will certainly come up. Especially my mom will ask me about my plans including marriage. But I am not going to get engaged or married either."

I heard what sounded like a sigh of relief from her.

"And if your mom or dad asks you why not, then what would be your answer?"

Oh boy. I almost felt like standing in the witness stand and undergoing examination and cross examination. Again I decided that I will give a very frank answer to her.

"I will tell them that I am not ready yet financially as well as mentally to take on a new responsibility in my life when I am not sure yet about my future here in the USA."

There was another sigh of relief.

"Any more questions Miss Graziano?" I asked her.

"No sir, no more questions. You may relax now."

"Have you thought about dinner yet?" I guess it was my turn to ask questions.

"Not really, but what do you want to eat? We can get a pizza or grab a sandwich if you want."

"Frankly Jen, I am not very hungry. Probably I can eat a small sandwich."

"Alright let me order a sandwich and I'll ask them to deliver. I guess you'll have some kind of chicken sandwich?"

She ordered for both of us and I did not bother to ask her the details. By this time, she knew my likes and dislikes.

"Bond, some more wine for you?"

"Yes, sure."

The phone rang as she was pouring wine in my glass. She almost ran towards the phone and I knew it must be her mom or more than likely her beautiful sister Emily.

"Hey, happy New Year," Jen said and then she was quiet for a while, trying to speak something but the person on the other side would not let her speak and I knew it was her sister. Emily was the only one in her family who talked more than Jennifer and while talking on phone she did not let anyone else speak. Soon I guess, it would be my turn to speak to her.

"Bond, Emily wants to say hi to you, do you want to speak to her?"

I knew that the answer to this question had to be yes.

"Sure." Jen handed over the phone to me.

"Hi, Emily, how are you?"

"Hi, Bond or should I say Dr. Bond?"

"Bond is good enough. How was your holiday?" I asked her.

"Very good. How was yours? I suppose you don't celebrate Christmas?"

"No, I don't. But I do enjoy the festive atmosphere. It almost feels like Diwali in India."

"Isn't Diwali the festival of lights you guys celebrate?" Emily asked me.

"Yes, you are right." I was bit surprised. "I have spent most of the holidays with your beautiful sis. So the holidays have been wonderful so far. How about you?"

"I am a senior resident now, which means less calls and more holidays. I also make the schedule so I make sure that I am off on the days I want. What is the scene with your residency applications?" Emily asked.

"I have basically applied over here only. I guess you know about Jen."

"Oh my god, you haven't applied anywhere else? Are you nuts?" Emily almost screamed.

"Listen, Emily, given the current scenario of the interest in radiology, I have no chance of getting accepted anywhere else because I am a foreign medical graduate," I explained.

"Oh I understand. I'm sorry about my screaming."

"That's alright. Most of the residents who are born here do not know about FMGs and their problems. Now, if I don't get residency, I have a very good chance of getting accepted in the neuroradiology fellowship program. I guess I have answered your next question too."

"Yes, Bond, no wonder Jen says that you are such a good mind reader, even on the phone. It was so good to talk to you and good luck for your application."

"Thanks, Emily, and good luck to you too for your fellowship application. I guess you want to talk to Jen," I said then handed the phone back to Jen.

Jen went to her bedroom and I started watching TV. I thought to myself, what are they talking about? God knows. Jen did not come out for a long time and I was getting bored.

When Jen came out with tears in her eyes, I knew something was terribly wrong.

I got up from the sofa, switched off the TV, put my arm around her and asked her, "What has happened? Why are you crying?"

"Emily broke off with her long-time boyfriend," she said, sobbing.

"Why don't you sit down here." I made her sit next to me. "Let me get you a glass of water."

I went to the kitchen and got her a glass of ice cold water and a most importantly a box of Kleenex.

She drank almost half the glass in one sip. "Thank you."

"Now can you tell me please what exactly happened with Emily?" I asked her while patting on her back.

"I don't know in great detail, but when Emily called her boyfriend to wish him and his family a happy New Year, he responded very oddly. He was not talking a lot so Emily asked him if anything was wrong upon which he replied that he wanted to end their relationship. They've been together four years." After saying this, Jen started crying inconsolably.

Frankly I did not know much about such relationships and I did not know how to respond.

If I would have kept quiet, I would have looked really dumb and Jen would have got mad at me so to say something I asked her, "Did he give any reason?"

"No. He simply said he didn't see any point in going further. Poor Emily, I felt so bad for her."

Even I was feeling bad now. When I talked to her a few moments ago, I had no idea about this event. Maybe I should have realized from her tone that something was wrong.

"Don't worry Jen, Emily is a very nice person. I am sure she will find a better person in the future," I said to console her.

"I know my sister very well, Bond. She is a great person. She took good care of me when our parents got divorced. She was there with me in all good and bad times of my life. She is simply devastated now. I felt so bad."

"I can understand very well, Jen. I am also feeling very sorry for her. I had no idea about this when I spoke to her. Maybe I will talk to her tomorrow some time."

"Yes, Bond that's a good idea. I'm sure she'll appreciate it. Let me write down her number for you." Jen got up and wrote down her cell and land line numbers on a piece of paper for me. I kept the paper in my wallet. I realized that she had finished the box of Kleenex I had got for her. She had not stopped crying so I promptly offered my handkerchief to her. She looked at it and then looked at me.

"Don't worry, it's clean."

"No, I was wondering if I can use it."

"Yes, of course. Otherwise I would not offer to you. Please go ahead and use it."

I watched as she somewhat hesitantly wiped her tears and gave it back to me.

"Thanks, Bond" she said.

"My pleasure."

After a pause, I said, "I think you are tired now and you should go to sleep and stop thinking about this whole thing." She just nodded. I went to her bedroom and put her in bed and said, "Let me know if you need anything even in the middle of night. Just call me and I will be there."

"Thanks, Bond, for everything. I'm glad you were with me today."

"No problem, Jen. That is what friends are meant for."

As she lied down in her bed, her hair falling all over the pillow on her side. She looked tired and drawn out but even in that state she looked beautiful. I could not resist myself and I leaned over and kissed her lightly on her forehead and cheek and softly said, "Good night." She seemed a bit surprised by my action but did not resist. In fact, I thought she blushed. I guess this was probably the first intimate contact between me and her, but it was not sexual.

"Good night, Bond."

I got up from her bed and switched off the lights and was about to close the door when she said, "Bond, you can leave the door wide open. In case I need to call you or something."

"Okay, no problem. I will leave it open."

I went to my bedroom and lied down in my bed. I was thinking about Emily. Such a nice girl, good looking, intelligent and witty. Why would anyone do such a thing to her? Why on earth would someone be cruel to her? I guess there was no answers, only unanswered questions. When I was about to fall asleep, I heard the fridge door. I got up immediately and rushed towards the kitchen.

It was Jennifer.

"You did not go to sleep?" I startled her with my question.

"Bond, you are still awake? I'm sorry if I woke you up."

"No. I was just falling asleep. What are you doing in the kitchen?"

"I was thirsty so I thought of getting some ice cold water. Do you want some?"

"No. I think I am fine. Are you . . . okay?"

"Yes, I am fine now. Don't worry. Life will go on, Bond. It's not going to stop for anyone. Why don't you go back to sleep?"

"I will, don't worry."

As I walked back to the kitchen door she said, "Oh, by the way . . ."

I turned around and looked at her. She was smiling a bit and looked at me and turned her gaze down to the floor and said, "Thank you for the kiss." She was obviously blushing.

I thought I missed a heartbeat, but I just smiled back at her. "You are most welcome. Good night again."

I was on cloud nine at that moment. I went back to my bedroom but could not go back to sleep for a long time. Next day I woke up early, had a shower and wore my scrubs again. I was wearing scrubs after a long break. I packed my items in the bag and went straight into kitchen. To my surprise, Jen was already awake and was fixing breakfast for both of us.

"Good morning, Bond. I'm making omelet for us."

"Good morning, Jen. Hope you had a good night's sleep. Let me make some masala chai for both of us."

"Thanks, Bond. Did you sleep well?" she asked me with a wicked smile.

"Not after I came in the kitchen."

She gave me a look.

"Once my sleep is disturbed I cannot sleep well," I tried to explain.

"Bond, you don't owe me an explanation," she said, smiling.

"Or maybe it was your comment in the kitchen." I spoke the truth.

"Bond, I like one thing about you," she said while sipping hot chai.

"And what is that?"

"Well, you are very honest and truthful. At least to me."

"I am honest to almost everyone, not only to you, Jennifer," I clarified.

"What are you planning to do today?"

"Frankly, I don't know. I will probably go over some unfinished small research papers and publications which I started writing with some med students but could never finish them. Why do you ask?"

"Nothing, I was just curious."

"What are you planning?"

"I'll probably go to the library and spend some time there."

"Good, maybe we can meet for lunch then, what do you think?" I asked her.

"Of course, we can. I'll come to your office," Jen said then took a bite of her omelet.

"Let us leave from here together and then we can depart," I suggested.

"Bond, you read my mind."

As we stepped outside, we saw it had started snowing a bit. We were going to take the subway so we were not bothered by the cold and snow. We traveled together on the sub, with Jen talking almost continuously and I listening. She had a habit of switching from one subject to another without any connection between the two. At one point she was talking about her sister Emily and suddenly she started talking about the New York Giants. I was her patient listener. She continued talking as we left the subway station and reached the campus of the hospital. At one point, I had to interrupt her and say, "Jen, I need to go to my room before I go to the hospital. Why don't you go to the library or wherever you want to go."

"Sure, I will. I'll see you at lunch then, bye."

"Bye, Jen, see you later."

I stayed there looking at her till I could not see her. I started thinking about her. Why is she so unlucky in love? She is so nice, sensitive, caring, smart, good looking, and most importantly, intelligent. She was kind of skinny but other than that she had a good figure.

Suddenly I realized that I was freezing in cold weather and snow. I needed to go back to my room and then to my office. I went back the tall dormitory building and was waiting for the elevator when I heard someone behind me and I turned around. It was Madhuri.

"Hi Bond, how are you?" she asked.

"I am great, how about yourself?"

"I am fine. I tried to call you many times and came to your room also. I had planned for a New Year party and wanted to invite you," she said as we entered the elevator.

"I had gone to New Jersey to my college... er... high school friend," I explained to her.

"You seem to have gone for a long time, Bond." She seemed suspicious.

"I was with Jennifer too for a few days so—"

She cut me short and said, "Your relationship with her is getting cozier, looks like."

"Madhuri, I have told you several times that there is nothing between me and her. We are just good friends and that's it."

"There is something cooking between you two. I can smell it. She is in love with you for sure."

"I think there is something cooking in your head, I think," I said and I was relieved that the elevator opened on my floor and I stepped out.

"Look, you are not even saying goodbye to me."

"Bye, Madhuri, see you later," I said reluctantly without turning back as I exited the elevator.

"Bye, Bond," she said as the elevator doors closed.

I was glad as the encounter was over. I went back to my room and was glad to find everything in its place. It had been a while since I had been in the room. I kept my bag in the bedroom and started unpacking slowly, keeping items back to where they belonged. Then there was this handkerchief on which Jen had shed her tears. I opened it and smelled it. It did have the distinctive perfume she wore. It almost gave me a feeling as being close to her. I folded it back the way it was and kept in in an envelope, sealed it, and kept it in a secure place that I could remember. God only knows if after June or July I would ever see her again! That handkerchief would stay as a fond memory of her with me, I thought.

# BACK TO WORK

As soon as I wore my scrubs and lab coat, I got into the mood to work. I gathered a few documents and went straight to my research office. None of the things in the office had changed. Only thing I noticed was bit of dust on the table, books, and the computer and my desk. I got a wash cloth from the department and started cleaning everything. My gosh, I hate dust and I like everything neat and tidy. I cleaned my table, I rearranged the books and cleaned the computer. After everything was nice and clean, I went to see Dr. Stein.

Mary, his secretary, greeted me. "Good morning, Dr. Bond. Happy New Year. How was your holiday?"

"It was great, how was yours?"

"Fine, too bad we have to work today. Right?"

Are you kidding me? Anyway, I was expecting this response. "Yeah, I know. I could have been lying in my bed for a while," I said to please her. I was thinking, I am bored of this vacation now and I want to get back to work. In fact, I was waiting to get back to work and do something productive. If I would have expressed my real feelings, she would have thrown a fit.

"Is Dr. Stein free?" I asked, finally coming to the point.

"Yes, he is. Wait a second, let me tell him that you are here," she said while picking up her phone.

"Hey Dr. Stein, good morning to you. Dr. Bond is here to see you."

I think by this time, most of the people who knew me, which includes me, had forgotten my real name, thanks to Jennifer rechristening me. I thought at one point that I should remind them about my real name. Otherwise when listing the residents for residency selection they will probably look for Dr. Bond instead of Dr. More!

I knocked on Dr. Stein's door.

"Come on in," Dr. Stein said in a burly voice. I think he had not had enough coffee.

I opened the door and saw him rearranging his office.

"How are you, Bond? Did you have a good holiday?"

"Yes, I did. Sir, how about you?" I asked him bit reluctantly and I knew that next five to ten minutes would be spent on how he spent his vacation in Europe and how the New York weather 'sucks.'

"I hate this cold weather," he murmured.

I offered my help to him to rearrange his office, which he happily accepted. While I was arranging the stuff, I briefly told him about my plan about what I was going to do for the next few days.

"That sounds good, Bond. The more you write papers, the wiser you are."

"Oh by the way, can I ask you something?" I asked him while rearranging books in his shelf behind his desk.

He stopped and looked at me wondering what I was going to say. "Go ahead, what's on your mind? Just speak out."

I was bit worried how he would react to this.

"I was wondering if the radiology department remembers my real name. Since Jennifer renamed me almost everyone in the hospital calls me Bond or Dr. Bond. I was worried that while ranking the residents, the program director may list someone with the real name of Dr. Bond, instead of me. My real name is—"

He cut me short "Dr. More, yes of course I know, and I am sure the program director will remember it. I'll make sure he lists you for sure, so don't worry."

I was relieved! Thank god someone still remembers my name!

"And can I ask you something?" Dr. Stein looked at me.

Now it was my turn to get startled. I almost dropped the book I was carrying but managed to save it from falling somehow.

"Are you okay? I have not even asked you anything and I saw you panicking!" Dr. Stein asked me while holding my hand.

"Yes, I am fine . . . I was . . . I was thinking of something else and your question kind of startled me," I said while keeping the book in my hand on the desk.

"Is there anything between you and Jennifer?" he asked me looking directly into my eyes.

I opened my mouth and looked at him, puzzled. I had to take a minute or so to recover before I said, "We are very good friends and that's it. As you know we never had boyfriend-girlfriend kind of relationship. I think we like each other, that's it!"

He did not say anything but took the big Starbucks coffee cup in his hand and sipped his hot coffee.

I gathered some courage and asked him, "Er . . . why do you ask?"

"Why don't you sit down and let me explain to you very briefly."

Both of us sat down. "As you know, our residency program is one of the top most in this country."

*Oh my god! Is he going to tell me that I am not getting into this residency?* Seems like he was a mind reader like me, because immediately he said, "Don't worry, it's not about you. I will personally make sure that you get a spot here, no matter what."

If it's not me then why the hell is he telling me? Lord, it must be about Jennifer! I shriveled.

He took a big breath and looked at me and said, "It is about your friend Ms. Graziano. That is why I asked you what kind of relationship you have with her. I am not at all interested in your or her personal life."

I could feel my small bowel contracting. I kept my face as expressionless I could, swallowed a big gulp of accumulated saliva in my mouth, and asked him, "What is it? She is not getting a spot here?"

"No. I never said that. She is a very good candidate, she has done research so that puts her ahead of others. But her USMLE scores aren't very high and there are many applicants who have higher scores than her and are eager to join this program. I am going to try my best to get her in because personally I also like her." I was surprised by his word 'also.' Does it mean you and me? God knows.

I uncrossed my legs as I realized my right leg was getting numb.

He took a pause and continued, "I thought I would call her and let her know but then I thought I would let you do the hard job since I thought you know her better than me."

At that moment, I thought the whole room was spinning around me. Me doing residency without Jennifer being in the same program? I could not digest the idea. She had been also assuming that I would be with her, maybe doing her calls or at least helping her survive first few brutal calls. How can I tell her? Impossible. I thought I would let Dr. Stein do the job and take the pressure off me.

No, but that is not correct. She had been with me literally from the first day in my office. I was stunned and did not say a word. I looked at the floor and was wondering what I should say.

I looked up and said, "Is there any way out? I mean, is there any way she can get it here?"

He took a long pause and then sipped his coffee and said, "Yes and no."

I was even more puzzled by his answer. I had to ask him "I don't get it."

"Well, Bond, she cannot improve upon her score now. But she can do well in other interviews and try to do her best. She should not take it for granted that she will eventually get in this program. I mean she has to take every interview as seriously as the one she did at our hospital. Would you mind telling her that?" he asked me in his gruff voice.

"Yes. I do. I will try to explain to her," I said very reluctantly and got up from the chair. I was dismayed and disappointed. "Thank you very much, sir, for your time. I appreciate it."

"You are welcome, Dr. Bond," I heard him saying as the door closed behind me.

From Dr. Stein's office I walked to the research area offices. Although my body was doing what it was supposed to do, my mind was somewhere else. At one point, I knew I would have to give the not so good news to Jen. How and when was a big question. As I was walking, I thought that I should probably ask her if she was done with her interviews and when she was going to do the final ranking. That seemed like a good idea. By that time, I would come back from Mumbai and then I could discuss with her in detail.

I reached my office and almost everyone was still in festive mood. We all greeted each other with a 'Happy New Year' and asked each other about their holidays. Looks like almost everyone had a good time. Some of the foreigners like me went for a short trip to their respective countries. Akio asked me if I went to India.

"No, I am going in few weeks now. It is a short trip for about ten to fourteen days," I replied.

"How about you, Akio? Did you do to Japan?"

"No. I will probably go at the end of this year. I don't have that much money right now."

After chatting with my co-research fellows, I checked my email. There was an email from Emily wishing me happy New Year. Gosh, I had not called her! I picked the phone and dialed her number and to my surprise she picked up.

"Hi Emily, this is . . . Bond."

"Hey, Bond, how are you?"

"I am doing well, how are you doing? Oh by the way, is it a good time to call you?"

"Actually a perfect time. I finished my rounds this morning, there were not many patients. The patients I have are quite stable and doing well. I have some time now before I go for lunch. Tell me, what's going on?" she inquired quite casually.

"I just saw your email and wanted to wish you a happy New Year too. I . . . don't know what . . . I mean, I am sorry about your break up. I mean . . . I heard from Jennifer and I thought I would call you to see how you are doing."

"Thanks for your call. Actually, I'm doing quite well now. I'm not still over with it but I'm much better than I was . . ."

Suddenly my pager rang and I had to cut short my conversation with Emily.

"Emily, I think I will call you in the evening, my pager just went off. Is it okay if I call you around sevenish?"

"Yes, that should be okay. If I'm not at home do leave a message so I can call you back. I would love to talk to you so do call me, bye."

The pager was from a weird number, but when I called I heard Jen's voice.

"Hey Bond, your number was busy so I had to page you."

"I was talking to your beautiful sister."

"Oh, how is she doing? I called her in the morning but got a voice mail."

"She is doing okay, but we did not finish the conversation so I am going to call her in the evening."

"Bond, thanks for doing that. Oh, I called you because I was going to the cafeteria and I was wondering if you want me to join there or should I come to your office instead?"

"I have not finished checking my hospital emails so why don't you come down in few minutes and then we can go wherever you want."

"Okay, sounds good. I'll be there in about ten minutes," she said and hung up the phone.

I went over the work emails pretty quickly. I took a look at the week ahead and realized there was not much time left before I headed to India. I didn't have much to pack, maybe a few gifts for Mom and Dad and for my brother. Anything I would buy here would be made in China anyway so there were hardly any items that were made in America!

I also looked at some unfinished papers and letters to the editor I had started writing. I wanted to finish at least few letters before leaving for Mumbai. Maybe Jennifer could help me in few. Just when I was thinking about her, there was a soft knock on the door and I knew it was her.

"I was just thinking about you, Jen," I told her as she entered.

"Really? You flatter me. Or did I do something wrong?"

"There are quite a few letters to editor which are almost done and I was wondering if you can help me finish them before I leave for Mumbai?"

"I should be able to do that, no problem," she said while sitting on the desk right next to my PC. "Shall we go for lunch, if you are ready?"

"Sure. Let me just shut off my PC and we should be on our way to lunch." I logged off and shut down my PC.

"Man, I feel like eating Chinese food today. Do you mind? Hope they have Chinese something today in the cafeteria," she said as we walked to the cafeteria.

"I don't mind at all provided they have Chinese food in cafeteria. I don't want to go outside to eat Chinese in this super cold weather!"

Luckily they had something Jen liked, so I also got some fried rice and chicken and we sat down in a corner table for lunch. As usual, Jennifer was almost continuously talking about something even with her mouth full of noodles. I wasn't really paying attention; at the back of my mind I was thinking about what Dr. Stein had told me about her. She immediately spotted that.

"Bond . . . where is your mind? You aren't paying attention to what I am saying. Tell me what's in your mind."

"Well, I was . . . I was just . . . thinking about my India trip ahead, I am sorry," I lied.

"Bond, you're lying to me. You know that you are not a good liar. Tell me what is going on?"

"I am telling you the truth. I was just getting nostalgic about my trip ahead of me," I firmly said and she seemed believed me.

Then I thought something and said, "I wanted to ask you something."

"Go ahead, ask me."

"I am going to submit my NRMP list after I come back from Mumbai. What about you? When are you planning to do that?" I asked after gathering some courage.

"I have few more interviews coming up. Also I don't want to wait till the last day so I think I'll submit it some time in the first and may be second week of February. Good you reminded me. Remember, don't wait till the very last day as the website gets really overwhelmed. So don't be a procrastinator. Maybe we can submit together after you come back from Mumbai so I can maybe help you while you do that."

This was exactly what I wanted her to do.

"I think that's a great idea. Just in case I am delayed or something, please wait for me to come back. And just in general, don't underestimate any interviews you have left. Prepare for them as well as you would do for any other interview."

"Yes, of course. But why do you tell me that now?" She seemed a bit suspicious.

"No, nothing special, I thought radiology is so competitive so I thought I will just reiterate what you are already doing." I tried to sound as normal as I could and it seemed to work.

There was a moment of silence and she said, "Bond, I'll miss you while you're gone."

"I will miss you too, Jen. I will have somewhat limited access to my email so maybe I will call you a few times. How about that?"

She looked at me and said, "That sounds great to me. I can hear your voice. Emails don't have a personal touch."

"Be aware of the time difference so it may be odd times like late night or early morning when I will call you, so don't get mad at me."

"Oh boy, you're getting too formal with me now. Of course I understand and I promise I won't mind. But do call me."

"Yes, I will. Do you have any doubts?"

"I have no doubts," she said. "And just in case, even if you wake me up in the middle of night, I won't mind for sure."

"Ok, let's go to my office. I have to finish some work. Let me show you some stuff and where you can help me, if you have time now."

"Yes, I have some time but I'm going back to library to study after that. I have a couple of interviews coming up," Jen replied.

"That sounds good to me. Where are your interviews, by the way" I asked while getting up from the cafeteria chair.

"There are few in Phili and one in Syracuse, NY. I'm also giving a few interviews for my internship in the city."

Later on, we went to my office and I went over some papers with her and explained to her what she needed to do.

"All right, I got everything I need from you. I'll work on these in between my interviews and let you know by email. I'm headed to the library now. Adios," she said as she headed toward the door.

"Jen, what was that you said in the end?"

"Adios means good-bye in Spanish," she said with a smile.

"Hasta la vista, baby." I also used my Spanish from the movie *Terminator 2*.

"I'm impressed, Bond. Maybe next time you should use some phrase from a Bond movie. I think that would be more appropriate. See you later." As she left, I made a mental note of calling Emily that night to conclude our unfinished conversation.

I started to work on one paper and decided I should submit the manuscript before I left for India. I did not realize how the time passed by. Oh boy, it was almost five, I thought to myself as I looked at the clock.

I quickly checked my hospital email before I switched off the computer. I rearranged my paperwork and left my office. It was very cold outside but my walk from the hospital building to my dorm was short and quick, even though it was quite freezing for me. I almost ran to avoid the biting cold. As I got to the elevator, I saw Madhuri waiting for the elevator.

"Hi Madhuri."

"Hi Bond. What's going on?"

"Oh nothing. I wanted to tell you that I am going to Mumbai in couple of weeks so if you want send something with me or get something from Mumbai, let me know."

"Sure, I will. Thanks for letting me know," she said as we entered the elevator.

"Why are you so formal with me? Both of us are from Mumbai so—"

She cut me short. "Are you going alone or Jennifer is accompanying you?"

I was bit annoyed by her question. But I decided not to elaborate on that and said, "No. Of course not. What would she do in Mumbai?"

She did not say anything. My floor came so I left the elevator and said, "Good night, Madhuri."

"Good night, Bond. I will let you know if need anything from Mumbai. Thanks."

"You are always welcome," I said as the elevator door closed behind me.

*Gosh, what is she thinking?* I thought to myself. I decided not to think too much about her. I entered my room and switched on the kettle to make tea. Soon the phone rang. To my surprise it was Madhuri.

"Hey Bond, it's me, Madhuri."

"Yes, tell me."

"Before you go to Mumbai I thought of inviting you to my room for dinner. *Ekdam* Marathi style food. You can bring your friend also with you."

"Which friend are you talking about?" I was a bit puzzled.

"Jennifer."

"Sure. Do you mind if I bring her?"

"No. Of course not."

"Let me know the date and I will ask her. I am sure she would love to taste Marathi food."

"Sure. Let me check my schedule and I will email you."

"No problem, thanks for inviting us."

"Not a problem. See you later, Bond"

I put the phone down and went to my kitchenette to make my tea. I switched on the news and suddenly remembered I had to call Emily.

I switched off the TV and looked at the piece of paper on which Jen had scribbled numbers for me.

I called Emily and she picked up.

"Hi Emily. This is me."

"Yes, Bond. I recognized your voice. I have your number, so let me call you back right away."

I put the phone down and within a minute or so the phone rang.

"Hi Bond, what's up?" It was Emily.

"Not much I guess. How are you?" I asked her.

"I am actually tired but we can talk. In fact, I would like to talk to you. Frankly, I had a long tiring day at work. A lot of patients with complications so I had to transfer a few to the ICU."

"Oh, I am sorry. But I called you in the morning and we did not speak for a long time." I started talking knowing that if I kept quiet, she wouldn't give me a chance to speak, so I continued without a break. "I am sorry about your break up and was thinking about you. How did it happen?"

"Everything was going quite well, at least that is what I thought. We didn't have any recent fights other than minor differences. When I called around holiday time he sounded very weird and cold to me. I asked if anything was wrong and he didn't say anything. Then suddenly out of the blue I get an email from him saying that he doesn't want to continue with the relationship. That's it. There was no explanation, no indication as to what went wrong."

"Did you try to call him or meet him?"

"Yes, I tried his phone several times. He won't answer his phone or return my messages. I wanted to meet him but not without talking to him first. I also emailed him several times saying that whatever has happened is okay but I need to sit with him and talk because I need to know what happened, what went wrong. Was there any mistake from my side? . . . And things like that. But I think he is trying to avoid any person-to-person meeting with me. I think just because he doesn't have a good reason to tell me."

"How are you dealing with the whole turmoil?" I got a chance to ask her as I thought she was sipping some drink.

"I am a very headstrong girl but I do have emotions like anyone else. I was very upset at first and I took a couple of days off, which I think was a big mistake. I just sat in my apartment and cried. I spoke to Jen and our mom and both of them supported me. I should have worked and not stayed home alone, that was sheer stupidity. So after a couple of days, I decided there was no point in sitting alone and crying and I decided to go back to work. In fact, I volunteered to work some extra hours to distract me from the whole thing. I'm much better now."

"I hope you are not drinking . . . I mean . . ."

"No. I don't resort to alcohol in my challenging times. No, absolutely not, so don't worry. Anyway, what is going on with you?"

"I will be going to Mumbai for a couple of weeks. When I come back I will hopefully start residency here in radiology."

"I am so happy for you. Jen is quite lucky that she will have a co-resident and a good friend like you."

At that point, I said, "Emily, can I share something with you about Jennifer?"

I thought she suddenly was more attentive than before although I could not see her.

"Sure, tell me. We're not only sisters but we are really good friends too. And we almost share everything with each other," she said in almost one breath.

"Dr. Stein called me in this morning and told me that there are many applicants with better USMLE scores than Jen. Although because of research, Jen has advantage over others, she does not have very high scores. He said that she may or may not get residency here in our hospital." I paused wondering what she must be thinking.

"Go ahead Bond, I am listening," Emily said.

"He also said that . . . she cannot and should not assume that she will get into residency into this program and should take other interviews seriously too and—"

She cut me short. "Bond, you know that she doesn't have a very high score. Because of her research, she was thinking she would have a good chance in your program. But looks like she may not. Gosh, this is serious."

Hearing her reaction, I thought that this must be a more serious matter than I thought.

She continued, "Jen has been dreaming about doing her residency at your hospital since she started this research with you. She thought her research would place her in high position ahead of others. I really don't know what else can she do to make her chances better."

There was no response from me so she continued, "I need to talk to her. Do you have any suggestions, Bond?"

I was clueless but decided to say, "I think she needs to take other interviews seriously and while ranking the programs, she needs to make sure to give preference to the programs in a thoughtful manner. I think you can convey this to her without disclosing the conversation between me and Dr. Stein."

"Yes, of course, I'll talk to her and don't worry, I won't disclose anything about our conversation or your conversation with Dr. Stein." After a brief pause she said, "Bond, I believe you are going to Mumbai, when are you leaving for your trip?"

"In a couple of weeks, in fact I planned my trip so I can be here well before the deadline for submission for match."

She did not say anything immediately and I thought she must be thinking about something so I asked her, "Emily, what are you thinking about?" I thought she was bit surprised.

"Bond, I know you can't see me. How did you know I was thinking?"

"I just guessed it since you did not say anything."

"Yes, I was thinking. So both of you plan to submit your preference list after you come back from Mumbai?"

"Yes, that is correct. I have told her specifically to not submit the final list until I come back. Once I come back from Mumbai, both of us will submit our lists."

"That is good. So Bond, what are your plans for Mumbai?"

"No plan as such. Just meet family and friends. That's it."

"Any plans to get married?"

I was taken aback by her question about marriage!

"No, absolutely not. Who gave you this idea?"

"No one. There was a girl in my residency program. She was from north India, Delhi to be specific. She went to India just before starting her residency and came back married or engaged to guy from Delhi who was also a doctor. So I thought it is a kind of tradition in India."

"No, you are wrong. There is no such tradition. But why do you ask?"

"I was just curious."

I thought there was something more than curiosity in her question but I decided not to dwell any further into this sensitive topic.

"All right, Bond, have a safe trip to Mumbai in case we don't talk. Thanks for your call."

"Not a problem, Emily. You can count me on this. You take care of yourself."

"I will and you too take care, bye."

After our conversation, I sat in the couch for a while. After sometime, I switched on the TV set to get some news around the U.S., and hopefully around the world. I finally got up from the couch and decided that I must start packing for my trip. I looked up in the closet and found the bag I had brought during my first trip to the United States, feeling quite nostalgic. I removed the bag and wiped off the dust that had accumulated over the past few months. I started packing slowly and then realized that I needed to buy a few presents for Mom, Dad and my younger brother. Looks like I needed to make a trip to the mall and buy some Chinese-made goods and carry them over all the way to Mumbai as presents from the United States. Although I decided that I will make a sincere attempt to buy goods made in the U.S., the chances of findings these things were almost nil. I went to bed a bit early and fell asleep immediately. I had a weird dream and I woke up. It was a bit early, but I got up and decided to go in to work. At around nine, my phone rang. I picked up wondering who would be calling me at this time; it was Jen.

"Hey, Bond, how are you? I'm at the airport waiting to board my flight so thought I would give you a buzz."

"Thanks how are you?"

"I'm great, just wanted to kill some time so thought I would call you."

There was nothing specific to talk about so I said, "I am fine. I woke up early due to a weird dream."

"Really? What was it?"

"Like Gandhi did in India to boycott goods from the UK, at one point Americans decided to boycott goods made in China!" I said and I could hear some giggling on the other side.

"So what is so weird about it?" came her question.

"We sort of burned all the goods made in China and made a huge bonfire of the things in the middle of Times Square like we do in the Hindu Festival of Holi, but guess what? Everyone was naked."

"Really?"

"Yeah, because there was hardly anything to wear as almost everything is made in China!"

She started laughing and said, "Who all were there in your dream then?"

"You and me some other random people we work with at the hospital."

"Oh my god, Bond, you saw me naked? Shame on you," she screamed.

I was sort of embarrassed by her reaction but in order to pacify her I said, "Don't worry, I don't have photographic memory of my dream and I only saw you from behind" upon which she started laughing hysterically.

"Bond, I was just messing with you. If you saw me in my birthday suit, I saw you too, right?"

Now it was my turn to get embarrassed!

"But it was my dream so theoretically you did not see me!" I clarified. As I was about to add something I heard some announcement in the background.

"Hey, Bond, I think it's time to board now. So see you later and don't get too cozy with your naked dreams! Bye." She hung up the phone without waiting for my reply.

# THE LONG GOOD-BYE AND MUMBAI

The next few days passed quickly. Jen was in and out of the city for her remaining interviews. I made every possible attempt to make sure that she took each and every interview seriously. I believe Emily had talked to her without divulging more details. She looked kind of depressed but told me she would do her best in the interviews. Unfortunately, some of the interviews she had were for intern positions so these were not so important as the radiology residency interviews. I did not see her as often as I used to, but we decided to meet over dinner one day before I embarked on my trip to Mumbai. Finally, I finished my little shopping practically in one day in the mall. As expected, I did not find anything made in the USA. Almost everything was made in China. Some goods were made in Indonesia, Thailand, and even India!

Finally, one fine morning my office phone rang. It was Jen.

"Hey, Bond, I'm back in the city and you know what? I'm done with all my interviews."

"Great, how did the interviews go?"

"Most of them were good. No big problems with any radiology residency interviews. But no one promised me to rank high or anything like that."

"Given the current scenario of heightened interest in radiology, I am not surprised at all."

"Bond, let's meet for lunch. I'll come to your office around noonish."

"Sounds good to me. I will wait for you."

I decided to wrap up my day's work and was checking my work email. There was a soft knock on the door and the door opened. I was so deeply engrossed in reading my mails that I was a bit startled. Jen burst in and looked at my reaction.

"Were you watching some porn when I came in?"

"No, of course not. I was just checking my work emails. Even if I wanted to watch the porn I am not stupid enough to do it here at work," I said while switching off the PC. I stood up and Jen grabbed me by my scrubs and gave me a warm hug.

"You smell good, Bond. How have you been?"

"I am great, how are you? Looks like you have lost some weight since I saw you last time."

"Yes, I might have. I guess I was traveling so much for interviews I didn't have enough time to eat, plus the stress of interviews. Anyway, let's go for lunch, I'm starving. I have to tell you a lot about the interviews."

I had guessed that part and was mentally ready for it.

We grabbed some sandwiches and were lucky enough to get a table near the window for the two of us.

Even before I could bite my sandwich, she asked me, "Bond, can I ask you something?"

"Sure, go ahead."

"Is there something you're hiding from me?"

I was about to choke on my first bite. "No, absolutely not. Why do you ask?"

"I got a call from Emily a few days ago and her tone was bit odd. She was trying to tell me how serious I need to be with my other interviews. It was kind of the same thing you were saying the other day when we met in the cafeteria. I don't know why there was such a sudden change in your and Emily's tone. Have you heard anything that my chances of getting residency here are low or something?" There came a direct question.

I took a deep breath and looked into her eyes, and said, "Jennifer, I have no inside information about the residency program and whom they are ranking higher or lower. Sometimes gut feelings are also important. It was just my gut feeling and Emily might have thought the same. That's it." She seemed to believe me.

"Tell me about your interviews now." As I expected, her description was detailed about each interview, including what impressions she had about the program director and chief resident. As usual, I finished eating since I was not talking much, mostly nodding and maybe asking a few questions in between. But she was not too far behind me, eating as well as continuously talking. Finally she described how her last interview went and described how she got delayed on her last flight due to snow.

"So what's up with you Bond?" she asked me.

"Nothing much, it was kind of lonely without you. I have been slowly and slowly packing for my trip to Mumbai. I bought some gifts made in China and will give them as gifts from United States!"

"How many more days before you leave?"

"About ten to twelve days. It is going to be a very short trip though. I will barely see my family and some friends and before I realize, I will be packing to come back to the United States."

"I can drop you at the airport. I suppose you are flying from JFK?"

"Yes, it is JFK. But no need to drop me. I will take a cab."

"Are you crazy? You will spend lot of money on a cab. No way. Now that the interviews are over, I have lot of free time. I'll drop you and pick you up. Just give me the returning flight details to me when we go back to your office," she demanded.

"Alright, I will go with you and come back with you, baby. I should consider myself lucky that a beautiful and sexy girl will be my escort! Let's go to my office," I said, getting up from the table.

"Yes, James Bond always has a sexy girl with him, so consider me as your Bond Girl." She seemed to like the idea.

As we were about to leave for the office, I saw John walking towards our table. He was wearing a large brown T-shirt with large ATM logo written on it.

He almost yelled at us, "Hey, y'all. I want to talk to you guys, hold on." From his voice and body language I thought he was in bad mood. Maybe the Cowboys lost again to the Giants, I thought. But it was something else, much more serious, at least for me!

He looked at me angrily and said, "Amigo, you cheated me. You are not for Texas, not even from the United States! Maybe you are not even from this planet." He came towards me in a rage and held my scrubs and said, "Tell me why lied to me. Why did you pretend to be a Texan when you're not even an American! Why did you play with my feelings?"

I was shocked but kept my cool. As promised Jennifer came to my rescue. "Hey John, cool down. It was me who made him do all those things so leave him and talk to me." He seemed to have little bit calmed down. He turned his attention towards Jennifer and gave her an angry look.

"You're my arch rival because you're a New York Giant's fan. Tell me why you did this!" he shouted at her.

"First of all, sit down here please," she requested and he sat down. "I just did it for some fun. Nothing else! Believe me, I like Texas and Texans, and for the record the Cowboys is a good football team. I think they're just going through some rough times. I told Bond to pretend he's from Texas and told him exactly what to say when he meets you. So don't blame him at all!"

John took a deep breath and said, "Thanks for the nice words about us and specially for the Cowboys! Now tell me truly where is Bombay and who is Bond?"

"Well, Bond is an immigrant from Bombay which is really not in East Texas but from west coast of India. His real name is Raju More." At that point even I was surprised that she could remember my real name, which I had almost forgotten!

"Bond is not even Christian but he is a Hindu, which is a different religion practiced in India and other parts of the world!" At that point John gave me a weird look which I totally ignored. "But the bottom line is that he is a very nice guy, extremely intelligent, and he's doing some awesome research here, which is going to benefit our country and all of us here!"

She continued, "He already is a radiologist and may stay here to do pursue radiology residency and is planning to enter academics, which is really nice of him because he is going to teach future residents and fellows."

That seemed to have changed John's mind a bit. He looked at me and said, "Wow, you came all the way from India to work here! I'm impressed! Probably I shouldn't complain so much about missing Texas. Anyway, I'll see you around but let me tell you: Don't mess with Texas and Texans!"

Then he got up, gave us a smile, and left the cafeteria.

I let out a sigh of relief and said, "Thank you for telling him the truth finally! By the way, why was he wearing a T-shirt with an ATM logo on it? Does his dad work in a bank or something? But I faintly remember that he is a farmer growing corn in Texas!"

"No, Bond, you are wrong. ATM actually stands for Texas A and M, which is the undergrad college he went to. If you had noticed the 'T' was larger than A and M letters! So it does not refer to the bank's ATM. Get it?"

"Oh yeah. I get it now!" I said, while trying to remember the logo on his T shirt.

After that interesting rendezvous, we went from the cafeteria to my office. I sat down on my chair and as usual Jen sat on the table next to my computer, crossing her legs. I pulled up my flight details and gave a print out to Jen.

"Let's see, you're leaving on Friday from here and coming back on Saturday. That's easily doable. I can drop you and pick you up too. No problem, Bond. That's a saving of at least a hundred fifty dollars or probably more for you, Bond."

"Great, thanks a lot Jen."

"Come on, don't be so formal, Bond. This is the least I can do for you."

"Do you want me to call you just to remind you?" I asked her.

"Aren't you going to call me anyway? I mean, I hope so."

"Yes, of course."

"Yeah, it might be a good idea to call me to remind me, although I'll note it down and track your flight online just in case it's delayed or something."

"Sounds good to me."

We chatted and after some time she said, "Bond, I'm going to my apartment and crashing. Would you like to come with me?"

"No thanks. I have to finish some projects and I would prefer to be in my room for at least a couple of days. Thanks for the offer though." Frankly, I was tempted by her offer but had to refuse. I was sure she was not very happy about it either.

After Jen left, I wrapped up my day's work and left my office. After making hot chai for myself, I sat down sipping it and started wondering if I had finished shopping for my India trip. I went over the list in my mind and realized that I had bought most of the items I needed for my trip. I looked at my pocket diary and checked my pending work. I had made a note somewhere in the diary about a present I was going to purchase for Jen from India. I was wondering what should I get for her. Maybe a small but elegant replica of Taj Mahal, I thought would be quite appropriate.

The next few days passed by fairly quickly. I was quite busy with my last-minute paperwork and packing. As my travel date came by closer, I was both sad as well as ecstatic. Ecstatic for obvious reasons and sad as I thought I was going to miss something, but I did not know what I was going to miss. New York City, my work, or Jennifer. Probably it was Jennifer. We kept seeing each other almost every day, most frequently during lunch hours. One day over lunch Jennifer said, "Bond, how about dinner tomorrow at my apartment or unless you want to go to an expensive restaurant?"

I was a bit puzzled. "Jen, we meet almost every day for lunch. What is this one for? Any special occasion?"

"Well, no special occasion as such. I thought I would give you a nice farewell dinner before you leave for Mumbai."

"That is very nice of you but I am not going forever, just for few days."

"I know Bond. But I thought we would have something together before you leave. Unless you don't want to. I'm not forcing you."

"No, no I don't mean that way. I am fine having dinner with you at your apartment. I don't want you to spend a lot. Keep it nice and simple. And you know what I like and what I don't."

"Yes, I do. I'll order some Indian food from outside if that is okay with you."

"Yes, that is fine."

"I'm sure you don't want me to cook Indian food. That would be a disaster. I wish I could cook like Priya."

"I would rather go to Indian restaurant in that case. Oh, one more thing," I said as I remembered something.

"What is it Bond?"

"I would prefer to have a farewell dinner with you at least few days before I leave. I mean I don't want to eat a full and heavy dinner the night before I leave."

"Let's see." She pulled up the calendar on her palm pilot. "You're leaving on this Friday, right? How about Wednesday night?"

"That will work for me, how about you?" I asked her.

"Perfect for me as I hardly have any work on that Thursday so I can come late."

"Great, I am looking forward to this dinner."

"Me too. Do you want me to remind you?" Jen asked me.

"No. I guess we will meet on Wednesday for lunch so you can remind me at that time. But I won't forget anyway. By the way…"

"Now what is it, Bond? Don't tell me that you can't make it on that day?"

"No, no. I suddenly remembered that my friend from Mumbai who stays in the same dorm, her name is Madhuri, I think you have met—"

She cut me short. "Of course, I remember her," she said with obvious distaste.

I was taken aback by her memory as well as her reaction.

"Whoa… whoa calm down, baby. I met her by accident one day and mentioned to her that I will be going to Mumbai. Anyway, long story short, she has invited both of us for dinner before I fly to Mumbai. She is going to cook authentic Maharashtrian food for us," I said in one breath thinking Jen might interrupt me.

"Really, I am surprised. Why me, Bond? You can go to her apartment and have a good time. I don't care."

I sensed some jealousy as well as some anger so I tried to convince her.

"She knows that we are friends so she invited you too. I think it is a nice gesture and you should meet her and maybe you will like her and the food she cooks."

"Alright, fine, as long as you guys don't speak exclusively in Marati, I'll go."

"Thank you, Jen. Don't worry, we will speak in English, I mean we will speak American. So may be Tuesday night we can go to her apartment and Wednesday we meet. Sounds good?" I asked her.

"Yes, but if she starts some nonsense, I won't keep quiet," Jen warned me.

"I don't think that kind of situation will arise," I said, trying to convince her.

"Well, I hope so."

"Alright then. I will confirm with her and maybe call you tonight."

"Alright. Adios."

"Hasta la vista, baby," I said trying to imitate the Terminator.

After the day's work, I went to Madhuri's apartment. Luckily I found her.

"Wow, Bond what a surprise! Come on in have some tea with me," she said.

I could not decline her offer.

Over the tea I asked her about Tuesday evening.

"That works out well for me too," she said while looking at her schedule. "In fact, I am finishing early that day so I will have enough time to cook. I suppose Jennifer is coming with you?"

"Yes, of course, thanks for inviting her too. She loves Indian food," I said.

"Not a problem, Bond. I will cook some chicken. I suppose you eat chicken?"

"Yes, I do. Listen, don't make too much food and cook something simple. I don't want you to—"

She cut me short and said, "Bond, come on, I am going to cook for me so two more people is not a problem at all! Don't be so formal with me."

I thanked her again and asked, "Shall I bring something?"

"Well, I don't drink and I don't understand about wines so if you want to drink you can get some wine of your choice," she replied.

"All right, sounds good. We will meet on Tuesday at seven or later if you want?" I asked her.

"That is fine with me but don't be late. I am working the next day and my shift starts pretty early," she warned me.

"No, of course we won't be late. I will let Jen also know. Bye, good night."

"Bye good night, Bond," she said and to my surprise gave me a warm hug.

Tuesday evening arrived pretty fast. Jen came punctually to my apartment. I opened the door and was surprised to see her in an Indian top. "Wow, you look fabulous!" I said.

"Thanks, Bond," she said while entering the room.

"I like your Indian top. Where did you buy this one?" I asked her.

"Emily and I went shopping in Chicago last year and I think I bought this then," she said as she sat on the love seat.

"Do you want anything to drink?" I asked her.

"Nope. Let us go to her apartment if you're ready."

"I am, so let us go. Let me get the wine bottle and corkscrew. Oh, and thanks for making it happen," I said.

"Anytime for you Bond! I hope we get along well," she said with a sigh.

"I hope too."

We left my apartment and went straight to Madhuri's apartment.

"Welcome, Bond and welcome Jennifer," Madhuri said. She was all dressed up.

"You look so pretty," Jennifer said.

"You too, Jennifer. Wow, I love your Indian top."

Thank god, I thought at least the beginning seems to be good.

"Here is wine and roses for you," I said, handing over the bouquet to her.

"Bond, thank you so much for the beautiful roses. Why don't you open the wine and start while I get my mango juice," Madhuri said.

We settled down and started drinking wine.

Madhuri got hot samosas as appetizers and Jen seemed to love them.

"Wow, these are awesome. Did you make these at home, Madhuri?" Jennifer asked.

"No, I got them from superstore. Try the other one, that is chicken samosa," Madhuri said, handing over the plate to her.

"Wow, this is one even better," Jennifer said.

Well my worry was slowly turning into a beautiful but unexpected dream! Both of them seem to hit off pretty well and started chatting sometimes totally ignoring me! At one point, Madhuri took her to show her wardrobe and saying,

"Feel free to borrow these if you like Indian tops. I have lots of them. I can pass it on to Bond if you want to wear these." I was about to faint. These girls were almost fighting in their first ever meeting and Jennifer was super mad at her. Now they are behaving like BFFs! Well that is how it is I guess. It won't take much time before I hear them calling each other with names, I thought.

The dinner was fabulous and uneventful

"Bond, I can't believe you grew up eating this kind of food," said Jen at one point.

At the end, we had dessert and it was about the time to leave. Believe me or not both of them were in tears!

"Thank you so much Mads," said Jennifer while hugging her. Well, there you go, Jen is good at christening or rechristening people. She changed my name from More to Bond and now it was Madhuri's turn.

"Jen, you should become a Christian missionary in future," I joked.

"Why do you say that?" Jen asked me with a question mark on her face.

"No. You changed me from Dr. More to Dr. Bond or just Bond. Now you baptized my friend Madhuri to Mads. I am sure you will be very successful being a Christian missionary!" All of us had a great laugh.

"You know what Jen? I think we should meet without Bond being present. We will have a great time together!" said Madhuri or Mads.

They hugged each other and exchanged phone numbers.

Finally, we left Madhuri's apartment and went back to mine.

"Do you want to finish the wine?" I asked her as I was carrying the unfinished wine bottle.

"I don't think so. I have to drive."

"You can sleep in my apartment if you want. I will sleep on the sofa outside."

"Not a bad idea," said Jen.

We finished off the wine quickly.

"Bond, I can sleep here if you want," Jen said, indicating the sofa.

"No. I think you should sleep inside and I will sleep here. I wish I had another bedroom like you have but this is what I have got to offer," I said apologetically.

"No worries, Bond. I was feeling bad for you that you have to sleep on sofa in your own apartment!"

I think we were drunk or tired or may be both because I fell asleep pretty quickly and I suppose she did too. The next day she woke up early and left to go to her apartment to get ready. We'd decided to meet in the office to finish off some incomplete work.

The next day, I spent the morning in my office doing some work and we met for lunch.

"Bond, you are not eating a lot," Jennifer said, looking at my plate.

"I am keeping extra space for the dinner," I said jokingly. "What should I bring for the dinner?"

"Nothing, just bring yourself and good appetite."

Soon we were joined by a bandwagon of Indian doctors, most of them were fellows or residents from different parts of India. I had met some of them but not all. As they joined us, I introduced them to Jen, at least the ones I knew.

Other guys introduced themselves.

"So how is the land of opportunity treating everyone?" I asked. "Sharma how was your day today?"

"I am on trauma service and at around five this morning I got paged from ER about a girl who was in a car collision and had a hand fracture."

"So why did they call you?" someone asked.

"This is the weird thing about American medicine. The funny part starts now, I had to go and do rectal exam on this young girl in her twenties," he said.

"You did rectal exam for a hand fracture? Are you insane?" I asked him.

"No I am not. My chief resident in trauma service paged me and told me to do it. Apparently, she was in a car wreck and someone in the same car had Level 1 trauma. It seems we have to fill up this so-called trauma sheet for everyone in the car. Everything on the trauma sheet was checked except for PR to look for fresh bleeding. So, I had to do rectal exam i.e. PR on her so that the sheet is complete and she can go home!"

"Wow, that is crazy"

"These crazy Americans," someone said.

I warned him "Hey, one white American woman is sitting next to me, so be careful."

"No worries, Bond, I admit we are a bit crazy," Jen said.

"Well, it was embarrassing for me and for her too," Sharma said. "I had to explain to her why I am doing PR on her for a hand fracture!"

Someone else pulled out a newspaper and said, "Look at this. Americans are rejoicing because home sales went up by point two percent last month and retail sales went up by point one percent and they are celebrating on Wall Street! I frankly don't know what to say!"

"In America, the economy is consumer driven as you know so these indicators are important," Jen tried to explain.

"Where is the manufacturing? China produces and America consumes. Who gains in this process? It's obvious," Vijay said.

It was my turn to jump in the conversation. "I am not an economist but I fail to understand how the American economy can improve when we don't manufacture anything but consume a lot."

And we all looked at Jen for her comment or explanation.

"Guys, I am just like you. Only difference is that I happen to be born here. So I cannot explain or defend what is happening. I'm a silent spectator like you guys."

Suddenly someone changed the topic. "Hey, Jen do you know if we can park in the parking garage on the weekend?"

"I guess you can park there on weekends and holidays. But if you park on a weekday, like I did once, you'll get a ticket," she explained.

"Ticket? What ticket? A movie ticket?" someone asked.

"No, sir. When you get a fined for a traffic violation, you get what is called a ticket. It is like a fine which you have to pay," Jen explained.

"Oh I got it," someone said.

"Even I did not know that you call that a ticket!" I said.

"Well, Bond, there is always something new to learn every day in America, you see," Jen quipped.

Suddenly someone got paged and he left to answer the page and everyone else also realized that the lunch hour was almost over and left to go to their respective assigned duties or shifts.

Soon the table was empty. We chatted a little bit after that and Jen got up and said, "I am actually leaving now so I'll see you tonight. Bye."

"Bye, Jen see you tonight." I too grabbed my plate and got up.

I went back to my office and checked and replied my office emails, grabbed some paperwork on the desk and went through it, shredded the old ones, and basically cleaned my desk.

I put on my coat and headed to my apartment. I wondered if I should buy something so I went to the grocery store across the street. I looked at their wine selection and grabbed a bottle of white wine. I went to my apartment had a shower and wore my blue jeans and a white turtleneck T-shirt and a navy blue sports jacket. I looked at myself and said, "I look pretty smart!"

I decided to take a cab instead of the subway. Luckily it was a relatively warm day so I could do without a cap and gloves. I reached her apartment building in about fifteen minutes and hopped out of taxi and went straight to her apartment on the fourteenth floor.

I rang the bell. When she opened the door, I was surprised to see her in a red velvet sleeveless dress. She had done very light make-up and had a different hair style. For a moment, I thought I was in a wrong apartment.

"Hey Bond. Great you're on time. Come on in."

After I heard Bond's name, I was sure that I was in front of the correct apartment.

"Hi Jen, you look beautiful in that red dress. And you look somewhat different today. Is it your hairstyle?"

"Yes, probably. Usually I don't have any specific hairstyle. I do whatever is most convenient and fast and most important, practical. And by the way you look sexy also," she said, giving me a hug.

"I got some white wine for you."

"You mean for us!"

"You are absolutely right. Let me open the wine," I said while entering the kitchen.

"Go ahead, Bond, you know where the wine opener is."

"Yes, I do. I know most of the things in your apartment."

I came back to living room with two wine goblets filled with wine. Looked like Jen had made elaborate preparations. The breakfast table was covered with a white table cloth. The dishes and glasses and cutlery were well arranged. The food was ordered from outside and she transferred it into her bowls and the *Nan* was covered. The room was well lit and Jen had a few scented candles burning.

"To our everlasting friendship," I said while clinking glasses.

"And to our future residency together," she said upon which I did not show any emotion or reaction.

"You look gorgeous and beautiful."

"Thank you so much."

"I am glad that we are not having a candlelight dinner," I said.

"I thought of it but I knew that you hate those. By the way, the wine is good. Is it California wine?"

"Yes, I believe so."

"I ordered some butter chicken and your favorite chicken biryani too."

"Thanks, I think by this time we pretty much know what we like and don't like don't we?" I asked her.

"Of course, we do. So what are your plans for Mumbai?" Jen asked, taking a seat on her leather recliner.

"No plan as such. Basically meeting family and friends. Many of my classmates practice in and around Mumbai. A friend of mine is arranging a small get together for me so I can meet all my friends in one place rather than going all around the town. There are some friends from my school and high school too and I will be meeting them too. I have sent emails well in advance to meet them."

"That sounds good to me. Are you planning any touring or sightseeing?"

"No, not really. I don't have much time in Mumbai. The time flies by very quickly," I said while finishing my glass of wine.

"Some more wine?" Jen asked me.

"Sure, if I drink too much, I will stay here," I said jokingly.

"Oh, were you planning to go back at late night? No way, I won't let you go. Of course you're staying here. So drink as much as you want," she said while pouring wine in my goblet.

"Are you serious?" I asked her.

"Hell, I am serious. You had some clothes here which I washed and kept back in your bedroom so you can wear those. Tomorrow morning you can go to the hospital from here or I can drop you if you want."

"I never thought about it," I said.

"Well, Bond you are going away for two weeks. I have not cooked but at least arranged this dinner for you. By the time we chat and finish the dinner it's going to be late. You're still too new in this city to go all alone late night."

"Why, is someone is going to rape me?"

"No, although I cannot deny that possibility. You may get robbed and killed and I am more worried about that than you getting raped." She was a bit furious.

"Come on, I was just joking," I said, laughing.

"I knew you were joking but I was just telling you the reality."

"Don't worry I will stay here and got to the hospital tomorrow morning. Are you happy now?"

"More than happy now. Oh, I forget to tell you that I have some small samosas I baked. Let me get those," she said while entering kitchen.

Frankly, I don't really enjoy appetizers. For me they mean killing your appetite rather than enhancing one. But I did enjoy the hot samosas Jen had baked.

"Wow, these are really good. Where did you get these?"

"I went to a nearby grocery store that carries a lot of frozen Indian stuff, and I asked the owner about some Indian appetizers and he showed me these. These are awesome!"

We sat down with bunch of samosas and finished them pretty quickly.

"I am already full. I am not sure how much I will eat now," I told her letting out a burp.

"Don't worry, we can have a late dinner. Some more wine?" Jen asked me.

"Sure. How is the wine?"

"Pretty good. I like it."

We chatted for a while before realizing that it was getting late and decided to have dinner and chatted over dinner. By the time we finished, I was so full that I did not have place for a dessert.

"I have ice cream and cheese cake. Which one do you want or you can have both?"

"Jen, I think I am going to skip that. I am really full. I hope you don't mind."

"No, I think you are right. I am full too. I think we had too much butter chicken. I'm going to skip that also. You can take some cheese cake with you if you want," Jen said while getting up from the chair.

"Let's clean up," I said.

"Thanks for helping."

"No problemo. I never feel that I am a guest in your place. When I meet someone, I instantly know if I can connect with that person or not. When I met you for the first time in the reading room and then we were walking to the cafeteria, I knew that we were going to be great friends. Our wavelengths match with each other's. Whereas with someone else whom I don't like so much, I have to struggle to understand him or her." Jennifer put down everything in her hands, folded her arms, and kept staring at me.

"What happened? Did I say something stupid?" I was a bit surprised by her response.

"No, keep talking. I like whatever you are saying. When you start talking I feel I should just keep quiet and keep listening to you. Usually I'm talking a lot and you are listening. So don't stop, keep talking."

"I know I don't talk a lot. But when I talk or say something, people have complimented me for my thoughts."

"Okay, I'm sorry. I shouldn't have stopped you. Let's clean this and we can sit down and chat till we feel really sleepy and then we can go to bed. How's that?" Jen asked me while picking up the bowls and dishes.

"Sounds good," I said.

"My only condition is you will talk and I will listen, which does not happen too often."

"Fine, I will talk. Once I start talking you can't stop me and don't blame me if you get bored," I warned her.

"No. I won't get bored although if it's too late, I may fall asleep."

"In which case, do you expect me to lift you and take you to your bedroom?" I asked her.

"No. But you can lift me, I'm not that heavy."

"You may not be heavy, but I am not very strong either!"

Finally, we settled down with me in the recliner and Jen in the love seat.

"Why don't you tell me about your childhood, your family, your life in Rochester, New York?" I asked her before she could ask me.

"I don't remember a lot. I have some memories. Some of what I am going to tell you basically comes from what my sister and mom have told me in relation to our childhood photographs I had."

"No problem, tell me," I said.

Jennifer got up from her sofa and went inside her bedroom and got an old-looking album.

"I can't show these unless you sit next to me, right here," she said pointing to the place next to her on the love seat.

"Alright." I sat right next to her. "Jennifer, you smell very nice. Is this why they call 'scent of a woman'?"

"Maybe, I don't know. You figure it out yourself," was her reply.

She started with the first picture in the album and it seems that there was story for each and every one. There was no picture of her dad. I asked her about it.

"I believe there were a few pictures of my dad with us but my mom removed them. I have seen his picture at home accidentally but my mom did not want us to see it. He was never in our lives. I think I told you that he left us when we were kids and never bothered to see us."

"Do you know where is he and what is he doing?"

"No, in fact I even don't know if he is alive or dead. My mom may have an idea. In the beginning, he used to send some money but later on he stopped even that."

Jennifer then continued with her photos and the stories associated with them with great passion. I'd had three to four glasses of wine and it was getting pretty late. I was feeling extremely sleepy and tired. At one point, I almost fell asleep.

"Bond, hey, Bond. Wake up. I think you need to go to bed. Why don't you go to your bedroom and sleep. I think you should have something for you to wear in your bedroon and a fresh set of your clothes and underwear. If you need anything just knock on my door. Come on, get up, I'm in no position to lift you up. Let me help you."

"No, I am fine, I am just too sleepy. I am sorry we could not even finish your first album."

"That's okay. I'll tell you the rest later after you come back from Mumbai. Anyway, we'll have four more years to hear stories of each other during residency."

"All right, thanks a lot," I said, yawning.

"Good night."

"Good night, Jen. Please wake me up in the morning."

I went in the bedroom and changed into my PJs, brushed my teeth, and crashed onto the bed. I fell asleep pretty quickly and was awakened with a knock on the door.

"Hey Bond, can you wake up? It's time to get ready."

"Oh really? Thanks, Jen."

"I'll fix breakfast for both of us."

"Good, let me take a quick shower and I will be ready soon."

By the time I finished showering and was ready, I could smell an omelet.

"Wow, the breakfast is ready," I said entering the kitchen. "Jennifer Graziano in action"

"Now I want to see James Bond in action making awesome chai for both of us."

"Of course and you don't have to say for both of us. I am not going to make only one cup."

Soon we sat down for breakfast.

"Did you go to gym already?" I asked.

"No, I'll go in the evening. Oh by the way I'll be at your apartment on Friday at eleven so we get to JFK well before your flight."

"Sounds good to me. I will be ready and waiting for you."

"Great. The chai is awesome, as usual"

"Thank you, so is the omelet," I said while taking a bite.

I took a small pause and looked at her and said, "Looks like you have changed a lot since I first came to this apartment. It was so shabby that I was shocked. It reminded me of Jennifer Aniston in *Along Came Polly*. And now it is always neat and tidy."

"It was you who made me change. I realized how important it is to be well organized. It makes life much easier! Thanks a bunch!"

"I am glad I could change you. The worst thing would have been me getting disorganized, like Ben Stiller."

"I know, I'm glad that didn't happen," Jennifer said while picking up the dishes and cups.

"Let me get my bag and other stuff and we should be ready to go."

"Bond, leave your unwashed clothes in the bag in the closet. I'll wash them and give them back later."

Soon we headed out to the hospital. Luckily it was not snowing, although it was cold.

As we were walking though the campus, I said "I will go directly to my office since there is no point in going to apartment right now. I think we have lunch with the department colleagues today so I may not see you till tomorrow."

"No problem. I wasn't planning to stay too long at the hospital. If I remember something, I'll send you an email or give you a buzz."

"Sounds good."

We stopped in the big hallway on the first floor of the hospital and departed after a quick hug.

I went to my office and checked the hospital email. There was nothing exciting. I went to Dr. Stein's office and chatted with him for couple of minutes. He wished me good luck on my trip and said he was looking forward to having me as a resident in the department. We met again at the department lunch. A lot of residents knew that I was leaving for Mumbai so they wished me well. I was glad that at least now they knew approximately where Mumbai was!

I cleaned my desk after lunch and took some of the papers and went straight to my apartment and took a good nap. I woke up and started packing up a few more things. I realized that the final packing would happen only on the day I leave. As the day of my departure was coming closer and closer, I was getting a bit restless and nervous too.

Finally the day of departure came. I woke up early without an alarm even though there was no need. I guess it was just a different state of my mind. I got ready too early and then sat down to watch some news. The weather was not too bad. At around ten thirty or so the phone rang and of course it was Jennifer. "Hey Bond, I'm about to head out, so depending on the traffic I'll be there in about twenty minutes or so. Are you ready?"

"Yes, dear, I am. I will come down in about fifteen minutes or so."

"Sounds good to me, see you soon," she said.

I switched off the TV and checked important documents such as passport, ticket, etc. I did not have to wait too long for Jennifer as I saw her car nearing the apartment complex shortly after I went down. It was cold and it had snowed little bit the previous night.

The car was warm and cozy. "You look great," I told her as soon as I sat down.

"Thanks. Let's go. You never know how the traffic is going to be."

Luckily the traffic was not bad. We reached the airport earlier than expected. On the way, she did not talk a lot as usually she did. She just said, "Hope you have your ticket, passport and other important documents."

"Yes, I do, don't worry."

Luckily we could easily find a place at the curb to park. Both of us got out and I took the bag from the trunk.

"Thanks for the ride. I will miss you."

"Of course, Bond, I'll miss you, too," she said and gave me a tight hug and also a kiss on the cheek. "Take care Bond and don't forget to call me."

"No, I won't. You too take care of yourself and be good."

"I will," she said and I could see her eyes getting wet.

"Bond, I can't wait too long here, so I better move. Don't stand here too long, it's really windy here," she said, releasing me from her hug.

I stood there like a statue looking at her car till it disappeared. The cold windy weather outside did not seem to bother me. My eyes started watering, not because of grief but due to the cold wind. With heavy heart and sad mind, I started walking to the airport check-in counter. There was a long line in front of the check-in counter, however much less what you would expect in the middle of summer or during the holiday season. I checked in my bag and collected my boarding pass. At immigration, there was not any problem. I realized that while leaving United States, they don't really bother, since you are leaving the country. The officer just looked at me and stamped my passport and handed it over to me, "Happy Journey," he said. The security check was quite painful. Since I was traveling outside the country for the first time after 9/11, I realized there were strict security checks.

"Thank you, sir," I said and collected my passport and went straight to the duty free shop to look at some stuff. Are you kidding me? The duty free shop prices seemed to be higher than regular prices but I had no way to compare. Anyway, I bought some Marlboro cigarettes and went to the liquor shop. While I was looking at the whiskey section, a young smart lady walked towards me and asked, "Are you looking for the Johnny Walker Black Label, sir?" I looked at her name batch which read 'Mitchell.'

"Mitchell, yes indeed. How did you know?" I could not hide my surprise.

"That is what most Indians buy or prefer to buy."

"Oh I see, market research, huh?"

"No sir, no market research, just common sense and observation. Here you go, sir"

She handed over the bottle to me.

"And if you want to walk with me, I will check you out at this counter, sir"

"Sure," I said and followed her.

"I'll give you extra five percent discount also."

"Wow. That's nice of you. Thank you."

"No problem, sir. If you don't mind, I need to check your photo ID."

As she bent down, she exposed her big cleavage, showing at least one third of her large breasts.

Great, I thought. Five percent discount plus free boobs show. Looks like I am having a great day!

She handed over the bottle in a big bag and the receipt.

"Thank you, sir, have safe journey."

"Thank you and have great day!" I said, and I left the counter.

I kept the box of cigarettes and the liquor in my hand bag and walked towards the gate.

Luckily, the flight was on time. There was a brief halt in London's Heathrow airport and then the next flight to Mumbai. The flight from JFK to London was uneventful. The service was good as the flight was not full. The halt in London was bearable. Again I felt odd as I was one of the few brown skinned people. Odd man out, I thought. The flight to Mumbai was almost full. Luckily the guy in the airline security did not harass me as they did to me last time.

Of course! I was traveling to India. While coming back to USA, I was sure they would harass me.

The flight to Mumbai was full of Indians, as I would expect, but I saw a few whites. The lady next to me was from Kansas City and had never traveled outside of her state or the country. She was going for some business in Mumbai and was freaked out. When she came to know that I was from Mumbai, she asked me, "Are there snakes or tigers on the roads in India?"

Now it was my turn to get shocked. "No, of course not."

"I heard you guys worship snakes and give them milk?"

"Oh that is just one day. And that tradition is sort of falling apart now. You should not worry about it at all."

After this conversation, I gave her a brief lecture about the greatness of Mumbai and gave her tips to survive in that city. Apparently, she was going to stay in Oberoi Towers in downtown.

"You are staying in one of the finest and poshest hotels in Mumbai. You should have great sea view from your room. You will feel as if you are in New York," I told her.

"New York? I have never been to Manhattan except when I had to catch a connecting flight from JFK to London."

"Well, then it would probably look like the downtown of the city you have lived so far."

She asked me if she could have my phone number, which very reluctantly I gave her.

"Don't worry, I won't call you unless it is absolutely an emergency," she said.

"Don't worry about your stay in Mumbai. I am quite sure that you would want to come again."

"Really? We'll see."

"Oh by the way, let me give you one smart tip also."

"What is it?"

"When you get a drink in any bar or restaurant, make sure they don't add ice."

"Why?"

"The ice as you know is made from water and we don't have any control over that. Many times the water may be dirty and I have heard people falling sick due to the ice. As almost everyone makes sure to drink good and safe bottled water but forget about the ice part."

She was impressed. "Thank you so much. You are so smart. You must be a doctor. I feel much better now."

After some chatting, both of us fell asleep and I was awakened by the lights in the aircraft being switched on.

Soon there was an announcement in English followed by Hindi that we would land shortly. I have realized that the Indian flight attendants who make the announcements in Hindi speak in such a manner as if they are born in some English-speaking country and are ashamed to speak our own national language. Come on, give me a break, gals. Can't you speak pure Hindi? Are you ashamed of being an Indian? No matter how much accent you put on while speaking Hindi, you can't hide the color of your skin. Anyway, while I was in these thoughts the plane landed at Mumbai airport.

I was glad that at the immigration counter I spoke in pure Marathi with the guy. It feels so homely now, I thought. I chatted with the guy for a while. He was originally from Kolhapur.

Customs did not give me any problem since I had nothing to declare. When I stepped out of the airport, I realized that the weather in Mumbai was really nice at this time of the year. There are only two seasons in Mumbai, summer and monsoon! There is no fall and hardly any winter. But January and February is probably the best time of the year to visit. In fact, whoever used to ask my opinion, I would say visit in those months. It is not hot, not too cold, and most importantly no rain.

I got the pre-paid cab and reached my home. We have a small two bedroom apartment in central Mumbai. In Mumbai lingo it is called a 'flat.' Our home or flat to be precise was in a nice somewhat upscale suburb of Mumbai called *Shivaji Park*. I could recognize the roads and buildings around our home. When I reached the building, I could not recognize it as it had been renovated and painted after I had left Mumbai. Although it was after midnight, my parents were awake and ecstatic to see me, so was my younger brother. My mom was wearing a household saree and I thought she had some more lines on her forehead since my last meeting with them. Both my parents were shorter than me but not overweight. I thought my dad had some more grey hair since I had seen him. Both of them were somewhat sleepy but warding off the sleep to see me and to hear from me. My Aai (mom) wanted to talk a lot to me. We chatted for a while and then all of us realized that it was almost two in the morning and decided to continue the conversation later on the next day. I did get a chance to show them the gifts I had purchased for them. The next day almost everyone including myself woke up late. We continued our chatting through the breakfast and lunch. After lunch, almost everyone including me were so sleepy that we decided to take a nap. I made sure that I didn't oversleep. As my clock was reversed, I was sleeping when it was day time in America and I was sleeping when it was bright and sunny in Mumbai. The next day, I realized that I had to call Jennifer. My parents had phone in our flat but we could not make international calls from home as they had opted out of that choice. There were many telephone booths which were managed by a live person in order to restrict the time of calls and number of people. I went out late at night and called her.

"Hello?"

"Hi Jen, this is me."

"Hey, Bond, how are you?" she almost screamed.

"I am great, how are you doing, babe?"

"I'm great too. How was your flight?"

"Very good, absolutely no problem. Both flights were less crowded. How is the weather in New York?"

"Oh, what do you expect! Another cold day here! How is the weather in your Mumbai?"

"Gorgeous! It is in seventies over here. Bright and sunny."

"Bond, I envy you and your Mumbai weather. Enjoy! Anyway, I was just going to the gym. Thanks for calling. Call me later. How is your family? Please give them my regards."

"I will, Jen. I will call you later. Bye."

The booth from where I made the call was managed by a big guy.

"Who, your girlfriend in America? Must be Gori."

I just gave him a look and I said, "No. Just a friend and she is not Gori she is Kali."

"Why, you don't like goris?"

"Black is beautiful," I said while paying him. He probably did not understand English!

*None of your business*, I said to myself. *Just tell me how much I owe you and let me go, man.*

Luckily I did not get any more questions from him. Why are these guys so crazy about white girls, anyway? None of my business too.

I was amazed and amused by the changes in Mumbai I had seen. Although there was development but it was quite chaotic. Mumbai was changing rapidly. There were tall towers in place of small buildings. Shopping complexes were being built. The chawls, the old tenement apartments in the Mumbai suburbs, were slowly being demolished. I was feeling somewhat sad that the charm of the old Mumbai was being lost. My classmates in private practice were flourishing. Thanks to a friend of mine, I could meet some of my classmates in one place. Most of them were questioning my decision to go USA.

"You would have been a practicing radiologist in Mumbai or wherever you wanted. You are talking about starting residency now? Are you crazy?"

"Yes, I am, maybe or maybe not."

Suddenly lot of my female classmates surrounded me.

"Do you have a girlfriend?" one of the girls from our class asked me.

"Nope. No girlfriend."

"Oh man, you better use your organ otherwise one day it may fall off due to disuse atrophy," one of the gals joked and almost everyone laughed.

"Hey, he may be having a boyfriend not a girlfriend. You know people stay in America and they change," said another gal.

Suddenly I realized that I am being ragged by these gals so I said, "Listen, I am a straight guy, okay? So no boyfriend. As of now, no girlfriend. Alright let's talk about something else, guys."

Finally, I was able to divert the topic of discussion into something else. I was amazed the way some of them had put on weight! The girls from my class were drinking wine and all sorts of alcoholic drinks as if it were water. Almost everyone was talking about their practice, how much money they were making, the expensive cars they owned, or even worst case, their neighbors owned, sending their kids to expensive private schools. Almost everyone complained about their sex lives. Basically, there was not time for sex! Although what amazed me most was that the girls from my class complained about their sex life more than the guys! Even some guys and gals had extra-marital affairs and had divorced. Anyway, by the late night when it was time to say good bye and good night, almost everyone, including me, was drunk. I woke up late next morning and realized I had not called Jennifer for at least a couple of days. I went to pay phone booth and I called her and spoke to her for a few minutes. She was happy that I called her.

"Hey Bond, it's so cold here and it's been snowing like crazy. I'm so jealous of you being in Mumbai. How's it going?"

"Pretty good. How about you, Jen?"

"I'm holding up. The weather is horrible here. It snowed pretty bad here the other day and everything came to a standstill," she started and kept talking and talking. Finally, I had to stop her.

"Jen, I am calling from a pay phone and there are people lining behind me. I need to give others a chance."

"Okay, no problem. But you never told me how you are doing." *Really, you never gave me a chance.*

"Bye, Jen see you soon."

"Bye, Bond. Call me or email me in case your flight plans change. I'll come to pick you up at the airport."

"Sure, I will. You take care."

I hung up the phone and people behind me heaved a sigh of relief.

"Sorry guys, I was talking to my mom. You know how moms are."

As I walked back home, I realized I did not have many days remaining before I flew back. Luckily, no one had raised a topic of my marriage or something like that. I realized I also needed to pack. I felt sad to leave my family and go back to the U.S., although I was also looking forward to seeing Jennifer.

The next few days passed off pretty quickly. Several relatives came over to see me, and some of them raised concerns about me getting older and not getting married. My mom and dad silenced them by telling them that they wanted me to settle down first and maybe start residency before getting married.

"Sir, what if he gets married to a white or black girl in the USA?" someone asked my dad, and I was pretty much annoyed.

"It does not matter. As long as both of them are happy and like each other, we are fine."

"Even if the girl is Christian?" someone asked.

"See, listen. I would prefer my son getting married to a Hindu girl, no doubt. But the religions, castes are only manmade barriers. If the girl is nice, we don't mind if she is black or white, Hindu or Christian or Jew. As long she keeps our son happy. We do not have many years left for ourselves. We don't want to force him to marry someone because we want it that way. Let him choose the girl. He is old enough and wise enough to make his own decision. If he needs advice, we are here to give him advice."

Wow! I was impressed by my dad's answer. I wish most parents were like my parents. After my dad spoke from his heart, no one dared to raise any questions. Soon almost everyone dissipated and my house was empty.

"Oh, by the way, do you have anyone in mind or do you have someone here in Mumbai or America whom you like?" my mom asked me.

"No, Mom, I am pretty busy with my work so I don't get much time to meet or get friendly with someone."

"I thought so. Make sure you get what you want. Then you can think about marriage. Oh, someone called Jennifer called the other day when you were meeting with your friends. Who is this girl?"

I was taken aback. Then I realized that I had given my home number just in case. But she never told me that she called here.

"She is a student doctor . . . I mean a medical student working with me on one research project. Maybe she had a question about a project or something. What did she say?"

"She was asking for you. She seems very nice. We almost spoke for about fifteen minutes."

Fifteen minutes! Oh my god! That means Jen was talking for fifteen minutes and Mom was listening to her.

"Really, what did she say?"

"She told me who she was, what she does, and little bit about her family too."

Which means Jen must have told her life's story in a nutshell, I thought.

"Did she give you a chance to speak?" I asked Mom and I knew the answer would be "No."

"No, not really. But I could interrupt her in between and asked her a few questions," my mom said.

That is a real success, I thought. Otherwise when Jen starts, the person on the other side of the line usually doesn't get a chance. Unless of course it is her sister. Then it is other way around.

"What did you ask her?" I was curious.

"I asked her about her family and what she wants to do in the future," my mom answered.

"Really, what did she say?" I was even more curious.

"Why don't you ask her all these questions instead of asking me?" There was a question to my answer which was unexpected.

"Sure, I will ask her . . . if she can remember when I reach there." I tried to play tricks.

"Of course she will remember. She is very sharp!" my mom quipped.

"She also said that she would like to visit us may be next time you come to Mumbai." And there came a bombshell.

"What?" I screamed. I did not know that the things would have gone so far.

"Looks like she likes you," my mom said after a pause and I was about to faint.

"Look mom, she is a white, Christian girl. There is no way she is going to like a *Ghati* brown boy like me. No way. And let us say hypothetically that she likes me, and she wants to marry me, would you like a Christian daughter-in-law?"

"Why not? If both of you like each other and she seems to be a nice girl. I strongly believe that religion is a manmade barrier. God creates all of us equally. Although some people are white, others are brown, and some are darker. These are all outside things. What is important is inside not outside. Do you like her?" I was about to get a cardiac arrest.

"No, of course not. She is too talkative, too nosy and . . ." I could not think anything else so I said, "Oh, there are so many things about her that I don't like. I only tolerate her because she is involved with my research project!" I knew I was lying and so did my mom.

"Then why did you give her your phone number?" I realized that my mom was much smarter than I thought.

I thought for a while and said, "Just in case . . . if she had any question about our research project. Nothing else. Our research project is very important. We are about to discover and reveal something great to the world. Why do you think there is something in between us?" I tried my best to explain but I had a feeling I was failing.

"I don't know about you but I had a feeling that she likes you," my mom said quietly.

I decided not to answer her question.

"I have to do some packing now," I said and left. I decided after going back I must warn Jen not to call here again. But why would she call here if I am going to be in New York? Yes, that is great thinking. She won't call here when I am in the U.S. That thought relieved me. I was glad the conversation did not go beyond this. Luckily my mom also never brought up her name or this topic again.

The days passed off pretty quickly and my departure date grew near. I made it a point to go to an exclusive shop in south Mumbai and buy a nice replica of the Taj Mahal for Jennifer and also for Dr. Stein. The shop owner was pretty smart and asked me, "Sir, are you carrying these to the USA?"

I was surprised. "Yes, how did you guess?"

"Sir, I have been in business for the last twenty years I know when my customer walks in what he or she wants and I can usually guess for who these gifts they are buying!" he said proudly.

"Really? tell me whom I am buying these for?"

"Sir, one for your girlfriend and other must be for your boss."

I was shocked! But I did not show my surprise. "You are right about one for the boss but the other one is for my immediate supervisor who is cranky and troubles me a lot" I basically lied to him.

"No problem sir, I got at least fifty percent right. I will pack these nicely for you and please carry these in your handbag not in luggage." I thought to myself, *hmm you are almost one hundred percent right, man!*

About two days before my departure, I went outside to give a call to Jennifer to remind her to pick me up from the airport.

The phone rang. It was late night in New York.

"Hello," I said.

"Hey, Bond! How have you been? You know the other day I called your home number and spoke to your mom. She is such a sweet lady and she cares a lot about you. We spoke for about may be fifteen minutes or so. I think we liked each other. You are blessed to have a mom like yours. Anyway, thanks for calling. I'll pick you up from JFK. So don't worry. It has been so cold here my ass is frozen."

I simply did not get a chance to talk! But anyway, I expected that.

"Do you want to say something?" she asked me. And really I wanted to say that I missed her but instead I said, "I miss . . . I am missing something . . . I think . . . you know what . . . I am missing New York City."

I guess she was disappointed as there was some silence on other side.

"Oh, of course not. You must be kidding. It's snowing here, dear. I'm sure you'll miss Mumbai when you come back," she said after a long pause.

"Anyway, Jen I will see you at the airport," I said and waited for her reply. I thought she wanted me to say something more, but I did not have courage to say that in reality I was missing her.

"All right, Bond, I'll see you then. You take care and have a safe trip back. Don't have an affair with a stewardess on your way back."

"No I won't because most of them will be fat, not so good looking, and much older than me anyway. You know the equal opportunity BS."

"Yes, you're absolutely right. I shouldn't worry then. Oh, by the way, in case I get stuck in a traffic jam or something don't try to catch a cab. Just wait inside."

"Don't worry. I will not run away with another chick. Bye."

She seemed to like my answer.

"Bye, Bond, see you soon."

Oh my god, I thought she must screaming into the phone on other side. I guess the person behind me also could hear her. He was smiling and asked me, "Who is she? Your girlfriend?"

"No, she is my supervisor at work. That is why she screams at me," I told him. I was bit annoyed. *Who the hell are you to ask me?*

Finally the day arrived and I left my house with a heavy heart. I knew for sure that my Mom, Dad as well as my younger brother were going to miss me dearly. My mom insisted on coming to the airport and I did not stop her from doing that. Our separation was hard and tearful, but she knew that I was leaving for a new start to my life. My success was more important to my mom than me being with her. She was tearful but delighted because I was going to start residency. She knew I would be successful and happy. She watched me walking away in the department lounge till she could not see me. After I checked in my bags in and went past immigration, I thought of leaving everything and coming back. Leaving Mumbai had always been a difficult thing for me. In spite of the bright future ahead of me, I knew I was going to miss Mumbai. Mouthwatering *pav-bhaji, pani puri* from Dadar Chowpaty or Grant Road's Delhi Durbar's chicken biryani and so many other things. Although probably New York is the only city that comes pretty close to Mumbai, it is not Mumbai. I did not realize how the time passed while I was indulged in my thoughts. Soon I was standing in the line to board my plane. It was a flight via London. Being off season, the flight was not full and I could find four seats in a row and slept all the way to London. The air hostess woke me up saying, "Sir, please be seated. We are about to land at the Heathrow Airport."

I was happy that at least half of the journey is over. I was fresh when we landed at Heathrow. I brushed my teeth at the airport and confidently ordered Starbucks coffee and I was ready for the next flight! The journey to New York seemed much longer, as I had decided not to sleep at all. In between book reading and watching movies, I chatted with my fellow passengers. Luckily the weather in New York was not bad, at least that is what the captain said. We were going to land slightly ahead of time. I thought about Jennifer who must have already started from her apartment. After landing, I decided to wait inside. I was surprised to see Jennifer waiting for me in the crowd.

She gave me a hug and said, "Bond, it's good to see you back in New York. How are you?"

"I am kind of tired from the trip but I guess I am okay. Feels like coming back home to me. How are you?"

"I'm great. Let's go home now, you must be really tired. I have so many things to tell you. I suppose you will stay with me in our apartment till you get over your jet lag. Your bedroom is ready, all nice and clean. Come on, let me push the trolley for you. Why don't you wait here till I get my car out here? I promise it won't take time. I have some food at home if you want to eat something." She continued talking till she left to get her car. Luckily, I did not see a lot of snow outside. Soon Jen came with her car and we were on our way home.

"Looks like you don't have much luggage. Did you do any shopping in Mumbai?" she asked me.

"No, not really. I think my baggage probably weighs less than when I left from here. I had many gifts purchased which were actually made in China and gave those as gifts from America."

"Oh, I called your home one day and I spoke to your mom. I think I told you when you called me, right?"

"Yes, you did. My mom seems to have liked you a lot," I said and I was waiting to see her reaction.

"Really? I thought so. I liked her too. I'm going to call her again maybe in a couple of weeks."

"What? Now that I am here, you don't have to call Mumbai. You can call me or meet me in my office," I protested.

"What is your problem, Bond? This is between me and your mom. I promised her that I would call her and I will."

"Alright, fine, whatever you want. Don't give out my secrets," I said.

"What secrets? You don't have any. Do you have secret girlfriend or may be a mistress? Wish you had a secret that I could reveal to your mom."

I kept quiet. She was right, I did not have any secrets. "Anyway, you don't have to tell me what you discussed in your phone conversations."

"Of course not, this is between two ladies, and you have no right to know even if you want to."

"Alright, Jen that is fine. Let us talk about something else."

"I have so many things to tell you. But maybe not right now. You look tired and jet lagged. After you get up tomorrow morning I will bore you with my stuff. Oh by the way, I may not be in New York City, you know," she said casually.

I was stunned. I could not imagine living here without her being around.

"What?" Now it was my time to scream.

"Yes, Bond. As you might know, my spot in residency may not assured here. I want to do radiology, but it does not have to be in Manhattan. It could be anywhere in the country. Maybe even Rochester. By the way, the University of Rochester has a very good radiology residency program. Plus my mom lives there so I'm sure she'll be happy too."

I decided to keep quiet.

"You are not saying anything, Bond." My thoughts were interrupted by her comment.

I decided to speak my mind, but then I thought not to for some reason. I spoke something probably I should not have said. "Well, you should be happy wherever you get radiology residency because it is in great demand now."

She was visibly annoyed. She did not expect this answer. Even I did not want to say what I said. Maybe I should have spoken my mind and told her that I was going to miss her dearly. But I kept quiet, I guess I was not bold enough like other guys.

She did not speak a word and soon we reached the apartment where both of us unloaded the bags. The guy downstairs, the concierge, recognized me and said, "Welcome back, sir. I guess you are coming from India? How was your trip?"

"Great. How are you?"

"I am good, sir. Do you need help with the bags?"

"No. I think we are fine. Thanks."

We went in the apartment and I put my bags in my bedroom.

"Bond, I washed and folded your clothes in the closet so you might want to wear them for the night if you want." These were her first words after such a long pause.

"Thanks, Jen. I don't know how I would survive here without you," I said spontaneously and we exchanged glances.

"Well, no one is indispensable," she said in a sour tone and some sarcasm.

I did not make a comment on that, but maybe I should have. I just put my bags in the corner and asked her "Do you want some masala chai? I have got some tea powder from India. I can make a stronger chai for you, not the dip-dip type."

"Sure, I don't know what I would do without you, Bond," she said.

"Well, no one is indispensable and that includes me," I replied and we both shared a laugh which somewhat made the moment a bit lighter.

I opened my bag and found a notice inside. I opened it and both of us looked at it. It was a printed note from TSA. All it said that my bag was one of the bags which was randomly checked.

"Well, Bond looks like you are under the scanner of the TSA and other anti-terrorist agencies. Hope you did not bring any bombs or guns from Mumbai," Jen said. "Jokes apart, did you have any problem in immigration?" she asked.

"Not really. It was pretty smooth, although there was a long line and they took my picture and fingerprints so it took more time than usual," I said as I headed towards kitchen

"Bond, I have a suggestion. Let us have chai in the morning. You must be tired now. Why don't you eat something and we can have cold beer. How is that?"

"Excellent. I like it. Are you not hungry too?"

"I'll have a bite. I am probably not as hungry as you are but I'll keep you company," she said.

We both sat down to eat but I realized I was more tired than hungry.

"I don't want to eat too much, but I will have little something and we can then sit down in the living room and have beer."

"Sounds good," Jen said and both of us went in the living room. "Here are some veg samosas for you and I'm having chicken samosas. Do you want a bite?"

"Sure. Let me taste it." I had a little piece of chicken samosa. "Wow, that was delicious," I said, then took a sip of beer. "So Jen, how have you been?"

"Good. Kind of lonely, though. I spoke to Emily a few times. But after you went to Mumbai, there was no one who listened to me as patiently as you do."

"Do I have a choice? I have been listening to you since I came here and continue to do so," I said jokingly.

"Yes, when I call Emily, I'm the one who does the listening."

"Have you thought about submitting your list for the match?" I asked her finally.

"Yes, but I haven't finalized it yet. I am seriously thinking about going to Rochester."

"You are going to leave the city and go to Rochester? Are you crazy? That place is no match for the life you are living here."

"Yes, but as I told you earlier, the University of Rochester has a great radiology program, plus my mom works at the Strong Memorial Hospital. There are so many additional benefits. I can stay with my mom and save on apartment rent, etc."

"Won't you miss Manhattan?" I asked her.

"Yes, of course I will. But I don't have many choices. The only other option is go to Chicago and stay close to my sister, which is not a bad option at all."

"Yes, probably better than going to Rochester."

"Well, Rochester is not a bad place at all," she protested.

"Yes, I know, I was interviewed for a research post at Strong Memorial Hospital."

"Really, you never told me." She was astonished.

"I did consider a research post in the radiology department at the Strong Memorial Hospital. But I thought that place would be too cold for me and pretty small for someone who is coming from Mumbai and Dubai!" I took a pause and said, "I am glad I chose New York City over Rochester because I met you."

She looked at me a little bewildered, I thought. When she did not say anything, I continued, "Plus New York can match something like Mumbai. Very lively city and always on the go."

At that point I realized that I was dozing off a little bit.

She finally opened her mouth. "Bond, I think you are too sleepy. Why don't you change and go to bed. I'll wake you up tomorrow."

"Yes, I think I am really sleepy. I better go to bed. Good night, Jen. And thanks for everything."

"Not a problem, Bond."

"I don't really know what I will do without you, Jen. Good night."

"Good night, Bond. Take it easy. Remember what I said?"

"Yes, I do. No one is indispensable, but you are!"

I went to my bedroom and changed and just crashed onto the bed. I never knew when I fell asleep and I was awakened by Jen's voice. "Bond, I think you should get up. It is almost ten."

I came out of the bedroom rubbing my eyes.

"Oh my god, I slept like a log. I did not realize it was ten!"

I looked at Jennifer. She was wearing gym clothes and looked stunningly beautiful.

"Looks like you are back from gym."

"Yes, I am and I'm dying to drink your masala chai," she said.

"Sure, let me boil some water and I will brush my teeth in the meantime," I said while pouring some water in the pot.

"Don't you want to use the kettle?"

"No, this is different way to make tea. You can say the Indian way! I will be back with the stuff I got from India."

I quickly brushed my teeth and got the tea powder out from my suitcase.

I poured two teaspoonfuls of the powder in the boiling water and let it boil for a few minutes as Jen watched intently.

I switched off the stove and let the tea powder settle down.

"We have to wait for a few minutes. The tea should be ready but it's going to strong. Do you have half and half?

"Yes, I do. I got the *Ilaichi* flavor from the Indian store." Jen showed me the can.

"Oh, that is great. This is how you make the real tea."

We sat down on the breakfast table for the masala chai.

"Wow, this tea is awesome. I would love to have it every day to head start my morning," Jen said.

"Yes, you can have the bag. I bought two."

"No I mean, I would love if you can make it for me. I'm too lazy to make it myself the 'Indian way' and I don't have the skills you have."

"Skills? This not rocket science. It is pretty simple. But I can make it for you if you want. No problem at all."

"How do you feel now?" Jen asked.

"Much better. Although it usually takes about a few days to get over the jet lag."

"Yes, I know, I can imagine. I've been to Europe once. It was horrible when I reached Europe. I still remember that."

"Yes, it is funny that it is pretty bad when you go from here to India but it is not as bad when you come back to the USA," I said.

"Okay, so what is your plan now?" she asked me.

"Well, get over the jet lag and then get back to work and then I guess I will submit my list for the match. What about you? When are you planning to submit your choices?"

"I'm not sure. Pretty soon. I can't imagine life out of New York City but I guess I don't have much choice."

"You still have a chance. You may still get into the program, you never know."

"Bond, if I get into any radiology program in this city, it is going to be this one," she said firmly.

"Yes, I know but you still have a chance here," I insisted.

"I don't know Bond. I feel kind of scared," she said and for the first time she sounded a bit nervous. I did not know how to console her. There was a long moment of silence which she broke.

"Anyway, Bond, how was your trip to India or I should probably say to Mumbai?" I was glad that she changed the topic of discussion.

"It was great. I met my family. I had a college, high school and medical school get-together. It was fun to see all the guys and gals."

"And your ex- girlfriends?"

"Yes, I saw a bunch of them too. But they all are married now."

"Did you have sex with any of them?"

"Yes, almost all of them. It was a kind of wild orgy," I said and we shared a moment of laughter.

We chatted for a while then I started feeling sleepy. I decided to take a nap and Jen went to shower and disappeared into her bedroom.

I woke up almost at lunch time.

"How do you feel now, Bond?" Jen asked me, still in her gym workout clothes.

"Much better now. The key thing is not to go to sleep in the afternoon. I think we can watch a movie or do something else."

"It's pretty cold outside so we have to do something indoors. We can watch a movie if you want. In fact, I would love to. Should I get a Jennifer Aniston movie?" I nodded yes. She seemed pretty excited.

We went to a nearby rental store and also grabbed a sandwich and got the movie home.

When we came back to our apartment, I suddenly realized that I had not given her the gift.

I opened my bag and got the carefully packed Taj Mahal out. I opened the wrappings and went in the living room.

"Jen, this is for you, the Taj Mahal."

She almost jumped from the love seat and grabbed it. "Be careful, it's delicate," I said.

"This is so beautiful, I wonder how it must be to see the real one. Have you seen it, Bond?"

"Of course. It is unbelievable . . . I don't have words to describe it!"

"Thank you so much, Bond. In case we have to part if I go to another place for residency, I will always remember you when I look at this Taj Mahal."

"Thank you but hopefully that situation won't arise."

"Let me keep it here." She made a space for the Taj Mahal on the entertainment center. "Okay, now let's watch the movie."

We started to watch and I started feeling sleepy.

"Hey Bond, wake up! Look, she is naked in this scene!!"

"Bond, wake up. Don't sleep or I'll pinch you!" That did not work well so she said, "Wake up, Bond. Look, Jennifer Aniston is naked in this scene." That seemed to work and I opened my eyes wide to see her but did not see her naked. "I was just joking to wake you up," Jen said while giggling.

Somehow I kept awake throughout the movie. I decided to make some strong chai to keep me awake through the evening. Finally at around eight I gave up and said, "Jen, if I don't sleep now I will either collapse or die."

"I definitely don't want you to die so you better go to your bedroom and sleep because if you sleep here I won't be able to lift you up and take to the bedroom. I'm not that strong."

"I am not that heavy either. Do you want to try?"

"No way. I can help you go to your bedroom if you want."

"No. I think I can walk back. I am fine otherwise. Good night Jen."

"Good night, Bond."

I went and crashed on the bed and within seconds I fell asleep. I must have slept like a log because I woke up with Jen almost shaking my whole body and screaming, "Bond, wake up!" in my ears.

"What happened? Why are you screaming? Is the apartment on fire?" I asked her.

"No. I am on fire. I tried to wake you up so many times but you wouldn't, so I had to scream and shake you. Are you awake now or are you still dreaming about naked Jennifer Aniston?"

"No. I am awake now. Thanks. Let me get ready and make some chai for us."

"Now that sounds like you. Great, I'll help."

While making tea, I realized that I had to go back and clean my room and get ready for the next working day.

"Jen, I think I will go back to dorm and clean my room. I will go there after breakfast and get ready for tomorrow. Hope you don't mind."

"No. Not at all. In fact, I'm quite bored of you and waiting for you to leave. Just joking, okay? Take your time. I think you should have bath and then go to your dorm. And I can help you clean your room if you want."

"I think I should be fine," I said. "Thank you for your kind offer, though. I think you need to concentrate on your stuff and make the list for submission for the match."

"That is what I don't want to do. I am so scared. What if I don't get a spot here?"

"I am sure you will. But let's say hypothetically you don't get residency here then you should probably get in Chicago or Rochester. I think you should be ready for any eventuality," I told her.

"Yes, I know but that thought itself scares me."

"What kind of thought?" I asked.

"The thought of leaving the city and studying in some other program."

I didn't know what to say, so I kept quiet.

# THE TENTH COMMANDMENT

After bidding her goodbye, I went straight to my dorm room. It was still cold outside. Jen offered to drop me in her car, which I happily accepted. I had my luggage with me which would have made riding the subway difficult.

When I got to my apartment, I cleaned my room and unloaded my suitcase.

After working for some time, I switched on the TV. On one of the channels they were talking about some Groundhog Day. I had never heard it before so I was watching with quite the interest. I frankly found it quite stupid. Then I thought to myself, "Groundhog Day is the day when the groundhog sees his butt or not. Depending on that the winter will be short or long!" After that I realized that the kitchen needed to be cleaned so I got up and switched off the TV. While I was cleaning the kitchen, I heard a knock on the door.

I opened and was surprised to see Madhuri.

"Hi, Bond, welcome back," she said with a big smile.

"Hi Madhuri, come on in."

She was carrying something in a plastic bag.

We sat down.

"How was your trip to Mumbai?" she asked.

"It was good. I met a lot of friends and my family. Had a great time. How have you been?"

"I am good. The weather was still cold so I spent most time in my lab and at work," she said. "I checked if you came back couple of times yesterday. You were not in or you were sleeping."

"Actually I have been here in town but I was—"

She cut me short and said, "You were staying with Jennifer?" I just nodded. "We called each other a couple of times and basically talked about you and Mumbai." After some pause she said, "I made some *puri-bhaji* so I thought I would get some for you too." She handed the bag over to me.

I was amused and happy too. My face lit up and I said, "Thanks, that is very nice of you."

"No problem, Bond. I will make a move now. Enjoy your food," she said, getting up.

"I am sorry my fridge is empty. I cannot offer you anything," I said apologetically.

"Never mind, I know that you just came from Mumbai."

I stood up and went to open door for her and said, "Thanks again Madhuri for the puri-bhaji"

She smiled and stopped for a moment and said, "Can I tell you something as a good friend?" I had a sense as to what she was going to say. "Bond, stay away from white girls. They are always looking for Indian boys. They know that Indians are hard-working, make good money, and most important won't cheat on them."

I smiled and said, "I will remember that but there is nothing between me and Jen."

She did not respond to that but to my surprise gave me a quick hug and left. I gently closed the door and went back to cleaning the kitchen. Afterward, I sat down and enjoyed *puri-bhaji* given by Madhuri. I was feeling sleepy so I went early to bed early and never knew when I fell asleep.

The next day I woke up early with headache, but once I got ready and was wearing scrubs I felt I was back to normal life. After reaching the hospital, I went straight to Dr. Stein's office. Mary greeted me with a big smile. "Hi, Dr. Bond. Welcome back. How was your trip to India?"

"It was great. I am just recovering from jet lag. I should get it over soon."

"Great to have you back. Do you want to see Dr. Stein? Let me see if he is free."

Soon she came back and said, "Yes, he is free. But he is about to go for a meeting. So make it fast."

"Sure, thanks" I said and I knocked on his door.

"Come on in, Bond. How was your trip to Mumbai?"

"Great. How are you sir? I got this replica of the Taj Mahal for you. You can keep it in your office or home."

"Oh, thanks a lot. I'll keep it my office. It's wonderful and I'm doing great. I guess you are going to submit your list for the match soon. I have put in my best recommendation for you. We are excited about the idea of you being a resident in our program. Even the program director is extremely pleased with your performance."

"Yes sir. Thank you so much. I am going to submit my list pretty soon. I am too excited about the whole thing. Although I am bit worried about the first year of surgical internship."

"Oh and I suppose you still remember about what I said about Ms. Graziano? She still does have chance although certainly not as good as you."

"Yes, sir, I do remember."

"Alright, I have to go for a meeting now. Why don't you take it easy for a couple of days and then we can meet again to see what project you can finish before you start your dreaded surgical internship."

I left his office and went straight to my office. I chatted with my research colleagues and then started looking at some unfinished papers and articles I had been working on with Dr. Stein and others.

The time passed by quickly and soon it was around noon. There was a soft knock on my door and knew it was Jen.

"Hey, Bond. Just wondering if you want to have lunch with me?"

She came in and swept aside the papers I had been working on and sat down on the table next to my computer with crossed legs.

"Hey, you just messed with the stuff I had been working on," I complained.

"Don't worry, Bond. I'll help you with that stuff after we come back. Where do you want to go for lunch?"

"Do we have lot of choices?"

"We can go to the big cafeteria, which is usually crowded at this time, or we can go to the small sandwich shop next to the gift shop and have a bite. We can even share a sandwich if you want."

"Sure, let's share a sandwich."

Once we were eating, Jen said, "I just wanted to let you know that I'm thinking of submitting my list today or tomorrow."

"Hmm," I said.

"Bond."

"Yes, I am listening."

"I will dearly miss you if I don't get in this program."

I was startled and looked at her. Our eyes met and I wanted to say something but I did not know what to say. I looked down and kept on chewing on my sandwich. I sipped some water to wet my tongue and I looked at her again. I thought I saw some tears in the corner of her eyes. My face was expressionless and we kept on staring at each other. Although I tried to hide my emotions, I thought I conveyed a lot through my eyes. Probably more than what I could have said. Finally after a long awkward pause I said, "You will get used to it, Jen."

She was clearly disappointed by my timid response. Although I wanted to say more, I did not. I thought the time and place was not just appropriate. We did not speak a single word till we finished our food and drink.

"Bond, I think we need to vacate as a lot of people are waiting for a table."

"Yes, you are right." We departed and I went back to my office, still thinking about my and her life without each other.

I could not concentrate. I barely finished editing a small online case submission and emailed it to Dr. Stein. After that, I shut off my computer and went back to my dorm room as I could not focus and work the way I used to.

I watched some news and was thinking about submitting my list for the residency match. I had only one interview so far and there was not much to be done. My internship was also promised by Dr. Stein and the chairman.

Suddenly the phone rang. I was bit surprised, as who would call me now?

"Hello," I said.

"Hey, Bond, this is Emily."

"Hi there. How are you doing?" I asked her casually.

"I'm fine. How are you, Bond?" She spoke in a cold, monotonous tone, which was somewhat unusual.

"You surprised me by calling me. What's going on?" I asked to start some conversation.

"Do you want to see Jen in a situation similar to mine? Distressed, unhappy, and sad?" she asked me and her tone suddenly changing from monotonous to a harsh.

I was confused. Did I do something wrong? After a pause, I said, "Of course not. Why are you asking me that? What did I do?"

"Bond, it is not what you did, but not what you are doing is causing a serious problem."

"I don't understand you, Emily," I said, hoping for a plain and simple explanation.

"Bond, gather some strength and go to Jennifer's apartment right now and tell her what is in your heart, before it is too late. Believe me, if you don't act now, you will regret it for the rest of your life."

"Emily, could you please explain me as to what do you want me to do?"

"Bond, you like her and she likes you and I want you to go to her right now and tell her that. Don't you love her?" she almost screamed.

There was a long pause. I took a deep breath and said, "Yes, I do. There is no doubt. How do you know?"

"I could feel it, Bond. I'm a woman. Plus, I'm her sister and more than that I'm her very good friend. I know you both love each other," she said emotionally.

"I would not have guessed it that you would notice something between me and her. Anyway, what should I do now?" I asked her my stupid question.

"Thank god you did not take long to confess. Okay, this what I want you to do. Dress nicely, buy some roses and some red wine or maybe champagne. Don't submit your match list, go to her apartment and tell her how you feel about her. Open your heart, pour your emotions. Just talk, okay? I know you can do it." She took a deep breath and said, "Once you told me that your great great grandfather fought against the Brits? Gather some strength from him, dear. Be bold like the man in your family who had courage to fight the British Rule in India. Once she also accepts you, both of you can submit the match list as a couple's match."

"Couple's match? But do we need to get engaged prior to that?" I was confused.

"Move your ass now and do what I said. Don't waste time or it could be disastrous,"

"No. Are you fucking crazy? Move your ass now and do what I said. Don't waste time or it could be disastrous," she screamed.

I was shaken to the core. She had never used the "f" word with me before and she never sounded the way she sounded today.

"Okay, Emily. I will do exactly as you have said. I just want you do a favor for me."

"Yes, handsome. What can I do for you?" she asked in a sarcastic tone.

"Could you call her and tell her not to submit the list?" I said in one breath.

"Bond, I already did. I called her before I called you because I knew you would not move your ass unless pushed by someone. I told her to hold off till tomorrow morning. But you need to act now. And most important, call me back to tell me what happened."

"It might be late—"

She cut me short and screamed "It does not matter even if it is fucking two a.m. Call me to tell me no matter what, okay? And get moving now!" She slammed the phone, leaving me shaken. That was second time she used the "f" word with me in less than two minutes.

It took me a few minutes to gather my strength and courage. I went to the bedroom and picked out a nice pair of jeans and a white button down shirt and a nice blazer. I quickly showered and shaved and put on a masculine aftershave lotion. I dressed and then looked at myself in the mirror. I thought I did not see the old Bond in the mirror. Old Bond was somewhat timid, frightened and naive. I saw a new Avatar of Bond, strong, determined and a man on a mission!

I took my big overcoat also as I knew it would be cold outside. I sat down for a moment and wondered what was I going to tell her. After thinking for a while I decided that I would just go to her and open my heart and say whatever came to my mind. I did pick up the envelope in which I had kept the handkerchief with her tears on it. I opened it and surprisingly it still had the faint smell of the perfume she usually wore. I kept the envelope with me in my blazer pocket.

I went down and decided to take a cab. On the way, I picked up the freshest roses I could find.

"Is it for someone's birthday?" the beautiful girl selling the flowers asked me.

"No, it is a Judgement Day!" I answered back to her and she was puzzled.

"Do you need a card also with flowers?"

"No. Whatever I am going to say today cannot be written on any of the cards you are selling in your shop," I replied curtly. She was even more puzzled and somewhat annoyed. I picked up some champagne and got a cab. The cab driver turned out to be a Sikh from Mumbai! He asked me, "Sir, do you like old Hindi songs?"

I was in no mood to listen to anything but I said, "Yeah, sure." although my mind was somewhere else.

He turned off his radio and turned on his cassette player. I immediately recognized the song from movie *Khamoshi*. I started listening intently to the lyrics as they were beautiful. The first stanza said,

"*Pyar Koi Bol Nahi, Pyar Aawaaz Nahi*
*Ek Khamoshi Hai, Sunti Hai Kaha Karti Hai*
*Na Ye Bujhti Hai Na Rukti Hai, Na Thehri Hai Kahi*
*Noor Ki Boond Hai, Sadiyon Se Baha Karti Hai*"

Love is not lyrics, love is not sound (or voice).
It is a silence that listens and speaks by itself.
It does not die, it does not stop, it does not pause.
It is a drop of bliss that flows for eons.

"Wow! What a nice song, I thought! I realized that thus far I had been silent. Silent love is not going to lead me anywhere today, I thought. I have to speak up and express myself! Khamoshi or silence is not going to work today. Soon I arrived at her apartment building. I paid the cab driver and said, "Thank you for the ride and the song too, Shukriya."

With confidence, I entered the lobby.

"You look great today, sir," the lady at the concierge commented.

"Thank you and I need your best wishes," I said while entering the elevator.

Standing in front of the apartment door, I felt a surge of energy going through my body. I was excited, a bit nervous too. I knew this was like the "do or die" mission for me.

Jennifer opened the door for me. She was surprised to see me at that time of the day and in that attire.

"Hey, what a surprise! Why didn't you call me? And what are you up to? Why are you dressed up, Bond?"

"Can I come in please and then I will answer all your questions," I said, smiling.

"Sure, of course. You smell nice. Come on in."

She was wearing an old tee shirt and jeans shorts, which were kind of torn at the bottom edge.

She looked at the stuff I was carrying in a bag quizzically.

"Jen, I have small request for you."

"Sure, go ahead," she said, still obviously confused about the whole thing.

"Can you please change into the red sleeveless dress you have while I keep these things in the kitchen?"

"Sure. Thank god you didn't ask me to change into a swimming suit or bikini! But if you could, please tell me what are you up to."

"I am going to tell you everything in a moment. Why don't you go and change and I want you to sit here when you come back," I said, pointing at the leather recliner.

While she went to change, I went in the kitchen and kept the champagne bottle in the fridge. I was nervous thinking about what was going to happen. I kept the flowers in the kitchen and came back to the living room. Jennifer came back in a red velvet dress. She looked stunningly beautiful, as always. She had put on some make up and lip gloss too.

She sat down in the leather recliner as I had requested her. She crossed her legs and then looked at me with a big question.

I took a deep breath and said, "Jennifer, I have known you for the past ten months or so. You have been my friend, my pal, my guide as well my guru since I have been here."

"Yes, Bond, I know that," she said quietly.

"You also promised to give to Ten Commandments to transform me from a Mumbaikar to become a true New Yorker." She kept staring at me.

"You have so far given me only nine commandments, do you know that?" I asked her.

"No, Bond, I lost count. I thought I had given you all ten."

"Jen, I have been counting. In fact, I have kept a diary and wrote down all the commandments so far you gave me."

"You must be kidding me."

"No, I am not. I am not kidding at all. Now listen to me, I have been mostly quiet for the last months I have known you. Today it is my turn to talk and you are going to listen." She was astonished by my attitude. She uncrossed and crossed her legs and looked at me curiously and seemed a bit nervous.

"I am here to give you the last or the tenth commandment."

"What?" She was shocked.

"Yes, this is my gift to you, also called a *gurudakshina* in Marathi."

"What is that? I don't understand."

"That is what a student gives back to his or her teacher, a gift, an expression of gratitude."

"Now I get it. So I am your guru and you are or have been my disciple so far?" she said.

"Yes, but before I do that I have to say something and I want you to listen to me carefully."

"I'm listening." She was amused and seemed eager to hear what I was going to tell her.

I took a deep breath and after a small pause I started talking. "I have been in this country for a relatively short time. Other than a few friends and classmates scattered throughout this huge country, I did not have a close friend.

I met you by sheer coincidence or luck should I say. We instantly hit off the day we met. Do you remember the day we first met?"

"Yes, I do. It was in the reading room. Right?" She was pretty sure.

"No. We met before that," I said confidently.

"No way! I don't remember meeting you earlier unless in your dreams," she protested.

"Jennifer, it was in the parking lot of the hospital. Do you remember it was a rainy day and I was walking through the parking lot and you got out of the car and yelled at me. You asked me if you could share an umbrella with me and I said yes."

She thought for a while and then said, "I kind of vaguely remember. Was I wearing scrubs?"

She asked me that question either to test my memory or to refresh her memory.

"No. You were wearing cream-colored top with dark brown skirt with matching dark brown high heel shoes," I said confidently and I could see that she was visibly shocked.

"Wow, you have a photographic memory!"

"Thanks. Yes, but my photographic memory works only for the people who are really special to me, not for everyone else! Anyway, within a day or two we met in the radiology reading room. You were wearing a sky blue top and dark skirt and tall black shoes."

"Yes, I do remember that! But of course I don't remember what I was wearing!"

Without responding to her, I continued. "I thought our wavelengths matched perfectly. I found a close friend and a buddy in you. You have been with me through thin and thick. You helped me literally from day one in almost every day-to-day affair from finding the social security office to teaching me how to buy coffee at Starbucks. You and I have worked on the research project together and without your help I would not have found success." I kept on talking and Jen was amused to hear me talking so much.

I took a small pause and I continued.

"Do you remember the night I was stuck in McDonald's? I was so worried when I called you that night as to how you would react. You came like an angel and rescued me, otherwise I would have been in big trouble. Thank god I could recollect your phone number! I landed myself in trouble due to my stupidity and you came to my rescue."

"Well, I would never forget that night," said Jen while I took a sip of water.

"I still remember the day of 9/11 attacks. You came to my office and literally forced me to stay with you in our apartment here."

Without knowing I said *our* apartment and she blushed a little bit.

"I was fine with staying in dorm and although I always felt safe, you insisted that I should come and stay with you in your apartment. You thought about me and my safety more than I thought about myself. It was not only friendship but your love which made you worried about me, but you never expressed your love for me. Although subtly you did it by asking me to move in your apartment. You did not think twice about asking a person like me who was totally unknown to you a few months ago, to move in for few days with you. Jennifer, it was your deep trust in our friendship but most important than that your love which prompted you to do that. I was a fool that I did not understand your feelings for me at that time." I took a small pause and looked carefully at her. I could see tears forming in her eyes.

"I have to say that you took really good care of me during that time and I did feel much safer with you than being in the dorm. The night you were sick in the ER, your friends called me to help you. I was so glad I could be of some help to you. Our acquaintance turned slowly into friendship and slowly the friendship turned into a close friendship and I haven't had a closer female friend other than you in past few years. You also gave me commandments to turn me into a true American and of course a New Yorker. I have transformed slowly from a Mumbaikar into a New Yorker thanks to you and your efforts. Because of you I turned from a nerdy and stupid researcher into a smart ass doctor."

I took a deep breath, took a little pause and started again. She appeared to be shell shocked and also more tearful than earlier.

"Jennifer, there is very thin line between close friendship and love. I never knew when I crossed that line. I did not even realize that was happening. We have spent innumerable breakfasts, lunches, and dinners together. I have to admit that when I went to Mumbai, one day felt like one year. I missed you every day, every hour, in fact every minute. When I came back I told you that I missed New York City. That was a blatant lie! The fact was I was missing you and so were you missing me."

I had to stop and gulp some water.

"We are about to start a new phase in our lives. I have gone through a residency in India so this one will be like a getting married again! Only difference, there won't be any honeymoon. In fact, honeymoon will be replaced by a year-long nightmare called surgical internship. I am physically and mentally ready for that. But I think at this difficult stage of my life I need a mate. You always jokingly said that you wanted me to be around during residency to do your night calls but the fact is that I cannot imagine doing this residency without you being around. I cannot imagine living in New York without you. You have been a part of my life and also a part of me. I have adored you since we met. You are beautiful from the outside and most important to me is that you have a beautiful mind. I love both your body and soul. I always believed that women are like cars. If you want a good car don't just go for the look of the car, look for what is inside the car. A car with a well engineered machine will run for longer time giving you a pleasure and company... maybe even forever. Your beauty is not only in your looks but it is inside, deep inside in your soul. You are more beautiful inside than outside. It is that inner beauty which attracted me to you the most. You are the good girl I have been waiting for. You are my Rachel Green. You are the object of my affection!

"We are inseparable, Jennifer. We are like conjoined twins, even if someone separates us by surgery, it is impossible to separate our hearts. We are two bodies but one soul destined to live and die together." At that point I couldn't think of anything else so I took help of my medical knowledge to make my point.

"If you are a primary tumor, I am like metastasis"

"Jen, if you are a primary tumor, I am like metastasis . . . if you are the left ventricle I am the aorta. If you are globe then I am the optic nerve. We are like the two strands of DNA intertwined together. We are born to be together, destined to live together and maybe die together. Jennifer, I love you from the bottom of my heart. Every red blood cell in my body adores you and loves you. My heart beats for you. I cannot do this residency without you, I cannot live in United States without you. I cannot imagine New York City without you. In fact, I cannot imagine my rest of the life without you. With my every breath, I smell your body scent. Please don't leave me and I promise you that I won't leave you ever." I stopped and I realized that even my eyes were tearful. I thought I had finished so I stopped talking and then looked at her carefully.

She was shocked probably because she had never heard me talking so much! While I was talking tears had been running down her face and by the time I finished my talk, she was sobbing.

"Bond, I never knew you could talk to me so much! Why did you wait so long? I cannot live without you either."

She got up from the sofa and we hugged and kissed each other with a great passion. She was still sobbing and I was trying to comfort her. We sat down on the love seat and she seemed to stop sobbing and said, "I am glad you came and told me today. I'm so happy. Today is the happiest day of my life." There was a long pause after she said that. "So what do you want to do?" she whispered in my ear controlling her emotions.

"Let us submit our match list as a couple's match," I said.

"Idiot, don't you want to have sex?" she asked me. At that point I realized how stupid I was!

"Of course I do," I said.

"Now with that answer you sound more like a true American to me," she said.

"Yes, interestingly the process started from my feet. From waist and below, I am a complete American. I still have an Indian brain and mind."

"That's a perfect man for me. I wanted someone with brain of an Indian and body and libido of an American." She grabbed my hand and said, "Let us go in the bedroom."

After we made love, she asked me, "So Bond, what is your tenth commandment? You never told me that!"

.

## 'TENTH COMMANDMENT'

"Thou shalt not love only the body...
But shalt love the body and soul!"

I smiled and said, "Yes, I forgot because you brought up sex! Thou shalt not love only the body but shalt love the body and soul."

She nodded and said, "I got it. Thanks for the gift of the gratitude." Then she paused and said, "Bond, just a hypothetical question. What you would have done if I had said no?"

I thought for a moment and said, "I would have gone to Texas, bought a huge corn field, a bunch of horses and become a Cowboys fan. I would have stayed there forever till either I would forget you or till you came and got me. Maybe bought a Ford F-150 truck and partied with bunch of hotties!"

She was shocked as well as amused by my answer. "I would not have wanted you to become a Cowboys fan. The rest, including Texas hotties, I guess would have been fine." We both laughed.

Suddenly she got up and put on a bathrobe and said, "Let me get some wine." I also started to get up and she protested. "Bond you stay in bed and I'll get glasses and wine and we can have wine in the bed."

"Jen, I have bought champagne for both of us. It's in your fridge. Why don't we open it?"

"Of course, let's celebrate with a champagne pop!" She brought the bottle and opened it like a professional bartender. I did hear that pop!

We had champagne together and although I must have had that brand of champagne, I have to admit that it tasted much better and different that night.

After spending some time in bed, we decided to go the computer and submitted our match list as a couple's match. I knew that she would get into the program unless something extraordinary happened.

"I am so happy today," Jen said.

"I have never been happier so far in my life," I told her. I suddenly remembered something and I got up. "Wait, stay here. I have to show something to you."

"Is there anything left that you haven't shown me yet?"

I knew she was being naughty but I ignored her and got the envelope from my blazer and handed over to her.

"What is this? A letter?" she asked me.

"No. Just open and see," I said without any emotion.

She opened the envelope and found a handkerchief and was thoroughly confused. "I don't get it. This is a handkerchief, probably yours, and looks like this one is made in India."

"Let me explain. Remember the night Emily broke off from her boyfriend and you were crying inconsolably?"

"Yes, of course I remember that!"

"So the box of Kleenex was over and you had to use my handkerchief."

"Yes, I do remember that." Suddenly she realized what she held. "Oh my god, Bond, is this the handkerchief I used that night?"

"Yes, absolutely. I had preserved it and it still has your perfume which you usually wear."

She smelled it. "Yes, it does."

I lifted a box of Kleenex and said, "This is American culture, use it and throw it." Then I pointed to the handkerchief and said, "That is our culture. Use it, preserve it, and cherish it! One of the answers to your question was if you would have rejected me I would have kept smelling the handkerchief to remind me of you. Although the perfume would have worn off, the sweet memories would have stayed forever."

"Oh my god, Bond," Jennifer said while getting up from bed. "I can't believe this. You are incredible," and she hugged me.

"Oh, by the way, I have to make a phone call." I just realized that I had to call Emily.

"Are you crazy? It's almost midnight. Who do you want to call?" she almost screamed at me.

"Well, it is your beautiful sister, Emily . . ." I said and she was astonished.

"How does she come in the picture? Wait, did she call you before you came here?" she asked me.

"Yes, she did. She was the one who told me to do what was in my heart but I had not expressed it so far," I explained to her.

"How did she guess that we are in love with each other?"

"I don't know. I guess she has a sixth sense. I guess she could understand you since she knows you since the childhood. But I don't know how she figured out about me."

"She is very smart! She must have felt the feelings I did!" Jen called her sister then handed the phone to me.

"Hi, Emily. This is Bond."

"So tell me quickly, did she accept you or she reject you?"

I looked at Jennifer and said, "Yes, she did accept."

"I knew it. I told you," Emily screamed into the phone and even Jen could hear it.

"Why did it take you so long to call me?" Emily asked and at that point Jen snatched the phone from my hand and waved me to step out of room.

"Bond, can you give us a few minutes? We need to have a heart-to-heart sister talk."

I immediately obeyed and stepped out of the room and sat in the living room for a while.

As I expected Jennifer came out with tears in her eyes.

"What did you tell her?" I asked her.

"Almost everything. Most importantly, I told her that we had sex." She smiled.

"What?" I screamed. "You told her that? I hope you did not give the details. What did she say?"

"She said Bond is fast, hot, and horny," and she burst out laughing. "Why don't you stay overnight. I think you still have your clothes and scrubs here for tomorrow."

"Yes, sure. Let us have dinner first. I am hungry."

"Oh, tell me about it. I am starving too," she said and we baked a pizza and few samosas from the fridge which was quite filling for both of us.

After the dinner, for the first time we slept together in one bed. The bed was smaller but that was good as it kept us even closer. The next day I got up early and got ready and Jen was ready soon. After breakfast, we went to the hospital and I went to my office.

"Jen, come around noonish and we will go have lunch and then go to Dr. Stein's office."

"Yes, sir, will do. See you later." She left and I started on my future project. Around noon there was a soft knock on the door. "Come on in," I said although I knew it was her.

She came and sat down at her usual place. Next to my PC on the table.

"So you want to go now?" she asked me.

"Yeah, sure. Let me save this document and I will be done," I said.

I saved the document and switched off my computer and looked at Jen.

"You are glowing, Jen. What is the matter?"

"I don't know. Maybe because I found my buddy."

"Or is it because of the wild sex we had yesterday?" I asked her and she visibly blushed.

"Let's go. I'm starving, Bond," she said, then got up, gave me a hug, and planted a kiss on my cheek. I guess it was my time to blush then.

While we were in cafeteria having lunch, suddenly I saw John walking towards us. He was with one Indian girl whom I had seen around earlier. They were holding hands and walking towards us. I was a bit worried as to what was going to happen.

John came to our table and sat down with us and also signaled the girl with him to do the same.

"Howdy," he said in his thick Texan accent.

"Hello, John, what's up?"

"Amigo, I want you to meet my new girlfriend, Kavita. She is originally from India but raised in Texas!"

"Hi Kavita," Jen and I said almost simultaneously and introduced ourselves.

"Bond, she's Hindu like you and we like each other and hope we can continue our relationship. She has Texas spirit in her and more importantly she's a Cowboys fan. In fact, that's what binds us," John said, turning his attention towards me.

"Great, football as you know is also kind of religion that binds everyone including you guys together!" commented Jen.

"Thanks to Kavita, I'm now learning more about India and little bit about Hinduism!" John said.

"Great, good to know that," I said, wondering what's next.

"I'm sorry about my outburst that day, Bond," John said.

"No worries, amigo. We have been and will be always buddies even though I am New York Giant's fan!" I said jokingly.

"Alright guys, I'll see you around," he said and both of them got up. Then he turned around and pulled out a small pouch from his scrub pocket. He opened it and I was astonished to see a small statue of Ganesha!

"Kavita gave me this. I'm going to keep this in my Ford truck when I go back to Texas," John said.

"Really?" I was surprised. "But you are . . ."

"Look, Bond, having an idol of Ganesha in the truck does not change my religion. Good luck can come from everywhere and anywhere, you just have to accept it! I am and will be Christian and a lifelong Cowboys fan," he said with a smile.

"Oh boy, what a turnaround, Bond," Jen said after both had gone.

"Yeah, Jen. I can see it. I am worried that with Kavita's continued influence he may well become a new Gandhi in the heart of Texas. He may come and tell us in few days that he has given up eating meat and drinks goat milk and eats Mediterranean dates for his lunch!"

"Jokes aside, knowing him that won't happen for sure," Jen said.

After that interesting rendezvous we went straight to Dr. Stein's office. Mary said, "Thank god, you came at the right time. Catch him before he buzzes off for another meeting."

I grabbed Jennifer's hand and went in Dr. Stein's office.

He was looking at some applications on the table. He looked up and saw me tightly holding Jen's hand.

"What's up, Bond?" he asked.

"We have submitted the match list as a couple's match yesterday. You might have seen it."

"No I haven't. But I am glad for both of you. When did this happen?" he asked us pointing at our joined hands.

Before I could say something, Jen opened her mouth. "Yesterday. Finally, Bond realized that he was missing something."

"I hinted to you, and I presume you did not get that!" he said, looking at me. Then he turned to Jen and said, "I thought you were training him to become an American, so it is all your fault."

"He has to learn quite a few things, sir. But he'll get there, I'm sure. He's a good student," she said smiling and looking at me.

"Thank you, sir," I said. We left the office holding our hands and Mary chuckled at us.

We both ignored her, but I turned around and winked at her.

"Looks like Bond now has finally met his sexy girl! Good luck."

"Looks like Bond now has finally met his sexy girl! Good luck," she said.

"Thank you," I replied and both of us walked out of the office still holding hands tightly.

# Epilogue

I was suddenly awakened from my thoughts by the announcement, "Ladies and gentlemen, we will be soon landing at New York's JFK airport . . ." I did not realize how time had passed by. I was lost in my thoughts during the flight, looking back on my life's journey. Wow! I thought!

Jennifer wanted to come to the airport to pick me up but I had told her not to. I was worried about our twins coming out in the cold and getting sick. Both of us had finished residency and were practicing radiologists in New York. Jennifer had done her fellowship in mammography and she was working only three days per week. I was a full time Neuroradiology faculty member at NYU (I guess less exciting than Professor of Sexology!). I was looking forward to see my family. We had twins, one boy and one girl! Thank god our daughter looked like Jennifer! According to her mom, she looked exactly like Jennifer had when she was young. Our son looked more Asian, more like me. Jennifer was balancing between her job and taking care of the kids and I was helping her to raise them. I knew that I had to take good care of the kids, raise them, send them to college till they find another alien like me! Or maybe they won't need or find an alien. Hopefully by that time, this country will quit calling immigrants like me an alien! Or maybe by the time my kids grow up they will meet a real alien from outer space, not a fake alien like me.

Printed in the United States
By Bookmasters